OLIVER & JACK—AT LODGINGS IN LYME

CHRISTINA E. PILZ

Cover Design by Bookfly Design
Logo by D. L. Pilz
Author Photograph by Bryan Sanburg

Oliver & Jack: At Lodgings In Lyme/Christina E. Pilz

ISBN Numbers:

- Mobi - 978-0-98-972734-1
- Epub - 978-0-98-972735-8
- Print - 978-0-98-972733-4

Library of Congress Control Number: 2015943715

This book is dedicated to...

Oliver and Jack
--My Dickensian OTP

And to all those orphans out there
--You know who you are

"We changed again, and yet again, and it was now too late and too far to go back, and I went on. And the mists had all solemnly risen now, and the world lay spread before me."

--GREAT EXPECTATIONS BY CHARLES DICKENS

CONTENTS

OUT OF LONDON AND INTO
THE WORLD

The world was not quite as it ought to be. As the rain came down through the ridge of almost leafless trees along the road, Oliver wrapped his arms around his books and walked. He could barely feel his feet, and water dripped off the brim of his hat and down his neck like the trail of an icy rope. The front of his trousers was soaked, slapping against his thighs as he walked. And walked. And walked some more, feet slipping in the mud, even when he walked along the edge of the road, along the path made by feet rather than by wheel. Shaking the whole while, not wanting to look over his shoulder, but feeling it, those unseen eyes, and hearing the truth so long ago spoken by the man in the white waistcoat that he was born to be hung. Noah was so likely to run to the constable the first chance he got and collect on his earnings for being an informant. Yes, he most certainly would, so at least that was as it ought to be, at least Noah would—

"Nolly, hang on now, it's uphill, this bit, come on then, would you? Nolly. *Nolly.*"

With a start as if he'd been slapped, Oliver jerked his head and allowed himself to look over his shoulder. Jack struggled behind him in the mud, his hands held out for balance. Oliver had given

Jack the red scarf to wear, and now the tail end of it slopped against his boots. His half top hat was dappled with mud, and the rain was sending each spot of muck into a faint grey tendril down the polished sides and off the brim.

It was raining so hard that for a moment, Oliver couldn't see Jack's expression, and imagined himself quite alone except for the stranger at his side. A stranger who came up to him, wiping his mud-streaked face with the back of his hand, and trying on a half-smile, as if that would make any difference. It did, in a way. Jack's smile was like that, a flit of a grin, and it made Oliver think differently, feel differently, as if he'd been warmed by that smile. Though, when Jack reached out to give him a pat, Oliver shied away and regretted it when he saw the look on Jack's face, for he had not meant to hurt him by refusing his touch.

"We must keep walking," Oliver said, trying to make his point calmly, but failing. "We have to keep going or they'll find us. Well, me, they'll find me, since they're not after you, are they."

He felt the brittle taste of the words as he said them, thinking he might take them back, if only there was a way. Jack didn't deserve his ire; Jack had come with him because he wanted to, though whether he would turn back was up to Oliver's temper. He looked at Jack, as the rain seemed to thin a bit, and could see his confused expression clearly.

"Where we goin', Nolly, eh?" asked Jack. "Just tell me that. We've been walkin' for hours, an' you've not said a single word, not one. I've been given the grace of the back of your head, an' them shoulders, all straight, as if they've already caught and haccused you. Well, they ain't. They ain't comin', an' they ain't behind us, so could you, for fuck's sake, tell me where we're goin'?"

The last village, Dulwich, had been some hours back, and now even the spires of the village church were obscured by the tall trees and the curve of the hill. It had been such a small village, so small and so still, that any stranger, even a law-abiding one, would have stood out. Both he and Jack had wordlessly agreed to skulk along the edges, coming upon only a single person, a young woman with a shawl wrapped around her shoulders and a bucket in her hands.

"You don't have to come with me, you know. You don't have to." Oliver said this to make it very clear what Jack's obligation was to him, that he had none, while at the same time, he wanted Jack to stay with him, so very desperately.

"'Course I don't have to," said Jack, coming up to him, thumping his shoulder against Oliver's. "What I want to know is why we didn't take that fork, the one that led east, to Chertsey. I reckon your aunt'd be glad to see you."

"I'll not be bringing the law down upon her head, nor saddling her with a criminal nephew I'm sure she'd just as soon not be related to." The words snapped out; it wasn't just the shame of it, it was the danger.

He'd seen Cromwell's eyes turn from glassy to flat; he'd smelled the warm bloodspray in the air, seen the mist of red as it landed on the table. He could hardly walk into Aunt Rose's tidy cottage with the echo of his actions, and these thoughts in his head. With the stain on his shirt cuff. If Aunt Rose was willing to hide him, she might be arrested as well, for wasn't there a law against that?

And, what was almost worse, if Aunt Rose and Uncle Harry could not be tasked to house a murderer, they certainly could not be called upon to give room and board to a street thief. And never mind what else Jack was to him. Acquaintance of long years. Fellow on-the-run. Close friend of oh-so recent days, his companion in the dark, in the quiet, soft parts of nighttime, where words went unspoken, and thoughts become translated into touches and sighs. He opened his mouth to tell Jack of it, but thought better of the details, tasting the rain on his mouth.

"I cannot task my aunt to accept any of this," he said, trying to make an apology of the words.

Jack's expression was solemn, as if to contemplate what Oliver had said, and indeed what he had not said.

Oliver thought to explain what it meant to have a family and a home, but Jack stopped him.

"So, then, where *are* we goin'?" Jack spread his hands wide, steadying his legs against the dip in the road.

Oliver followed where Jack's hands pointed. Both back along the road, a ribbon of grey and brown through the stark grey trees, down the hill to the village of Dulwich. And then along what lay before them, a road that wound through a copse where the trees snugged full up to the road, hiding the direction of the road behind their reaching, dripping branches.

They were south of London, and of course they couldn't go back, so the only way was forward. By Oliver's recollection of the map pinned to the wall of his old room, the direction they were headed was to the sea. He'd never seen the sea; Uncle Brownlow had always thought it was a good, healthy destination, but circumstances had typically kept the household close to the country and the City. So beyond what Oliver knew there was the coastline, and beyond that, lay the world.

"Nolly."

Oliver hefted the books in one hand, and wiped the rain out of his eyes. It was colder standing still, with the rain pushing through the damp cloth of his jacket to his bones. A shiver took him, forcing his bones to rattle and his teeth to chatter. Jack didn't look any more at ease and perhaps worse, with the bruises on his face, laced with rain, and the narrow squint his eyes would sometimes exhibit, as they did now. The uncomfortable way Jack's shoulders were tight, even as his smile came and went.

"My mother's people came from Lyme Regis," said Oliver. He began to walk, balancing the weight of the books against this chest. "Perhaps we might go there."

"An' how?" asked Jack, walking beside Oliver in the rutted mud, his footsteps squelching in tandem with Oliver's. "Walk the whole way? 'Tis a hundred miles or more, that'd take weeks, an' on empty stomachs an' in this rain, forever."

Shaking his head, Oliver walked on, *made* himself walk, face numb with cold, feet as heavy as ice blocks, not even bending properly, making him slip all the more.

"Nolly." Jack's voice was low and close in Oliver's ears, and was much softer and warmer than the rain.

"We could—" said Oliver. "We could sleep under the hedgerows when it grows dark, and in the morning, just keep walking."

He licked his lips and tasted the cold and shivered, a deep internal shiver that did nothing to warm him. And looked at Jack, his eyes drawn again to the curve of a bruise along the side of his face from Cromwell's fist, the wan color beneath that bruise. And knew that this, too, was his fault, though he didn't imagine that Jack would say the same.

"If it's all right by you, *young master*." Jack used the back of his hand to wipe the icy rain from his dripping forelock, and his tone was beyond mocking. "You can just stop goin' on about findin' a nice cozy hedge to huddle under. You know as well as I that they ain't cozy, even if it ain't rainin'. An' do you *hactually* mean to tell me that you want to go on without a nice hot supper? I could get us money for that. It's as easy to do as anythin' else, if you let me."

Oliver shook his head again. The conversation was going in exactly the direction that it might go with Jack leading the way. For all that the reason for their exodus from London lay upon Oliver, he had no conviction as to where they should go; Lyme Regis was only an idea. It was Jack who stopped him again, this time with a hand on his shoulder, a touch to Oliver's raw, cold cheek.

"We *could* get there, I should think," said Jack. "There's bound to be a village big enough to have a coachin' inn, to be on the line. We could do that, you know, take a coach. I could get us some brass so we could do that."

That they had come to this moment was not as much of a surprise as it ought to have been, and it took Oliver a full moment to keep himself from shouting that he wasn't a thief, that he wasn't like that. But of course he was, and much worse. He chewed on his lower lip and let himself look at Jack fully, noting the rain dripping from Jack's hat, and that Jack's lips were turning as blue as his own felt.

"At the next large village," said Jack, "we'll brave it an' stop an' inquire. An' we'll get some brass—no arguin', mind. I expect at any moment to hear your stomach start complainin', an' I don't think I could bear it."

The last thing Oliver wanted was to linger in a strange place while Jack practiced his quick-fingered skills. But there was no other choice and, besides, Jack didn't look his bright self; even the sooty streak of grime along his jaw didn't seem as jaunty as it usually did.

"But only—" Oliver began. "Only just don't—" His stomach began to growl with the thought of food, though he could not imagine being a party to something so low as stealing to get it. "If you must, pick someone who has more than enough—"

"Look at you, already you're naggin' me. What a fussy miss you are."

But even though Jack strived to act as though he were cross, he seemed as though he was going to abide by this advice, simply because Oliver wanted it. It was somewhat bewildering that Jack would do this for him. There had not been another in his life like that. Not anyone.

The idea of it distracted him for a moment, but then it began to rain harder even as they stood there, as if someone had undone the sluices overhead and let all the water through all at once. The woods loomed in, close under the weight of the rain and the chill spring afternoon that would soon wear to dark.

"The next village, then," said Oliver. His jaw felt sore as he spoke, from having been clenched so tightly. "And Jack," he asked, unable to stop himself. "Are you unwell? You look pale. Is it the cold?"

"No, no," said Jack, waving this away with a rain-darkened and soaking cuff. "It's just all this fresh air, my lungs can't take it."

It might be a lie or it might be the truth; Oliver wasn't feeling like himself either at the moment, so perhaps it would be worth it to get some money and find a room to rent for the night. Clutching his books to his chest, he trammelled his fingers over the edges of the damp cloth covers, the pages.

"Well, we won't get there if we don't keep walking," said Oliver. Scolding, as if the delay was entirely Jack's.

They began walking and continued on until they came out of the wood, where, at the bottom of a hill, there were three painted wooden signs, all pointing to Croydon but in different directions. One sign pointed the way to Croydon through College Water, another sign pointed to Croydon through Whitehouse Farm, and the third sign pointed to Croydon through Woodside.

"Always to the left," said Jack, smoothly, as if this wasn't the very same statement he'd made at Camberwell, when they'd taken the left-hand fork in the road and ended up plodding through mostly open countryside, and then slipping along the muddied tracks of Norwood Forest. But this time, they were close to a village, and Oliver nodded.

Jack had offered to take the books, but it was better this way, with the solidness of them pressed close to his chest. Jack had given them to him, and he wanted to keep them close, when so much around them was changing. Even though they were heavy, they were his.

The road became macadamed along about the time that the slope leveled out, and cottages began to dot the roadside, with their stone chimneys roiling with smoke, and fat drops falling off rooflines to plop into the soaking black earth beneath. Oliver saw that beyond the green common, where a small herd of brown cows had tucked themselves beneath some spreading oaks, and beyond the tree line, a spire rose. Even from this distance, it looked sturdy and respectable, which might not be the most suitable place for Jack to ply his trade.

"Can you do it, Jack?" asked Oliver, as they walked close together along the road. "And not get caught?"

"Caught?" Jack laughed, but then he winced and this seemed to turn the laugh into something else. "Me? The last time I was caught was for a tuppenny ha'penny snuffbox, an' I'll not likely make that mistake again."

"And what should I do?"

"What you do best," said Jack, and this time his smile was real and deep. "Stand by an' watch me work my wonders. And oh, yes, be beautiful, as you always are. It'll make a very useful distraction indeed."

As they came forward, the trees broke ranks to reveal a high street, indicating that this was more than just a mere village, it was a byway of some repute, and therefore likely to be, as Jack put it, on the line.

2

NEEDS MUST WHEN THE DEVIL DRIVES

The idea of merely watching Jack steal, as opposed to stopping him was, of course, the issue at hand. What Jack proposed to do, in the coaching inn yard of the King's Arms, amidst a pair of six-horse, long-distance coaches, one coming, one going, was to pick someone's pockets. He was rubbing his hands together, pulling at his knuckles to warm them up, and looking out across the cobblestoned yard through sheets of rain as they spattered into the hillocks of grey-pitted snow. All business, focused on the task at hand. If there was a single word in all of the Queen's English to stop him, then Oliver did not yet know it. Besides, after only a single afternoon's trudge in the rain, he was already cold right through; the idea of a hot meal promised by Jack's notorious employment was battling hard, and winning, against the sin of it.

As they stood beneath the crooked balconies of the coaching inn, Oliver looked at Jack. The both of them were too road-spattered to be completely unobtrusive, but Jack had insisted that no one would notice them. But what was worse than standing out, if Oliver allowed himself to think about it, was the condition of the red scarf around Jack's neck. The walk from London, and the grime from less-than-salubrious stopping places, where they'd sat upon hard rocks, or climbed over lazy fence stiles, all of them had left their mark. And now the scarf was not only tattered along the edges, it was suffused with grey. No longer red, no longer cherry. No longer a resplendent representation of anything good, or snug, or safe. Oliver made himself turn away from these dismal thoughts, and made himself remember that he was in the wide, wide world, out beneath a bleak, weeping sky because he had chosen to be.

"Don't forget you said you'd—" He paused to consider a moment, not wanting to be in charge of this mad plan. "You promised to pick the right person. Like the gentleman in the bottle-green coat—"

"Do you actually think it makes a difference, Nolly?" Now Jack was laughing at him outright, mouth wide, with only a small wince as his split lip cracked open. "Stealin' is a sin, no matter the reason. Ain't that in the Bible?"

"As if you've ever read any of it," said Oliver with a snap, even though he knew that he could not deter Jack from this plan.

But Jack merely winked at him, and began to move toward the center of the courtyard, rain leaving hard, silver streaks on his hat. He said, as bold as he ever was, "You might as well come with me; you'll be a great foist, if I needs one."

Jack strode the sleek cobblestoned yard, jerking his head back to set his half top-hat to rights, cracking his fingers with his thumb, the furtive movement hidden beneath the too-long arms of his coat sleeves. He tugged on Oliver's jacket, drawing all of Oliver's garments close, reminding him how cold and damp he was, and how much more cold and damp he would be if he forced them to sleep under a hedge. He did not want that for himself. Besides, Jack looked pale with that dark bruise on his cheek, and as he turned, he moved with some stiffness, which caused his movements to be jerky, not like the usual smooth ease that followed Jack's every move.

So Oliver let himself be led, ducking his head as he stepped out into the splattering rain, clutching the three books. He told himself that he was doing this for Jack so that Jack could have a hot meal and a dry place to lay his head, but not for himself, no, never that. And particularly not because of his fear that Jack, not being a tame and sensible companion, might leave him otherwise. Not that Jack had said or in any way indicated that. But Oliver had no tether to hold him, and if Jack left, then Oliver would be alone in the wide world, standing out of the rain beneath the balcony of a coaching inn.

But while he could not hold Jack, he would much rather travel to Lyme Regis, from whence the Flemings had come, with him than without him. For he could not imagine walking along the road without Jack, without Jack's green eyes and that ready smile. Even Jack's mockery had become necessary in his life; he could not manage without all of that, so he would manage to do with it. Not that he would ever inform Jack of his trepidation, for Jack would only mock him all the more.

He followed close behind Jack, the brim of his hat tipped down so that he did not have to meet anyone's eyes. Nor see the face of the gentleman in the bottle-green jacket, the silky scarf wrapped snugly around his neck.

The gentleman was shielded from the damp gusts of wind by his manservant, who, taking one look at Jack, nonchalantly looked the other way. It was a nice coat that the gentleman wore, and Oliver envied its fine, somber lines, which were thick enough to withstand even the most insistent gales. Of note, the gentleman, top hat shedding the rain with ease, the cravat around his neck a dense and spotless white, appeared to be quite well off. Enough to have, possibly, afforded his own coach and four but who, for some reason, had determined that a conveyance departing from this lowly country coaching inn was the way to go.

It was truly going to happen, then, as it had so long ago, with Jack on the job and Oliver standing by, an observer and half-hearted participant, only this time, not so innocent.

⁓

Jack felt the weight of his jacket cuffs on his wrists, the rain on his cheekbones. It didn't matter the rain, nor the fact that the back of his shoulders felt as though they'd been slammed with an iron bar, for he had his sights on a score: a rich old gentleman, the best kind of mark, puffed up on his own importance, and distracted by the difficulties of getting to his destination. This was made even better by the fact that, in spite of his disapproval, Nolly had picked the mark out, just for Jack. The theft would be easy; Jack would be able to deal with Nolly once he'd presented him with a good hot supper, and something sweet besides.

It was too bad if Nolly didn't like the task at hand, for how else were they to eat, to get shelter? Besides the fact that Jack refused to sleep under a hedgerow, did Nolly truly imagine that they'd be taken in by some kind soul who would not question from whence they came, or why?

Glancing over his shoulder, Jack looked at Nolly, at those blue eyes round and scared as he followed Jack, and that mouth clamped tight over whatever timorous warnings of dire consequences that were surely running rampant just beneath the surface. Nolly was licking his lips and clutching his books, as if he was afraid that Jack might want to trade them for something far more useful. But didn't he know that Jack would never do such a thing? Those books were Nolly's heart, and Jack would never break that. Though it might be useful if Nolly didn't look quite so nervous.

"Hey," said Jack. "This will only take a moment, right? I'm on my game, you'll see."

He was proud of what he could do, and Nolly would be more pleased with him, he was sure, once this was over. So he was going to make it quick. He was going to do a grand job, one that Fagin would have been proud of. And besides, he was picking the richest gent in the yard, in spite of there being easier marks, like the pair of gentlemen who had their heads together in a conversation that Jack suspected was not altogether legal, but that left them without a single shred of defense from Jack's agile hands. Or the lady in the blue cape, with ermine at the collar; she was holding her little white dog in her hands, and was paying a great deal less attention to the beaded reticule hanging from her gloved wrist. She would have been a much easier take, indeed, but the gentleman in the bottle-green coat it was, as per Nolly's request.

"Excuse me, mister," said Jack in a grand way, going right up to the gentleman in question. Being an obvious idiot in the ways of the world was the truest of distractions. "Is this the coach to Exeter?"

Jack stopped so short that Nolly walked into him, and causing Jack to bump into the gentleman, as planned.

"Watch what you're doing there," said the gentleman's manservant loudly, though he moved not a muscle to settle his master.

"I beg your pardon," said the gentleman, "but no." He tugged on his lapels to set himself to rights, and then Jack's hand was a blur, a flash of white against the green, and all of a sudden Jack had turned to Nolly and thumped him in the chest.

"How many times have I told you to get your head out of the clouds?" Jack asked this as loudly as possible so that even the tavern boy lounging in the doorway of the inn could hear him. "Ain't it enough that you keep bumpin' me with those damn books?"

Nolly jumped back, as if startled at the clarity of Jack's voice, the loudness of the words fairly bouncing against the dripping balustrade. Doing it as perfectly as if he'd been trained to it for years, though he never had. One of Nolly's background didn't bump into strange men willingly, nor ask questions in loud voices, especially not in public places. Nolly's mouth was open because he'd seen what Jack had done; the shock on his face was natural and convincing.

Jack turned back to the gentleman. "Beg your pardon, mister, but can you tell me if this is the coach to Exeter?"

"No indeed, as I believe I've already told you," said the gentleman in formal tones. "It goes to the south, to Plymouth."

"That's not the one," said Jack, shaking his head, the rain dripping from the brim of the hat onto his face. He turned back to

Nolly, allowing himself a bit of a grin, because couldn't a fellow be proud of himself once in a while?

"Come on, Nolly," said Jack now, "we'll get the right one in the mornin'. Good afternoon, mister."

Jack tipped his hat and, ignoring the smirk of the manservant, walked them back across the yard. His hand remained firmly on Nolly's arm, as if Nolly was indeed the culprit responsible for the brief, unwanted collision and needed guidance. As Nolly let himself be led, Jack patted his chest, assuring himself that the wallet was now securely tucked inside Nolly's jacket. To continue the pretense, Jack tipped his head toward Nolly's, as if continuing to scold him for the accident.

When they were once again beneath the balustrade of the inn, Jack stood close to Nolly and pulled out the wallet from his jacket. It was worn but had a new clasp and was thick with money. Hefting it, Jack smiled as he watched Nolly's eyes widen even further. The fact that Jack had not, in all the years he'd been away, lost any of the skill in his fingers that had made him Fagin's best and brightest, seemed to leave Nolly a tad breathless.

A moment later, the evening coach clattered into the yard, and six sweaty horses scrambled to a stop. The gentleman, along with his manservant, and the woman and her dog, nodded at the driver's apologies for being late, and then all clambered aboard. Before even a moment's grace to water the horses, the coach shot off. It probably would be miles away before the gentleman thought to check his pockets. As the clatter faded and the slats of mud slipped back into their cobbled cracks, the yard of the coaching inn grew still and empty, leaving only Nolly and Jack.

Jack pulled out a handful of shillings and a single gold crown from the little change purse sewn inside the wallet, showing off a little as he looked up at Nolly. Jack smiled, feeling a flash of plea-sure run through him, in spite of Nolly's dour expression that displayed his dismay quite clearly.

"Well, I reckon you can select for us fried mutton or even beef an' chicken roasted, if you've a mind to." Jack held out the shillings and some pennies to Nolly, a gift of skin-warmed coin. "An' you could get us tickets on the next coach to Lyme or anywhere near it. Then I've a mind for a dry bed to sleep in. Want to join me?"

Nolly took the coins, and folded his fingers over them without a word, as if stunned at how easy it had been. While he might be considering the difference between right and wrong, let alone how he'd let Jack use him as a plant, he was even more easily led to the main entry of the inn.

3

THEY ATTEMPT TO PASS FOR
RESPECTABLE GENTLEMEN

The King's Arms was very grand on the outside, even in the pouring rain. The front of the building was of pale, creamy stone, which seemed warm, the yellow thawing through the damp. The window frames were painted white and the heavy sign with the name of the establishment looked to be gold-gilt.

The inside showed the King's Arms to be a series of low-ceilinged and dark rooms, with the passageway from the entrance too narrow to do anything but proceed slowly, shifting sideways when another person was met along the way. The lintel proved to be so low that Jack had to duck his head to go through the doorway to the main room, but once inside, Jack could smell something roasting and see the flicker of several fires reflecting against the low, age-polished post beams that sheltered travelers while they rested and ate.

Nolly took his hat off, and Jack unwound the red scarf, and patted the wallet that was now tucked into his own trouser pocket. He could feel the warmth of coal fires, and gratefully absorbed the acidy smell into his skin, thinking of a meal, and of bed, somewhere quiet and dark where he could shake off his headache, and the lurid memory of blood on the stone floor of the kitchen of the Three Cripples, and of Nolly standing there with not a spot of it on him.

With Nolly in front of him, Jack steered them both to the wooden counter, where they were met by a white-aproned clerk with almost no expression on his face.

"Might I help you, sir?" asked the clerk, as if Nolly had been attired as a young gentleman instead of a dripping vagabond. This appraisal didn't surprise Jack in the least; Fagin had always considered that Nolly's face would be his fortune, and this could be turned to their advantage now.

"You ask," said Jack, whispering into Nolly's ear. "You've got the face for it."

Jack took Oliver's hat and held it, completing the picture of Nolly being a gentleman with a servant standing by. Then he leaned in close, almost brushing his chin on Nolly's shoulder to still the shivering that had suddenly overtaken Nolly. Not on account of the sudden warmth of the room, but rather on the prospect of spending money, just feet from where it had been stolen.

"We'd like to inquire if there is a coach to Lyme Regis hereabouts."

There was a slight tremor in Nolly's voice, and Jack had to admire him for carrying on when all of this duplicity must have felt overwhelming. As for himself, well, certainly picking pockets was as familiar to him as anything, but typically he'd handed over the take to Fagin's waiting hands, or purchased something at Fagin's direction. Never this, spending for one's own benefit. It held a quick thrill, but instead of grinning, Jack made himself remain the sturdy, serious companion to Nolly's grace.

"Indeed there is," said the clerk, "but not from here."

"Where can we get a coach from, then?"

"If you were to apply at The Bush in Staines," said the clerk, "then I believe straightaway you could get a coach to Exeter and, along the way, alight at Lyme."

"And how much is the coach to Lyme?"

"Oh, I don't rightly know," said the clerk, completely uncon-cerned that now that they were standing still, Jack's head had started to throb, and Nolly was shivering head to toe, hard enough to click his teeth. They had money for plenty, it seemed, but there was no coach that was gong the way they wanted, when they wanted t. Jack pressed his body close behind Nolly's, to give him some comfort, felt Nolly press back, gratified that Nolly trusted him to be so close in public.

"Why don't you—" asked Jack, his chin almost resting on Nolly's shoulder, but Nolly held up his hand.

"Is there a coach we might get to Staines?" asked Nolly, and Jack could see that he was doing his very best to be polite, but it was getting more difficult with each passing moment. Had Jack been the one speaking, he would have handed out more than a few choice profanities at the clerk's dull mind.

"Indeed there is," said the clerk. "It leaves in under an hour, and I have available two inside seats at a two and four each."

"Two shillings fourpence each?" Nolly's dismay was plain, even to those customers seated on benches alongside the walls, who looked up with interest at the sound of Nolly's voice, who must have forgotten the fat wallet that Jack had just stolen. Just the same, Jack knew it was highway robbery, in the most basic and literal sense. The hard, amused glint in the clerk's eyes confirmed it.

"'Tis a very popular route," said the clerk. "And those are the only seats left."

There was nothing else to be done. And as well, running in a straight line, as they had been doing since they left London, was a sure way to be caught, whereas taking a sudden and inexplicable left or right, was sure to shake the peelers off their arses. Jack kept his mouth shut, as it would have caused Nolly to fret a great deal were he to become aware of it.

"Then I'd like two tickets, please," said Nolly.

Jack saw him swallow, Jack's brave boy, and he wanted to

whisper something that would ease Nolly's shaking, but did not, as there were too many ears that might overhear him.

From the money that Jack had given him in the yard, Nolly presented five shillings to the clerk in a clumsy way that would surely tip off the clerk that the money being given to him was stolen. Nolly half-looked back at Jack, as if to make sure he was still there, though Jack was pressed up flat against him. Jack suspected he'd done this so he wouldn't have to focus on the moment that the clerk took the money to a box under the counter and made change, handing over a mere sixpence, and two stubs of paper upon which he wrote the date and destination. To watch their stolen money being spent was probably more than Nolly could bear.

"Ask at The Bush for rates and a room; the coach to Exeter comes early in the morning."

The clerk passed their vouchers over, which Nolly took, nodding his thanks, and shifted his attention to Jack as he stepped away from the desk. As if wanting to sigh with Jack in relief that there was yet another hurdle overcome.

But Jack could not sigh with him, he could only droop against Nolly as the warmth of the room overtook him. A sudden quick pain arced up his back and then vanished as, tight-lipped, he tried to think of what they should do next.

Nolly turned to him, not pushing him away, as Jack would have expected, but, hefting the books to one side, leaned his head close.

"Jack," he said. "Are you all right? I know you said it was the fresh air, but—"

There was a hand upon his shoulder as Nolly tucked the scarf close to Jack's neck, his eyes looking Jack over, and however much Jack might ordinarily enjoy such solicitude, his headache, which had come and gone since morning, now made him wince and turn away. Black spots were forming in front of his eyes.

"All this smoke," Jack said, ducking his head, looking for a place to sit. "We can wait for the coach by the door, you see. It'll be as simple as that. Come on, you an' me, right over there."

He took Nolly's arm, as if he were in charge, and as if his legs weren't about to wiggle out from under him and send him crashing to the floor.

Nolly, seemingly distracted by the newness of all that was about, was obedient, as he had been in the yard, clenching his books, following behind. He sat next to Jack on the bench, and looked around the room, and that gave Jack a moment to rub the back of his neck when Nolly wasn't looking. When Nolly turned back around, Jack dropped his hand, assuming an air of innocence, and doffing his hat, like a gentleman, to show Nolly that he could be one, when he wanted to.

"Jack," said Nolly, with a sigh that seemed to not relax him at all. He still sat up, his back not touching the back of the wooden bench, the books on his knees, his fingers sliding up and down the edge of the cover of the book on top. "Will it be all right? Will we get away?"

Nolly looked as though he very much needed a kiss *and* a cuddle, and Jack wanted so very badly to give it to him, in part so that he could himself get the same. But however much this might have helped his headache, there was no reaching for it. They were in a crowded place, and in addition to Jack's headache and the gnawing pressure across the tops of his shoulders and the back of his neck, Nolly was strung tight, eyes wide, face white. Jack imagined that it might take until they were at their destination before Nolly relaxed. Until then, touching him would be like touching a barbed hook, and Jack would get stung.

"It'll be all right, Nolly, upon my word it will," Jack said.

"Will it, Jack?" The words came out bitten, as if Nolly might have spat at him for being so foolish.

Jack was about to draw back; he did not know what to do with Nolly like that in this closed space, with so many strangers around. But in spite of this, he touched Nolly's knee with the tips of his fingers, reaching out. Whereupon, Nolly's shoulders came down, and he ducked his head to look at where Jack's fingers were brushing his knee. And even though his hands were shaking, he actually gripped Jack's fingers in his own. Not to stop Jack, but to touch him back in the only way that he could, with their hands low on the bench, between where their knees almost met.

There was a look in Nolly's eyes, as he gazed up at Jack through those dark, fanned lashes, as if he didn't realize he might be flirting. And if they weren't in a crowded room with strangers all around, Jack might have had both the kiss *and* the cuddle. And found in his arms a Nolly who wouldn't snap or spit or strike out.

The day had rattled them both, and yet Jack had hardly heard one word of complaint out of Nolly, in spite of the mud up to his ankles and the damp that had eaten them both quite through. That deserved more, so Jack scooped his palm around Nolly's hand and squeezed it gently. It was only then that Nolly drew a deep breath, a spark to his eyes, and Jack smiled, just a little, to answer that spark, even though his headache was coming on hard now, pounding behind his eyes, a scratch-claw scraping over his skull. Black sparks blossomed in his vision, and he looked away, as if interested in the comings and goings of travelers, so that he could blink hard and fast to clear his sight. To take a breath, as if that would ease his headache. It didn't.

"Will you say it, Jack?" asked Nolly.

"Say what?" Jack's lips felt almost numb now.

"That it will get better, by-and-bye. Like you do."

Now Jack *had* to look at Nolly, or Nolly would know how ill he felt and want to do something about it, when there was nothing to be done.

"It'll get better," said Jack, unclenching his jaw. And he said it, even though he didn't know that it would. "It'll get better, by-and-bye."

When the horn for the coach sounded, they scrambled up, the scarf tangling, refusing to uncoil so that Jack could wrap it properly again around his neck. Oliver almost forgot the books, and had to turn to grab them. They raced out the front door and into the yard, and without looking back, they ascended the coach. The rain determined to keep falling, except for the single moment as they raced outside, when the clouds whisked over each other, and the sun streamed through, only to be swallowed up in the grey and moving tumble.

The air was crisp as the door was clicked shut after them, leaving Oliver and Jack sitting in the backward-facing seats. They were silently greeted by a little family of three, who occupied the frontward-facing seat. They wore grey silk, the trio, and the little girl had lilac flowers on her bonnet, and the mother and father had matching grey gloves.

Oliver knew this for what it was; the family had been in mourning for some time and were only coming out of it. Out of it enough to take a journey, in this case from Croydon to Staines, their final destination that required, it seemed, the most formal of dress.

No one said anything. The coach sped up, tipping forward as it went down an incline, a hill that Oliver glimpsed out the window, with a row of trees, and a narrow lane that looked as though it was leading out of town.

Jack slumped in the seat beside Oliver, legs sprawling. When Oliver looked over, Jack was eyeing the family, his lip curled, one eyebrow cocked. In another moment, Jack was going to say something quite unseemly, perhaps about his desire for a good clay pipe. And while that wouldn't exactly have been out of place, his next comment would be about playing a hand of cards, or a remark about the thin pallor of the woman.

Oliver had not been with Jack in polite company, at all, up to that moment; if true to form, Jack would have no compunction about being rude, and while Oliver might care, Jack had no stake in being civil. But Jack surprised him, as he had a way of doing, as he merely leaned against the wall, taking off his hat to rest it at his feet, and making a small pillow out of the scarf. As Oliver looked at him, Jack, blinking slowly, like a cat, nodded, as if in agreement with a conversation they'd been having for a while.

"This coach rocks a bit, eh, Nolly?"

Oliver nodded in agreement, though he was unsure of how they were being perceived.

"All this country air is sure to bring on the fever," said Jack.

"Surely not," said the young father solemnly. "'Tis good for you, the country air. It will bring you to health, sure enough."

"If you let it," said the woman, in a slightly scolding way. The little girl, holding fast onto her mother's hand, didn't say anything, but just stared at Jack. The little flowers in her bonnet, which, amidst the smell of damp straw strewn along the floor of the coach, gave off a faint flowery scent and bobbed with the motion of the coach.

But Jack didn't answer. His eyes slid closed, and he hitched up his arms to wrap them around his chest, keeping one hand on the scarf, his fingers trailing among the weave. His cheeks were flushed, but the skin around his eyes was tight, and it alerted Oliver to the fact that Jack was truly not himself; he was not well, even though he'd denied Oliver's queries. Hopefully the time they spent in the carriage would be enough to give Jack the rest he needed, and Oliver as well. Though he was used to walking great distances, that had been in the City, with the pavement beneath his boots, and not the rutted, muddy track they'd been following for most of the day.

Over the hills outside, the lace of the leafless trees was stabbed by shafts of sunlight as it cut through the clouds along the horizon. All else was falling into darkness, as though a slow, swirling blanket was coming down upon the landscape. Oliver shivered with the chill of his clothes, still damp against his skin. The weight of the books on his lap bit into his thighs. He looked down to stroke the covers, using the cuff of his jacket to erase the damp. The books were on the verge of being ruined by the exposure, but he could not have borne leaving them behind.

The coach rocked and jerked and lurched as it left the cottages behind to traverse open country, and went into the bottom of a small valley, where the rain pounded on the top of the coach and the chill air built up beneath his feet. The little grey family pushed close together and Oliver considered asking them where they were bound, but decided against it. He'd only be making himself and Jack more memorable than they already were; two young men, lashed by rain and spattered with mud, who were able to afford inside seats on a rather posh local coach were bound to be memorable. There was no sense making it worse.

So he kept his eyes on Jack as he dozed, and rocked with the coach, and pretended he was warm.

✣ 4 ✣
EATING SUPPER IN A STRANGE
PLACE

It was after some time that the horses' hooves clattered against the surface of the road. The sound was high and sharp, as if the horses went across cobbles rather than a macadamed surface. Then there was a whistle and a horn, and all of a sudden the coach was pulling to a stop. Oliver looked out to the yard; it was an inn, rather trim and bright, with lanterns in the sconces, and a sheltering overhang. The ostler was running alongside the coach, cast in shadows of the candle-lantern a young boy carried as high as he could. Oliver tucked his fingers around Jack's elbow to waken him.

"Jack, we're here, wake up."

Jack had not stirred the entire journey, but he woke now, eyes flitting open, focusing only on Oliver. There were rings under his eyes, and his mouth looked tight.

"Nolly?" Jack asked, but only that, and nothing more, as if he couldn't bear to talk.

They waited for the grey family to alight from the coach, which they did, assembling in the inn yard before being led away by someone with another candle-lantern. Then Oliver and Jack alighted, following the direction of the ostler's pointing hand to beneath the low-hanging roofline. As they entered the inn, they were able to stand up straight only when they were on the other side of the door, in the short passageway that led to the main room of the inn.

Though the air was clouded with smells of cooking and unwashed clothes, and the tired skin of travelers, the change from the damp courtyard to the warm room was a welcome one. Smoke tumbled along the darkened beams and once-whitewashed ceiling and over the forms of damp travelers bent to their meals.

Jack guided Oliver by his elbow up to where a man was standing behind a counter, handing out keys and wooden chits and giving change and briskly writing it all down. Oliver didn't have to ask to know why he should be the one making the transaction. He already knew, but Jack told him anyway.

"Quick like," Jack said, "an' use that pretty smile for us. Supper an' breakfast an' the coach to Lyme, provided it don't leave too early."

Before Oliver could even begin to unravel this litany of information, he was at the counter.

"Sir," he said politely, his face beginning to tingle from being in the warmth, "might I inquire as to—"

"Hold up a moment," said the man. He wiped his pen with a cloth and ran his eyes along a piece of paper in front of him. By the way he was looking, a fixed stare, Oliver knew he was going back over a list of sums, double-checking his own arithmetic. Then he looked up.

"Yes, then?" he asked. "Hurry on, I've not got all day."

"We'd like meals, supper and breakfast, my friend and I, and a room for the night, and a coach—"

The man began writing in his ledger, focused on that and not on Oliver, but he nodded. "Go on."

"A coach to Lyme Regis, in the morning, if it's not too early," said Oliver. He was dictating Jack's orders to the letter, not knowing of a sudden whether he really wanted to go to Lyme. For what would he find there? A family? A home? His nerves, jumpy and wrangled, had taken him this far but could not go further. From behind him, Jack gave him a gentle nudge with his elbow; Oliver felt that he could do it, if Jack were close, if Jack *stayed* close—

"We've got the coach, The Comet, that leaves at six in the morning, and if you get up at five, we've got bread and small beer."

Before Oliver could say *yes* or *no* or even ask for clarification, Jack nudged him from behind.

"How much, then?" Jack asked, from over Oliver's shoulder.

"Well," said the man, considering. "You want four meals, two coach seats, and one room with a bed. That'll be 16 shillings for the coach, two for the meals, one shilling for the room, I'll throw in extra bedding, and we'll call it a pound even."

Oliver's eyebrows rose at the cost, and, wanting to protest, felt Jack pressing a heavy coin into his palm. Oliver brought it up to the light and saw that it was a gold sovereign. He placed it on the counter with a heavy clink.

"That should pay for all and return me a shilling's change," he said, meaning to demonstrate that he could do sums in his head as well.

The clerk wrote the information down and looked at the sovereign somewhat askance. Old-fashioned gold coins were remarkable enough in London; at a coaching inn in the country they were even more so.

Oliver opened his mouth, searching for something plausible to say that would keep their movements from any gossip when Jack saved him.

"Oh, Nolly," said Jack, pushing up against Oliver from behind, peering at the coin with his chin just about resting on Oliver's shoulder. "That be the coin your Gran gave you when your Mam died, ain't it?"

As the clerk looked at him, Oliver attempted to make his face suitably grief-stricken, but since he'd never practiced in a mirror, in fact, avoided them when he could, he could not be certain how successful he was.

"Don't be brave, Nolly," said Jack, patting him in an obvious show of support. "Surely she'd want you to spend it to visit your uncle, as he ain't long for this world."

If allowed to go on much longer, it was readily apparent that Jack could and would invent an entire passel of relatives, either dead in their graves or lingering in a sickroom. Oliver wanted to duck his head, for he had a small laugh building, the first one in days, which would not be seemly, given the circumstances of his, wait—who had died?

"Give it over, then," said the clerk, sweeping up the coin with ink-stained fingers. "Here's your shilling, chits for your meals, and a key. There's only one bed, so you'll have to share. There will be a bell at five for breakfast, and a horn at six, to announce the coach. And we don't hold the coach for stragglers."

With this rumple of instructions, Oliver's fingers felt nerveless; he let Jack scoop up the key and the shilling and took the wooden meal tokens, which he cupped in his hand. He clutched his books to his chest and wanted to stand and gawp at the gathering of people, none of who had any idea what type of boy he was. But Jack would not let him stand still. No, Jack hooked his arm through Oliver's and led them both to a spare spot at one of the long tables. Jack pointed at a chair facing away from the majority of the crowd, so that Oliver would be looking only at Jack.

"But I don't want to—"

Jack made him sit down and then walked briskly around to the other side of the table.

"That sweet face of yours," said Jack, as if this face were something Oliver should be aware of and tend to. "You'll leave a trace of you, memorable as you are. Besides." Jack added a smile. "After being shoulder to shoulder with you all day an' neither of us talkin' much, I want a chance to look at you. Make sure you're all to rights."

He found Jack's eyes upon him, a small, pleased curve on Jack's mouth. But the bruise on Jack's face that swathed like black and green ink, and the split lip, were too distracting for Oliver to be pleased. He himself had barely a mark on him from his altercation with Cromwell. Yet here was Jack, who'd ostensibly done everything that Cromwell had required of him, looking as though he'd been plowed over by a team of runaway horses. But in spite of this, Jack seemed more worried about Oliver.

"No, Nolly," said Jack. "Don't think of it. We're here now, on our way to Lyme, though God knows why. It's a backwater where we shall find nothin'."

This was a distraction; Jack intended him to get agitated and focus on these dismissive comments instead of his own thoughts. So Oliver took a breath. They removed their hats and put them beneath their chairs, and as Jack took off his jacket and laid the red scarf upon it on the back of the chair, Oliver took off his own jacket, even though it was impolite to do so in public, so that he could lay it along the back of the chair to dry.

As he sat back, he was still shaking slightly, but concentrated on the biting taste of coal smoke that filled the corners of the room. Then he looked at Jack, who was looking less well now that they'd sat down, though the room was warm and jostled with brown-coated travelers, drinking and laughing, which by Oliver's reckoning, ought to make Jack feel more at home than he'd been in the fresh, damp country air.

It was strange to think of it, but in the many years since he'd met Jack, he'd never envisioned this moment, him and Jack together, though not in London. Oliver's escape from the law and his search for the Flemings precluded Jack being involved. And yet, here he was, no more than an arm's length away. Closer than that even, for upon the narrow, scarred brown table, Jack now planted both his elbows.

Oliver might have snapped at Jack to mind his manners, while he himself set the better example. But that was not his old life; this was a different life into which Oliver had, literally, chopped his own pathway. But he did not regret his ferocity; Cromwell had hurt Jack to prove some meaningless point, and Oliver was still angry about that.

As he made himself not think about Cromwell, he noticed again, in the stillness between them, Jack's nearness. Oliver could have reached and touched the bruise on Jack's face. Pushed the locks of rain-streaked hair back from that pale and smudged forehead. Or he could have moved around the table to sit beside Jack, so that they might brush shoulders in the noisy room and be together that way.

But more than the desire to sit next to Jack, he earnestly wanted to find a warm bed, so that Jack could curl beside him and they could sleep together until they had actually arrived at Lyme. Oliver's regard—his *affection* for Jack, a street thief, was still new to him. And though this relationship would bring shocked looks from anybody he'd ever known, he realized the cared very little what opinions they might have.

In the midst of these thoughts, a serving girl came up to the table. Her dress was brown, with large circles of greasy stains near her hips, as if she frequently wiped her hands there instead of on her crisp white apron. Which itself was probably the point. The apron stayed white for the customers and, as for the brown dress, the poor wretch probably didn't have anything else to wear. He didn't quite want to look up in answer to her mumbled greeting, so that she would not see the pity in his eyes, when he realized that he, too, only had one outfit to wear. Goodness knew when he'd get another; probably never, so what did it matter? It was the one he had on now and would sleep in that night. He raised his head, but before he could manage a hello, she held out her hand.

"Give us your chit, then, sirs."

Her hand was begrimed at the knuckles though the palms seemed fairly clean. When Oliver handed over two of the wooden tokens he had, she curled her fingers around them.

"You get one serving of food an' drink each; anythin' else is hextra."

Extra meant nothing sweet for after the meal, unless they paid; Oliver found himself suddenly, truthfully, grateful for the distraction from much darker and more complicated thoughts.

"We'll pay you a good solid shillin'," said Jack, with a sly, quick smile at Oliver as he reached into his pocket. "If you can locate anythin' that comes with pourin' custard all over it."

"And extra beer, two pints." Oliver added this as Jack handed over the shilling, for it seemed too much to pay for only one serving of pudding.

"Make that one beer, an' one gin with sugar an' water," said Jack, winking.

"Just two beers," said Oliver, shaking his head. He would take just a sip of the beer and give the rest to Jack in the hopes that it would bring some color back into his face. And there he was again, mentally fussing over Jack. Jack who had survived many years on the street while under Fagin's less-than-tender tutelage, and five years in a penal colony, for God's sake. Jack surely would be less than pleased to comprehend that his old mate, the cosseted and fair-faced Oliver Twist, did not think that Jack Dawkins could take care of himself.

"You're far too serious for a lad who's on such a great adventure." Jack was scanning the room, a habit he seemed to have brought with him from London, but he flicked Oliver a glance, and then away, at the room again.

But it wasn't an adventure. Or at least, it didn't feel like one. There were no helpful and magical talking dogs or crones who were really enchantresses in disguise. There were no sun-dappled glades to shelter them from a bit of wind as they made their way along a well-marked path to Lyme Regis. No, there was only snow-slatted rain, and a mud-splatted coaching inn, and his empty belly and his aching heart. Pining for the life he had wanted, the one he'd been living. All gone. Soaked to the bone, and shivering where he sat.

"Nolly," said Jack, focusing his attention directly on Oliver now. "There will be puddin' for afters, I promise."

For one long moment, it seemed as though Jack was a horrible street urchin, just as he should be after years of dirty clothes and chancy food, and a roof that leaked, if he had any roof over his head at all. And he thought that he had the right to mock Oliver that his needs were so simple? So easily met?

Then Oliver caught the dance of a laugh in Jack's eyes, and he had to duck his head and yes, plunk his elbows on the table to cover his face with his hands. He felt so new to the world, so unexposed in comparison to Jack. He was not used to being teased in this way, and he'd just about laid into Jack. Just as he had—

After a moment, he took a deep breath, uncovered his face, and looked at Jack. Solidly and plainly. "It's not like it is in the books."

"The what?" Jack asked, as if completely confused, though Oliver considered that Jack knew what he was talking about and was pretending not to.

"I want a hot meal in a quiet place, and a hot bath, with a servant to tend to my damp clothes—well, our damp clothes," he added, thinking that if this was all a fantasy anyway, he might as well be gracious and add Jack's needs to those of his own. "And then I want a newly made feather bed with wide, white sheets and then—"

"What you wants is fuckin'," said Jack suddenly. "Only I'm too tired, y'see."

Oliver's face grew hot. It made him feel somewhat better to see the streak of blush across Jack's face as well, though Oliver suspected that it was less to do with his bold profanity than the actual intimacy of what he was suggesting. Though, to that, Oliver couldn't imagine either of them in such a provocative closeness. Couldn't *imagine*—

Jack laughed deep in his throat, but then stopped, again wincing, tucking his chin down to his chest, his face going pale.

Without regard to the stares he drew, Oliver scraped back his chair and hurried round the table to sit beside Jack. He did not know what was wrong or how to mend it, but he attempted to soothe, his hand on Jack's arm, fingers curled around the crook of Jack's still-damp elbow. Had they been elsewhere he would have pulled Jack over to the smoky coal fire and called for the nearest servant to bring blankets and a chair and, yes, some hot water and gin and sugar for Jack to drink while he sat near the warmth of the hearth. But to do that would call more attention than Jack would probably want.

"Jack," said Oliver, low. "Are you unwell? You look so pale."

Jack's eyes looked a little glazed, narrowed, his forehead stiff, as if with some internal pain. He looked as though he were trying to laugh at his own lubricious comment from earlier, though there was an expression in his eyes that was new to Oliver. There were things about Jack with which Oliver was unacquainted and this just one of many.

"Cromwell hits hard," allowed Jack, "but I've been hit harder, so leave off your fussin'."

Then as if to stave off any continued concern on Oliver's part about this, or perhaps merely as a distraction, he added, "It's all this country air, it ain't doing me no good atall. You might as well give me a hot bath an' dress me up in a gentleman's suit, for all this clean air is makin' me so miserable."

Jack shrugged him off gently. "Go on, go an' sit back over there; the servin' girl is comin' our way."

Jack looked as tired as Oliver felt, so he did as he was asked, and went around the table to sit in the wooden chair that had gone cold in his absence. He didn't imagine that Jack was embarrassed by Oliver's sitting so close; as far as he knew, Jack didn't care about common, everyday niceties such as a polite distance between two young gentlemen traveling on the road together.

"Never you mind," said Jack. He leaned back to let the girl lay down two plates, steaming with hot food, the heavy china clunking on the wooden surface of the table.

"Here's your cutlery." She reached into her clean apron pocket. The knives and forks clattered next to the plates.

"You find somethin' sweet for my friend here?" asked Jack, looking up at Oliver, some good humor coming back into his eyes.

"Still lookin', mister," she said, moving away. But it was easy to see that she was flattered by his small attention as she sashayed away, touching her neck, brushing back her hair. Jack had such a way with people, speaking with ease, making them want to talk to him, do things for him. Yes, he'd already paid the serving girl for the sweet, but still, with the flirty words, she was more likely now to do as he'd asked.

"Why, Jack?" Oliver looked at his plate, which contained an array of boiled meat, boiled potatoes, and boiled carrots. The food was steaming hot, for all it was so plain, and he looked for the bowl of salt and the bowl of pepper, and pulled them to him. "Why must we sit across from each other like this?"

"Because," said Jack, poking his knife at a potato, "I can see you an' the room, all at the same time. Right?"

"Is that important?"

"It is if somethin' happens, an' I ain't seen it comin'."

Oliver was about to ask why *that* was important, but Jack waved him off with a fork.

"Just eat," Jack said, and began to nibble at a bit of carrot, his elbows splayed out on the table, as if this were the most ordinary of occasions. Him and his mate Oliver at a coaching inn some distance from London. As if there were nothing amiss, no dead body cooling in the dank cellar of the Three Cripples. No Noah Claypole, a registered informant, who could so very easily call a constable and turn the whole of that morning's events over to the law. Or that any of Cromwell's coterie might think of tracking Oliver Twist down. It might not happen now, or tomorrow, or even a week from now, but it would happen. The law would find him, and this time he would *hang*.

There was a clicking sound in his ears, and he realized it was his hands rattling the cutlery against the edge of the plate. Jack looked up, briefly glancing at Oliver's hands. Then he went back to his plate, back to taking very small bites as he chewed rather slowly.

"If you don't finish that," said Jack, "then the girl will never bring you puddin'."

In a way, it was the best thing Jack could have said. Oliver made himself cut up the meat and potatoes and start on the carrots, even if they were boiled and wanted for a large dollop of butter. Acting as if all were right in the world, though the food tasted as pleasant as wet dust and the pint pot that the girl presently brought over to them had thin, dull beer that did not quite begin to wash down the tasteless food. But he ate because Jack had directed that he should. And because it was sensible to eat even if the panic in his belly that simply would not subside.

As he ate, cutting away parts of the potato that looked spoiled or felt underdone beneath the blade of his knife, he looked over at Jack, whose plate was mostly full.

"You're not eating," said Oliver. "Don't you like it?"

"This beer tastes like rat's piss," Jack said, tipping the pint pot towards him. "I've had better from a pig's trough."

Before Oliver could think to ask how Jack knew what rat's piss tasted like, and whether he'd eaten from a pig's trough, the serving girl plunked down two plates of a cozily steaming pudding. There was jam at the top and custard oozing down the sides, and for the first time that day, Oliver felt himself relax.

She handed them each a broad, flat spoon. "From the cook's special shelf," she said, at which point Jack reached into his pocket and pulled out another shilling and gave it to her.

As she pocketed the coin and returned to the kitchen, Oliver turned away from the remains of his supper, and began to eat his pudding. His sweet tooth was one of the things known between them, and thinking to share his appreciation of Jack's taking care of him like this, he put the spoon down and lifted his head.

"Mind your puddin', if you please," said Jack, tapping his spoon on the edge of Oliver's plate. "Or I'll eat it myself."

Dutifully, and smiling to himself, Oliver ate the entire pudding and wished for hot, cream-laced tea to polish it off with. But there was none to be had. Besides which, Jack's shoulders were slumped; he was curved over his mostly full plate, as though he meant to fall asleep right there.

As if he could feel Oliver's eyes upon him, Jack looked up. The bruise on his cheek was black and green, and his face was an odd shade.

"It's my head," said Jack.

"It ails you, I know it does," said Oliver. Jack was terribly pale, his eyes narrow, as if even the dull gloom of the room was too bright for him to bear.

"It don't matter, it just aches. Need to lie down, that's all."

5

NOT BEARING UP IN FRONT
OF NOLLY

Nolly was looking at him, and Jack considered pointing out that though the tavern was dark and furled with smoke, it was better than standing in the rain, begging for shelter. It was better than watching Nolly eye the hedgerows, as if he imagined that they might seek shelter beneath them, because, to Nolly, suffering was always a better option than stealing. Not that he could help it, it was just the way he was.

"Did you like the puddin'?" asked Jack, wanting a distraction from his own thoughts, which had suddenly taken such a dour turn, and the pain in his head, which refused to go away. He pointed at Nolly's bowl with his spoon. "It looks all clumpy, but you ate it quick enough."

Nolly always sat upright and polite, as if he were at a tea party with the Queen herself. But the giveaway, now that they were sitting down and Jack could concentrate, was that Nolly's hands were quivering.

But Jack was off his game, and couldn't attend to Nolly, as he'd like to, because his head had a dull thudding echo in it that made it hard to listen, hard to pay attention. Which meant that Jack couldn't look at the room, and watch the folk coming and going. Couldn't keep his eye out for danger.

Which was important, because while Nolly was, evidently, aware that there was danger to be found, he seemed not to know how to spot it. Such as the two gents who'd come in after them, doffing hats and shaking out their fancy frock coats. They'd been looking at Nolly as if he was something good to eat, both of them. But Nolly wasn't aware of them at all. He just seemed focused on his food and, sometimes, on Jack.

Jack's head throbbed; he tried not to lift his hand to press the back of his neck and soothe it, but he lost that battle time and again. Knowing there was a coach ride coming in the morning was its own kind of hell. Jouncing about with strangers, being next to Nolly for hours without being able to say what he wanted. Watching those blue eyes skip over him and look at anything else. Not that Nolly was ashamed, no. He was terrified, and lost in his own worries.

"I'm lookin' out for you, Nolly, I'll see you safe." Jack meant this as he had nothing before. He wanted to shout, to remind Nolly that he'd bloody left London, hadn't he? Would he do that if he'd not meant to look out for Nolly? His best mate?

With this, and the tension in his back, the headache blossomed again, weaving up like smoke, an unstoppable tendril that moved into a fist, clenching his head and not letting go.

"Nolly." Jack kept his voice down but reached across the table with it, wanting Nolly to look at him, just for a moment, just for now.

Nolly blinked with those long lashes of his, the light in his blue eyes coming to crispness as he finally seemed to wake up. Then he looked at Jack.

"Yes, Jack?" he asked, as if they'd been in some long and casual conversation, only Nolly'd been thinking of something else there, just then.

"You finished with your supper? Do you want anythin' more?" asked Jack, instead of saying what he really wanted to say. "I'll get you extra bread an' butter, if you'd like. Do you want extra bread an' butter?"

Those smoky brows furrowed together, and Nolly tipped his head to the side, graceful, as if for hours he'd studied that pose. Only he hadn't, that was just how he moved. As though guided by some angelic hand, or a sculptor's direction. And completely unaware that every time he moved, Jack wanted to hide him away from anything harsh or unpleasant, or the staring eyes of strangers.

One of God's most beautiful creations should not have to suffer any of the world's misfortunes, though this particular creation had a temper to match a fallen angel's, and Jack had been there to see it. Or the end of it, when he'd blinked his way through the blackness, and seen Nolly standing in the kitchen of the Three Cripples, swinging a meat cleaver as though he'd studied how for years. Swung it right into Cromwell, and as agile as anything, had stepped back, avoiding the pool of blood that was forming on the floor. Standing out of the way of Cromwell's body collapsing to the floor, he'd hefted the cleaver in his hand, just the once, frowning at Cromwell's body, as if considering what he might do if Cromwell did not stay down. It was a good thing he had; Jack knew he could not have borne hearing metal hit bone again, hearing the bone crack.

And in that moment, Oliver had put the cleaver down, on the table, perhaps, Jack wasn't quite sure, because Oliver had turned to where Jack was and a filament of expression had simply lifted from his face. And back he had turned, into the gentlemanly Nolly that Jack knew, the haberdasher's apprentice, a regular boy. But until then? He'd been terrifyingly strong, and angry, and focused. Would that he'd put that much effort into becoming a thief, and paid attention when Jack and Charlie and Fagin had been teaching him, then none of this would ever have happened. But this was a secret opinion that Jack could never share, for if he did, Nolly would be affronted, and take on that expression that said to the world how very right and proper his way of life was, and how very wrong was Jack's. Not that he said it outright, but it was in the little things he said and did and mostly that expression, the one Jack hated to see.

He was on the verge of seeing it now, and looked down to where his own cuff was dragging across the leftover puddle of grease. Not that it mattered to Jack, as the brown would match the cloth and no one would care. But it mattered to Nolly, so Jack sat up a bit, and tried not to wince as his shoulder muscles jumped in an ungainly way, and the throbbing in his head rose to a higher pitch.

"Jack, you are not all right. Please don't tell me you're fine when I can see that you're not."

Now that he had Nolly's attention, he didn't want it. Not like this. In Nolly's mind, in that picturesque storybook world that he seemed to believe really existed, an unwell boy was due for a good, hot bath, clean sheets, and a mug of warm milk with honey drizzled in. Jack only had to look at him to know it. And the exact moment when Nolly realized that there was none of this to be had, and that it was his fault. But then, even guilt looked sweet on Nolly, causing that droop to his lower lip. And he didn't even know how beautiful he still was.

"Just need some rest," said Jack. "Which I can get, if you're finished with your supper. I just want to lay my head down somewhere that don't move."

That was better; now Nolly was distracted by the lie, so Jack took a swallow of his beer. He had to fight against the sudden urge to puke all over the table. He stood up, ears ringing with the sound of the legs of the bench scraping against the flagstone floor.

Nolly looked up from his plate, a spoon of sponge and custard halfway to his mouth.

Jack's stomach felt pummeled, as his mouth filled with saliva and an ache in the back of his throat as he struggled to free himself from the gravity of the room.

"Where are you going?"

But Nolly's voice bounced off the walls, adding to the cacophony of the room. Jack could barely make it through the entryway out into the cold, dark, cobblestoned yard. With the rain streaming down, silver-cold, making him blind for a moment as he searched for a dark shadow to hide in before he would be forced to empty his stomach all over the ground.

After a few tripping steps, his hand grazing the wooden side of a shed that was set against the brick wall of the inn, he found a spot. There was even a ledge under which he could shelter as he bowed low, hand on his stomach to keep the red scarf out of the way, and the contents from within splattered all over the rounded humps of wet cobbles.

He could feel the hot acid in his throat and closed his eyes as the smell of his sick rose up in the damp rain. He willed his stomach to settle, but it was a battle already lost, and his stomach churned and he almost keeled over with the pain in his head as he vomited a second time. When he thought he was done, he turned away, covering his face with his hands for a moment before pressing against the dark wooden planks, burying his head in his arms, heaving breath foul, plastering itself all over his rain-drenched skin as his head pounded.

His body shook, even as he tried to still it, even as he heard footsteps behind him, distinct, careful. *Nolly*. Who was to have been spared any trouble or concern.

"Leave me be, Nolly, just leave me be." His voice cracked as he said the words, the rain dripping down his neck. He tried to push himself away from the wall but his hands slipped and he ended up with the cold wood pressing against the side of his face.

He felt Nolly's hands upon him and jerked away, but Nolly would not be stayed. He tugged on Jack's rain-damp shoulder and made Jack turn towards him, and then used the back of his own sleeve to wipe Jack's mouth. It was almost too much, this intimate thing that he did. Then Nolly smoothed the hair away from Jack's forehead, looking at Jack with grave eyes.

"I'll say it for you now: It'll get better, by-and-bye." Nolly said in low tones, as befitted the growing gloom of the yard, the dark speckles of rain that pattered on Nolly's hat.

"I've got your hat, it came off, and you've got the key to the room," Nolly said. "And I left the books at the table. Come along and we'll get you to bed."

This was all said as though there were nothing more amiss than Jack being in control of the room key and this was all that was keeping Nolly from his well-earned night's rest. But the quick, gentle pat that Nolly gave his cheek and the nudge of Nolly's shoulder against his belied that simple statement.

Jack wanted to say something, to thank him, but his knees went weak beneath him and he stumbled on the slick cobbles, grabbing onto Nolly's arm, as if he had no more strength, could not hold himself upright. His whole body felt slack when Nolly gripped his upper arm, fingers curling tightly.

"Jack."

Nolly's face was so very close now, and Jack thought that he would, as he normally did, pull back and regain his distance. But he did not. Instead he bent close, and Jack kept his mouth shut and attempted to calm his breathing. To focus on Nolly's nearness, so close and so tender it made Jack's heart ache that he had not the span of attention to appreciate it.

6

A ROOM AT THE INN

L eaving Jack in the dim entryway, Nolly hurried over to get the books, then came back, the weight of the them in one arm, Jack's hat dangling from his fingers. That Nolly could take charge as easily as Jack was made plain as Nolly stopped at the front counter to ask for a candle to take to bed with them. The clerk lit one for them, and this Nolly took. Jack let Nolly lead him across the main room to the slender stairway at the far end, darkened by railings and slanting up into the half-beamed ceiling.

Feeling only a bit better, now that his stomach was empty, Jack felt in his pocket for the key. It was an ordinary brass key that would have been so easy to copy and a metal ring tag as well, which clattered in his hand as if he shook.

Jack could almost hear the concern in Nolly's breathing as they mounted the stairs as to whether the air in the room would be foul, if there were rats behind the wainscoting, and, assuredly most concerning to Nolly, whether or not there would be water to wash with. There was nothing to be done about any of this, but since Jack wanted nothing more than to lie down, he held his tongue.

Toward the end of the passage, Nolly stopped, and Jack

unlocked the door to open it upon the darkness that was banished but the circle of candlelight

It was a narrow, white cell of a room. The floor was bare, but swept, the walls unadorned. There was no fireplace, but the window, a narrow, grey slice in the thick wall, seemed tightly hove to and did not let in the slightest errant wind, even though it was pelting rain just beyond the panes of glass. There was a small table to hold the candle, and the single low bed was tucked with the head of the bedstead against the wall, but shore-to from the wall on either side. Jack could smell no rank scent that signaled an overabundant number of rats or other vermin, and as the bouncing candle-flame cast bright circles upon the walls and floor, he could see it was a dry and clean room.

Not that Nolly couldn't sleep on old sacking; Jack had seen him do that often enough to know. But the fewer reminders of the harsh reality of the world, the better Nolly would do. They were on a mad plan anyway, searching for family that was long gone. Nolly's Aunt Rose would have written and found them, had there had been anyone to find. But Lyme Regis was as good a location as any, and would get them far from London and the threat of Noah Claypole. Jack didn't think he'd ever get over Oliver and Noah having met before. Ever.

Nolly put the candle on the table, and then went to stand at the foot of the bed, the books in his grasp, a bit of rain glinting on his half top hat. Shaking the rain off his hat, Nolly put it and Jack's hat at the foot of the bed, below the foot rail, along with the books, and straightened up, his attention drawn again to the bed. Though the bed looked more comfortably appointed than the bed that they had shared at the Three Cripples, Nolly's expression seemed to indicate that he thought the bed would bite him, were he to approach it.

"Nolly," said Jack, as gently as he could manage, considering his head was pounding, and all he wanted to do was tear off his damp clothes and throw himself on the bed and not move for many, many hours. "It'll be all right."

Jack pulled the key from his pocket and locked the door. The lock was only stout in the most casual of ways, and would only keep out the less determined of intruders. He left the key in the lock, as once the tumblers were set, the noise of the tin tag alone would be the sharpest alarm.

Nolly was looking around for a washstand and basin, and would soon be confronted with a bed where there were no silken sheets nor eiderdown comforter, never had been, never would be. Jack knew the signs and supposed he could go downstairs and ask one of the servants for a basin of hot water, he certainly had coin enough. But his head ached, and he couldn't bear to. Instead, he took a breath to say something to soothe the worried look from Nolly's brow.

"There's nowt to worry about," said Jack. "There's only you and me, an' no one followin' after. Understand? It's just you an' me now."

Jack tried to unwind the red scarf, to untie his neckerchief, but his fingers felt numb and kept slipping on the knot.

"Besides, you want sleep, an' if you do that, I can lay my head down, which is all I want at this moment," he said, giving up on the neckerchief. "Let tomorrow worry about tomorrow, eh?"

Nolly was looking at him, as though he felt that Jack was about to dole out some dire punishment. Therefore, Jack's slightly scolding tone was not working. Something softer was on order, then.

Jack moved close to Nolly till a single circle of candle-lit shadow engulfed them both.

"The bed's only to sleep in," Jack said.

Nolly sighed deep from the center of his breast, shaking his head, as if remonstrating himself for some deep, untenable fault.

"Nolly, my dear," said Jack, laying the softest of touches on the back of Nolly's wrist. "Come along, then, 'twill be all right."

He took a step, till his boots were touching Nolly's and their chests almost touched. Now he had Nolly's full attention, could see the flicker of his blue eyes in the half light, see the query in the lines of his brow.

"You're damp through," said Jack, as he touched Nolly's jacket collar.

"So are you," said Nolly, shivering at the touch of Jack's fingers, which seemed to rouse him to the point where he was attentive to his surroundings, the room, the flickering candle, the distant sounds of the taproom below. The scent of dust and wood oil, and damp wool, the red scarf around Jack's neck, curling as it dried.

Then Nolly flung his arms around Jack's shoulders. Jack's hands came up, a start of surprise making them jerk before he slid them around Nolly's waist.

Nolly was saying something against Jack's neck, his lips a warm softness against all the cold and damp. With a final tight press, Nolly tried to step back, but Jack held him fast.

"What're you sayin', Nolly?" asked Jack.

"I'm sorry, Jack," said Nolly, barely meeting his eyes. "To bring you all this way with you feeling so ill, when I don't half know what I'm doing."

"I reckon nobody does," said Jack, drawing the edge of his palm across Nolly's brow. "Besides, we do know what we're doin', we're for Lyme in the mornin', an' when we get there, we'll figure it out, you an' me."

Though his head felt foul and his body felt battered by some unseen hand, Jack was rewarded by the small lift of Nolly's smile.

"You and me," said Nolly in return. He leaned in, as if to kiss Jack on the forehead the way a friend might, but Jack clasped Nolly's face in his hands and gently kissed him on the mouth.

"There," he said, rubbing his thumb along Nolly's jaw. "That'll send you to sleep right enough. Now, out of them clothes, quick as you can."

The brisk order seemed to help; Nolly took the red scarf off of Jack and draped it along the headboard. Then he helped Jack with his neckerchief, and together they took off their jackets, which Nolly spread out on the floor. Then their boots, putting them near the door to catch whatever passing draught might dry them. They took off their trousers and waistcoats, which Nolly laid over the end of the bedstead to dry. Stockings were hung on the low rails of the nightstand.

Jack stood shivering in his shirt while Nolly pulled back the bedclothes, as hesitantly as if he were expecting something to jump out at him. As if for courage, Nolly turned to take Jack's hand, but then he stopped.

"Jack," said Nolly.

If Jack had felt better, he could have fully appreciated Nolly's attention, and the hands that Nolly lifted to both sides of Jack's face. The soft stroke of Nolly's thumb, the tender, concerned expression in Nolly's eyes. As blue as the southern sea—

"You must sit down. Here, come and sit down."

Jack let Nolly lead him to the bed, and sat, the stiff edge of the mattress biting into his thighs. He felt numb, as though he was floating, as Nolly coaxed him to put his head on the pillow, to lie down, to be still.

He felt Nolly pulling the blanket over him, tugging at the sheets, and moving the counterpane. It was delicious to be still, for once, and the sight of Nolly bending over him was all the medicine he needed.

"You're so hot, Jack, your skin is on fire," said Nolly, hurtling back into his trousers, his boots. "I'm going to go fetch some water. You'll be all right till I get back?"

Jack closed his eyes, and listened to the clank of the key tag, the patter of feet in the corridor, and let himself drift, and tried to let go of the tenseness in his neck. He'd almost succeeded, when he heard the door open, and Nolly's breath. Beyond his half-closed eyes, the candle's light flickered across the ceiling.

"I tried to hurry," said Nolly.

There was a clunk, and a scrabble, and dripping water, and suddenly, quite gently, someone was laying a cool cloth on his forehead.

"Nolly?"

"Your skin is very hot, yet you are quite pale," said Nolly's voice. "I don't know what to do, whether I should fetch—"

"Don't fetch nobody," said Jack. His mouth felt dry, but the cloth was nice. "Can I have a drink of water?'

Quickly, Nolly's arm slipped behind his back and lifted him up a little. Nolly tipped a tumbler to his lips and Jack drank. Then, Nolly took the cloth away, and brought it back, cooler now, and laid it again on Jack's forehead.

Jack sighed, and let himself drift. He felt much better, now that he was lying still.

"We can arrange to take the coach another day, when you're feeling better." Nolly's voice came from a distance as if muffled by a low hum

"No," said Jack. "We'll get there all the sooner if we leave in the mornin'. Like we planned."

"But what can I do to make you feel better?"

Jack opened his eyes, just a little way, to see Nolly on his knees beside the bed, half-lit by candlelight. If Jack had asked him to run into the street and sell his soul, he believed that Nolly would do it, in that moment. That moment right there.

"Just be with me, now," said Jack. "Put out the candle an' come to bed. Let me rest my head on your shoulder, like we've done, you an' I."

With a quickness that rather gladdened Jack's heart, Nolly snapped the wick with his fingers. The candle went out and there was a shuffling sound as Nolly took off his boots and his trousers. Then he slithered beneath the sheets, pulling the blankets up over them both. Pulling Jack to him, with a gentle care.

When Jack's head came to rest in the hollow of Nolly's shoulder, and the sweet smell of Nolly circled all around him, like roses and ash, then Jack closed his eyes fully and tipped his head forward. Had he not felt so sore, his head dully pounding, this might have been the grand opportunity to pull Nolly into his arms and elicit a more pleasurable response. But the warmth of Nolly's body, the beat of his heart beneath his slowly drying shirt was enough for Jack. They had all the world to travel, with roads before them and adventures to be had.

They were well away from the stew of London and though Jack would miss it, for it was home after all, he was with Nolly and they were tucked into each other's arms beneath the roof of a snug and dry inn, a proper inn, rather than the hedgerow that they would have been curled beneath, had Nolly had his way about the stealing.

"Ain't you glad I still got the grace of my fingers?" asked Jack, low, in the dark.

Nolly turned toward Jack, sending ripples of kind heat that Nolly was now sharing, warm and slow. There came a kiss and a sigh.

"You are a wicked lad, Jack," said Nolly. But he pressed his hand against Jack's face to belie any sense of a scolding. "And I hope you never become any less so, for we would be freezing out of doors if not for you. Just promise me—" Here Nolly stopped to swallow. "Don't ever get caught. I couldn't bear it if you were taken from me."

In the dark, it seemed that Nolly could speak what was in his heart, in the quiet dusk of night when there was no one to see or hear. Would that he had shouted the words in daylight, the sentiment could not have pleased Jack more. For it bespoke of the fact that of all his regrets, and it seemed that Nolly had many, being with Jack was not one of them.

This warmed Jack from within, and he shared that warmth by sinking a little lower in the bed until Nolly became his pillow and Nolly's arms around him became his blanket. The night became dark and still, and he listened as Nolly's heart slowed, and his breath leveled out. Jack was warm all through as he soaked it in and tried to ease the back of his neck and willed his headache to go away.

"You an' I," Jack said.

∾

The room was somewhat less wild and insalubrious than the one at the Three Cripples. The ceiling creaked overhead, though Oliver didn't imagine, didn't want to imagine, that he heard roof rats scuttling about. As it was, he felt the need to jump out of his skin and get out of bed and walk around the whole of the coaching inn to look for constables, and the skulking ghost of Cromwell. To see if Noah Claypole had indeed followed them, to perform his office of informant with his usual élan and style. There were too many details he'd not attended to, too many shapes and outlines he'd not thought to be wary of. Something needed doing; with Jack's ragged state, the bruises on his face, as well as Oliver's own disheveled person, they could not have been taken for young gentlemen on a simple outing. That they'd not been arrested for vagrancy straight away was a small miracle; tomorrow might not bring the same luck.

For Jack, all of this must seem so easy; compared with the worry of being caught as a thief, compared to the worry of being homeless, attempting to convince Oliver to shut up and go to sleep seemed to be his main desire. That Jack had followed him this far, had not turned back to London in despair of Oliver being sensible enough to keep his mind in the moment, well, that was worth something. Jack deserved more, for simply coming this far with Oliver, so Oliver would give him that.

Jack lay still now, next to him in the bed, in his arms. Where Oliver's hands were tucked, he could feel the sweat under Jack's arms, the rise and fall of Jack's chest full of warmth and heartbeat and simmering fatigue. And Oliver thought that in spite of Jack's protestations, he should have called for a doctor. Jack had said he only wanted to sleep. He might have said it for himself, for his own sake, but he meant it for Oliver's as well.

Jack knew how to be on the road, to be on the run, to play hide and seek in plain sight. If he was worried about what Oliver had done, he didn't express any squeamishness that Oliver had killed a man with his bare hands. Though the heft of that cleaver as it hit bone still rang a ghostly vibration through his hands, to Jack it was nothing, a mere trifle. If he was worried whether they would be discovered and arrested in the morning, he showed no sign of it. Whether he was still hungry or full of complaint at his own discomfort, he had barely spoken of it.

It was only the heat of his body that soaked into Oliver's bones that gave him pause. Jack was almost too warm to be near, too warm to so easily fall asleep, but yet he had. Oliver felt the start of Jack's body before it calmed; the deepness of his breathing told Oliver that Jack was indeed exhausted, that the fever of his body or no, Jack was fast asleep.

For a moment he wanted to awaken Jack, to ask him again whether it would be all right, but he stilled the thought even as he stilled his hand, still lightly clasped around Jack's shirt collar. Had this been only a day or so ago, Oliver would not have hesitated to ask for soothing words, but Jack didn't deserve to be woken merely to calm Oliver's nighttime fears.

The world he'd been in, had come so far from, was much darker now, and shadows on the walls, the unease of thought now that the day had come to an end, were only the small steps of a child. He had more things to worry about than that. Besides, after the day they'd had, he'd rather lock himself in a coal box than waken Jack. Jack had come with him from London, after all, something he'd sworn he'd never do. Oliver owed him a good night's sleep, at least. So he tucked his chin, and burrowed beneath the blanket and thick sheet, let his eyes drift closed, and matched his breathing to Jack's, his grasp on Jack's collar never loosening.

7

BREAKFAST AT DAWN

Oliver was already half awake when the bell clanged in the yard outside. He sat up and crawled over Jack's slumbering form, and on his hands and knees searched in the dank dark at the foot of the bed for his trousers, his stockings. When his fingers caught the edges of them, they were chilly but almost dry.

As he sat on his backside on the floor and pulled on his stockings, his heart hammering, fingers blind with haste, he realized that Jack wasn't moving.

"Jack," he said, his voice stumbling over itself. "Jack, there's the bell, you must get up now."

Jack wasn't answering, so Oliver stood up to pull on his trousers and sat on the bed to lace his boots, throat parched all the while and aching for something cool to soothe it.

And still Jack had not stirred. Oliver stood up and, at the window, pulled the back thick drapes. The room grew brighter as the dawn gathered over the grey rooflines.

Oliver pulled Jack's garments together in his arms, as he stood above Jack and considered how to wake him gently. Jack rolled on his back and opened one eye then closed it again.

"Nolly, dear," Jack said, voice gravel-low. "Let me sleep, only five more minutes, be a good lad, then."

Of course, there wasn't any real need for concern; they had time.

But the anxiousness that pattered like a confused rabbit beneath his breastbone refused to allow Oliver to be at ease. Yet even as he meant to roust Jack from the bed, he could see that Jack was still pale, bruises standing out with green and black starkness, as though painted there, a countenance of ill health that presaged nothing but dire consequences.

"Starin' at me again, are you, Nolly?" Jack asked, both eyes closed. "Want to crawl back in an' join me, eh?"

Jack remained curled up beneath the sturdy blanket, now divined as workaday brown, with thick calico sheets. Jack's dark hair sprawled across the pillow, the length of his neck white, despite the smear of flush along his cheeks.

"Jack," said Oliver, bending close. "You are unwell, tell me true—"

At that instant, Jack pushed Oliver away with the back of his arm and sat up, grubby from sleep, scrubbing at his eyes as a small child might whose nurse has woken him in too abrupt a manner. Of course, Jack had never had a nurse, nor any kind hand to gentle him out of sleep, at least none that he'd spoken of. But then, in an eye blink, Jack became the young man he was as he shoved away the bedclothes and stood up, naked feet curling from the chill of the wooden floor, his shirt, with its ragged hem, barely coming to his knees.

"You got my trousers?" Jack reached for them without waiting for an answer as he tugged them on and buttoned them at his waist. Tucked the shirt in and grabbed his stockings and sat to pull them on.

"I'll get your boots, said Oliver, anxiety momentarily soothed by the sight of Jack tugging at his tattered stockings. He could make believe, for a moment, that it was just the dawn of an ordinary day.

But it wasn't an ordinary day. They were scheduled for Lyme Regis on a public coach with tickets purchased with stolen money. He'd spent another night in Jack's arms and nothing would ever be ordinary again.

"Stop looking so damn peevish," said Jack, striding to the foot of the bed to pull on his jacket, to step into his books and to jam his half top hat on his head. "Grab them books; I'd kill for a half-pint of beer afore we set out."

But, as Jack wound the red scarf about his neck and clomped across the room to unlock the door, he bumped Oliver's shoulder with his own. As if to indicate that while his complaint about Oliver's expression was true enough, he did indeed have sympathetic regard for Oliver's confused state.

"Say now, is that another bell? Or is it the horn?" Jack gave Oliver a crooked grin to show he was teasing, and he looked somewhat better after a night's rest. "Reckon you could do with some beer as well. Yes?"

At Oliver's nod, Jack tugged on Oliver's jacket, and pulled him along into the passageway and down the narrow stairs.

The ground floor of the tavern was chilly; the serving girl was building the fire in the grate at the far end of the room. There was a small knot of gentleman sitting around the tables by the fire. They had pots of drink and slices of bread in their hands, and as Jack strode to the bar, Oliver clutched his books to his breast and watched them. Nobody seemed to give him any notice at all; they weren't yet awake, as was right with any sensible person at this hour. When Jack came over with the beers, he handed one to Oliver.

"Sip it, or you'll be pissin' it out before the hour is up an' these coaches don't stop, except for the horses."

Glad, even if only for a moment, to have some guidance amidst the madness that had become his life, Oliver did as he was told, putting the books on the table Jack as he sat down.

The beer was fresh and cool from being kept in the cellar and soothed him almost as much as had watching Jack don his stockings.

Over the rim of the tin pot, and through the thick bulls-eye windows, Oliver heard a brass horn seconds before he saw a coach rattle into the yard. It was way too early to be theirs, and he wondered from whence it had come. London, probably; the inn was on the main coach road to Exeter, after all. And it was along this route that he and Jack were bound, to search for a family that might not even acknowledge him. And even if they did, they would have not the slightest notion of what to make of Jack.

Even with the fire burning in the hearth, the chill of the room made Oliver's teeth chatter. Neither he or Jack was dressed for travel; everyone else in the room had stout coats and cloaks for riding outside, with warm boots, and packets of food. And no fear of being arrested on the spot.

Oliver's shoulder blades were almost meeting at the back, he couldn't hold himself any straighter. Nor could he change the judgment of the servant, who slammed a plate of cold meat and bread in front of them.

"That's to share. Coffee's extra."

Oliver looked at Jack, who shook his head, and was toying with a piece of butter-less bread. Oliver knew he should eat, but cold ham first thing in the morning had never been his favorite. Neither was bread without butter, but he picked up a slice and bit into it. It had a strange country roughness to its texture, but it tasted fairly good. He ate the entire thing, and then, since his stomach had woken up, he reached for the slice of ham.

"Jack, you're not eating," said Oliver, with his mouth full

"'Tis only a headache," said Jack.

"Be true to me, Jack, it's more than that."

"Stop fussin' an' pass me some ham afore you eat it all."

Pushing the plate toward Jack, Oliver felt his chest ease a little bit. He would feel better when they further away from London

Jack ate a little of the bread with the ham, but then gestured with it, as though he meant to put it on Oliver's plate so that Oliver could have it.

"No," Oliver said. "You need to eat; you cannot travel on air."

"I agree," said Jack, and the little smile on his lips turned real. "That's why I'll be travelin' in a coach, with you at my side."

He said it as though it were a good thing, something to be treasured. Oliver was about to demand why being on the run with a murderer was a good thing when the horn for an approaching coach sounded, and the whole room scrambled to its feet.

Jack turned to Oliver, with that smile and sparkling green eyes, the beer having brought some good color to his face.

"Ready then, Nolly?" he asked.

Oliver grabbed the books and followed Jack along the narrow passage to step out into the rainy yard of the coaching inn. Jack could not be faring well, and indeed, Oliver saw him shiver as they neared the open door of the coach. Reaching out, Oliver tucked the red scarf tighter around Jack's neck, which earned him a quick smile over Jack's shoulder.

Oliver handed their chits to the man at the door of the coach; again, they got rather corrosive looks as they, in their muddy and wrinkled clothes, clambered inside to sit facing forward, while the outside passengers, in thick cloaks and hats and gloves, grimly climbed on top. The coach rocked on its heels as all the passengers settled themselves. Leaving Oliver and Jack in the faded interior of a coach that had seen better days. It was solidly paneled with wood, but the edges around the window were scuffed, and the cushions had pokes of wool coming out, and more than one button was hanging by a mostly shredded thread.

Their fellow passengers were a man and the woman, who were sitting in the backward-facing seats. And while they were dressed in black garb, as if they'd just been to a funeral or were going to one, there was no presence of sweet flowers and they did not hold hands. They stared at Oliver and Jack, as if personally offended, and Oliver knew that had Jack been in better spirits, he would have made several unconscionable remarks that would have left Oliver quivering with irritation and shame.

There would have been no righting a folly such as that, but Oliver was left with nothing to worry about. Jack clamped his mouth tightly as he adjusted himself in the seat. He attempted to unwind the red scarf to give it to Oliver, but Oliver waved him away as the coach jumped into motion. They were rocked together, their shoulders banging, and Oliver did not miss Jack's wince.

"Let me take your hat," Oliver said. "You can use my shoulder as a pillow." He quickly stuffed the books and Jack's hat behind his back and coaxed Jack close. He unwrapped the scarf from Jack's neck, and, using it like a shawl, smoothed it around Jack's shoulders. He pulled Jack to him, and, as Jack relaxed, Oliver looked out the window at the sheets of morning rain. Anyone sensible of propriety would not want him anywhere near. Except for Jack. There was always Jack.

For the first quarter of an hour, the rocking motion of the coach through the narrow lanes of Staines at speed felt quite heady. But after those first fifteen minutes, Oliver realized that the coach did not so much roll along as lurch, banging the side of Oliver's head against the thinly padded edge of the window. The window's leather flap let in damp gusts of air, which did not improve the fug of moisture and exhalation of their two fellow passengers bundled to the cold. The whole atmosphere was unhealthy, at the very least.

He tried to distract himself with the glimpses of view beyond the rain, how the mud from the cantering horses flicked up in the air. How the trees, as much as he could see them through the foggy air, were green, tipped with stirring life, much brighter than had been seen in London—

He jerked his mind away from that place, which grew more

distant with every passing moment. That was behind him. Now he was here, with Jack close beside him; they were thigh to thigh, knee to knee, with the roll of Jack's shoulder fitting into the curve of Oliver's. Jack's body was warm against his.

The flash of Jack's blue waistcoat glowed against the gloom of their two fellow travelers, with their solid frock coat and sensible bonnet and cape, black and grey and brown-trimmed all. Jack was again the bright bird, and while Oliver wanted to reach over and tug Jack's jacket closed, he thought better of it.

For while them sitting so closely side by side, with Jack's head lolling against Oliver's shoulder, might be explained by the close quarters of the coach's interior, if Oliver posed a question to Jack about his comfort, it would not make the right impression. For then Jack would reply with his eyes, so very expressive, as he thanked Oliver for his care, right before he said something teasing and provocative enough to curry notice.

But where did his loyalty lie, with Jack or with people to whom he'd not, and would never be, properly introduced? While the answer to that might seem clear, that he should not act as fond of Jack as he should like, he decided to rebel.

"Sleep if you will," Oliver said to Jack, as he tugged Jack's jacket closed. "I won't mind." His voice was low, but Jack heard him.

"But if I do that, an' you see anythin' good, then I'll miss it."

"Then I shall wake you," said Oliver.

He shifted the scarf around so that it covered Jack more. Pulled up Jack's collar and touched his neck before settling back against the seat, though the books bit into him. And he hoped, that in anyone's eyes, they were just two young men traveling together. A little brightly dressed and ragged at the edges, perhaps, but just two young men, close friends and nothing else.

Though *close friends* was not enough of a description to encompass the tumult in Oliver's heart. He felt unable to pin down what Jack was to him. Someone of intimate acquaintance, to be sure. Someone who professed derision at Oliver's civilized ways, and yet who watched Oliver with careful eyes and pulled Oliver to him when the night grew dark and the world too wide a place. Someone who had insisted that London was his only home and who had followed Oliver out of it anyway.

All of these things, was Jack to him, dozing warm and still against him as the coach lurched on.

8

ALONG THE ROAD TO EXETER

Jack almost slid off the bench seat as the coach went rollicking over a hill and down a stone-guttered lane. There was an earsplitting warble of a horn toot-tooting their fucking arrival, and the clatter of horses' hooves on stone, and all of a sudden the coach came to a stomach-jerking stop. That, along with the screech of iron and wood, thundered in Jack's head. He knew he was grinding his forehead into Nolly's shoulder, as if that would stop it. But it didn't; nothing had, all the long morning. Only now the coach was still as the funeral people got off, stomping out of the coach, as though being with the likes of him and Nolly was more of an affront than their delicate souls could bear.

Nolly, just coming out of his own cloud of misery, turned to Jack.

"I'll go first and help you, no—I will, I tell you. We'll rest. We'll eat. Here."

With unconscionable gentleness, of a sort that would have made the angels weep, Nolly alighted from the coach and turned to Jack, as he scrambled to his feet. Nolly didn't make a big show of it, as someone else might have done. Instead, he stayed right by the leather-padded door, as if needing to hold onto it himself, leaving his arm there for Jack to use. Positioning his whole body so that if Jack stumbled and fell, Nolly would be there to catch him. And all without a single word, not that anyone in the coaching inn could hear, at any rate. It undid Jack to the point where he felt quivery all over, and did stumble, on the last wooden stair-step. But Nolly's arm was around him, and Nolly was nuzzling his ear as if they were the best of chums, and Nolly had a secret to tell.

"Easy, there. Shall we walk to that bench under the window? Or go inside?"

Unable to reason whether he was hot or cold, Jack shook his head. But Nolly needed to eat, even if Jack didn't feel like it. And from the pace the coach was setting, they wouldn't have long for anything much.

"Inside," he said.

He could not quite unsquint his eyes to see, stumbling over the smallest rough spot in the courtyard, and again Nolly was there. Brushing up against him, tugging on his sleeve. Leading him into the building without seeming to lead him. Taking him to a small table out of the way, once they were inside. And sitting close beside him.

Leaning close. Almost catching Jack unawares with his closeness, when Jack was able to open his eyes in the semi-gloom of the inn.

"Jack, we can stay here. Just a few days, and then you can rest." This was said in the utmost earnest, with the sweetest voice. It made Jack want to weep.

"No," he said, his teeth gritted. "Just want to get there, quick as we can. Then I'll lay down."

"Very well," said Nolly. "I'll wave the girl over. It looks as though they've got beer, beef, and potato. Will that do you?"

"Just the beer," said Jack. "Don't care for no beef or boiled potato."

He could smell the food as it was brought, an assault of grease and salt that made his stomach turn. He needed to collect himself or Nolly would be overriding all of Jack's careful lies. Yes, he was fine, yes, they should go on. Frankly, the thought of being stuck in an inn, especially one in the middle of nowhere, with Nolly and the idea in his head that his remaining family could be found somewhere beyond the horizon, well. It would take a better man than he to endure it with much patience.

It was better to keep moving, besides, and put as much distance between them and London as possible.

When the food and drink came, Nolly urged Jack to take a sip of his beer, before turning to his own meal. Jack listened to Nolly eat, and eventually was able to open his eyes without feeling as though someone had stabbed him through each one, and look around. It was an old-fashioned coaching inn, to be sure, with thick cross-beams in the walls, and showing through the plaster in the ceiling. Time had polished those beams, from rough oak to a silken, smoke-scented patina. The coaching inns in London looked much the same, except for they had grubby stains in the plaster, and the spit-streaked walls, and the constant smell of cow shit reeking through the air.

Maybe Nolly wouldn't mind staying at a place like this, though it would be foolish to stop their journey now.

Jack drank his beer, slowly, thinking the taste odd, and putting it off to country brewing habits. It didn't make him feel much better, but he didn't want to alarm Nolly, so he stood up slowly, as if needing to stretch his legs.

"I'm going outside," he said. "Fresh air, an' that."

"What?" Nolly's mouth was half-full of food, and he stopped mid-chew to look at Jack.

Which made Jack queasy all over again, even though he'd had nothing but a little bread and some beer for breakfast. He made for the door, and once outside, took as deep a breath as his lungs would permit, and willed the pounding in his head and down his neck not to take over. He found he was leaning against the corner of the main building, where the inn's yard met the road, and staring at the low hillock rolled over itself until, just beyond, there was the sight of a row of large grey stones, set in a circle.

It was only a little way off, and there seemed to be a narrow, dusty road leading up to it, and beyond the stones, the road led off, becoming a small brown path before it disappeared over a long, green mound.

Before Jack had time to suss out what he was looking at, Nolly was at his side, warm and solid in the wavering air. The feel of Nolly's shoulder against his was steadying; Jack leaned back into it, and liked the idea of it. Their shoulders together; them together.

"Are you all right, Jack? You got up so suddenly, I had to pay—"

"What's that?" asked Jack. He pointed at the stones.

"Oh," said Nolly. He lifted his head to look where Jack pointed, silent for a moment. "It's a henge," he said. "I don't know which one, but I've read that they're very old."

Someone came up from behind them; he was dressed as a stablehand might be, with a filthy apron and grease on his arms.

"It 'tis," said the stablehand, in his country accent. "'Tis very old, from the time afore writin', they do say."

Jack very much doubted that the fellow could himself write, but Nolly seemed interested, so Jack kept his mouth shut.

"The Exeter coach don't come from London this way, very often," said the stablehand. "But the matter appears to be that the direct road, goin' through Salisbury, had a washout in the rain. 'Tis bein' fixed now."

"But what's it called?" asked Nolly.

"What? Oh, them stones? 'Tis a henge, you see."

"Yes," said Nolly, sounding as though the edge of his patience was wearing thin. "But does it have a name? And if we're not in Salisbury, like it says on the schedule, then where are we, exactly?"

"Oh, that's easy enough. This here's Amesbury, and that henge over there," the boy pointed at the stones. "That there's Stonehenge."

The name meant nothing to Jack, nor to Nolly, as far as Jack could tell. But Nolly nodded in his polite way, and the stablehand went off, just as the coach's horn toot-tooted into the damp air.

"We have to get back on the coach," said Jack. He needed Nolly to get moving, but he was still looking at the henge.

"I know," said Nolly. "Can you manage? I don't know how many hours we have to go."

"Don't matter," said Jack. He wanted to add that as long as Nolly was by him, he'd do well enough. But as they neared the coach, the funeral people, their black crepe ribbons fluttering in the brisk wind, were coming close, and would most certainly hear, so Jack kept quiet. It wasn't any of their business what he felt for Nolly anyway.

Nolly politely let the funeral people get on and get settled, and Jack did his best to ignore all of the traveling folk in the courtyard and atop the coach who were staring at them. He knew what they were thinking. Two lads such as themselves should allow two ladies who were riding on top to take their places in the inside seats. But Jack was no gentleman, so he didn't recommend it to Nolly, because Nolly was. And would have offered to change seats, had he thought of it. Only the distraction of being on the run for cold-blooded murder was enough to keep him alert and focused. And selfish. Which was all right by Jack.

They were barely seated when the coach started up again, with a hard rock forward and a bang backwards. The wooden panels rattled, and the coach swayed as the coachman cracked his whip, and the horses broke into a gallop.

And that was the beginning of his headache all over again.

The only thing he could do was to endure it.

The road went up and down, and no sooner than Oliver had settled himself to going up, with his head plastered to the back of the seat, then the coach would chuff almost to a halt and tip forward and race on. He didn't have to look out the window to know that they were going downhill again. He could only hope and pray that the horses wouldn't slip on any flints and that the harness would hold.

They seemed to be going at a terribly fast pace. They had to get where they were going, to be sure, but if the coach were to tumble down a hill, they'd all break their necks before they could think about it. That, at least, would cheat the hangman of his due, so when the coach lurched upwards again, Oliver gritted his teeth and did not complain.

Jack, for his part, was quiet, his eyes closed, looking a little lost and a little pale. They'd stopped for a short while for some dinner, but Jack had only had a little beer, which couldn't be enough to give him any strength for the remainder of the journey.

The black-garbed lady and gentleman were still staring at them, and Oliver couldn't determine whether it was Jack or himself who drew their eyes, or whether it was Jack's impoliteness at dozing off, his splayed legs, arms crossed over his chest, or at the bruises on his face. Regardless, those eyes were eyes of condemnation, though, since the couple was dressed all in black, as though they were on their way to or from a funeral, it could be that they were merely sad. But when the older gentleman huffed under his breath and pretended to be very concerned with his gloves, Oliver knew that it wasn't the funeral that was distressing them.

It was as the coach mounted the top of a pass that Jack began to look grey around the edges, his jaw clamped shut, his eyes half slits, skin warm with fever. Suddenly, as the horses cantered down-hill, the coach pitched sideways, with a yawl to the left like a small ship skulled in a storm, and Jack slumped all the way forward, half across Oliver's lap, and vomited between his legs.

The warmth of fluid, the remains of beer, which had been all Jack had been able to manage at dinner, sank into the cloth of Oliver's trouser leg and splashed onto the floor as the coach tilted roughly backwards and forwards. What made it worse was that Jack was now utterly slumped across Oliver's thighs, his fingers curled clawlike into the cloth of Oliver's trousers. And then, instead of sitting up, Jack sagged there, drool trailing from his mouth. A dank smell rose inside the coach, and the two black-garbed passengers drew back, clutching at each other.

The man in the black top hat looked disgusted, his lip curled, as his lady companion moaned in horror.

"That had better not be cholera, young man," he said. As if Oliver had any control over a disease caught by breathing the foul air of sewers.

Just at that moment, Jack pressed his forehead against Oliver's knee. "What'm I doin' across your lap, Nolly?" he asked, sounding as if he were very much struggling not to be sick again.

"You just vomited between my legs," said Oliver. He'd meant to explain that it was better than anywhere else, for it had shielded their fellow passengers from the worst of it, but he was distracted by Jack's low, thick laugh.

"What is it, Jack?"

"I only meant to say," said Jack, with a slight cough to clear his throat, "that there are better things I should like to be doin' between your legs than vomitin'."

The man gasped aloud, and the woman made a sound that was well on its way to being a shriek. The man sat forward.

"I say, you're far too crass to be in a coach with a lady—"

"He's drunk," Oliver snapped, desperate to stop the man from making the most obvious of conclusions. The back of his neck felt hot with what Jack had said, as clearly as if he'd announced it to the world, and to hell with what it bestirred deep within Oliver's belly. To distract himself, he bent over Jack, wiping his chin gently with the back of his hand. The books fell forward, jamming into his lower back as he leaned over Jack.

"If he is drunk then he should not be on this coach, nor any public conveyance."

It was a rough scolding to be receiving with so many eyes upon him, yet it was more acceptable to be faulted for drunkenness than cholera. Which would surely have seen them tossed off the coach into the nearest ditch. As to the other thing Jack had said, his breath hot against Oliver's thigh, Oliver made himself focus on grasping Jack's shoulders to gently pull him upright once more. But the gentleness was wasted; the coach swung sideways as the wheels slipped in the mud, banging everyone against the insides of the vehicle, with Jack smacking right against Oliver's side and leaving a trail of vomit all over Oliver's shirt bosom. Jack's face was sallow, his eyes rose-tinged with exhaustion. The man and the woman turned their faces away.

"Well, is he drunk, or does he have the cholera?" The man demanded this, drawing his woman to him, as though he and he alone could protect her from the miasma that Jack had brought with him. The woman clutched at her man's arm.

"No," said Oliver, not quite certain he was right. He knew what cholera was, everyone did, but he'd never witnessed it up close. Jack was as feverish as any fever victim, but the mess on the floor was only beer and what Jack had eaten that morning; he'd had nothing at Amesbury at dinner, professing his distaste for beef and boiled potatoes. Which was rubbish; Jack had no food fancies, he ate everything put in front of him. "He's unwell because—"

But Jack interrupted him with thick heaving sounds as he leaned forward, the weight of his chest pressing against Oliver's knees. Jack gasped, grinding his forehead against Oliver's thigh.

"Dreadful boy," said the man. "It's simply dreadful that such people are allowed to ride inside, when good people are suffering the weather."

He stared at Oliver and lifted his glove, breathing in the scent of the leather rather than the sick on the floor. The woman looked as though she might faint, so instead of incurring further condemnation by punching anyone in the nose, Oliver took Jack's hat out of the way of the vomit, and placed it behind him. Then he took the scarf from behind Jack's back, where it had slipped, and, reaching between his knees, wiped Jack's mouth with it.

Jack tried to turn his head, but Oliver wiped the spit and vomit away; he'd do a better job in a moment with the cuff of his sleeve and a lick of his thumb, but for the moment, he pulled at Jack's shoulders.

"Nolly, what's wrong w'me?" Jack slurred, as if half drunk.

"You just finished throwing up, but never mind that now. Sit back, just rest your head." He cupped Jack's face in his hands, pushing away sweat-streaks of hair from Jack's forehead. He pulled out his cuff and used it to wipe Jack's chin. Then he licked his thumb and swiped it along Jack's lower lip.

"There," said Oliver. "Better?"

While Jack nodded, lashes almost fanning closed against his pale cheeks, the man watching them snorted.

"What about the mess on the floor? Are we to be expected to suffer the entire journey with that mess at our feet?"

"No indeed," said Oliver, with the sternness of a rebuke, narrowing his eyes at the couple.

There was nothing for it but to pull the length of the red scarf and scrabble to the floor to wipe up the vomit as the coach swayed and shook over the macadamed road. He bumped against everyone's knees at each turn in the road, and, when he was finished, he climbed back into his seat. Sliding open the window on his side, he tossed out the red scarf, watching the ragged ends land against the muddy hedge along the roadside. Leaving the window open for the fresh air, he looked over to where Jack was watching him, not quite wide-eyed, but with stark surprise that Oliver would do such a thing.

"I'll get you another," he said, uncaring that the man and the woman were listening.

"I'll get *you* another," said Jack, in return, his eyes closing with the effort of speaking. He tipped his head back, resting his cheek against the thinly padded wall.

"You're disgusting, the pair of you," the man snapped, drawing Oliver's attention away from Jack's welfare and into the reality of an uncaring pair of people.

"You're the one who's disgusting," said Oliver in return, unconcerned with their start of shock. He reseated himself so that he,

Oliver, would be against the hard wall, with Jack in his arms. "It would be more Christian of you to realize that he can't help being ill."

They went silent then, but their respective glares increased. At least the fact that they'd stopped talking left Oliver in peace; he didn't have to pretend to be polite anymore. Instead he could concentrate on Jack, clasping his hand, stroking his forehead, and mourning the loss of the red scarf.

9

A BRIEF RESPITE IS HAD AT
BRIDPORT

They had reached the near-coastal town of Bridport, coming down from the high plains of Salisbury and into the valley, where the green-turning hills humped themselves into rocky ledges, and the sea air came bitingly through the trees. They had stopped at the George Inn to freshen the horses, and Oliver clambered out of the coach with the black-garbed man and woman.

Jack, whose comments had devolved into the silence of a gritted and stony stoicism, did not move. Oliver wanted to get him some water at least, if there was nothing more to be had. But before that, he walked up to the ostler, who was doing something clever with the buckles on the lead horse's harness.

"Excuse me, sir," said Oliver, his voice clogged with road dust and want of rest. "Could you tell me—I could not catch the coachman, and perhaps you do not know, how long till we reach Lyme Regis?"

The ostler, a small man, with spare movements and spots of grease on his sagging linen shirt beneath his leather waistcoat, turned to Oliver, puzzled. "This coach 'ere? The Comet?"

"Yes, this coach." Oliver didn't allow his temper to take full rein; the man probably saw many coaches come and go through the day, perhaps he only meant to be sure before answering. "This coach, the one to Exeter." *The one I have just disembarked from*, he wanted to add, but didn't.

"Oh," said the ostler. He finished his business with the harness, and then gave the horse a hearty pat along its flank. "This 'ere be the coach to Exeter, fine enough. But it don't go nowheres near Lyme."

"But we're going there, the coach is headed *through* there and will stop so we can get off." The words came fast and frantic in spite of his determination not to panic. "We've purchased tickets. We've been on this coach *all* day, and should arrive after nightfall." At least he thought he had the facts right. It had been a long day, with Jack looking worse, his forehead tight against the pain, with every passing hour. "We're meant to alight there, so I can care for my friend."

"The coach is goin' *past* Lyme," said the ostler firmly. "I don't know who has sold you yer tickets, lad, whether they lied or you weren't a-listenin', but this coach." He jerked his thumb at the rocking, lurching conveyance, now still, for all the horses moved within their harnesses, as though they meant to keep the wheels rolling, in spite of everything else, in spite, even, of gravity. "This coach is bound for Exeter and don't go *through* Lyme. See that letterin' braced in gilt? Hit says The Comet. That's the name of the coach, the coach that goes to Exeter and don't go through Lyme. There is a coach to Lyme, but it ain't this one."

But before Oliver could open his mouth and ask, even if a trifle faintly, where he might catch the coach to Lyme, the ostler held up his hand. "The coach to Lyme come from Brighton, through Plymouth, Yarmouth, an' along the coast, see? But you can't catch it 'ere. The best you could do, the best you *should* do, lad, is to ask with that pretty face of yours if the coachman will let you off somewhere along the way. Wait—there he is. Mr. Weston, will you come close a moment?"

The coachman, with his tan tri-caped long coat, the red braid along the edges dark with time, his dust-flecked top hat, and his long, stiff-handled whip, came striding over the cobblestones in his tall, black boots, looking like something out of an old-fashioned print that Oliver'd once seen in a shop window back in Chertsey. He was the romance of the road, covered in dust and looking at the ostler with a purposeful eye.

"What's amiss then, Willie, m'old friend? This here lad a-botherin' you?" The coachman eyed Oliver as if he were the most preposterous of people to be bothering the ostler. "You ain't keepin' Willie from his work, are you, lad? Why, him and me, we've got a bet on whether this harness'll hold till the next stop, a full shilling, is it? Willie means to patch it and I am to let it break apart an' all of us go flying, an' that'll teach the owners not to reinvest in their gear. Why, they—"

The coachman meant to go on, but Willie held up his hand to make him stop. "The Comet will never fly apart, sir, not as long as I'm here to tend it."

"An' how long for will that be?" The coachman looked as though he wanted to spit, and an old argument simmered between them, for all they seemed so at ease with each other to speak so plainly. "When the train'll be growing between here and the coast, covering the old road with iron, and us left with nothing to say about it?"

The ostler shook his head and looked at the coachman with the flesh crinkling about his eyes, though he didn't allow himself to smile. "When that day comes, my friend, and isn't there always change a-comin'? When that day comes, then you and I will find that cottage along the shore, above the deep caves built into the rock, and smuggle brandy—"

"Don't need to smuggle brandy n'more, Willie," said the coachman, seemingly sad about it, but he was smiling instead of frowning now, as if somehow stirred by the idea of it. "How you live in the old days."

Willie smiled fully now, crooked, a tooth missing on one side, but unabashed to be seen doing it, for all they were in the yard, and the coachman towering and vibrant and far more powerful than he. "It's so easy to go there, nowadays, but never mind that now—this lad, somehow, thought The Comet was a-goin' to Lyme, but it ain't."

"Of course it don't go there, what foolishness is this?" The coachman turned on Oliver with a flick of his whip, seemingly on the verge of giving him a good thrashing for bothering his ostler friend in such a manner. "It ain't never gone there, where does he want to go?"

"He wants to go to Lyme, says his friend is ill."

"Ill, you say." The coachman looked at Oliver without any sympathy whatsoever, and his eyes narrowed. "Has 'e got anythin' which might be catchin' and dangerous for my other passengers?"

Oliver took a step back, his whole body feeling tight. "N-no sir, that is, I don't think so. He'd hit his head yesterday, and it's coming on in a fever, and I thought—"

"You thought this coach was a-goin' to Lyme, like some simpleton."

"Now, there, that's true enough, but Mr. Weston, it ain't as troublesome as all that. Why, you could drop this lad and his friend off at the Hunter—"

"Best be dropping them off at Penn Inn, though it be closed now," said the coachman, eyeing Oliver up and down. "If you're a-goin' to Lyme, it'd save you a full double-mile, if not more."

"That's right enough, Mr. Weston, straight down the hill from the Penn, even in the dark, it'd be only the walk of ten minutes. If you'd be kind enough, Christian enough, to do it."

While he waited, Oliver imagined that the two men had had many a conversation such as this, about where the road went, and how fast a man or a coach could go. How long the harness would last; whether this horse needed new shoes; whether the clover was sweet enough for the mare. He wasn't a part of this conversation, and never would be; he was only the latest matter deemed inter-esting enough to discuss. Realizing this was rather like stepping out of a painting that one felt one was a part of but wasn't. He was only the watcher; aware but apart.

"Kind enough, eh?" The coachman took off his top hat, and holding the long whip in the crook of his elbow, smoothed his oiled black hair. "I'll show you kind. Boy!"

With a start, Oliver thought that Mr. Weston was shouting for Oliver to do something, but a boy came running from the inn, wiping his hands on his long apron. "Yes, Mr. Weston?"

"Get a jug of water for this gentleman here, and you." Now he pointed at Oliver, "Find it in your heart to dig up a penny for his troubles. You've got a mite over two minutes to tend to your friend."

Then he jammed his top hat back on his head, and flicked his whip in the air, just beside Willie's ear. "I'll show you kind." Then he marched off.

Willie just smiled, and reached out to make a last adjustment on the harness. He looked at Oliver briefly, and returned to watching Mr. Weston march into the inn. "Never underestimate the tender heart of a newly converted Christian," he said. Then walked off himself while Oliver gaped at him, turning only to accept a thick jug full of sloshing water from the boy.

"You don't 'ave to get me a penny, mister," said the boy. "I get plenty, Willie makes sure of it."

For a brief moment, Oliver felt the tug of a familiar longing. And jealousy of this boy, working in a venerable inn, one that had a tidy roof and clean windows that bespoke of attendance and pride. Wiping his hands on his apron after a small errand, being willing to turn down a penny, because there was someone looking out for him who would make sure there were many more of those in his future. Who probably had his own room, or one to share, and a series of tasks to keep him employed in a steady way so as to make his nights clear of tossing and turning. Who probably dreamed of owning an inn such as this himself one day—

"Here," Oliver said, taking the jug with one hand, and digging into his pocket with the other. A few coins still jingled there, and had they the time, he'd rent a room for a small while, and lay Jack in the bed with a cold cloth for his head, only while they'd money a-plenty, they had no time.

"Take this," he said, handing the boy a shilling. "I know it's too much, but give the ostler a penny when we've gone, and buy the coachman a cold drink when the days get hot. Can you do that?" He somehow knew that the boy would do just as asked, that Willie would be pleased with the penny that would be his, and that Mr. Weston would roar with astonishment at the pot of beer, and that he, Oliver, would be miles away, and would know nothing of it. Would not be, would never would be, a part of the convivial circle of acquaintances here at the George Inn.

"Sure thing, mister," said the boy, and he tossed the shilling in the air as if testing its weight when he caught it, and turned on his heel back to the inn, his tasks, his cozy life.

Oliver took the jug and climbed back into the stuffy coach, ignoring the stares of their fellow passengers, who stood in the small shelter offered by the lee of the building eating slices of bread. As he sat on the bench next to Jack, Jack was leaning against the window, his neck lax on his shoulders, his eyes closed, his mouth white and tense.

"Jack," said Oliver, low, his voice not as tender as he would have liked it to be. "Jack, wake up a moment, I've some water for you."

"Water?" asked Jack, sourly, keeping his eyes closed. "What's water when what I want is beer?"

"Water's what's best, it's what I've got for you, Jack, now. Please sit up a moment."

Jack did as he was told, eyes opening to narrow slits. One hand grabbed at Oliver's thigh, and Oliver let it, feeling the heat and damp of Jack's hand through his trousers.

"Where'd you get the water?" Jack asked.

Oliver held the jug up to Jack's mouth with one hand, and clasped the back of Jack's head with the other, gently pulling Jack further upright so the water wouldn't splash all over him. He tipped the jug till it rested on Jack's pale lips, and thought of the ostler and the coachman and the boy from the inn, and didn't say anything. "I got it for a penny, because you needed it; now drink up. Just enough, mind, we don't want you needing to piss before the horses have stopped."

Jack half smiled at this, eyes closed all the way now as he tipped up the jug further with one hand and took a swallow of water. His throat even sounded parched as he drank it down, and took another swallow because Oliver made him. Then he pushed the jug back, and flicked his eyes open to look at Oliver.

"Take a drink yourself, an' then give the jug back. We don't want to be haccused of stealing in this fair village an' have the local law following us on horseback to retrieve their jug." There was a flicker of a laugh in his eyes, as if he knew his jocular comments would distract Oliver. Well, Oliver was not distracted; Jack was ill and needed to be off the coach and resting.

"We'll stop here for the night," said Oliver, growing warm with the thought of it. "We'll continue on to Lyme in the morning." He didn't mention that they'd actually be getting off at Penn Inn, wherever that was, or that he was terrified of walking that far in the dark; it would be of no use to trouble Jack with this small and unavoidable detail.

"No," said Jack, shaking his head, though even this small movement made him wince. "I couldn't sleep with the notion of havin' to get on this coach again first thing in the mornin'. Couldn't abide the hanticipation of it. Would rather take the 'angman's noose straightaway than that."

He pushed at the jug, at Oliver, and there was nothing Oliver could do but alight from the coach, and walk to the inn to give the jug back.

As he stepped into the relative darkness of the inn, he held out the jug. "Can I give this to someone?"

Someone's hands took the jug, and the coach's horn blew.

"You'd better be off, young master," said a voice. It wasn't the boy from the inn, nor a young serving girl, and for a moment, Oliver felt he heard the scolding tones of Mrs. Bedwin. Then he heard the clack of a whip from out in the yard. "He won't hold those horses longer than he has to."

Oliver nodded, half-blind, and hurried to the coach under the stern glares of Mr. Weston, as well as the collective glares of the passengers riding on top of the coach.

"Hurry on, boy, an' if you don't, not even Willie's sly comments will save you a seat. I've a schedule to keep!"

With that he flicked his whip, causing the horses to jump forward, their hooves clattering on the cobblestones. Oliver flung himself into the coach, slamming the door, fumbling against the knees of the lady and gentleman, stepping on the edges of her cloak as it trailed on the floor. He chivvied himself between Jack and the wall and pulled Jack to him, smoothing back Jack's hair, circling his arm around Jack's shoulders.

"We'll be there soon, Jack," he said, thinking that with the darkening afternoon that it might only be a few hours, two or three, but he didn't really know. Hadn't thought to ask. "Can you manage till then?"

"I can if you can," said Jack, with some acidity. "But you'll prob-ably have to piss afore I do, what with all that water."

The comment seemed to give him some amusement, for beneath the grey cast of his skin was a curl of a smile. Which, in its turn, gave Oliver some courage, as it was probably meant to do.

"Here, now," he said, almost under his breath. "I've got a shoulder for your pillow, and I'll keep you steady as I can, and we'll be there before you know it."

"That we will, Nolly," said Jack, equally low, as if by the power of his desire he would have them there already, at a destination he truly wanted no part of, but was going to for Oliver's sake. Oliver gently chafed the length of Jack's arm, as Jack's weight settled against him. He would concentrate on that, on taking care of Jack, and hang the world. Hang them.

10

ALIGHTING AT PENN INN

In the growing twilight, amidst the rattling of the coach, Oliver could tell that they were going uphill even without needing to look past the leather flap tied over the window. For one, the coach had slowed. Also, he could hear the snap of the coachman's whip and the whistle of encouragement, the shouts to the horses.

"Up there, Bramble, go on there, lead them on, lead them on, for God's sake."

Mr. Weston sounded particularly fierce, and just then, the coach shot forward, the wooden benches banging in their frames, the leather padding shifting, smacking Oliver's head on the wooden panel behind him with a sickening thump. Then the coach began to rock and speed up.

"We're approaching the top of Penn Hill, I'll be bound," said the black-frock-coated gentleman, as if he'd traversed the way many a time before. He patted the gloved hand of the woman. "Only one other hill before Axminster, dear, you remember."

Rubbing the back of his head, Oliver eyed the couple almost idly. He didn't care where Axminster was or why they were going there. Only that they would be getting off the coach soon, leaving him and Jack in peace. For in spite of Oliver's determination to disregard the couple, the man had continue to rudely stare at them, as though he were sure there was something amiss. Maybe he meant to impress his female companion with his authoritative forthrightness, or perhaps he was only a busybody.

But there was no way for Oliver to move out of that gaze. In some accounts he'd read, traveling by coach could be a jolly affair, with well-travelled old grandfathers sharing a story or two, and a kindly woman opening her basket to share a slice of cold meat pie or some such. Of course, none of that had happened, and Oliver was starving and desperately thirsty, in spite of the jug of water at their last stop.

The coach slowed to a jerky crawl across rough ground, the jangle of harness, the clack of hooves on the flint road almost making the panels on the side of the coach vibrate. Then the coach bounced and chuddered to a stop, and at long last, every-thing seemed level. Oliver leaned back in his seat, his backbone aching, his head still ringing with the snap of the whip and the horrible breathing of the horses. He longed to be still, to be on a soft bed somewhere, with the sounds of crockery and cooking coming from the kitchen.

Oliver gritted his teeth, settling Jack's head more firmly on his shoulder. He wanted to pet Jack's head once more, to feel his pulse. Oliver knew nothing of medicine, but the heat swamping from Jack's body, pressed close to him, was unnatural. It felt dangerous. He hoped the coach would start up soon, longed for the end of their journey, part of his mind scampering on to the mundane details of a place to sleep. For Jack to be able to rest.

But the coach did not move on. Instead the door was cast open, sending the worn leather shade to rattle against the window frame. Mr. Weston stood there with his whip in his hand as he let the rain in. The ease of twilight into darkness made it still bright enough to see his impatient expression.

"This is you, then," Mr. Weston said, holding the narrow door wide open.

"Is this Lyme Regis?" Oliver asked. His voice felt stiff, his throat dry.

"No," said Mr. Weston. "The Comet don't go to Lyme, as you've been told. Horses can't make it down and back up the hill and still keep to schedule."

Feeling foolish that he'd forgotten, Oliver opened his mouth ask as to whether an exception might be made, but before he could, Mr. Weston tapped his whip at the door frame.

"This 'ere's the Penn, lad. Your stop, if you still want it. But better make your mind up quick, for I can't hold the horses longer than a moment."

The couple opposite stared at Oliver, as though he were to blame for the rain coming in through the open door, which he was. The passengers on top looked at him as if he were to blame for the delay in their journey, which he also was. But he turned away and attended to Jack, gently pulling him upright.

"Here we are, Jack, time to go."

"Where, then?" asked Jack. He lifted his head, as if to smell the rain, his eyes narrowing.

"We've got a mile or so to go, can you make it?"

With a jerk of his chin, Jack shrugged off Oliver's grasp and pushed himself to the edge of the seat. "Leave off. I'm fine to go, if you'll just—"

The leather seat crackled a bit as he got up, and as Oliver grabbed up the books and stood to follow, Jack shoved himself out of the narrow door and into the wet slant of rain. Oliver followed him, shivering all over as Mr. Weston closed the door behind them, turning the narrow handle with a click.

"Now, you lads just go along here; see that chalk track? Takes you down, over a bit of water, as there should be a bridge, and through some woods. Then you'll see the road, take it left, straight down to Lyme. You can't miss it."

The tip of his long, curled whip made it seem so easy. Oliver looked down the hill and over the trees, and, in the gloaming of late twilight, came a sliver of silver that might be the sea. He wasn't sure; the rain was thick and the darkness seemed to be swooping down at them.

"I'm off, then," said Mr. Weston. "Good luck to you, and remember me in your prayers." He tapped the brim of his rain-spattered hat with the curve of his whip, and ascended to the driver's bench with a flick of his buff-colored coat. Remembering what Willie the ostler had said about Mr. Weston's recent conversion, Oliver nodded.

"Yes, thank you, Mr. Weston, we will."

Jack seemed to snort at this, but the sound was covered with the clank and jingle of the horses shifting in their harness, and the crack of the whip over their heads, the creak and groan of tired wood as The Comet leaned back against the pull of the horses, and then, at the last moment, snapped forward and shot into motion. With a fly of wood and muck from the horses' hooves, The Comet sped on, and, in a moment, was lost to view, over the other side of the hill, on its way to Exeter.

Without the coach to shield them, the wind came over a hump of dripping rocks and flung itself at them with cold arms, as if it meant to scoop them up and fling them into the sea. The rain was coming sideways, dashing itself through the budding trees that stood in a line along the road, their branches like starving fingers, reaching into the rain.

"But hey," said Jack, looking at Oliver with widened eyes, as if he'd just come up with a clever idea. In the next moment, his legs twisted beneath him as though he meant to sit down, and as Oliver tried to catch him, the books crashed to the road, smacking open, their well-loved spines breaking with high, thin cracking sounds. Oliver half reached for the books, but Jack's body thudded against him, and Oliver grabbed Jack instead; there were always more books, but there was only one Jack.

His knees hit the dirt with Jack's weight in his arms, Jack's head pulled close to keep it from smacking on the rocks. The rain thundered down on the top of his head, his hat somehow having been blown off his head, and Jack's as well. The hem of his jacket flew up his back, and he heard the faint tinkling sound of coins hitting the stones.

He heard a small keen from Jack, perhaps of pain. With one white hand, Jack gripped at Oliver's coat, and pushed into him, breathing heavily, his legs splayed out as if they had no energy at all.

"Jack," said Oliver bending close, shifting a bit to adjust Jack against him. But no matter how much he tried, there was no shielding Jack from the rain.

"Will we die on this bloody hill, Nolly?" Jack asked, his voice moving up and down.

"Not if I can help it," said Oliver. He pushed wet locks away from Jack's eyes as Jack looked up at him, rain dripping down his temples. "But we must walk. About a mile, downhill, into the village. Can you stand?"

With a slowness that made Oliver's heart ache, Jack nodded. He gripped Oliver's coat even harder for a moment, and Oliver pulled, his hands cupping beneath Jack's arms, and, as Jack stood, he leaned heavily into Oliver for a moment.

"Alone at last," Jack said, with a shadow of his regular smirk. "Except for my head, I'd kiss you right here an' now."

This almost made Oliver smile in return, but only almost. Jack, in the fading light, was too white, his mouth thinned with pain, and Oliver longed only to have Jack, and himself besides, lodged somewhere warm and dry and still.

"We walk, and *then* I'll kiss you."

He was willing Jack not to see the ruin of the books, the pages already curling and spoiled by in the rain. The light was going; Oliver's heart thudded at the prospect of traversing unknown woods in the complete dark.

"Is that a promise?"

"Yes, of course it is, now, come on, enough of that." He knew he sounded like someone's governess, fussy and ill-tempered, but Jack only smiled.

Oliver felt a fondness surge through him, a warm current from his belly. Jack hadn't made any signs that he wanted off the mad course that Oliver had set for them both, and here he was on the top of a rainy, stony hill, smiling at Oliver, as though all was well.

They began walking, Oliver noting that Jack saw the ruin of the books, but wasn't saying anything about it. The track led into the undergrowth, beneath the dark swirl of the canopy of young trees, somewhat more leaved than could be found at the top of the hill. It was less windy amidst the trees, though the leaves were dripping with rain. The light was going, and Oliver felt that he should push Jack to go faster. He did not like the dark at the best of times, and here in this unknown forest, with the track headed downhill into more darkness, he felt as though he was falling.

"I should walk in front," said Oliver, trying to keep his voice steady. "That way, you don't have to concentrate so hard on where we're going."

Jack didn't respond to this, and Oliver knew that he needed to stay close and catch Jack if he stumbled and fell. With that in mind, he walked a little faster until he could reach out and wrap his arm around Jack's waist, and walk beside him.

"So I don't lose you," he said, at the motion of Jack's twitching shoulders.

"Never, Nolly," mumbled Jack, as if unconsciously, without thought.

It was far too dark now to do anything but focus on the path ahead, and wend their way downward, amongst the fern, and the low, slapping branches, and the rain dripping down from overhead. The path itself was uneven, and not well trod, and Jack seemed to slip and stumble every other step. Oliver's breath was forever in his throat, as he held tighter and tighter, until his fingers curled in on themselves, and he was sure that Jack would remark that Oliver was a worrying ninny and that he, Jack, was fine.

But the remark never came, and while their pace wasn't exactly slow, neither was it steady. It seemed to go and stop, crawlingly unpredictable, but always downward, as if they were descending into the darkest of mines where the light never shone and the wind always would be whistling past their ears.

And then, abruptly, there was water at their feet. Oliver heard it rushing over the rocks as he heard Jack's feet splashing. He pulled on Jack's coat with a sharp jerk, his feet slipping in the mud of the bank. He wondered if it was a river or a brook, and couldn't tell even as he squinted over Jack's shoulder, his cheek brushing the cold curl of Jack's ear.

"Shouldn't there be a bridge?" asked Oliver, but Jack was silent.

The path had led them here, and so there must be a bridge to take them across. Otherwise, why would so many have taken the same way?

"Do you see something darker across the water?" Oliver lifted his chin as he spotted it: a narrow reach of a blacker grey than the curling foam of water. "Just there, beyond that hump."

Jack said nothing, and Oliver's heart fluttered with panic, a cold stone in his belly, because he knew that he had to take care of them both.

"Here, let me—" Oliver stepped in front, pulling Jack's hand as he did so. "Hold onto my jacket, and let me see if—" Gingerly, he stepped forward, letting his toes bump against what felt like wood. "Yes, it's a bridge." He bent down, with the tug of Jack's hand now on his jacket, and felt across the wet planks with his feet as drifts of spray curled up and smacked him in the face.

With Oliver leading, they crossed the footbridge and followed the path until it took them to a wide road, where the wind was swift and chill and the rain came in sideways. Then they came to a break in the trees, and Oliver felt the crunch of gravel beneath his feet just as he bumped into something solid and waist-high. As he reached out, he felt brick, good English brick, it seemed, and well tended for all that it was dripping with rain. The sky above was free of trees; the fat drops, water coming straight down, was enough to tell him that they were in a clearing.

A darker gloom gave the sense of a building rising some height above them. And beyond, through the streaks of silver rain was a light, burning in the cross-hatch of a small window. It would be an oil lamp; he could almost smell it. The lamp was steady and the glass it shone through was clean, and as the rain came down, Oliver dragged Jack across the wide yard and right up to the window.

The light flickered across the yard to show him a door. He went to it, tugging Jack in his earnestness to find shelter for them both, somewhere to lie down, someplace warm and still. Jack had not said anything for the last half-mile, and he was mild and obedient beneath Oliver's hands. The obedience, more than anything, was worrying. Jack had followed Oliver as a trained hound might, and it was that placid state, so unnatural to Jack, that made Oliver actually pound on the door, and consider the prospect of being arrested for trespassing well worth the risk.

After a moment, more windows brightened, as if someone had lit a candle to carry to a door. That a house had so much light for what appeared to be the side entrance was a message in itself. And when the door opened to reveal an older man, dressed as a butler, and carrying a brass candlestick with a beeswax candle in it, Oliver knew. This was not merely the home of a local tradesman, no. It was a manor house, with a thick door, and a butler dressed fine and carrying a candlestick for his own use.

"It's rather late for beer," said the butler, as if he'd been expecting someone else altogether. Then he saw Oliver, and his eyebrows beetled together. "I say, what do you want? Come on, speak up, what are you about?"

Oliver opened his mouth to answer; his experience with butlers, however slight, told him that this one had enough clout to allow a beer-drinking companion entry during his off-duty hours, and that he wasn't worried that Oliver might be anyone dangerous. He'd opened the door wide, and hadn't quite closed it, even upon discovering that they were nobody that he knew.

He clung to Jack's shoulders, as it seemed that Jack's knees were giving way beneath him, and indeed a moment later, they did, sending Jack slamming into the wall beside the door, slipping out of Oliver's hands, as if he'd been yanked. With a cry, Oliver was upon him, pulling him upright, and the butler, heedless of the rain, was at his side, helping with his free hand to stand Jack upright.

"What's going on, what's wrong with him?" The candle flickered as a gust of rain pushed against it.

Oliver cradled Jack's head to his shoulder, trying to soothe with petting hands the small sounds that Jack probably didn't realize he was making.

"My friend has a fever—we were on the coach to Exeter and they let us off at Penn Inn. Could you—"

"Penn Inn?" said the butler. "You're not going to tell me that you walked all that way in the rain?"

"We'd nowhere else to go," said Oliver. "Is there a chance you have a place I could lay my friend down, get a cold cloth for his head, he—"

The butler, whose shoulders were getting marked by the rain, tilted his head to one side, appraising them. "That's not like the coachman," he said finally, "to abandon a couple of lads in this weather."

It was almost a question, the way he said it. As if he wanted them to prove that they'd been on the coach, rather than being two miscreants playing some sort of foul trick on him.

"We were in Bridport, at the inn, and I asked the ostler, Willie, how long to Lyme, and then he and Mr. Weston talked about the railway, and that The Comet didn't go into Lyme. Or something like that. But we asked him to let us off; I'm looking for family here, and my friend Jack—"

"It's not the cholera, is it?"

Oliver shook his head. "No, at least I don't think so—" He stopped, fighting the panic rising in his breast. If they didn't get shelter here, they'd have to keep going, find a hedgerow or something to crawl under. But that would be damp and muddy and no good for Jack.

"All right, come in. I'll check with Mrs. Heyland, the house-keeper, but you'd best come in out of the wet. She'll likely be able to arrange something, though you've picked the worst night for it, as the master and his family are packing up to leave in the morning and there's so much to do."

The butler stepped back to let them cross the threshold and the stone-floored passage and into a small room, nodding as they slid past him, as if relishing the clout his position offered him.

As Oliver stepped into the room, he found waves of warmth rushing at him. He pulled Jack to the chair in front of the fire, and without stopping to ask, pushed Jack into it. It was a wooden chair, with thin, old-fashioned legs, a doweled back, and an old cushion, and barely looked sturdy enough to hold Jack, let alone the butler, who outweighed him by some years and no fewer stone. Jack sighed deep in his chest, and doubled over, not to vomit again, but to clutch at his knees and keen into them, his hair slipping forward, dripping rain onto the braided rug beneath his feet.

Oliver knelt in the glow of the tidy, crackling fire, the light from it making gentle waves about the room, the soft air soaking into him as he took Jack's hands in his.

"Jack," he said. "Jack, I've got you somewhere warm, for the moment, so you can rest." He chafed Jack's hands, slipping his fingers along the side of Jack's temple, pushing the wet hair back. "Jack?"

"I'll get Mrs. Heyland," said the butler. "She'd just gone along to answer a bell, but should be back in a moment."

Before Oliver could turn around, the butler was gone, closing the door behind him, as the china knob slipped shut and the brass fittings clicked closed.

If Jack were alert enough to appreciate it, then he would be telling Oliver what should be obvious to a blind man. This was a rich house. There were shiny candlesticks, two of them, even for a servant's sitting room, both lit and blazing. There was a good fire, and a bright, polished kettle on the hob, pulled to one side. The rug, though made of rags, was new and clean. The floor was slabs of stone, well-scrubbed and snuggly fit together. The sideboard was old, but of fine wood, and upon it were china dishes, and platters stood on their edges to show them off. There were no doubt spoons in those drawers, probably old, but of serviceable silver. The far end of the room, under the window, had shelves of crocks, and books, and a basket that might have yarn or sewing things.

The butler had left them in a room full of riches, and had Jack been awake he would have advised Oliver to grab what he could and make a run for it. But Oliver could not leave Jack. Not while he was ill, and, indeed, not ever. He should not have thrown his lot in with a street thief; even one as clever as Jack was bound to get caught one day, and Oliver would be found in that same net. Though while there was no future in it, Oliver knew he would stay. He would convince these people, these comfortable, well-servanted people, to take Jack in. He, Oliver, would stay in the barn, or the shed, or wherever there was room for him, leaving Jack to have the best of what was available.

"Jack," he said, low. "Can you hear me, can you lift your head, just a little?" With slow pets, he stroked Jack's head, wondering when the last time was he'd seen Jack so still. "Jack, please—"

"Oh," said Jack. It was almost a whisper. "Will you—enough, eh, Nolly? Why is it so hot?"

Gratified to hear Jack's voice, Oliver leaned forward, his hands on Jack's shoulders, to push him upright. Jack felt so heavy, but he sat up, wet jacket slapping against the wood, his eyes going to the fire, and the shelves, before alighting on Oliver himself. "Looks like a cave for plunder."

"You would think that," said Oliver, only half scolding. "But the butler has gone for the housekeeper, and they're likely to give us shelter, even if it's only for one night. You can rest, lying still."

"Where are we? In Lyme?" Jack seemed a little dazed for a moment, but he pushed his hair back from his eyes, and sat up a little straighter, as if the warmth of the room had given him some strength.

"Just about," said Oliver. "We didn't get quite that far, but we got halfway down the hill, and I couldn't, well, you kept stumbling, and your skin is so hot—"

He reached out to touch Jack's forehead, but Jack smacked his hand away. "Stop fussin', Nolly," he said, but Oliver could see, by the furrow of Jack's brow, the taut line of his mouth, that Jack's head hurt him dreadfully. To prove this, Jack's hand came up to rub at his forehead, his eyes squinting to narrow slits as he did so. "I could use a draught of gin, if you have it," he said, faintly, then his head tumbled forward till his chin touched his chest.

"Jack," said Oliver. "*Jack.*"

The door behind him opened, and from the dark passageway came a woman, undoubtedly Mrs. Heyland, the housekeeper. It wasn't just the thickness of her skirt and apron or the jangle of keys on her belt. It was the way she held her head, the way everything about her was tidy as she folded her hands in front of her and appraised them both.

"You've caused Mr. Archie some concern, this night," she said. "Making him run to fetch me when I was a-waiting on the master."

"I beg your pardon, ma'am," said Oliver. He got to his feet, and stood between her and Jack. Jack was disreputable without being drenched in rain; it would do him no good, no good at all, if he was to be tumbled back into the storm after only a few moments out of it. "I didn't mean to make him run, but I'm asking for shelter for my friend, for he has a fever and I'm unable to carry him further—"

"You're soaked through, the pair of you."

She had the acerbic tones of a nanny, who is just about to plunge her charges into a useful bath and scrub them well with soap and send them to bed early for daring to play in the wet weather. His mind raced on: *yes, yes, a hot bath for Jack, he's been quite reckless out of doors of late, and a dose of treacle if you please, to settle him*

*down and help him with his head, right before you pop him into a warm,
clean bed.*

Mrs. Heyland moved closer, peering at Jack, slumped to one
side in the chair.

"Has he a fever?"

Oliver could hear the anxiety in her voice. "It's not the cholera,
ma'am, he complains of a headache—I think he hit his head
yesterday."

Of course, *think* was the wrong word. He *knew* that the blow
from Cromwell had sent Jack crashing into the wall and caused
Jack to hit his head. Why had it taken Oliver so long to figure it
out? Jack had been unconscious for only a moment, but it had
been enough, and now he was paying for it. Actually Oliver was
making him pay for it, by forcing Jack into a jouncing coach,
forcing him to walk in the dark, in the rain, when his head ached
so much he'd thrown up more than once. Oliver's mouth began to
quiver with the thought of it, that he'd caused Jack so much extra
discomfort; he clamped his jaw tightly, but not before Mrs.
Heyland's sharp eyes caught him.

"Mr. Archie says you came down from Penn Inn. Did you carry
him all that way through the forest, young man? And in this
weather?"

Before Oliver could speak, he heard Jack stir behind him.

"I'm a dead weight to 'im, missus," said Jack in a low, gravelly
voice. "But he wouldn't leave me, no, not Oliver."

Oliver looked down. Jack's hands were claws around the arms
of the wooden chair, and it was with an effort that he was sitting
upright. His jacket was stained with mud, his hair still dripping
into his face, and his eyes blazing with fever. But Oliver realized
that Jack was creating a story about the two of them, making it up
as he went along, something to give to Mrs. Heyland so that she
would let them stay.

"No," said Oliver, very gently, "no, I would not leave you."

Mrs. Heyland's gaze turned to Oliver now, scanning him up and
down in a manner of a trader looking over unknown stock. Of

course she was seeing what she wanted to see, what everyone seemed to see: a beautiful young man, now in shabby clothes, but with a face so well graced in spite of the dirt and exhaustion that there could be nothing but goodness behind it. No one ever believed differently, and Oliver could not let Mrs. Heyland believe it now. So he stood there and let her look at him, and kept any dark thoughts from showing in his eyes. This was the place that Jack needed, under the ministrations of such a woman, for one night, at least. For two or three if he could manage it.

"I think a good night's rest somewhere warm and dry should do him well," said Oliver, ducking his chin a fraction, looking up at her through his eyelashes. "That's all he needs, truly."

That did the trick. Mrs. Heyland's expression softened, her head tilting to the side. "He needs a good deal more than that, I think," she said. "What did you say your name was?"

"Oliver, Twist," he said, just as he realized he should be telling them a lie about what their names were. "And this is my good friend and companion, Jack Dawkins."

Oliver laid a hand on Jack's shoulder, to include him in the circle of Mrs. Heyland's growing goodwill, when Jack surprised him by straightening up and pushing his hair back from his over-bright eyes.

"I used to be his manservant, but the money's gone a bit thin, so now we're just travelin' together."

So that was the rest of the story. Oliver had not ever had a manservant before, but it was unlikely to be any more of a complex relationship than having a maid of all work personally bring him his breakfast tray when he'd been lying abed from some illness, so he should be able to carry it off with some aplomb.

Mrs. Heyland nodded at the two of them, their relationship set in her mind, their circumstances understood and filed under the category of *respectable but down on their luck*. And their story was accepted.

"Mr. Archie," she said through the open doorway. "I know it's late, but if you would, please, get that worthless Peter to take a message. I know the doctor is still here for the master; when they are finished, can you have him come?"

The butler nodded and was gone before Mrs. Heyland could even touch Jack's forehead. This Jack was not expecting and he flinched. Oliver had never seen him do that before, not even in the face of Cromwell's fist or the bloody cleaver in Oliver's hands. It was not that he was afraid of Mrs. Heyland, it seemed, rather what she represented. A good woman of respectable virtue, older, wiser, confident, and no mark for his thievery; she might have been fooled by the general story, master and manservant, but her expression when she touched Jack's forehead with the back of her hand told its own story; she knew a reprobate when she saw one.

"We'll get you both out of these wet things, and the doctor will look at your servant."

Jack's eyes flicked up to meet Oliver's. In a house that could afford such services, there were probably *many* sets of silver plate, and a bag of money besides. That's what Jack's eyes said. Oliver frowned; stealing was not the way to pay for such kindness, though he was almost past the verge where he cared about the cost. What mattered was Jack getting the care he needed.

11

THE SICKROOM

The sickroom that Mrs. Heyland led them to was on the ground floor, on the far side of a wide, warm kitchen, near the end of a narrow passage that followed a series of twists and turns, which again bespoke the largeness of the house. It was a small, narrow room with one window at the far end, set into the wall at least a foot, leaving a wide ledge beneath. There was a small table tucked into the far corner, a bed with a narrow, iron bedstead, and that was it. The walls were whitewashed, glowing pale blue in the light of Mrs. Heyland's candle as she set it down on the table.

"Can you put him on the bed, and get his boots off, at least? While I—there you are, Edith, did you bring him a dry shirt?"

Edith was in the doorway for only a moment, crisp and tidy in her broad white apron and cap, gawping open-mouthed at Oliver while she handed over a shirt to Mrs. Heyland. Oliver waited for her to leave before he helped Jack sit down and then knelt at Jack's feet, with Jack's hand gripping his shoulder. Jack's head clearly hurt him, for the arm behind the grip shook, and his weight was heavy on Oliver's shoulder.

Moreover, as Oliver worked at damp laces, and slipped off

Jack's boots, Mrs. Heyland was busy with Jack's muddy jacket and shirt. It seemed she meant to strip him bare, and then when the jug of hot water arrived, via the worthless Peter, who set it down with a clank inside the basin, and put both down in the doorway and departed, Oliver realized that she meant to give Jack a good scrub as well. Oliver could barely stop her, but at least he could make sure that Jack was never without his shirt. Even with Oliver in the room, it was far from circumspect. Although, Mrs. Heyland went about it as though Jack were her young charge, her wet and naughty charge, caught gadding about in the rain for the fun of it.

"Did you walk all the way down that hill in the dark, then?" she scolded as she tugged Jack's shirt over his head.

Oliver waited until she'd slipped a clean, dry shirt over Jack's head before tugging off Jack's trousers and drawers all the way, for modesty's sake. Though he knew, somewhat, the curve of Jack's hips with his hands in the dark, he'd never seen Jack in the altogether, and he imagined that Jack might not want Mrs. Heyland to see him that way either.

But as Oliver straightened up, trousers over one arm, Jack's face looked bland, not crimsoned red as Oliver's would have been, had he been stripped bare by a woman old enough to be his mother. But in the warmth of the room, Jack's eyes were glassy and his jaw was tight. Mrs. Heyland saw it as well.

"Oh, my," she said. "Grab that basin that Edith brought, we can rinse it out directly after. Here, hold his head, or—"

But Jack, as if wary of being an inconvenience, grabbed the basin with both hands as he vomited into it. Mrs. Heyland was quick to dip a cloth into the jug of hot water to wipe his mouth with, taking the basin from him as she stepped away.

"Get him into the bed, Oliver, while I take this for Edith to clean."

With that, she was gone, leaving Oliver and Jack in that airless little room, with the jug of hot water steaming the air, and the candle-flame standing aquiver in the corner. Jack sat on the edge of the narrow bed, crumpled against the white sheets, curled forward, his hands on his knees, the wrists of the borrowed shirt flowering with tucked edges that bespoke of a graceful hand that had sewn it together. Oliver wanted to get Jack into the bed, where he would be more comfortable, but first he needed to bathe the grime from Jack's skin, and to keep more smears of grease and mud from imbedding themselves into the counterpane and the clean, thick sheets beneath.

"Shall I wash your feet first?" asked Oliver. He lifted the jug and basin, and carried them over to where Jack sat. Then he knelt down.

"No." Jack's voice was thick. "I don't want that, you're a—"

But whatever Jack meant to say to dissuade him, Oliver grabbed a flannel cloth from the bed and dipped it into the jug. Wringing out the flannel most of the way, he took one of Jack's bare feet, the left one, onto his bent knee. Then he stroked the flannel cloth along Jack's ankles and then his foot, the sole of it blacked with the length of time since Jack had had a bath. There was a line of reddened skin around Jack's ankles from where the edges of his boots had been biting through the worn, woolen socks that Oliver had pulled off and draped at the bottom of the bedrail.

"I would rather do this for you than to let her," Oliver said, as he drew the flannel down Jack's calf. He fought down the hysterical laughter that shot up inside of him; him washing Jack's feet in a sickroom in a manor house in the middle of the country was not, and had never been, something he'd ever imagined.

He tried to be circumspect by not staring, but he had to look to see what he was doing. He'd never seen Jack this way, in a state of nature. The dark curl of hair between Jack's legs was much darker than Oliver's own, when he'd been brave enough to look. There was simply so much about Jack's body that seemed still a mystery; their nights together had been in the dark, with candles that guttered and went out, rather than the steady, beeswax one that now cast a golden light and left a trace of honey in the air.

But no one would see Jack this way but him; he would make sure that Jack was clean and decently covered and not left for eyes that would find shame in such a thing, Jack's naked form, laid out as if for death, but still breathing and alive. Oliver would see to it.

"Bloody hell," said Jack. His shoulders slumped. All the light was gone from his eyes.

"It's all right," said Oliver, cleaning what must be years of grime from Jack's ankle. A long soak in a large tub of hot water would do Jack a good deal more good than a damp flannel, but it was all they had for now. "You'd do the same for me, then. Wouldn't you?"

As he nodded, Jack's eyelashes flickered down, as if he meant to hide something. It was a shy look, that of a small child keeping secrets. Swallowing a rise of something he could not quite define, Oliver sat back on his heels to dip and wring the cloth again. He patted Jack's left foot, and pulled Jack's right foot to his damp knee.

With his own clothes still damp on his skin, Oliver wanted to shiver, but he concentrated on Jack instead, and washed his foot and calf up to the knee, where the hem of the shirt waved in graceful curls. It was a fine garment indeed, and that it was being given to Jack, a stranger in the night, to sleep in, was a mark of a fine house that had shirts to spare.

When he was finished, and had rinsed out the now quite grimy cloth and laid it on the edge of the jug, he tugged the bedclothes back to get Jack into bed. He straightened Jack's feet along the mattress so that he could lie comfortably, adjusting his head on the pillow and pulling the linen sheet and coverlet up. Jack's eyes were closed, his forehead drawn in wrinkles, as if his head were killing him from within, every time Oliver moved him even the smallest inch. This alone stayed Oliver from washing Jack's hands and face as well.

"I'll wait with you," said Oliver. He sat on the edge of the bed, fitting his hip into the slight curve of Jack's waist, and took Jack's hand.

"Doctors are killers," said Jack, his eyes still closed, lips barely moving. "Except the one in Port Jackson, when the mare went down in the wire. Do you remember that, Nolly?"

"No," said Oliver. It took him a moment to realize that Jack was speaking of another time, another place: Port Jackson, where he'd been deported to, and now this was the story of a doctor and a mare strung up in wire. It was more than Jack had ever revealed of his time in that place.

"Tell me about it. Was the mare all right in the end?" Oliver asked this as though the subject were commonplace between them.

"Some marines had determined to go for a race, through the hills, you know, like they liked to do, in the evening—" Jack opened his eyes. They were a brilliant green now, blazing with fever; Jack couldn't quite focus on Oliver, though he seemed to try. "They charged the horses along the path between the sharp grasses, and when they came back, well, one of them bumped the other and the mare went through the wire they had brought on the ship to keep out the kangaroos. It never did, but they strung the wire just the same—the marine wanted to put the mare down, but the doctor said no, and he tended her for weeks afore she got well."

"But she did get well," said Oliver. He clasped Jack's hand between both of his; Jack's skin was on fire, and if he could have, Oliver would have sucked all of that heat into his own body and gone out and stood in the icy rain to put it out.

"That she did," said Jack, distantly, as if combing through his memory to find what had happened next. "That wasn't the marine who—well, never mind, that's behind me now."

Jack's voice trailed off, and his head lolled to one side against the clean pillowcase, his dark hair spilled ink. He was so silent that Oliver began to think that he'd fallen asleep, in spite of the fact that his hands and face were still unwashed and that the doctor was coming. The candle was still, and the rain pattered against the four leaded panes of the small window. Oliver considered opening the window for the fresh air, but it was likely to be wet as well as fresh, and besides, he couldn't bear the thought of letting Jack's hand go. Jack might think that Oliver had left him, and he didn't want that.

"Nolly," said Jack, in the semi-darkness.

"Yes, Jack," said Oliver.

"You got that snuffbox?"

"The *what?*" His voice was sharp in the stillness. Whatever was Jack talking about?

"The snuffbox." Jack opened his eyes to look at Oliver. They blazed with fever, and sweat was trickling down the side of his temple. "Fagin's going to thrash me when 'e finds out I got pinched for it. So maybe we could tell him *you* took it, an' me gettin' pinched was a mistake, so I won't have to go so far from home in the mornin'."

All at once, Oliver knew what he was talking about. It was the snuffbox, a *small* two-penny, half-penny, snuffbox, the one which had gotten Jack deported for stealing. A bit of folded metal, and nothing to make a fuss about. And yet there had been a fuss, to hear Noah talk of it, which he had, at length, about Jack's day in court, where even all of Jack's tale-spinning skills had not been able to get him released from the arms of the law. And yet, his biggest concern was Fagin's disappointment in him, and the tragedy of being removed from his beloved London. The latter of which Oliver had done to him as well, with impunity and a complete disregard for Jack.

Oliver swallowed, and then swallowed again. If only he'd been there that day, and stepped in to say to Jack, *no not this one, not today, let it go, Jack, there are more snuffboxes where that one came from.* And have saved Jack from the ignominy of Fagin's disapproval and a five-year exile.

"Yes, Jack," he said, as clear as he could manage over the lump in his throat. "We'll tell him that, you and I, when we next see him." Oliver clasped Jack's hand tighter. "You know I was only ever good at picking initials out of handkerchiefs, and washing them to be ready for sale. We'll tell Fagin that it was me who got ahead of myself, and really, all the training in the world won't make me good for—"

Jack smiled at him, and Oliver stopped talking.

"Your face will be your fortune, but you weren't meant to pick pockets," said Jack. "No, you were made for the big shill. Only Fagin can't see that—"

Jack looked at Oliver as though he was were something good to eat, or to sell, whichever came easiest. As though they were back in the old days, where barefooted boys shared a fire and a pint of gin and whatever bread could be toasted on a stick, and Fagin was still alive.

Oliver could not stop the sharp pangs of fear that raced through him. Such talk meant that Jack was out of his head, and if the fever were to take Jack, if Jack were to *die*—

He bent forward, slipping his hand behind Jack's neck, and tipped close to kiss Jack on the cheek.

"I'll tell Fagin," he said, all in a rush. "I'll tell him it was me and apologize. He knows I'm hopeless with these things, and he'll come at me with the cane and not you. And we'll find the snuffbox, we'll remember where we put it—"

With a rough hand, Jack pushed him back, and Oliver sat up. The light in Jack's eyes was dim, his face white.

"What're you on about, Nolly?" Jack's frown was like a slash across his face. "Fagin's dead." Then he sighed and closed his eyes. "Ain't your fault, anyhow. Ain't anybody's fault."

The doctor, when he came with Mrs. Heyland, was a small man, wiry and quick, as if every movement agitated him. His hair was slicked back and matched his dark eyes that darted from one face to another without pausing, as if he were running out of time at every moment.

"Did you wash him, Mrs. Heyland? Oh, mercy, you did not. I

cannot abide filth, though it's to be expected with the lower orders. Can a manservant afford my fee? I tend to gentlemen, not paupers." He went to the far side of the bed to glare at Jack, as if in despair over the existence of pauper, but he took Jack's wrist in one hand.

"The bill will be paid, Dr. Rudge," said Mrs. Heyland. She seemed unruffled by his haste. Oliver knew, from his experience with Uncle Brownlow's doctors, that Dr. Rudge was taking the measure of Jack: how fast his pulse beat beneath his skin, how hot he was. "This is the young man's master, Oliver Twist, and he said that his manservant hit his head, was it yesterday, Oliver?" asked Mrs. Heyland.

"It was against the wall," Oliver said, as Dr. Rudge's sharp eyes glanced at him.

"Was he unconscious for any length of time? A moment? An hour?"

"It was several moments," said Oliver. "He seemed to wake up slowly from the floor, and was well, until later in the day. He had a headache, he said."

"Has he vomited? Usually in cases such as these, there is a great deal of vomit. Can I see the vomit? I need to examine it."

Oliver looked at Mrs. Heyland and she at him.

"Once in the coach on the way here," said Oliver. "And once at an inn, when we stopped for dinner."

Mrs. Heyland nodded. "He vomited once here as well," she said, slowly, as if to counterbalance the doctor's speed. "But we've cleaned the basin, so there's nothing to look at. The question is, what can you do for him? And where is Dr. McMurtry? Did he not come with you to see the master?"

"He's too busy practicing his newfangled medicine, imagining he can make a difference where I cannot." Dr. Rudge barked. "But in the meantime, we need to dose this one with laudanum—do you have any wine, Mrs. Heyland? Something rough that you can spare? And then we need to bleed him."

As Mrs. Heyland went out to get the wine, Dr. Rudge lifted his boxy-looking leather bag onto the bed and began unpacking his equipment. Out came a galvanized green tin bowl, with a half-moon curve along one edge. Dr. Rudge showed it off to Oliver.

"You see this basin? See the curve there? I had it made to order, to allow the arm to lie flat, so I can get at the vein. It's easier to bleed them, when the arm is flat."

He drew out a knife and flicked it in the air. The blade glittered in the candlelight.

"My knife is sharp, sharpest in the business, cuts right down to the bone if I want it to." He laid the bowl on the small table and the knife within it, shattering the stillness of the candle's flame. Then he withdrew a small brown bottle and a spoon with a curved handle. "This will settle him; have you ever been dosed with laudanum, young man?" But Dr. Rudge wasn't looking at Jack or Oliver; he was opening the bottle to take a sniff of it, as if to assure himself of the contents. The bottle was unmarked, and the liquid within could be anything.

"They gave my uncle laudanum sometimes," said Oliver, more to indicate that he'd been listening than to answer any question.

"Well then, you know it's a miracle cure for fever, mental incapacity, or any sort of foul illness your body might dream up."

The doctor took Jack's wrist up again, standing beside the white bed in his proper dark suit, his shadow moving against the wall as he looked sternly at Jack. As if he felt his gaze alone should be enough to rouse the patient and make him walk.

Oliver waited, not speaking, his heart pounding, until Mrs. Heyland came in with a glass of wine. She carried an actual glass with a curved lip and fine stem; perhaps the butler had refused to pour wine into anything else, he didn't know. Dr. Rudge's eyebrows flew up, but he took the glass and placed it on the table. Then he took the open bottle of laudanum and tipped out several drops onto a spoon, which he stirred into the dark wine.

"Young man," said Dr. Rudge, "can you help him sit up? He needs to drink this; it will help to calm him."

As Jack looked to be actually unconscious, Oliver felt the first stirrings of doubt. But it wasn't his place to question a man of such learning, so he did as he was told. He curved a hand under each of Jack's shoulders, and leaned down to speak to him.

"Jack, can you sit up for me? The doctor is here, he's got some medicine for you to make you well." As Jack didn't answer, Oliver tightened his grip and pulled Jack up to a sitting position, gratified to see Jack's eyes opening.

"The marine ain't comin' back for me, is he, Nolly? Tell me he won't come back?"

Horrified that Jack seemed to be babbling nonsense, Oliver attempted to soothe him just the same. "The marine is far away, Jack, in Port Jackson. He got eaten by a kangaroo, I expect, and won't be troubling you any more."

Moving closer into Oliver's arms, Jack actually smiled, his nose crinkling up. "You're daft, Nolly. Kangaroos don't eat people."

The smile made Oliver's heart jump, and the doctor used that moment to bring the glass of laudanum-laced wine to Jack's lips.

"What's this?" asked Jack against the curved edge of the glass, his eyes narrow, his hand up as if he meant to push it away.

"It's wine that this very good lady has given us. You're to drink it, drink it all, mind. Then you'll sleep, and when you wake up, we'll go walking in the sharp grasses and look for kangaroos." Oliver wasn't quite familiar with what those actually were, but his words kept Jack focused on him, even though he got another one of those looks, the one where Jack thought he was mad.

"There ain't no kangaroos in England, thank God," said Jack, shaking his head. But when Oliver nodded his head at the wine, Jack obediently put his mouth to the glass and drank the contents of it in several long swallows.

"He's used to putting it away, I'll wager," said Dr. Rudge, frowning. He opened his mouth as if he meant to go on like this, disparaging Jack while Jack's condition went untreated.

"Jack is Oliver's manservant, if you please," said Mrs. Heyland, "and a guest in this house, Dr. Rudge."

Oliver didn't let his surprise at Mrs. Heyland's sharp remark show, and besides, Dr. Rudge was ignoring her, rolling up Jack's shirt sleeve.

"Lay back, boy," said Dr. Rudge, as if they were the only two in the room. "This will hurt a bit, but then you'll sleep, and it will all feel better in the morning." Without waiting for an answer, he pushed Jack back into the pillow, leaving Oliver's hands empty and useless as the doctor placed the moon-cut bowl beneath Jack's arm. Then, pausing to display the shine of his blade, he stuck it into the crook of Jack's elbow.

Jack cried out, and Oliver felt his whole body jump. Jack's eyes started to haze as he looked toward Oliver, and Oliver, telling himself he didn't mind that the doctor was watching him, leapt forward to sit on the bed to curve his arm around Jack's shoulders, and take Jack's free hand in his. His heart raced in panic at the spurt of blood that splashed bright red on Jack's pale arm, turning to a dark ooze that sprang up and slid, a round, dark line, down his skin and into the bowl. Then, looking away from it, he looked at Jack instead, swallowing hard.

"It's all right, Jack, sleep now. I'll watch over you."

"What about Fagin?" asked Jack, his voice young and troubled. "He'll be so cross with me, so *angry*—He'll throw me back in the streets when he finds out. He'll sell me back to the gypsies for sure, an' I won't amount to anythin', won't have any riches bein' a tinker's son."

Aware of the curious glances sent their way at Jack's hurried words, his quavering tone, Oliver leaned forward.

"I'll explain it to him. You know he was always fond of me—"

"Yes, that's so," said Jack, his voice falling off. "You always could manage him, right enough. He liked your pretty face, would have sold you if he could—"

"I'll tell him," said Oliver again. "Rest now."

He reached out to touch Jack's face. Jack's eyelids slipped closed, and his body stilled, and his elbow slid into the bowl of blood.

"What a mess this one is making," said Dr. Rudge, shaking his head. He pulled out a cloth to wipe the blade and as he tucked the cloth and the knife in his leather bag, he nodded at Mrs. Heyland. "He should have nothing, not even water, for the next twenty-four hours. And would you be so kind as to rinse out my basin? I'll be upstairs tending to the master and having one last bit of sherry before I head home."

Then, with his heels clip-clipping on the stone floor, he left in some haste.

Mrs. Heyland busied herself with the basin, taking Jack's arm out of it, attempting to wipe it dry of blood, but leaving a streak on the sheets anyway. Mrs. Heyland made a noise under her breath. It wasn't quite the *tsk tsk* that Oliver used to hear from Mrs. Pierson, but it held the same dismay, the same disapproval. But whether it was directed at him or at Jack, Oliver didn't know. Sighing, she took up the basin, and covered it with the corner of her apron.

She stopped for a moment, to look at Jack, and then at Oliver, not quite in a motherly way, but not quite sternly, for all that.

"I've always been known as a steady sort of woman, not given to new inventions or fancies."

Oliver made himself listen, though his eyes were on Jack, who lay quite still, his head tilted on the pillow, the creases in the cloth running away like old memories.

"But Dr. McMurtry, who was not available tonight, he would know how to tend to your manservant. He, like my second oldest boy, has been trained at the most modern of medical colleges, you see."

For a moment, Oliver thought to correct her, that Jack wasn't his manservant and that indeed Oliver had never had a servant totally devoted to his needs. And that if it were to be anyone, Jack would be the last to volunteer. But Oliver stopped himself; that was their story, their reason for traveling together. It was hard to maintain the parts of it, so late at night; he rocked forward on his feet, and grabbed the bedstead to stay upright.

"I'll take this," said Mrs. Heyland. "Then I'll be back with some bedding; will you mind sleeping on the floor, young man?"

Now Oliver had to look at her, at her round face, and clear blue eyes, and the flop of the lace of her cloth cap on her forehead, and the way her mouth tilted down to one side. "No, ma'am," he said, his voice a little thick. "If you have a chair, I could sit up with him, for a while, tonight. And maybe a blanket if you have it."

"We can do better than that, I think."

Then she left the room, her skirts brushing the side of the bed and the white-washed walls at the same time, the room was so narrow. She did him the courtesy of shutting the door behind her, and for the moment, Oliver was alone with Jack. Jack, who looked like a corpse, with blue splotches under his eyes, and his lips white and chapped. There was grime on the bed sheet, where Jack's hands now lay, a streak of blood that had sprayed from the doctor's knife, and grit on the pillow.

How could he have come to this? Alone in a room with Jack, who was dying. It was Oliver's fault, as it usually was, that Jack was ill. Oliver should known; he'd seen Jack hit his head when Cromwell had thrown him against the wall. Jack had seemed all right afterwards, and Oliver too eager to leave London with the specter of Cromwell, and the worry as to what Noah might do with what he had seen. It was only a matter of time until the death of Cromwell caught up with him; until Oliver could get him and Jack far enough removed from those events, there was no telling, no telling at all, when the hangman's noose would find them.

The door opened and in walked Edith, her hands full. Oliver jumped to take the bundle from her, and she turned to just outside the door and brought in a chair.

"You can sit here if you like, and that's clothes for you to change into, and blankets. It's not very much, but we're washing the bedding for the whole house. I've got a flocked mattress for the floor, but is there anything else you need?"

"It's very good of you," he said, as she bent to grab the mattress and hand it to him. But he was talking to the shut door, she was gone that quickly. Of course, it wouldn't do for a maidservant to be alone in a room with two young men, even if one of them was unconscious. That spoke well of the tone of the house, to be sure, but he wasn't used to servants running away from him.

Feeling tired beyond measure, Oliver put the mattress and bedding in the corner, and moved the chair against the wall. Then he sat on the chair, and took off his shoes and stockings, all of which were soaked through. His trousers were damp and smelled of Jack's vomit, and when he took off his jacket, he discovered his shirt stank. He needed a bath, but couldn't call for hot water, not at this hour. Not when he'd not a penny to pay for any of this; in checking his pockets, he realized he'd lost all the money Jack had handed over to him. It must have blown out of his pockets in the wind on the hill.

Instead of changing into the clean clothes that were waiting for him on the chair, he sat on the bed next to Jack. Jack's hair was oily beneath Oliver's fingers, and against the clean sheets, Jack's skin was still somewhat begrimed and streaked. In London, this hadn't been apparent, hadn't mattered. But here, in the country, where the air was salted, and crisp with cold, with the clean sheets and the clean floor that they'd trudged mud over, it was now a focus.

He'd seen the looks they'd received, from Mrs. Heyland, from the maidservant, from Mr. Archie. It was the type of look he'd given many a street urchin in his day; it was the way he'd looked at Martin, in the beginning. It was the way Mrs. Mann used to look at him. As if he were nothing more than street dirt come to life and the most expedient thing to do was to be rid of it. That, or wash it with some strong lye soap and a stiff brush.

Jack should have something more gentle than that to make him more comfortable, though really, it was because Oliver wanted the judgmental looks to stop. But there was no one to say this to; Jack was unconscious, asleep on the pillow, and, without those bright and knowing eyes to spark unspoken words into Oliver's heart, alarmingly youthful.

"Jack," said Oliver. "You're asleep now, but when you wake up,

I'll be here, and Mrs. Heyland will be armed with hot water. I'll be wanting breakfast, as I'm sure you will also. So don't lollygag about as you usually do, you must be sure to get up in time—"

His throat closed up like a sudden fist, choking off the air, making his eyes water. Had Jack been awake, he might have mocked Oliver for this show of sentiment. Or, as he sometimes did, he might surprise Oliver with commiserating with him, about their chances of making it out of this in one piece. And about how Mrs. Heyland looked a little bit like a man, for all her flounces and lace. About how Oliver had been drooling over the hot water that had been brought for Jack, and it was too bad that there was none for him.

"I'll sit here for a while, Jack," said Oliver, swallowing and then swallowing again. "And if I fall asleep, and if you wake up, you must be sure to wake me, wake me in time for breakfast. Will you do that for me, Jack?"

Oliver touched his fingers to Jack's face, curving along the small bruise alongside Jack's mouth, noting the flicker of Jack's eyelashes as he turned toward Oliver's hand. Oliver almost gasped at the moment, the reaction. Did Jack know he was there? Oliver didn't know how it felt to be dosed with laudanum, but Uncle Brownlow had never reacted in this way. He'd always slumbered on, no matter who was at his bedside.

Making himself take a deep breath, Oliver settled further on the bed, tucking his hip into the curve of Jack's side, pulling his legs up a bit, one knee resting on top of the bedclothes. He was alone with Jack in this narrow room, so close to the sea and so very far from home. Then Jack sighed, his head lolling sideways on the pillow, the creases in the case spreading out like unwanted thoughts.

"Jack?" asked Oliver. He leaned forward, taking Jack's hand, rubbing his thumb along Jack's palm. "Jack, are you awake?"

Jack stayed still, his eyes closed, slumbering on.

Oliver leaned close, close enough so that he was whispering in Jack's ear, gently, quietly, so as not to disturb Jack from his cocoon of sleep. "We're out of the coach. I found us shelter, and a doctor has seen you. Do you remember the doctor?"

Oliver cupped Jack's face in his palm.

"The morning will come, Jack. By-and-bye, the morning will come."

But Jack did not answer him. The laudanum and the bloodletting had left him not just listless, or even relaxed, as the doctor had intended, but had pulled him into unconsciousness. That he was breathing shallowly also added to Oliver's fears, but at least Jack's brow was smoothed from pain, and the heat of his hand in Oliver's had abated.

"I'll stay here, shall I?" This said in a whisper as the candle flickered as it shrank, tainting the air with the smell of burned wick and the melted beeswax. The shadows of the quavering candle-flame made the circles beneath Jack's eyes seem black, and the strands of hair across his forehead, inky and dark. Only his throat was white against the grimed muslin of his shirt, and the bandage, white with a red sear across the crook of Jack's lax elbow.

All through the night, Oliver stayed awake and watched over Jack, sitting in the chair, so very still, in case any movement that he made might startle Jack. When the candle burned to a stub, he replaced it with the one he found in the drawer, and lit it with the last flame of the first candle. At some point, when he was about to fall off the chair, he changed into the clothes that the maidservant had bought him. These were dry at least, and the movement of getting into them kept him solidly awake for a good hour or more.

The scent of the candle was sharp in the damp, sea-salted air, and the texture of the walls, pale blue with the coastal version of whitewash, crackled with age. And beyond that, through the casement, though tightly bound, came the smell of the sea and, perhaps, some thin, faraway sound of waves banging on the rocks along the shore.

He had never seen the sea, never been to a place so wild as the seaside and the high hills beyond. But he was here now, with Jack, and the hangman had not yet caught up with him. That was enough. Would have to be enough, for now.

Even the mightiest of oaks might be felled in a powerful wind, Jack knew. And try as he might to stay upright, and not cry like a baby with the pain in his head, he felt himself begin to fail. At first the headache encircling his head made him want to shut his eyes. Then, it made him unable to speak, because he couldn't bring himself to rattle his head further and beyond what the coach was doing, and even the smallest whisper was too much to bear. He found himself curled up against Nolly's side, way over on Nolly's portion of the bench seat, with no remembrance as to how he got there, and only a vague glimpse of the funeral people and their looks of disgust and dismay.

But then Nolly's arm was around him, pulling him close, and a hand, so gentle, pushed his hair back from his forehead. Which told Jack that Nolly didn't care about the funeral people and what they thought, or what stories they might carry with them to anyone who might care about where they were and where they were going. He knew he must be truly ill for Nolly to go that far, in not giving a squirt of piss about what a proper gentleman and his lady thought. That was love right there. The truest kind. The kind Jack wanted.

Only he couldn't say anything, for even if Nolly was willing to ignore some proprieties, there were others he would not want to cross. So Jack only pressed his head to Nolly's chest to say thank you, in his way, and to let that closeness, Nolly's hand on the back of his bent neck, be enough.

And it was enough, for a good long while, the rhythm of the coach echoing the ebb and flow of his headache. It lasted until the coach went over a hill, and he found his stomach taking over, and the only thing left to do was to empty it. He barely remembered doing that, and found himself bent over Nolly's knees, with the splash of vomit between Nolly's feet, and a string of spit hanging from his mouth.

Oh, the funeral people had not approved, not at all.

Jack had the vaguest notion of Nolly using the scarf to clean his mouth and the floor, and the hard words he'd had in response to some remark from the funeral people. And then as Jack sagged against Nolly, the coach rolled on and nothing seemed to make any sense.

In one moment, Nolly was holding his head and giving him a drink of water. The next moment, they were on the top of a windy hill, stung by the rain, and somewhere, in the back of his mind, Jack realized he could smell the sea. A salty smell, bitter with seaweed, and something old that rolled and rolled over itself, until it knew all of the secrets, but never shared them. Deep within the belly of the sea, while the ship's sails flapped in the wind and almost tore, and the wind turned warm, and the sun baked the earth and Jack had no idea how far he'd come.

Only that he was now sitting in a chair, and Nolly was kneeling at his feet, looking up with wet hair and eyelashes, and where on earth was Nolly's hat? He couldn't be a gentleman without a hat, that was for certain. But Nolly didn't seem to care about that at all. He was saying something, his hands on Jack's knees, kneeling on a stone floor, on a bit of rug that had a nice warm, red pattern in it. Jack tried to focus on that, on the rug, and the winding threads, tried to hear Nolly's voice, like a sweet prayer, in his ears. And while he could feel the warmth of Nolly's skin through his damp trousers, he couldn't hear Nolly speak. Only the whisper of some faraway sound, like the scratching of rats in the wainscoting in the house but one over.

At least he was warm; he sensed he was out of the rain and under someone's roof, and there was stillness. When had they gotten out of the coach? Where was the rain?

There was movement in the room, a shred of air across his face as he sensed a door opening and closing. Then Nolly got up and was pulling Jack to his feet, and Jack saw spots of black in front of his eyes, felt a chill race over him and his whole body shivering as though he'd been dashed with ice. He went where Nolly pulled him and sensed the pillow, the mattress, the dry blanket. And the words, always in whispers, in hissings, being spoken over him. He wanted to reach out for Nolly's hand, to feel that Nolly was close to him, and tried opening his eyes.

There was Nolly, standing by the bed that Jack realized he was lying in. It was a moment of clarity, that moment only, when Nolly looked down, a glint of blue, and the sweet curve of his mouth.

"Jack, you're going to be all right, the doctor is here now."

But Jack couldn't see anything after that, only sense whether it was warm or cold, when something hurt, and when it stopped. And finally, when the room was still, he could catch the scent of rose and ash, and wanted to lift his hand. And then, suddenly, Nolly was there, a weight on the bed, warm against Jack's hip, the only warm spot on him, on his whole length.

"I'll stay here, shall I?" said Nolly. "The morning will come, by-and-bye."

And then it was dark, so very dark, and Jack was alone.

12

ON A PRECIPICE, NEAR DEATH

The light from the rising sun brightened the room by increments, so slowly that Oliver thought he was imagining it. But yes, the walls began to glow a pale blue, and the outline of Jack's body beneath the bedclothes became more distinct. His face was turned toward Oliver, as though Jack knew he was near, but his eyes never opened, and he never stirred. It was like sitting in a room with a corpse, which Oliver had done a time or two, back in Hardingstone, under Mr. Sowerberry's watchful eye. This was different, though, for Jack was still alive and might pull through, *might*—

At some point, mid-morning, one of the serving maids had brought Oliver a cup of tea, and he made himself drink it. Then, quite soon after, as he sat in the chair, and watched the shadows and light coming through the windowpane to mark the sad passage of time, Mrs. Heyland opened the door and stuck her head in.

"Parson Wheeler's come to see you," she said. "You can take a bit of tea in the kitchen with him, he won't mind that."

"I shouldn't leave Jack," said Oliver, his voice gritty, unsure as to why a parson would want to speak to him.

"He's heard about and your manservant, from the talk in the

village," said Mrs. Heyland. "He wants to pray with you for your manservant's well-being. He's very involved with his flock, you see."

Oliver wished he could say no, but there seemed nothing else he could do but get up and follow her into the kitchen, though he worried about Jack all the while.

He wished he could have had time to wash, but in a moment, he was in the kitchen, which was wide and bustling. And there, sitting at a well-scrubbed and rather large table, was the parson. His white collar gave him away, as did his attentiveness on his cup of tea, and plate of cakes. He was a small man, as Dr. Rudge had been, but his hair was bright silver and his moments were slow, and as he looked at Oliver coming towards him, his expression was kind and thoughtful.

"There you are, young man. Gussie, could you bring another cup and some more cakes, these are very good, and I've eaten more than my fair share, I believe." Then, to Oliver, he said, "Come sit down, young man. I've just seen the master and mistress as they drove through town; they're bound for their house in Brighton, where the sea air will pour through their windows and make Sir John quite well again."

There was not a true answer to this flow of words, so Oliver sat down in the chair next to the parson. He took the cup when it was offered to him, and let the parson pour him the tea. He didn't touch the cakes, not because he wouldn't have enjoyed them, but because they couldn't hold a candle to even the meanest of Mrs. Pierson's cakes. And he didn't feel like eating anyway.

"Now, young man, Oliver Twist, is it? I'm Parson Wheeler, I'm the rector at St. Michael's, where we hope to see you come Sunday? And your manservant as well, if he is able."

"Certainly," said Oliver, somewhat discomfited by the obvious fact that the parson knew the whole of Oliver's story, even though they'd just been introduced. "I should like to, if Jack is well enough."

"Oh, I'm sure he will be, and I shall pray for him every day."

The parson took a large mouthful of cake, and washed it down with a swallow of tea. "And wasn't it good of Mrs. Heyland to take you in? She's a good Christian woman, that's for certain, made evident by her sheltering of you, without so much as a proper introduction."

A little silence fell about the kitchen, though the maidservants went about their duties, which did not seem to take them elsewhere than the kitchen, as if Oliver and the parson weren't even among them. And that was the crux of the matter, who Oliver was and who Jack was, and why they were there, in Lyme Regis, when no one knew them or had expected their coming. The parson was looking at Oliver with wide, expectant eyes.

"My Uncle Brownlow died this past winter," began Oliver, "so Jack and I—"

"Jack, your manservant," said the parson.

"Yes," said Oliver, hiding his sigh of worry; it was, it seemed, the lie that never stopped needing to be told. "My manservant and I came here to seek my family."

"Your family?" The parson asked, his voice rising with surprise. "Well, I can tell you right now, there are no Twists in the village."

"Well, no," said Oliver quickly, feeling the need for some haste. "My father's people are all dead, and Twist is my—well, it's my adopted name." It would take too long to explain the alphabetic method that Mr. Bumble had used to name the paupers in his charge. "My mother's people, the Flemings, came from here, or from around here. My Aunt Rose is married and living in Chertsey, so I've come to see if I can find our people. On my mother's side."

"Has your mother passed away?" asked the parson, a little more gently, and vaguely distracted, as if he were thinking of something else.

"She died when I was born," said Oliver. He did not add the bit about the workhouse, or the locket, or the machinations of Fagin and Monks, but if it was a lie to leave that part out, then so be it. He didn't need his reputation sullied from the start. "She died giving birth to me."

"Oh, dear, I am so sorry to hear it." And indeed the parson looked sorry, but Oliver could see, also, that there was some romance in it, and wished that Jack were here, in the seat beside him, slurping tea in a rude manner, and adding the veriest details that would give the romance even more heft.

"I only know that my mother's father was a sea captain. At least my Aunt Rose referred to him as Captain Fleming, though of course he might have only been a common seaman, for all she was so young when her sister, my mother—"

"Fleming," said Parson Wheeler. "Why, I *do* know that name, for I have been in this parish all of my parochial career. I don't even need to check the burial lists, nor the rents and tithes." He took a large gulp of his tea.

Oliver waited. He was close to finding out about the Flemings, and not at all sure what he might feel about it. Were they all dead, and what should he do? Were they all living, and then what should he do? And, if Jack were to get well, what would he say? What would Jack *want*? Would he stay with Oliver if Oliver were to start up his bookshop in this part of the world? His head was dizzy and he was overwhelmed with the sheer fear that if Jack died, he'd be left on his own.

"Drink your tea, young man," said Parson Wheeler. "It's not good news, I'm afraid."

Oliver could not have expected more, and somewhere deep inside, in a place that could harbor only truth, he was not sorry. It wouldn't make any difference in his life, if there were no living relatives in Lyme, but it might have been nice. Only now he didn't have to convince Jack to stay because of that family. Or would it have made a difference? Would they have wanted to take him and Jack in?

"The tale, as you probably know some of it already, is sad. It was 1828," said Parson Wheeler, "as I'm sure you're aware. Captain Fleming, your grandfather, was the last of his line; his own mother having died, he took up with the Navy, running messages and supplies. Nothing very dashing, but certainly useful in the war.

Afterwards, when he was sectioned out, he worked on the ships as they came in to the Cobb, helping with repairs, ordering sail. But everyone called him Captain Fleming."

It didn't sound like an exciting life, but perhaps it had suited his grandfather, so Oliver nodded, all the while listening for any sound coming from the sick room.

"Then, a group of gentlemen came down from Brighton in the early spring, having tired, I suppose, of the activities of the bon ton, to take a dip in the ocean, though it was far too early in the season for that. Your mother, Agnes, *shockingly* took up with a man in a long blue coat, and a month later he was gone. In January of the next year, Agnes left town, and Captain Fleming and Rose Fleming left soon after, presumably to follow Agnes, who had been great with child. Who, it turns out, has become yourself, a young man of some breeding and education, which is the Lord's blessing, considering who she was."

"Is anyone buried in the churchyard here?" Oliver ignored the slight against his mother, and tried to think instead on how it might feel to be connected to some bit of earth, even if it was a plot in a graveyard.

"Your great-grandmother is buried in the yard, but that was some years ago, and the records as to exactly where are lost. Your great-grandfather died some years before her, but that was at sea, and so—"

"No headstone."

Parson Wheeler shook his head, almost sadly. He seemed kind, for all that he had no good news, and gentle with Oliver, even though he was, after all, merely a bastard of the workhouse.

"Thank you, Parson," he said. "I truly appreciate your telling me the story."

Taking a last gulp of his tea, and putting the cup in the saucer, the parson nodded. "Is there anything else I can help you with? I feel badly that I was not able to offer you more."

This part of his journey was a dead end, in more ways than one, though for some reason, Oliver almost felt relief at the lack. The connection to Lyme was proven: his family had lived here, but had all died off. It meant, however, that he was free to roam, he and Jack.

"Would you be able to assist me with Jack's family?" asked Oliver.

"Assist your manservant? In what way?"

Oliver straightened in his chair. Of course a stranger might not warrant time or attention from a parson in such a tidy village as Lyme, so again, Olivier had to use the lie, which came up to smack him in the face.

"He's been very loyal to me," said Oliver. "And to hear him tell it, he was stolen by gypsies when he was quite young. In the village of Barnet."

"So you want to determine whether or not he's lying?"

The tone of the parson's voice changed, as though catching a servant in a lie was a laudable pursuit, for some reason. But this was Jack, and now, suddenly, it became very important to find Jack's family for him.

"No," said Oliver. "He's very ill, and I want to find out if he's got any family, in case—in case—" Oliver stopped, unable to go on with this line of thinking.

But the parson, approached with such sacred task, appeared to make up his mind. He pulled out a fold of paper and a stub of a pencil from his pocket. "Give me the details and I'll see what I can do."

"Jack says he was three or four when the gypsies took him, so, say, fourteen years ago." Oliver said, doing the sum in his head. "In 1832, in Barnet."

"They have a fair there every year," said the parson, somewhat unexpectedly. He didn't lift his head, but kept scribbling as he wrote. "Sometime in September, a horse fair. A dreadfully licentious event, as I am told. If gypsies did take him, that would be when. I'll write to the parson at Christ Church there; if a child went missing, he'd be the one to know, or he would know who to ask."

"Jack has said he doesn't remember anything except that day; he had been sitting on the stone lip of a fountain in town somewhere."

The parson continued to scribble. When he was done, he folded the paper and put it in his inside breast pocket. "We should hear in a week," he said. "The postal system is remarkably fast, wouldn't you say?"

The parson smiled at Oliver, who made himself smile in return. He supposed the post was fast; a parson wouldn't lie about a thing like that, after all. But he found that he was tired of making conversation. At least he might be able to help Jack.

"Thank you for your time, Parson Wheeler." Oliver stood up and shook the parson's hand. "I'll call on you, if that would be all right, to hear what you might have found out?"

"Yes, that would be fine. And I'll see you in church on Sunday, and your servant, presuming he is well enough to attend."

Of course the souls of servants were much less desirable than that of young gentlemen. Oliver could see it in his eyes.

"Yes, sir," said Oliver.

But that was that. As he watched the parson bid Mrs. Heyland farewell, he realized that he had no family besides Aunt Rose and Uncle Harry. And then he had Jack, who was not family, but he was somebody who Oliver was coming to know. And would continue to know, if Jack did not—

Without saying anything to anybody, Oliver went back to the sickroom. Jack was still lying very still, as though fast asleep.

Someone had removed the Oliver's cup, now empty of tea, and wiped up the blood that had splattered on the stone floor the night before. The flocked mattress was neatly rolled up along the wall, with the blanket and the pillow on top. Jack's blankets had been pulled up to his chin, and the whole room had a tidy, well-looked-after air.

Oliver closed the door behind him, and leaned against the wall. He could sit in the chair again, of course, but this position gave him the best view, and he could see all of Jack, every breath, every movement. But although there was breath, there was only stillness.

~

When Jack woke, it was vaguely bright behind his closed eyes. His throat was dry, as though it had been coated by sand whirling in a storm, gritty and dry. He tried to swallow, tried to feel various parts of his body, but when he moved his arm, it hurt, a sharp, quick pain that told him to remain still. Then he opened his eyes.

The room about him was narrow and pale blue, lit with a grey light from somewhere behind his head. The room had an odor about it, a spicy, dark smell, like old wine and poison. From beyond the closed door, he could hear the clank of pots, and a dull thud of something being set down, and voices talking brightly.

Jack wanted a drink of water very badly.

When he turned his head, there was Nolly, who was standing against the wall near the door, and was fast asleep. His head was tilted sideways, blond hair slipping over his forehead as though he'd scrubbed his hand through his hair and left it there. His mouth was open, and he looked so very tired that Jack vowed not to wake him. The trousers he had on, Jack knew, were not his own. The shirt he wore was plain, made of thick cloth with thin, blue stripes, not Nolly's style at all. The buttons on the straight collar were undone, and the cloth fell away from his neck, leaving it bare; if Nolly knew he were so disheveled, he'd be very cross indeed. Jack thought that then he might wake Nolly so he could put himself to rights.

But just as he was about to do so, a woman opened the door without knocking and came into the room. From her crisp white cap to her enormous belled skirts, she was every inch a bossy housekeeper.

"Oliver Twist, are you awake?" This was said in a loud whisper, and Nolly jumped up and went to the woman.

"Yes, Mrs. Heyland? What is it?" asked Oliver, in a more hushed tone than she had used.

"I've brought Dr. McMurtry. He's very good, for all he is so young. He thought he would stop in to see your manservant."

"Yes, thank you." Nolly said this with less conviction than he might have done, but Jack got a good look of his backside in those country trousers, which were laughable not only for their double buttons at the high waist but for the *suspenders* too, as they set off Nolly's bum very well. Not that Jack would ever tell him that, for the only reward besides a blush would be Nolly's reticence for hours afterward. Best to keep it to himself. In the meantime, he would stare, though his head was starting to pound a bit, and the ache in his neck was making itself known.

Just then, Nolly turned, his eyes lighting as he saw that Jack was awake. As Nolly rushed to his side, it was rather like a vision, with the sweet expression and the simple clothes, and Nolly's shirt collar undone, as though he were a country boy.

"Jack, *Jack*, you're awake."

Nolly sat on the bed, and for a moment, it was as if they were alone together, and Mrs. Heyland wasn't at the door, and a doctor wasn't soon to come.

"Thirsty, Nolly," Jack said, the sand in his throat rattling around.

"Yes, Jack, yes," said Nolly. "Let me fetch it—"

Before Jack could speak, Mrs. Heyland was chittering about the doctor having just come, and then she flew away to fetch him, leaving the door ajar.

Nolly looked at Jack with a sad expression in his eyes. "I hope this doctor is better than the last one. And we'll do everything he tells us and you'll get well."

"There's nowt wrong with me," said Jack. "What's wrong with me?"

"You've got a fever," said Nolly. He reached for Jack's hand and squeezed it. "You weren't yourself since we've left London, and I've been terrified that—but you're going to get better now."

At that moment, the blue and white china knob turned, and the door opened all the way. In came a young, bespectacled man, in a trim brown suit and sensible white cravat, bustling into the room with a bulky leather bag, pushing his glasses up from where they'd slipped on his nose. Jack suspected by the bag that he carried that the young man was a doctor. On his heels was Mrs. Heyland, her hands clasped together in front of her breast, beaming at the doctor in a very motherly way.

The doctor squinted through his spectacles as he went to the far side of the bed and put his bag down on the edge of it.

"This is Dr. McMurtry," and Mrs. Heyland's smile for him seemed quite genuine. "He's just been at the finest schools, wasn't it last year, Dr. McMurtry? Why, my own boy, my second eldest, went to Paris over the winter; he's there still. Learning the French as fast as he's learning all those things a modern doctor needs to know."

Mrs. Heyland's smile was warm, and she let both Nolly and Jack have a bit of it, though mostly the smile seemed to be for her second eldest, the clever one, on his way to becoming a doctor.

As for the doctor, he came right up to Jack with some confidence. Rather like a shyster who's got the perfect coney in his sights. Jack couldn't help but clutch at the bedclothes. This made the doctor have to tug a little bit to pick up Jack's wrist and check for his pulse.

"You say he had laudanum, Mrs. Heyland, and was bled last night?"

"That was Dr. Rudge, I'm afraid. My son has told me that—"

Dr. McMurtry shook his head; he was quite young, but the shake was enough to make Mrs. Heyland close her mouth with a snap.

"I'm sorry," she said, quieter now. "I don't mean to tell you your business. You know as much as my son does, and I'm sure if he were here, he'd agree with everything you're about to say."

Dr. McMurtry's lips quirked a bit, as if he were trying not to laugh. "Indeed," said Dr. McMurty, "and I thank you for the confidence of it. Now, what do we have here?"

"This is Oliver Twist and his manservant, Jack Dawkins." Mrs. Heyland nodded at each of them. "Young Twist has fallen on hard times and—"

"He *was* my manservant," said Nolly, stumbling over the words, as if hesitating over the lie. "But, with hard times, I can no longer pay him—"

"And yet he has stayed at your side," said Dr. McMurtry, smiling even more broadly now. "That's loyalty for you, and it says something about you as well."

The doctor had sharp eyes as he looked at them both, and made a little sound that seemed to be a sigh.

"Actually, I wanted to know about the patient. Jack, is it?"

"Jack hit his head, yesterday—no, the day before yesterday," said Nolly. "He was unconscious for a moment or two, and then yesterday he became feverish, and then—"

"And then he vomited?" As Nolly nodded, the doctor took Jack's pulse, then touched his head. "Where did you hit your head, Jack?"

Before Nolly could answer, Jack reached up with his left hand to cup the back of his head on that side. "He hit me, an' then I hit my head," Jack gestured toward the pillow with his thumb, "back there."

He didn't mention any other ills, not being keen on having the doctor do anything to him, and certainly he didn't want to be bled —though, by the rough scab on the inside of his elbow, it seemed he already had been, which explained the pain he'd felt earlier. But this doctor seemed different. The single question focused in on Jack's ills, as if he were a person, rather than merely someone's manservant. Jack couldn't figure out whether or not to trust this.

"He only had some beer, and then he was sick—"

"Young Twist," said the doctor. "Would you give me a moment to converse with my patient or I shall have to ask you to leave the room."

For a moment, Nolly seemed startled, his mouth open, as if in surprise, and Jack didn't blame him. This was not the way strangers talked to Nolly; they usually stared and said nothing at all, or cooed and flattered. But the doctor was still looking at Nolly with a steady gaze that indicated he meant what he said.

"Yes, sir," said Nolly, sweet as a lamb. He was standing so close to the edge of the bed, tucked in quite close, that his hand was brushing against Jack's. Jack determined to stay very still indeed so as not to lose contact.

Dr. McMurtry put Jack's arm gently on the bed, then put his hand on Jack's forehead.

"Do you feel as though you might want to vomit now, or do you feel more steady than that?"

"No," said Jack. He frowned, wondering at this doctor, who asked so many questions. "My mouth tastes like dirt, though."

"That would be the laudanum," said the doctor.

He used his thumb to pull Jack's eyelids up, and immediately stopped when Jack jerked his head away. "That would be the headache."

Then the doctor nodded, looked at Jack, as if for permission, before taking his hand, very slowly, to cup it behind Jack's head. The hand stayed there for a moment, and though Jack winced, he kept his mouth shut by sheer will.

"There's a bit of a lump here, which probably aches. And your headache, is it sharp or dull?"

"Mostly dull," said Jack. He was feeling quite tired from the questions, and the constant touching from someone he did not know made him feel prickly all over his skin. "But in the coach, all that movement, it got very sharp indeed."

After a moment, the doctor took his hand away, and took off his glasses to rub his nose. He put his glasses back on, and looked at both Nolly and Jack, and at their connected hands.

"He's hit his head," said Dr. McMurtry. "And the laudanum did him no good in the slightest."

"I thought not, but there was no stopping Dr. Rudge."

"And there's to be no more bleeding. A hit on the head is not a disease."

"Oh, I agree with you completely."

"I should think, Mrs. Heyland, that some willow bark tea would do this young gentleman a great deal more good than either laudanum or wine. And some beef broth. Let's say, willow bark tea every two hours, and beef broth every four. And as much water as he'd like; it will rinse the bad humors away. A few days in bed, till he feels himself again. Can that be arranged, Mrs. Heyland?"

"Certainly," she said, almost bobbing a curtsey at him.

"After that, you can get out of bed on Thursday. How does that sound?"

Mrs. Heyland nodded, beaming with her slanted mouth. "My son would agree with you, I'm sure."

This made Dr. McMurty smile again, a genuine, deep-dimpled smile that made him seem younger than his years. "I'm sure that he would. Jack should have rest and care and as much quiet as you can afford him. As for Oliver, here—"

"Yes, sir?" said Nolly promptly.

"You can be his nurse and save the good lady from too many steps while the master is gone. What is it, to Brighton?"

"Yes, and a shame, too, with Sir John's room just painted a lovely green over the winter." Mrs. Heyland shook her head, flopping the lace across her forehead, with her hands folded in front of her. "He won't get to come back to it until halfway through summer, though there's not another who deserves to enjoy it more."

"That is a shame, indeed. But Oliver will lend a hand, will you not, Oliver? You can make it up to your manservant for the help he has given you, eh?"

"I'd be proud to do it," said Oliver. "Whatever I can do, I will."

"Very good. Well, then, Mrs. Heyland, do you have the willow bark tea, or shall you send someone into the village for it?"

"I do have some," said Mrs. Heyland as if affronted by the

notion that hers was not a well-supplied medicine chest. "Dried just last autumn, so it will be very strong, the way I make it."

"All to the better," said Dr. McMurtry. "Now I'll be off; do call if you need me, and no more bleeding, do you understand? Not in a concussion such as this."

"Of course not, Doctor."

"Can I give him some water now, sir?" asked Nolly.

"Yes, indeed," said Dr. McMurtry. "Did Dr. Rudge say no water?" Without waiting for an answer, he took off his glasses and cleaned them with his handkerchief. Then he put the glasses back on. "You shall give him water as he asks for it, and when he feels like eating, keep the food simple at first. We don't want him throwing up on Mrs. Heyland's clean white sheets."

He patted Jack's leg, gathered up his bag, and strode out of the room. The set of his shoulders told Jack that the doctor was confident in his diagnosis, and as long as Jack was going to get a drink of water, he would agree with him. The doctor and the housekeeper moved into the hall, leaving the door ajar; Jack was glad to see them go.

"I'll be right back," said Nolly, and he dashed out of the room to return with a tumbler and a small jug. He poured water into the tumbler and put that on the little side table.

"Can you sit up?" he asked. "Let me help you."

It hurt to sit up to a straighter position, but Jack couldn't let Nolly know that, so he gritted his teeth and let himself be helped. His reward was Nolly's hand on the back of his neck, so gentle it made Jack shiver.

"Are you cold?" asked Nolly. "Here, drink some water, and we'll get you under the covers where you'll be warm."

"You're quite affectionate when you're worried," said Jack. He wanted the cheer the seriousness away from Nolly's expression.

Nolly blinked at him, his hands stilled. "I was worried—*am* worried. About you." It seemed as though it took a lot for him to admit this, but his eyes were soft.

"They'll be bringing tea," said Nolly now. "But drink this for now."

Nolly brought the tumbler to his mouth, and pressed it to Jack's lips, and Jack was never so grateful for a simple drink of water as he was then. And with Nolly's eyes, quiet and blue, looking at him, with a lift of a smile at the corner of his mouth. The mouth that Jack wanted to kiss all the time, if Nolly would let him. But Nolly had notions of propriety in matters of kissing, with the housekeeper only steps away.

When Nolly took the tumbler away, Jack licked his lips.

"That was nice," he said, keeping his voice low. Then he heard swishing skirts in the passage. "Here comes the missus. You think that tea will work?"

"It should, since the doctor ordered it. Here, have another sip of water."

This Jack did eagerly, watching Nolly's eyes as they watched his mouth and throat as he swallowed. It was hard not to smile, for Nolly was so easy to bestir and half the time had no idea that Jack was doing it on purpose. Though Jack supposed it was cruel, when the missus of the house was just coming in the room with a mug of tea.

Mrs. Heyland came in, her stiff skirts swishing; Jack could almost hear the starch in her cap crackle. She carried a tray upon which there was only a single mug, out of which the steam rose. Jack might have told her that it was foolish to carry a tray that large and bring no beer or gin on it, but he knew that it would fluster Nolly, but in the wrong way. So when she came close and took the mug from the tray and placed it on the table, reaching over Nolly to do it, he let Nolly do the talking.

"That's very kind of you, Mrs. Heyland," said Nolly. "Very kind indeed."

"Only the charity that our Lord would himself give, were he here," she said. "And before his departure, I was able to get word that Sir John gives his leave for me to shelter you, so you are here on the charity of a great man."

And with a snap of a nod, she left, shutting the door behind her. It was Jack lollygagging in bed that she did not approve of, that was for sure. Had it been Nolly in the bed, with his sweet curls spread across the pillowcase, she would have been cooing and running to fetch and carry for him. Nolly had that way about him, which was perhaps a good thing. For if Nolly had been the one in the bed, Jack would have been tossed out of doors.

But those were such dark thoughts when Nolly was just there, near at hand, bending to blow on the liquid in the mug, in case it was too hot for Jack.

"Will you take some of this?" Nolly stood up, one hand on the mug and looked at Jack.

Jack nodded. When Nolly had that expression, that blue-eyed way of looking at Jack as though he were someone Nolly adored, Jack would have eaten bramble stew.

Nolly sat on the edge of the bed, a little primly, rather than curved in the hollow of Jack's hip. But perhaps that was for the best, since he lifted up the mug full of hot tea.

"It doesn't smell very good," said Nolly.

"Medicine always smells bad," said Jack. "It'll probably taste bad, too."

When Nolly lifted the mug to his mouth, Jack found out he was right. It tasted worse than a witch's arse, but with Nolly looking at him so expectantly, he swallowed the mouthful, trying not to make a face and failing.

"Does it taste terrible?" asked Nolly.

"Worse," said Jack with a gasp. "But if it works, I won't care. Give us the lot."

Tilting the mug to Jack's mouth, Nolly watched him as he swallowed, and Jack found that it was a very nice thing to be waited upon like this, with Nolly close to hand, and everything feeling settled and calm. That was the way Nolly liked it at any rate, and so Jack wasn't above living the tame life for a while.

"You should rest now. That's what the doctor said."

Nolly put the mug on the table, and Jack let himself be shifted down in the bed as Nolly tucked the bedclothes around him and settled the pillow beneath his head. The headache seemed to be easing somewhat, the tension leaving his neck and floating away. Not far, no, but away, so that he felt he might fall asleep.

"Nolly," he said.

"Yes, Jack?" asked Nolly, as he sat on the bed.

Jack kept his eyes open, but just barely.

"I see how we're here, you n'me, in this nice place, but no doctor comes for free."

He felt Nolly's body stiffen.

"We ain't got any more money, have we." Jack didn't need to ask it, for he already knew it was true.

"You're not to worry about that just now," Nolly said.

He was fiddling with the sheet, not quite looking at Jack, and Jack knew that there was no money, that whether they'd spent it or it had fallen out of pockets during their bumpy journey, there simply was no money left. And him not able to get up and amble into town to pick some pockets.

But Jack didn't say anything about it, and Nolly seemed to relax as he continued to sit at Jack's side. He looked at Jack, studying him, as if he'd never really done so before today. Though Jack knew that wasn't strictly true. Nolly often had odd moments where his eyes would go unfocused, and he would look at something without really seeing it. As he was now.

Jack wondered what was passing through Nolly's mind. Perhaps it was about where they were and from whence they'd come. Or perhaps, as the circles beneath his eyes might attest, he was tired. Jack knew he was troublesome to be with. Always laughing at Nolly, and making him go places and do things that he didn't want to do. It was good for Nolly in a way, when Jack did things differently; it would keep him sharp, keep him safe. But it also made Nolly cross, and gave him that little crinkle between his eyebrows. As there was right now.

Jack turned on his side, and pulled up his knees so that they connected with Nolly's backside, curved around his hip. He saw

Nolly twitch and thought that he might be shoved away and told to go asleep. But then Nolly's face softened, and he bent his head down. Laid his arm along Jack's hip and waist, his hand along Jack's shoulder.

"I'll just sit with you while you fall asleep, Jack. I won't leave you alone."

Funny, that. Nolly seemed to know what he needed, and why he needed it. Jack closed his eyes, and swallowed hard; he was too tough to need soft touches, but when he got them from Nolly, it seemed to melt him, and render him to a point where all he could do was breathe through that moment, and the one after that. And wish that he could ask, out loud, that Nolly never take his hand away.

Jack realized his eyes were closed when he felt Nolly's hand on his forehead.

"You rest, Jack," said Nolly, low, his voice rumbling low, like a slow river. "I'll be right here. Right here."

Jack dozed between being given doses of tea and having a cold cloth put on his forehead, and dozed some more as he felt Nolly watch him sleep. Not once had he woken alone, and he had only to make a gesture for Nolly to be at his side, giving him a drink of water or tea. At some point Nolly woke him up to give him beef broth from a fine china bowl, which tasted quite nice, and then Jack floated off into sleep again.

He felt better as it started to get darker, when Nolly came in the room, as if he'd left it, though Jack had never noticed him leave.

"The doctor's here again," said Nolly.

"*Again?*" asked Jack, mumbling as he tried to pull himself to a sitting position. The village of Lyme Regis must be very small indeed if the doctor had time to visit a scoundrel like Jack twice in one day.

And indeed, there the doctor was. He came through the door and right up to the bed as though the room, perhaps the whole house, belonged to him.

"I was on my way back from Axminster workhouse, and thought I'd check in. How are you feeling, young man?" asked Dr. McMurtry, touching Jack's forehead with the back of his hand. "Is the tea working?"

"I reckon so," said Jack. The doctor looked entirely too sure of himself for Jack to want to praise the tea. "Tastes terrible, though, like a witch's behind."

Too late he realized that Mrs. Heyland was standing just outside the door. He heard her gasp and stride off and Jack winced, but pretending it was the doctor's prodding, rather than in antici-pation of Nolly's opinion of Jack's behavior. But that's who Jack was, someone whom a woman like Mrs. Heyland would always disapprove of. Leastways, he'd mind his manners till they let him out of bed, but beyond that, he could make no promises.

"A witch's behind?" asked Dr. McMurtry, his eyebrows rising. "Now that's a good one. I'll have to share it with the boys at the tavern."

Jack almost laughed at this but even the slight movement tested the edges of his headache, as if wanting to bring it back. And as for Nolly, he was trying not to laugh because that wouldn't be polite, no matter how much he wanted to. He had pressed himself along the wall near the door, watching everything the doctor did. Jack hoped the doctor realized what scrutiny he was under; it would be better for him in the long run if he did.

Mrs. Heyland came back in the room with her most disap-proving glare; it would have put the best of Nolly's expressions to shame.

The doctor took Jack's wrist, his eyes unfocused as he concen-trated on testing Jack's pulse, though what good that might do, Jack didn't know. Then the doctor felt the lump on the back of Jack's head, and cupped Jack's head in his palm. Jack remembered this from before, and thought that his head wasn't as sensitive to the touch this time. Then the doctor took his hand away, nodding, as though satisfied.

"Young Oliver, I will tell you this." Dr. McMurtry looked over the top of his spectacles, first at Nolly, then at Jack. "Your manservant is young and healthy, and he will be well soon; I have seen it before, many times, in my practice. The headaches will abate in time, and he will be himself again. A full recovery, I assure you."

There was a moment of stillness, and while Jack was glad of the news, and though he had been fairly certain he would be well, it was nice having it spoken aloud so that Nolly could hear it. Only his beloved boy did not quite look relieved.

"C'n I get out of bed now?" asked Jack. "Since I'm soon to be well an' all."

"No, Jack," said Dr. McMurtry. "You've got quite a lump there, so I still think you should stay in bed till Thursday. If that can be managed, Mrs. Heyland?"

"It's no trouble at all," said Mrs. Heyland.

But of course, that was a lie, and she was very good at it. The last thing she wanted was someone like Jack in her sickroom. Even a moment of his presence would have been too long and now she was being asked to suffer him for longer. But Nolly was there, right at Jack's side, and there wasn't a thing Mrs. Heyland could do or say about it. Not with the doctor there. Not with Nolly there.

"I'll go brew more tea, and see you to the door, Dr. McMurtry."

"Thank you, Mrs. Heyland," said the doctor, as the two of them left the room, closing the door behind them.

When they were gone, Nolly tested the door, turning the china knob slowly in his hand to make sure it was closed. Jack got the idea that he was wishing there was a lock on the door, so he could shut the world out.

But in that moment, instead of turning to look at Jack, Nolly pressed his hands flat against the panels of the door, and slipped his arm up to hide his face in the crook of his elbow. He stood there, hip cocked, fist clenched over his head, legs shifting beneath him, as if he were prepared to run a great distance, or as though he already had, for his ribs heaved, and Jack heard him take a long, shuddering breath and let it out slowly.

"Nolly, whatever is the matter? *Nolly?*"

Jack pushed back the bedclothes, feeling hot and cold all at once, and knowing that when Nolly saw it, he'd be telling Jack to get right in the bed, and he'd be insistent about it. But Nolly scrubbed his face on his upper arm and tried to look at Jack, but failed; his eyes were wet, and it was this that made Jack stop short.

"You're going to be well, Jack," said Nolly. And to anyone else the words would have lacked all passion and feeling. But it was the lack of ease as Nolly spoke them that told Jack what he wanted, perhaps needed, to know.

"Certainly, I am, Nolly, that's what the doctor said, but I knew it afore he even said it." Jack patted the bed, wanting to draw Nolly to him before he fell down. "Come an' sit by me, there's a good lad, come an' sit."

Nolly did as Jack bade him, but his shoulders were bowed, and after he'd pulled the covers back up over Jack, there was a movement as he reached out to take Jack's hand, then withdrew it, as if whatever emotion had urged him on was discovered to be forbidden.

"Nolly, 'tis goin' to be all right, you know it is."

"There was a great bit of time, in the night, when you were quite still and burned with fever."

Nolly's fingers gripped the counterpane fiercely that he might have torn them, had not Jack placed his hand on top of Nolly's. The bones in his hands were white and shaking, as Nolly blinked, his eyes unfocused.

"You were so still, Jack. So *still.*"

Nolly's voice was low, drawn like a hard line in the air over which he might dare anybody to cross. Usually none dared, or if they blundered, they fared rather badly. Except Jack was not anybody and the declaration served as less of a warning than an indication of the purest love. Nolly need not even have added the last, for it was evidence enough to Jack that had he actually expired, then Nolly would have paused only long enough to find the person who was responsible and deliver him the most dire consequences. It was for them a fairer fate that Jack still breathed, to amend this disaster from happening. Moreover, there was yet any line in sand or stone that Nolly might draw that Jack could not step over.

"Were you afeared I'd perish, my dear Nolly?" Jack shook his head, albeit gently, prepared to temper this kind of question with some statement, perhaps more taunting, to break Nolly of his mournful expression and give him another.

But Nolly beat him to it.

"Yes," said Nolly, his shoulders slumping down, as a wash of grey air seemed to descend over him. "Yes, I did."

It had been bad then, for Nolly, sitting alone in the dark with his dying companion.

So Jack did away with sitting still, and reached to pull Nolly to him. Nolly was stiff in his hands, resisting for that second, for propriety's sake, before what must surely be an indecent impulse, and let himself be pulled. Right to where his head rested on Jack's breast, and his arms looped around Jack's waist as Jack leaned back on the pillows.

Nolly rested there, no doubt listening to the steady pound of Jack's heart, letting himself be stilled by Jack's hand along the curve of his back. Finally, he felt Nolly sigh against him.

"'Tis all right now, Nolly, for I am quite well, quite well, you see."

There was no remark of response from Nolly, save for the tightening of his arms around Jack and the deepening press of his face against Jack's chest. And that, for Jack, was answer enough.

13

AND THEN, HAVING SUPPER

The smells of cooking wafted down the hall as Oliver sat in the chair in the sickroom and watched Jack doze. He was grateful for so many things, for though it was raining outside, he was warm and dry, and Jack was getting the care that he needed. Granted, it was at Oliver's untrained hands, but it was so much better than it could have been, so he should have been more grateful.

Through the slightly opened window, he could hear the rain pattering on the glass in a heavy, sleepy way that bespoke nothing of winter. Instead, the smell of wet earth was laced with salt, and there was a faraway roar of what he could only presume was the ocean. Lyme was the last home of his family, so would he be willing to settle down in here and continue the family line?

But sitting there, in the dry clothes that Mrs. Heyland had lent him, the darned stockings, the thick muslin shirt, he felt as though he was a stranger in his own skin. He knew nothing of the sea, and Jack, were he by himself, would never consider staying in such a clean, innocent place as Lyme appeared to be.

Jack stirred on the bed, distracting Oliver from his thoughts, which were wayward twigs in a twisting river that led to the sea.

He'd never seen the sea and Jack had. Would this one be like the seas that Jack had sailed upon?

Oliver stood up, and brushed Jack's hair back from his face; the tangle felt oily beneath his fingers. Jack's skin was damp with perspiration. It was not as bad as it had been the night before, but it meant that he needed to rouse Jack to make him drink more tea.

Oliver traced a path down Jack's neck, thinking to cup his hand along the back of Jack's head, and allow him to gently wake up, so he wouldn't jerk with surprise. But just then, Jack opened his eyes, which were hazy with the remains of his fever. He blinked at Oliver as though he would, at any moment, start spouting more memories of the old days. But at least there was no one to hear, not in the slow dip of late afternoon. They were all alone.

"Nolly, is everythin' all right?" This came out a whisper and Oliver leaned in close to answer it.

"You need to wake up, Jack," he said sweetly. "Please, can you wake up and sit up a little bit? You should drink some more of this tea."

Jack rolled over on his side, and pushed himself up on one elbow. "Just give it to me," he said. "I'll drink it. There's no need for you to pull that sad face on me."

It was Jack's game attempt to act as if everything was normal, that his skin wasn't once more overly warm, a sign that the fever could rise if they didn't tend to it. Well, Oliver could play that game as well, and he took the mug of tea from the table and held it to Jack's mouth. The tea was cold, but Jack took several large swallows, and if he sloshed it over his mouth and onto the bedclothes, there was no harm in it. The sheets would wash, at any rate.

Oliver took the flannel cloth that had been left with him and wiped Jack's mouth with it. Or tried to. Jack pushed his hand away, now sloshing more of the tea, and lay back on the pillow with a flop and a sigh.

"You're like a bleedin' nursemaid, you are," said Jack. His eyes closed, and the dark furrow between his eyebrows eased as the tea took hold.

"That's because I *am* your nursemaid," said Oliver, as he adjusted the bedclothes.

"Can you open the window a wee bit more, Nolly? I'm on fire here."

Oliver stood up and pulled the latch on the window frame out all the way until it clicked. The rain came into the casement, just a little bit, fresh-smelling along with a brisk current of air. Oliver could taste the salt air on his lips.

He looked down at Jack. "I could cool you down some more if you like, but you mustn't get out of bed."

With a flicker of his eyelashes, Jack looked up at Oliver and then away.

"How's that, then?"

"I've got water, and a cloth. Mrs. Heyland thought it might be better if I did this, rather than one of the maidservants.'"

"You goin' to give me a bath, then, Nolly?"

Oliver felt the heat on his cheeks, just as he felt something spark inside of him. "Of course not," he said. "I'm just going to— here. I'll make you feel more comfortable, and then you can go back to sleep."

Oliver leaned to get the cloth from the bed, and wet it in the depths of the jug that a maidservant had brought some time ago. The water was only lukewarm, but that couldn't be helped. He wrung out the cloth and wiped Jack's face with it, going slowly, pushing Jack's hair aside, gently taking up some of the heat and sweat, at least. He dipped and wrung the cloth again, to wipe the back of Jack's neck and the part of his chest that could be reached through his the open shirt. Then he bathed Jack's hands, taking Jack's fingers betwcen both of his own hands, to hold them there with the cloth folded over.

"'S'nice," said Jack. His lips barely moved.

"That's good," said Oliver. He soaked the cloth and reached over to wash Jack's other hand.

When he was finished, Jack looked a good deal more relaxed, with his neck tilted to one side on the pillow, and his forehead, finally, was smooth and peaceful. The cloth was quite dark, but what did that matter. That's what soap was for.

"You starin' at me, now, Nolly?" The question was asked with the rain building to a steady thumping sound on the pane.

Oliver ignored the question and reached up to close the window, pushing in the latch, leaving only the barest crack for fresh air.

"Nolly."

"Nobody's staring at nobody," said Oliver.

He felt overwhelmed by the responsibility of Jack's care, terrified he was going to make a mistake, do the wrong thing, and make Jack ill again. Yet at the same time, when he was in the middle of it like this, wringing out the cloth one last time, or pulling up the sheet to tuck over Jack's chest, it felt better. It felt good. It wasn't Jack's fault that he was ill, if anything it was Oliver's—oh yes, that was true. He should have walked away and taken Jack with him, and left Cromwell without Cromwell's ever knowing it, he should have—

"You can stop thinkin', an' give us a kiss then, an go off an' get somethin' to eat. I c'n hear your stomach growlin' from here."

"It's not suppertime yet."

"Women live to feed, an' you the sweetest thing to grace their table. Go on, kiss me an' go; I'm sick of your hand-wringin' ways."

Jack didn't mean it, of course he didn't. His eyes were closed at any rate, so he would hardly be able to see whether or not Oliver was wringing his hands.

"Kiss first," said Jack.

This wasn't an order, it was a request, made in that low tone that Jack used when he was being honest with himself as well as the world. There wasn't an ounce of the street thief in it, a tone Oliver heard only once in a while, such as when they were alone and there was no one to hear. And it was no hardship to give Jack this, no hardship at all.

He bent close, taking in the scent of the oil in Jack's hair, the smell of his sweat, the desperate, lyrical mess of his dark hair on the pillow. Then Jack opened his eyes, turned his head, and looked at Oliver.

"It's goin' to be fine, Nolly, truly it is. I promise. I'm goin' to be fine, so you won't have to look at me like that n'more."

The sweetness of this, the innocence of it. The promise. It all clenched at Oliver's heart, a hard fist around a tender thing, and he had to swallow, not understanding why such a thing would make him feel this way.

And then he kissed Jack. Not in passion or in haste, not in the darkness, hiding from the day. But on the lips, touching Jack's with his own, paper light, and soft as a rose petal. It was new, felt sweet, and as he pulled back, expecting a scowl from Jack, because that's not the way he imagined people kissed, he was surprised anew. Jack had a small, secret smile curling at the edges of his mouth, and a swath of color along his cheeks that spoke nothing of fever or illness.

"Oh, you *are* the tender one, aren't you. C'mere, give us another'n."

With a jumbled sense of heat along his jaw, Oliver thought to pull back, but stopped. It had just been a kiss, after all, and a chaste one at that. And good, tendering the rumble in his belly with something far more pleasant. So he sat on the bed, and curved his hand gently around Jack's head, and bent down for another kiss, tasting the willow bark tea, as Jack's mouth opened to his. A touch of Jack's tongue startled him, though he did not want to admit it. That would only bring more teasing, and Jack needed to rest.

So, Oliver sat up straight, and smiled down at Jack, running his thumb along Jack's jaw.

"You should sleep now," he said, keeping his voice quiet. "I'll go along, and when you wake up, I shall be at your side with more terrible tasting tea."

Jack's eyes were already closing as he drifted off, with that same small, curled smile.

~

Oliver rubbed his eyes, and tucked in his shirt as he left the room, traversing a narrow passage, before turning into a bigger one, following all the while the sounds of cooking and talking. The kitchen, when he found it, was enormous, and more vast and airy than many a kitchen he'd seen, due to it being on the ground floor instead of a cellar. Not only did a door lead directly outside, there was a huge bank of windows all along one wall. Splotched sunlight from the setting sun made its way through, hitting the copper pots hanging from the opposite wall, and the well-groomed stove gleamed black as night against the white-scrubbed stone floor and the clean, white wooden counters.

He found Mrs. Heyland by the stove talking to one of the serving girls. She turned to him at once.

"Yes, Oliver?"

"Mrs. Heyland, I—"

"Just a moment," Mrs. Heyland said, nodding at the serving girl. "You could have gone to Brighton, had you tended to your tasks better than you were."

"Yes, Mrs. Heyland," said the girl, with a small curtsey.

Then Mrs. Heyland stepped away, as if Oliver wasn't even there.

"Mrs. Heyland," he called to her back, and she turned, though she looked somewhat cross.

"What is it, Oliver? I must get supper on and I need to organize the servants for spring cleaning. What is it?"

"It's about the bill for the two doctors, Mrs. Heyland," he said. "I do not think it right that you should pay it."

"And I will not," she said, with something much less than the kindness she'd shown before. Then, shaking her head, she went on. "I do not mean to be cruel; I took you both in out of Christian charity, as is proper. But I won't be showing Sir John the bill, that's for sure. And I myself cannot afford three shillings and sixpence per visit, so you must. There's a man in the village, a Mr. Thurly, who could use a good hand with packing fish and the like, so you could earn money that way."

"But I know nothing of fish," said Oliver, thinking about how close they were to the sea, so of course there would be fishing nearby. "I've only ever eaten them."

This seemed to amuse her, for she smiled at him, eying him anew. "You're a young man of good breeding, it's easy to see. But a few days of low work won't do you any harm. You'll earn your keep, and Jack's besides. I, in turn, will earn Mr. Thurly's good wishes by providing him with extra hands. Which means that he will sell me his very freshest fish, which is a very good thing when it comes to providing this house with the best. So you see? A good turn for a good turn."

"I would like to stay near Jack, till he's better," said Oliver.

"And so you shall. You can help with the spring cleaning until I can secure you a position with Mr. Thurly; a sturdy lad like you will make a difference."

"Of course, Mrs. Heyland," he said. "I could not continue to stay if I did not contribute to the household."

This softened her, he could see it at once. Though he was not quite the clean-cut lad he'd been at the haberdashery, his looks and bearing, and perhaps Jack's story, had won him the moment, if not the day. Should there be a day when that was not true, well, he would deal with it then. In the meantime, he needed to take care of Jack.

"Would you like something to eat? The servants are about to sit down to a bit of supper. And then, tomorrow, we'll put you to work. You can check on your manservant between times, but since Dr. McMurtry's declared him on his way to health, he will soon get better, don't you worry."

She turned toward the center of the kitchen, her skirts swishing about her feet. "Come, have a seat, and I'll let you meet the maidservants, we have three—"

Three young ladies who had been working at the counter turned toward Mrs. Heyland, straightening their starched caps and twitching their aprons. He only recognized Edith, and nodded at the serving girl who'd just been scolded, but meeting new servants was always like this. They all seemed cut from the same cloth until some aspect of their looks or personality would find a way to jump out at him. For now, they were all comely and slightly shy, and well groomed, and they all dipped a curtsey to Mrs. Heyland and to Oliver.

"Girls, this is Oliver Twist, who came to us last night with his manservant Jack, who is quite ill in the sickroom. Oliver, this is Melinda, Edith, who you've met, and Gussie. Oliver has been tending to his manservant, who is getting better. Melinda, heat up water for the young man to tidy himself with."

With a swirl of white aprons and strings tied behind, the maidservants went to work, while Oliver watched, feeling a bit out of place and useless, besides.

"When did you last eat, young man?" Mrs. Heyland asked.

"Oh, I'm not hungry—"

"You've been up all night and all day," she scolded, only a moment's distance between her and a sound *tsk tsk* that would have made him feel right at home. "I'll make you a cup of tea, and by the time you finish that, everything will be ready. Come and sit here."

He could hardly disobey a direct order like that, not when she was pulling out the chair, and tugging on his arm to get him to take a seat. So he sat, and for a moment, slumped forward as rudely as if he were in a tavern, straightening up only at the last moment, when he felt her eyes upon him.

"How far have you come, then?" she asked.

"From London, ma'am," he said. "There was nothing for me in the City, and I couldn't keep a manservant there." His skin prickled as he told the lie, but while there might not even be a need for it at this point, there was no way for her to check. It might distract her from the real issue of why they had had to leave London in the first place. Besides which, one of the maidservants came over with a cup and saucer and handed it to Mrs. Heyland, who then handed it to Oliver.

He took it, and brought the cup to his lips, tasting the tea, which was a little bit weak, and not quite sweet enough, certainly nowhere near the way he liked it, but it would give him some energy at least. He drank it, and handed the cup and saucer to her.

The kitchen was warm and the serving girls bustled with pre-suppertime preparations. Oliver sat at one end of the table, and he let his exhaustion relax him; Jack was going to be all right, and that was all that mattered. He wasn't near the warmth of the fire, but it was better that way, as he could watch everyone, and think about their lives, distracting himself to settle his mind. It was amusing to watch the three maidservants not tripping over each other's skirts.

As for Mrs. Heyland, she did not have the same firm, self-assured hand with either her kitchen or the servants that Mrs. Pierson had. She would make polite and soft requests, and then turn to a different task, regardless of whether what she wanted done was done to any standard. Still, the girls helped her prepare the meal on the stove and the long white table, while Oliver sat there, doing his best not to fall asleep.

Presently, through the rain-dappled glass windows, Oliver saw two figures, a man and a boy, who entered through the kitchen door, stamping their feet and shaking off the flap of oilskin the man carried over them. The man was broad shouldered and brown from the sun and air; he took off his rough jacket, hung it on a hook on the wall, and ran his hands through his hair, before gesturing to the boy to do the same. The lad was dressed as the man was, with dark woolen trousers and a rough jacket, and he imitated the man, shaking the rain from his hair. They both regarded Oliver with some reserve, the man politely, the boy shyly.

"Who's this, then? Is this our visitor, come to supper?" the man asked. The question was asked with no malice, though it might have been that Oliver was sitting in someone's favorite chair.

Oliver hopped to his feet with a little bow, quite forgetting that the man was a servant, as was, most likely the boy, neither of whom were used to being bowed to.

"Was I in your chair?" he asked. "I'm terribly sorry."

"No, no matter," said the man. He came up to Oliver, bringing the young boy, who could not have been more than ten, with him. "I'm Gerald, and this 'ere's Timothy, Tim as we calls him. I'm the second groomsman, and Tim is our latest acquisition as a stable-hand, just last autumn before the first snows came. Say hello, Tim."

"'Ello," said Tim, in a quiet voice. "Have you come to help in the stables?"

"Now, never mind that, Tim," said Mrs. Heyland. "He's come for a visit is all, and you need to wash before you sit down to eat. Mind me now, there's the basin."

Both Gerald and Tim washed, while the serving girls whirled in their white aprons to dish up supper. The meal was plain, much simpler than Mrs. Pierson's cooking. There was boiled mutton and boiled potatoes, and something that looked like a fish pie but that turned out to be chicken and peas beneath an underdone crust. Oliver made himself take a small serving of everything and, after the short grace delivered by Gerald, ate as much as he was able. He longed to know where the salt cellar was, and whether there would be pudding, and whether or not it, too, would prove to be barely edible.

No one spoke much during the meal, or at least it seemed to Oliver; he could barely keep his head up far enough so that it didn't drop into his plate. Halfway through his slender slice of chicken pie, he heard someone say something and tried to focus.

Then he felt a slight touch on his shoulder, and looked up to see Mrs. Heyland standing there.

"Why don't you go on to bed. I'll leave a plate for you in the cupboard under a bowl so the mice don't get it. If you're hungry in the night, it'll be waiting for you.

Oliver stumbled to his feet, and made his way back down the passageway to Jack. He made it to the door and had turned the china knob before he realized that he'd not said thank you or even goodnight. Not thought to ask about more tea for Jack. Could not even remember what he'd eaten. His exhaustion landed hard on his shoulders the moment he stepped into the room.

A low gloom oozed in the air, and it was almost too dark to see, so he lit the candle, too late aware that this might wake Jack. But Jack slept on, and Oliver unrolled the mattress and spread out the blanket. But once it was ready he determined to sit in the chair, so that if Jack awoke, Oliver would be available to bring him anything he needed. He sat down, blinking against the tiredness of his eyes, the glare of the candle, and thought about how he should take off his boots, but before he could bestir himself to do this, he fell asleep.

✀ 14 ✀
TO BE TENDER IN THE
NIGHTTIME

Someone was calling Jack's name. At least he thought there was. A voice calling, because it was after dark and there was work to be done. Jack opened his eyes with Fagin's name on his lips, and an apology ready, and as he scanned the room, he looked for his hat and coat. Where were they? He needed to go out.

A single candle on the table beside the bed cast a low, sputtering light on the far wall, and Jack licked his lips, thinking that he knew where he was, after all. Somewhere in Lyme, in the sickroom of a grand house. The day had been marked with long stretches of a headache that seemed to get better with every dose of willow bark tea, and the sleep that had followed after, deeper than he was used to. Waking up now was like climbing out of a well, one with slippery walls and not enough handholds.

But the bed was dry and warm, a still, clean island amidst the dark; he moved his hands along the top of the counterpane, a quilted coverlet, one that was, perhaps not good enough for upstairs, but still too good to cut up for rags. Good enough for the sickroom. Good enough for Jack, the collarless dog that he was.

And there Nolly was, asleep, sitting on a broad-backed wooden chair by the door, only an arm's length from the bed. He'd been sitting closer to the bed before, when he'd brought Jack soup and tea, every hour on the hour, shoulders ratcheted up, and when Jack had been alert enough to focus, Nolly had been all tight around the eyes, taking on something that Jack knew that Nolly had never done before. And yet he'd done it, for Jack.

The candlelight cut through the dark, spreading a smudged glow over Nolly's slack form, his arms balanced on his spread thighs, chin tucked down to his shoulder. Mouth open, breath even in the silence, but hard, as if Nolly were slowing down from running a race. And his face, all lined with grey exhaustion, with a strand of hair across his forehead, ungainly, like a wayward child. Even when drunk, Nolly never sprawled like this, unconscious, almost beckoning with the way he was splayed.

It was late; Jack didn't know the hour, but it was late enough so that the house above them contained only a dignified, weighty silence. Everyone else must have gone to bed, and Nolly had stayed on duty, a lone soldier. Not that Jack was really surprised, in spite of the fact that Nolly was a fluid beast, prim and snotty one day, bossy the next moment, and in dire times, a fearless thing to be reckoned with. And now a dovecote in a storm, a place for wild birds to hide behind.

Nolly was many things, but he never shirked what he felt was his duty. Duty took precedence in Nolly's world, and Jack sighed. He could not bear it if his care was merely a favor for a friend, a debt owed, support given to anybody who might have needed it. But the leap from London had been so quick, so hasty. Not thought out in any manner that Jack would normally have associated with Nolly. Nolly and his dear little job at the haberdashery that he was so very proud of. Strutting down the street like a schoolboy in that sturdy brown uniform with its touches of green and white. Looking well fed and confident, almost whistling to himself in spite of the cold weather, whenever Jack had followed him.

Which had been often. Enough so that Cromwell had made a

crack or two about it, and certainly he'd used Nolly's pull on Jack to his own advantage. But before that day, before the bloodbath of the kitchen, Jack had worked hard enough at night, taking the silver to be melted, doing stints in the early evenings at the bottom of Field Lane, and into the slightly better parts of London far from the surrounds of the Three Cripples. Going far afield had been a part of his job, and so, with grace divine, he'd been able to skim behind Nolly on his deliveries.

Oh, but the lad had legs, Nolly did, long strides, and a careless handsomeness that drew glances and double-takes and flat-out stares. Nolly, focused on his own thoughts, on some tuneless tune he'd probably not known he was whistling, strode along, hefting his basket, dodging the wide skirts of the ladies, slipping between carriages when he'd crossed the street. Always in a hurry, always focused on the next step, and if Jack had chanced to move ahead, on account of Nolly being blocked by something that delayed him, a sandwich man, or a governess with a stroller and a well-dressed charge, Jack would look straight at Nolly, but Nolly wouldn't see him, his eyes, blue and sharp, but somehow unfocused as if he were thinking his own thoughts, dreaming about his bookshop. Wondering what delightful repast would be his at the next meal-time. But never, Jack noticed, did Nolly's attention linger on the blind beggar in the doorway, or the urchin with her broom and her battered bonnet, the wind whistling through the holes in her coat, her stockings. No, Nolly looked away, if he did anything. Looked at something else. Simply didn't see.

Not that Jack had any heart to take pity on those wretches, he had none to spare. He'd made it, had succeeded in the stew of Fagin's dens, among house breakers and the petty immediacy that devoured coins with a mouthful of gin and never thought to the next day's needs. But to not even *see* them? This was a purposeful blindness that Jack couldn't quite understand, especially with Martin. But he was not bold enough to bring it up. It might make Nolly furious, or it might make him draw back, and Jack didn't want either.

Him and Nolly, coming out of London like that. It was something that he'd not thought to experience. Nolly had not even really asked Jack to come; he was going whether Jack would or not. But perhaps he'd seen it in Nolly's eyes, that longing for a companion while he went out into the unknown to escape the hangman's noose. *Perhaps* he'd seen it. He hoped that he had. Nolly had seemed glad of Jack's company, at the start, at least. But as they'd neared Croydon, it had started to feel as if they were tied together by melting strings, that Nolly had rather he'd been on his own, without Jack to remind him that he'd never survive without petty theft. Or maybe it had just been the headache that wore Jack down and was now making him see the devils dancing where there were none. Or wondering what price he would pay for this simple moment, in the dark, where he could stare at Nolly without Nolly getting prissy about it.

Perhaps he should wake Nolly up, so that Nolly could sleep without cricking his neck like that, which would surely make him cross, come morning. Craning his neck, Jack could see a bed of sorts had been assembled on the floor, with a flocked mattress and some blankets, a pillow. Rather flat for Nolly's liking; Nolly liked his comfort, oh yes. But someone had determined that if Nolly was to play nursemaid, then all he was due was a few layers of blanket to ease him into sleep. But that was not good enough, not after all the work he'd done. Carting Jack across the country, practically carrying him down hill for miles, in the rain. And there'd been something about the books that Jack couldn't quite remember, but he'd seen no sign nor mention of them.

"Nolly," said Jack. His throat was dry, so it came out as a rasp. He swallowed, or tried to, his throat sticking with every moment. Wished he had something soft to throw. "Nolly, wake up."

Nothing. Nolly snored on, in a gentlemanly way, his head rolling on his neck toward his shoulder, as if looking for a pillow that simply wasn't there.

"Nolly," Jack said a little louder, then added, "I need some water."

Which, actually, did the trick. Nolly's eyes opened with a snap, and directly his attention was on Jack.

"Do you need something, Jack?" He stood up, rubbing his mouth with the back of his hand, pushing at his eyes, staggering a bit. "What can I get you?"

"Is there water?" asked Jack. He hated to ask, but his throat was truly dry, and in a moment he'd have Nolly's hands on him. This came to pass, quite quickly. Nolly went around the bed to the table, and took up the small jug and poured water from it into a glass. Then he sat on the bed to help Jack drink it, which he did, swallowing large mouthfuls, and a bit of it slid down the corner of his mouth in his greed. But instead of teasing, Nolly only wiped it with his thumb, blinking slowly, as if this focus were the only thing keeping him upright.

"Now you drink some, Nolly," said Jack. "Then come to bed. You've been nursemaid long enough."

"I should stay awake, in case you needed anything."

"You must come to bed," said Jack, taking on the governess tone that Nolly seemed to like to use to get things done his way. "This instant. You can have the pillows an' I can have you. You're so tired, I can see it. Please come to bed."

"Will you be all right?"

"Only if you come to bed, Nolly." Then it occurred to Jack how he might get this to happen. "I can't sleep in this strange place. Havin' you near will make it less strange. Now, c'mon, don't you want me to be able to sleep? I know that you do."

This was the ticket, indeed it was, for Nolly bent to unlace his boots and slid out of his suspenders, and yanked off his trousers. And then stood there in only his shirt, taking up the glass and finishing off the water.

Jack thought that it might be nice to have a kiss from that wet mouth, but the way Nolly fumbled with the candle wick before dousing the flame told him that Nolly was too exhausted for anything so tender, and Jack would be cruel to ask him.

The weight on the bed next to him, Nolly's fussing with the

bedclothes, soothed Jack more than he imagined it might. Nolly even went as far as to steal the pillows, which Jack had expected, but in doing so he shifted his body to curve his arm around Jack, so that Jack could make a pillow of him, as Jack had requested. All without a word, or a complaint, or even a sigh.

As Jack relaxed against Nolly, he could smell the sweat of the day's efforts on Nolly's skin and felt some pity, for there was nothing Nolly liked less than going without a wash every two minutes. Jack smiled, curving his neck to press closer to Nolly's breast, where his heart beat and his lungs moved, and in this quiet dark, he was all Jack's. Every bit of him, even the restless fingers that curled around Jack's arm, and squeezed and let go, squeezed and let go, over and over, as if Nolly was assuring himself of Jack's presence, of his safety.

"Sleep now, Nolly," said Jack, "I'm here, I'm here." And though he knew his voice was barely audible, there was a low rumble of ascent from Nolly's chest, exhaustion wearing it thin before it became an actual form of speech. "Kiss me in the mornin', promise me you will."

Another sound, faint and light, and a gentle press from Nolly's chin to the top of Jack's head. It felt as good as a kiss, anyhow, and as sweet as any lullaby.

Oliver woke up with an icy start, sitting up, his shoulders cold, the darkness hovering like a pressing weight. He peered into the gloom, shifting his weight to kneel up, when he realized that what had awoken him was the rattling of the pane in the window frame. Perhaps the latch had come loose in the wind. If the rain leaked in, it would get on Jack, so Oliver shifted his weight on the mattress, and leaned toward the wall to reach for the latch. He had to find his way by touch, his fingers finding the cold pane, and the iron latch, which he twisted shut, then pushed down on again, for good measure. The wind stopped moving about his shoulders, and he was about to shift back into bed, when Jack stirred below him.

"Nolly," said Jack. "What are you doin'?"

It was good to hear Jack's voice sounding much more like its normal self, but it was too late in the night for Jack to be concerned about anything.

"You should be asleep," said Oliver, not really scolding, his voice low so as not to unsettle Jack.

"You too," said Jack, turning it back around, as if that settled the matter. "Are you cold?"

At Oliver's hesitation, he heard Jack rustling with the counterpane. "Come on then, under you go; we'll keep each other warm."

Oliver let his hands fall to his sides, searching for ways to explain that this was not a good idea. But Jack reached out to him, grasping his wrist with the lightest of touches, giving Oliver permission to pull away, if he so wished it. But the sensation of Jack's hand on his skin, with the darkness all around, and the thought of a warm, soft bed and Jack to share it with, pulled at him. But when he tried to adjust the pillow behind Jack's head, Jack pulled Oliver close enough to whisper in his ear.

"Don't need that; you're my pillow."

The cloak of darkness made Jack very bold indeed, seductive with his whispers and the ghost of his breath behind the words. Jack was on the mend, but he needed more rest to get better. Were Oliver to resist, Jack would keep insisting, now that he was awake and had the idea in his mind. Oliver slipped lower into the bed, the warm hollow next to Jack's body, their legs sliding together. Jack was so warm, and shivered even as he pulled Oliver to him.

"Better than sleepin' on the floor, eh, Nolly?"

But there was nothing to say, not when his whole body was soaking up the warmth, his skin sighing with the nearness of Jack's skin, the scent of the fading fever across Jack's brow, the sweet bite of salt. How could he resist this, why would he resist this?

"Never mind that," said Oliver, low. He moved near the center of the narrow bed, and tucked Jack into his shoulder. "You should rest. I'm warm enough now; it wasn't this cold last night." He would not explain that he barely remembered the previous night, the images all rushed together like badly assembled puzzle pieces.

"'Tis rainin' again, ain't it."

"Yes," said Oliver. Tipping his head, he brushed his chin across the top of Jack's head, feeling the scrape of dark hair on his neck, the press of Jack's shoulder, the long length of Jack's side. His toes were bare, and warming up nicely with Jack's feet upon them, sending streaks of pleasure up his legs with the soft shimmy feeling of skin on skin. "Will you sleep now? I'm sorry I woke you."

"Bloody rain," said Jack, behind a yawn.

This was better, so much better than it might have been. Jack's illness might have been something worse, something so fatal and infectious that the both of them would not have been given shelter.

15

CHORES IN THE MORNING

I n the morning, Oliver woke up with a lighter heart than he'd
carried in days. Jack was still asleep, so Oliver kissed him on
the forehead before he slipped out of the bed to pull on his
clothes, and lace up his boots. Then he made his way into the
bustle of the kitchen, where Gussie showed him a basin and towel
with soap standing by where he might wash.

It was a bit of a blessing to feel the warm water around his
fingers as he pressed both his hands to the bottom of the basin.
For a moment, the noise of the kitchen faded away, leaving him
with the shivery feel of the warmth moving up his arms and into
his shoulders. Then the moment was shattered by the clang of a
pot and the scrape of a chair against the stone floor. There were no
benches; in a house as grand as this one, each servant had their
own chair to sit in. Oliver quickly washed, dried his hands, and,
checking the buttons on his shirt, straightening his suspenders,
moved towards the table.

"Sit there, Oliver, and come in, Tim, did you wash—did
Gerald? Oh, the mud. Never mind. Melinda, will you pour? I've got
the porridge."

The bustle and Mrs. Heyland's snapped-out remarks made

Oliver want to jump up and show her how Mrs. Pierson would have done it, Mrs. Pierson who had a general's heart and a long spoon for a sword. His throat ached with remembering her; how she would have been glorious in such an expansive, bright kitchen as this, the sweet things she could have baked in such a stove. But no. Mrs. Heyland was dishing out porridge that slopped in their bowls as glue might have done. The bread was sliced thin and crumbly, and he couldn't locate any honey. But there was sugar already scraped from a cone into a bowl with a spoon. Oliver made himself wait while the bowl was passed around; even with butter to soften the porridge, there was no way he could eat it without something to sweeten it.

Meantimes, the maidservants had brought the tea and some slices of fried ham, and settled down at the table, which was only half full, even with Gerald and Tim. Oliver was now more awake and aware to realize that it must be a fairly huge house, then, if the table for the servants could hold so many and have places to spare. But Oliver kept his observations to himself, and wolfed down the porridge, which, for all its formidable dull looks, didn't taste too bad. He was lucky to get this meal at all, that was for certain, so what should he be complaining about. Nothing, that's what. Though he did long for a slice of fried bread with salt sprinkled on. His stomach was still half empty, even with the meal inside of him.

"That's fair enough, Melinda," Mrs. Heyland was saying as she sliced up her ham with her knife and fork, making screeching sounds against the plate. "But you must take turns with Edith and Gussie; the harder work must be shared by all. And Oliver, would you mind, then?"

"I beg your pardon?" Oliver looked up, startled at being suddenly spoken to; perhaps part of the conversation had gotten away from him.

"There are sheets in the laundry, they need to be carried up to all the floors, five at least for each room; the girls will put them on the furniture once everything has been dusted and wiped down. Except for the library, I don't know what I'm going to do about that. Then perhaps Gerald'll have something for you to do in the yard."

Oliver put down his knife and fork, having finished the last of his fried ham. The porridge was long gone, and still his stomach was growling. Underneath that was a swamp of guilt; he'd taken from house, and now he should give back, not for himself, but for Jack's sake.

"I must see to Jack first, Mrs. Heyland," he said, standing up, shoving back his chair. "And I need to bring him some tea. Shall I come back for the—"

"No, I'll have Gussie bring it to you, and she won't be a moment, never fear."

With a nod, Oliver turned and hurried back down the passage and into the sickroom.

Oliver went back into the little room, to see Jack in the bed, dozing, his lashes dark on his pale cheeks. But he was resting, warm and dry, not out in the weather, or being jounced along in a public coach. That Oliver had done for him, at least, even if it would mean days of playing the servant, and more days of cutting open fish like a fishmonger's son.

"Are you starin' at me, Nolly?" asked Jack, his eyes still closed. Then they opened to look at Oliver, a little quirk of a smile in them. "What magic have you wrought, I say? I've had not one but two doctors come to see me, an' got the mistress of the house waitin' on me, as if I were the lord of the manor himself."

"Mrs. Heyland would never stoop to wait on anyone, save the master of the house," said Oliver, trying to be stern. But he came over to Jack and his heart felt a little lighter as he sat down on the bed. "But she's taken us in, so we should be grateful for her kindness to a man and his manservant. His *former* manservant."

"That was a good one, eh?" said Jack, smiling, his eyes opening to look at Oliver, teasing. "With you lookin' the part and me tailin' after you."

Oliver shook his head, but he didn't want to argue. At least not about that. Or about anything. There would be time enough to ask Jack about the snuffbox and about the marine, and to get him to explain about the gypsies and Fagin.

"Hey," said Jack, breaking into the stillness of Oliver's thoughts.

"Yes, Jack?" asked Oliver. He patted the back of Jack's hand, only to have him take it away to push at the bedclothes. "Is there aught I can get you?"

"With all this tea an' such, I need to take a piss," said Jack. "Can you fetch it?"

For a moment, Oliver could only look at him. In the nursing done for Uncle Brownlow, Oliver had only been required to sit by the bed and hold his uncle's hand, or to fetch a tonic from the kitchen. Anything more intimate had been done by the nurse that Mr. Grimwig had hired. Still, this was *Jack*, whose feet Oliver had washed, and whose body Oliver had become acquainted with, even if only in the dark.

"Give me a moment," said Oliver, and he slid from the bed to kneel on the floor, lifting the bedclothes to scan beneath the bed. There, toward the head of the bed, almost against the wall, was the chamberpot. Oliver pulled it out, and dusted it off with his fingers. It was of sturdy ceramic with painted blue flowers on the rim and on the inside; only a house such as this could afford such a finely decorated thing for a sickroom. He put it on the floor next to the bed, and turned to Jack, his hand held out.

"I'll help you," he said, only a little anxious that he should get this right, that he would be what Jack needed when he was so vulnerable and sick.

He helped Jack stand up, putting his arm around Jack's waist. Jack swayed on his feet, unsteady, and his body beneath the shirt was still overly warm. He smelled like dank sweat, and a bit like willow bark tea, but Oliver held him close, just the same.

"Brace your hand on the wall there," said Oliver, and he swept his hand along Jack's arm to guide him, and when Jack's hand was splayed on the whitewashed wall, Oliver, with the toe of his boot, nudged the chamberpot closer to Jack's feet.

Jack's breathing was a bit ragged, his eyes glazed. The high color of his cheeks came from the fever and nothing else.

"Can you manage, Jack?" asked Oliver quietly. "I'll lift your shirt for you."

Which he did, the feel of it familiar enough to offset the sudden intimacy between them. He lifted the shirt far enough, halfway up Jack's belly, just past his private hair, so that Jack could reach down and hold himself to piss in the chamberpot. The stream of urine splashed against the blue flowers, smelling like salt and tea, and when Jack was done, he gave his cock a shake, and Oliver took a bit of a hard breath as he dropped Jack's shirt back down. Then he used his foot to push the chamberpot out of the way; he'd tell one of the maidservants to come for it, or take it himself, if need be.

"Is that better now?" he asked, helping Jack back into bed. He eased the pillows beneath Jack's head and soothed Jack's dark hair from his forehead, and pulled the bedclothes up, tucking them beneath Jack's chin.

Jack's eyes were closed, though he was not asleep. "Just sit w'me," said Jack.

And this Oliver did, one leg up on the bed, Jack's hand in his, watching with careful eyes as Jack dozed. Counted Jack's breaths, each rise and fall of his chest. Except for the rain pattering against the window, the room was quiet and still, and Oliver thought that he would be content to sit with Jack for a good long while yet.

But now the door was opening, disrupting the balm of solitude in the sickroom. Gussie came in, with her hair cap in place, and her tidy apron wide across her skirts. She carried a mug on a small tray with the willow bark tea.

"'Tis for the manservant, Jack," she said, looking at them both, somewhat astonished, perhaps, to see Oliver lolling on the bed. So

Oliver got up, and nodded to her, and she went to Jack's side. Oliver helped Jack to sit up, and Jack, all sleepy-eyed and tousled, seemed amused to find so many waiting upon him.

"More tea?" asked Jack.

"Yes, and you must drink it," Oliver said. "I know it tastes nasty, but you must drink it all."

"That's right," said the Gussie. "It tastes like wood shavings, but it'll help your head ever so much. Your head'll stop stop aching soon, I promise."

Trying not to smirk at the maidservant, Jack let Oliver tip the mug to his lips and drink from it. When Jack had finished, Oliver put the cup back on the tray. He settled Jack back down on the pillow, and pulled up the bedclothes once more.

"You rest now," he said. "I'm going to ask this kind maid to take me to Mrs. Heyland so she can put me to work."

"Work befittin' a gentleman, I hope," said Jack, in what he probably hoped were suitably aggrieved tones. "Can't have my master muckin' about like a common stablehand."

"Indeed not," said Oliver, playing along. Then bent to pick up the chamberpot, and, straightening up, said to Gussie, "If you could assist me, miss, as to where I might empty the slops, so I don't get lost along the way."

"Indeed, it is a big house," said the maid with a little coquette of her lashes. Oliver ignored Jack rolling his eyes, and followed her out into the passage.

After he'd attended to the chamberpot, Mrs. Heyland directed Oliver to the laundry. It was a rather grand room for a laundry, the walls all whitewashed with a narrow bank of windows high up along the long wall, and a deal table at one end. There was a shelf full of laundry gear, from bins of lime, a slat full of spindles of different colors of thread, to various washing blades, and tucked in the corner was a small mangler. There was a large copper boiler with a fire blazing beneath to churn out enough hot water to launder an army's worth of uniforms; currently, he was told, there were various household linens soaking.

Finding the piles of starched and folded sheets, he gathered a small armful and, at Mrs. Heyland's direction, carried them to the top of the house. He used the narrow, dim servants' stairway that folded back and forth on itself, all the way to the penultimate floor of the house. He left the pile in front of one room, the door to which was slightly cracked. It was a lovely room, done in pink and rose, more like a sitting room than a bedroom, but there, indeed was a bed, and Melinda, on her hands and knees in front of the grate, scrubbing away though the grate already sparkled and the bricks were as clean as pale bone.

"Stop staring, and don't leave them sheets there, they'll get tumbled. Come in, then, and put them on the bed. And mind, don't get any smudges on the counterpane. It's silk."

Melinda was almost snarling at him, no doubt because she'd not been given whatever easier work Gussie or Edith had been assigned to. It was of no matter to him, but he did as he was told, and backed out of the room as quietly as he could so as not to disturb her. When he went down the stairs to the laundry for more sheets, he checked on Jack, who was fast asleep, curled up beneath the counterpane, his face no longer quite as pale as the linen of the sheets. Then Oliver closed the door, finally able to take a good, deep breath.

Oliver carried more sheets, and after that, the work continued. Mrs. Heyland sent him all over the house with odd tasks to do, and assistance to give to the servants, who already knew their jobs but who needed a little extra muscle. An extra pair of hands. A pair of arms into which to hand clean, folded laundry from the line, or buckets of ash to take to the ash barrel, or coils of rope to take down to the storage room. A flagstone floor to sweep.

The floor was polished from years of wear, and the broom went easily, even though his fingers felt tired and cramped after a few moments, and his head got dizzy with all the twists and turns.

Then she sent him up to the servants' bedrooms at the top of the house to take apart the metal bedsteads and carry them out into the stable yard. There, Gerald was painting the black frames with something thin and green from a bucket.

Then Oliver went out again into the yard, ready to take up a shovel and a pail, or a rake or a broom, and right away, a pony, being led by young Tim, tossed its head and took itself for a small canter around the stable yard and through the open gate that led to the orchard. Without thinking, Oliver slipped through the rails of the slatted wood fence, and slopped through the spring mud, to find the pony behind some newly budded apple trees. The pony started, then bent its head to nibble at the young green grasses around the roots of one tree.

While it was distracted, Oliver walked up to the small, well-groomed beast and caught the lead in his hand before the pony could even lift its head and blink at him with its ridiculously long-lashed and deep brown eyes. Young Tim was only footsteps behind him, mouth open, tears streaking down his face.

"Oh, thank you, Master Oliver," he said, taking the lead with shaking hands. "This is the mistress's favorite pet, and in my charge while she's away. I don't know what I'd do if I 'ad to tell her I'd lost her little pony."

While Oliver didn't think the boy was calm enough to be in charge of any beast, let alone a small pony, he handed the lead over. He was glad to see Gerald, now covered with a leather apron, coming over to them. For a moment, Oliver feared for Tim's well-being; Gerald was a large man and his belt was ready on his waist. Oliver contemplated saying that he'd startled the pony, and that this had been the cause of the pony running off. But Gerald looked gratified to see the pony under control once again, and when he came up with quick strides, he only clapped the boy on the shoulder.

"That's the way, lad, you'll hold tighter next time. Daisy here has an independent spirit, and we don't want to break that out of her, do we. So gently on, give her a tug and some kind words and we'll show her where her sugar comes from, eh?"

With a nod at Oliver, the man led the boy and the pony through the gate and out of the apple orchard. Leaving Oliver to wonder at the gentleness of the man, and the desire of the boy to please. Some servants were like that. Uncle Brownlow's had been, for the most part, quite keen to see to their master's pleasures.

And now, watching the boy and the man, and standing in the orchard, with the apple trees not quite to blossoms yet, he remembered those times, where everything had been of gentle ease, and he the young princeling. Who now, to think of it, was grateful to have a flocked mattress on the floor, and a pillow and blanket, one of each only, down enough on his luck to appreciate a place to sleep and work to do. But it was good work, honest work, with Mrs. Heyland directing everything.

Could he stay in a place such as this? Could he be a servant, as he was now? Or work with fish, as he was bound to do soon? He had no idea what that would be like, but if it needed to be done to take care of Jack, then that's what he would do. He heard Mrs. Heyland's voice coming from the house, calling his name. So with a sense of belonging, and the smell of damp earth and early blossoms filling his lungs, he went to answer it.

Oliver came into the sick room, expecting that he'd need to bring more tea, but found Jack sitting up with an empty mug in his hands. He looked about the room, but it was a clean room, well-kept, so there was not much for him to do. Jack watched him out of the corner of his eyes, as Oliver took the mug from Jack and put hit on the table.

"Will there be prayers soon?" Jack asked.

Jack was smirking and of course, he was poking fun at Oliver tucking this and straightening that.

"Bloody hell, Nolly, just sit down. Wish you had a book to read me, too bad those—"

Then Jack stopped, as if he'd only just realized that the reason the books were gone was because Oliver had dropped them to save Jack's head from being caved in by several ragged and slippery stones.

"And I'm lonely," Jack said. "Got nobody to talk to, except them maids, who came in together to bring me my tea, as if I was dangerous, and then they tittered—" Jack waved his hands in the air, the curly cuffs of his shirt falling back to his elbows as he expressed just how annoying those titters were.

Oliver smiled at that, the thought of Jack being dangerous. Which, perhaps he was, being a street thief and ex-convict. But Oliver had never seen him angry, never seen him strike out, as Oliver had done. That wasn't Jack's way; the maidservants had nothing to worry about.

"The doctor said you'll be up by Thursday," said Oliver.

"And then what do we do?"

Coming over to the bed, Oliver traced his finger along the iron bedstead. "Well, I'm waiting on a reply to a letter I had the parson send. It'll come in a few days, he says."

Disgruntled, Jack flopped his hands on the bed.

"There is a library. Mrs. Heyland told me I could help her give the place a good dusting, and other work besides. After that, and whether or not the letter tells us anything, then we can leave."

"And after?"

"I don't know." Oliver shook his head. "I honestly don't know. I've not thought that far ahead."

"Well that's not like you," said Jack, but he didn't seem cross.

Oliver's stomach tightened at the thought, the realization that he, indeed, did not have a plan beyond making inquiries to the local parson. He was about to go back to chores, when Jack looked at him.

"I'm too weak to straighten the counterpane, dear Nolly," Jack said, "so could you come here an'—"

It was not too much to dance to Jack's tune, being bored to tears in this small room, so Oliver did as he was asked, walking around the bed, to bend and tuck Jack in more firmly. Then, in that same moment, he felt Jack's hand on his arm.

"We could always go to your Aunt Rose's in Chertsey, you know. She misses you and I'm sure won't mind that you—"

"Don't say it, Jack. *Don't.*" He knew Jack meant only to tease, but the thought of telling Aunt Rose any of this made him cold inside, made his shoulders stiffen up. He must have telegraphed this to Jack, for Jack gave Oliver's arm a squeeze and then dropped his hand to brush his fingers across the back of Oliver's hand.

"You could lie with me, awhile," said Jack, softly.

Oliver wanted to say no, to spell out quite clearly that it was inappropriate, seeing as they were a guest in someone's house, and besides which, Jack was only now getting better and it was important that he rest. But he was drawn in by Jack's smile, and the jerk of his chin toward the bed, where he wanted Oliver to sit. There was only so much Oliver could resist.

"I will," said Oliver, almost swallowing the words. "If you tell me about Port Jackson."

"Port Jackson? Why would you want to hear about that for?"

"You went on about it," said Oliver. He sat on the edge of the bed, straightening the covers over Jack's chest.

"I never did!"

"Yes, you did. On and on you went about the snuffbox, and the marines, and the horse that got cut in the wire, and the doctor that healed it." He reached out; his fingers met the edge of Jack's shirt collar. "You never talk about it. If you tell me something about it, I'll lie with you. Just for a little while."

Within that moment, Jack was pushing Oliver off the bed and pulling back the bedclothes.

"C'mon, then," he said, tugging at Oliver's shirt.

As Oliver slipped into the narrow bed, and placed his head on Jack's chest, he knew that this was what he'd been missing all morning. It was not like being with other people. It was Jack, with his warm skin and slow breaths, the sweet oil of his hair, and the way he curled his arm around Oliver's shoulders. Oliver shuddered at the slight pressure of it as it soaked into him, filling places inside of him that he'd not known were empty. He tucked his head close, and circled his arm across Jack's waist. He hardly dared breathe, as he felt Jack go still above him, as if he were trying to observe Oliver.

"What's got you riled then?"

Oliver didn't quite know what to say; Rhode Hill House was no worse than any other place he'd even been, and in some ways a bit better. Certainly the air was fresher than in London, and—

"I went outside today," he said. "And from the hilltop you can see that the buildings are limestone white, and all the streets run down to the sea. The air smells like salt, and every surface is crusted with a rime of white. There are trees in the low dells, along the old roads, and some places, there's only brambles and low bushes, and no trees at all."

He stopped, closing his mouth over any further ramble, and listened to Jack's heartbeat, and heard him take in a breath.

"It's so far from home, ain't it," said Jack, and immediately Oliver felt a pang run through his chest. "An' you so exhausted, takin' care of me an' all."

"I'm sorry, Jack, I shouldn't have let you come with me, it's not fair, it's not—"

"Oh, bloody hell, don't be daft. I wanted to come, I told you. Yes, it's strange here, but you're with me, an' I'm with you, an' that way, at least part of it's familiar, eh?"

Breathing slowly, in and out, matching his pace to Jack's, Oliver nodded against Jack's chest. "You are," he said. "But the trees, the smell—"

"People pay good money to come to the seaside," said Jack, as if this were the most reasonable rebuttal in the world. Which it was.

"Now, about Port Jackson," said Oliver, wanting to distract himself from dark thoughts. "You used to talk about that tattoo you never got, and how clever the blacks were. Was that doctor who cured the mare a black?"

"No," said Jack. "But they worked in the house an' in the stables, which was where I worked, when I wasn't at the soldier's billet, tendin' on them, polishin' boots, sewin' on buttons, makin' coffee—"

"Sewing on buttons, Jack? You?"

"Well," said Jack, his voice scruffy, as if he wasn't willing to be embarrassed by that particular fact. "Mostly it was rough work, because I got no skills, see. An' them blacks, why they could talk English as good as the Queen, an' I couldn't speak their words atall."

"What language did they speak, then?"

"I don't know, black?"

"There's no language called *black*," said Oliver. "I'm sure of it."

"That shows what you don't know," said Jack. "Because if it ain't black, what're they talkin'?"

Oliver tipped his head back till he should see, in the soft light, the curve of Jack's chin. "I expect it's like French," he said. "If you spoke to someone who knew it, then you would learn it. Did you ever even try, Jack?"

"That I did," said Jack, stoutly. He folded his arm so he could stroke Oliver's temple. "There was this girl, Kayema, her name was. She had skin the color of dark mahogany, an' hair even darker. She wore a sack, an' no shoes. She could walk among the sharp grasses an' all them snakes, an' never be the worse for it. She worked like I did, in the garden an' such, an' she would talk her talk an' I would talk mine. She taught me her name, an' I gave her mine. She would make gestures, you know, like she was talkin' to the sky, an' the sky was answerin' her back. There was an older man, maybe her pa or somethin', an' she went with him to where the blacks slept at night."

"Did she teach you any black words?" It was all so very exotic and different, not just the faraway world where Jack had been, but who Jack had been while he was there. Working in gardens and sewing buttons and waiting hand and foot on some marines.

"Maybe a few," said Jack. "I don't remember any now. Maybe that's enough about Port Jackson."

"But what about the marines, you said you looked after the soldiers, what did you do—"

"Enough about Port Jackson, I says," said Jack. "My throat is all tired with this, an' I'm sure to get my headache back any instant."

Oliver was about to poke Jack in the side to keep him talking, but there was a warble in Jack's voice that Oliver had not heard before. Perhaps he missed Kayema, perhaps the marine had been kind to him. Perhaps the whole memory of Port Jackson was simply too much to bear.

"Very well, Jack; I should go back to work soon."

"Only a moment more, Nolly, just stay. Just like you are. It makes my headache better, you know, havin' you near."

This made Oliver smile in spite of himself. "Just how long," he said, in mock disapproving tones, "are you going to take on airs about your headache?"

"As long as it gets me what I want," said Jack, and he didn't sound sorry about it, not even the least bit.

And Oliver wasn't sorry either to be staying still for another moment or two, at Jack's side, in the warm curve of the mattress, with the cool air circling overhead.

After a little while, Jack stopped petting Oliver's temple, and his hand fell lax against the back of his head. Oliver stayed where he was, feeling Jack's slow breaths beneath his cheek, feeling the heartbeat through his breastbone, smelling the sweat from Jack's skin. He didn't feel so lost, being in Jack's bed like this, being near Jack, with their feet tangled beneath the covers. He would try and remember this feeling in the morning, so he wouldn't feel so lost as he walked down the roads, to the village by the sea.

In a moment, he would move. In another moment.

~

Jack woke up when Nolly got up to go back to his chores, but didn't let him know, or try to keep him from going. Nolly had such a keen sense of obligation that even a short rest was probably making him feel guilty. So Jack blinked slowly at the ceiling, not feeling guilty at all, or not much, to be at such leisure.

It felt odd to have Nolly asking questions about Port Jackson, let alone be interested in what language a young black girl spoke, and whether it was something you could learn like French. Oliver might have been appalled, had he ever met Kayema, on account of her soiled shift that had been her only garment, or that she wore no stockings with her ratty pair of men's boots, when she wore anything on her feet at all. Or that her skin was constantly dusty, her hair tacky and stiff on account of she only washed when forced to. That she ate with her hands as well, unless indoors and sitting with the white farmer's servants, yes, Nolly would have winced to see it.

But had he met her—and the image of Nolly standing handsomely beneath the ball of blue sky, the hot dry air whisking through his flaxen hair was rather distracting—but had he met her, he would have looked at her for a moment or two, his eyes appraising, with that solemn, thoughtful set to his mouth. He would have given her his name, as Jack had done, and she would have taken it like a gift, her dark brown eyes tracking the outline of his form, tracing it against the sky so as to commit it to memory. And from then on, night or day, she would have known him whether in coalmine darkness or snow-storm white. Then she would have given Nolly her name in return. Kayema. Just that, no surname, in spite of the farmer who insisted frequently, constantly, punctuated sometimes with blows, that she was now Kayema Wilson and she'd better get used to it.

No, Nolly would have taken her single name and accepted it for what it was, as an invitation to a story about her that would never be written down.

Thinking about her was always hard, rather like what it must be like for Nolly, whose eyes still harbored the cloak of guilt brought on by the death of wee Martin.

Jack had seen the orphan, glimpsing him in the yard at the haberdashery or out front, whilst Jack had skulked about, hoping for a moment with Nolly. But while Nolly had been the rare jewel amidst the fog of coal smoke that constantly sifted from the sky, Martin had been as common as the filth in the street. And, as had been easy to note, was as underfed and underdressed as befitted those who are expendable. Jack had seen it directly and had been surprised that at first, Nolly had seemed blind to it.

Then, of a sudden, that had changed and Nolly had turned concerned and fretted a great deal, as evidenced by the tightness of his shoulders, and the bit of fist he would make whenever he would mention Martin's name. The poor wee thing had taken on a bit of rosy cheek before he'd died, and Jack imagined that Nolly had had a hand in that, though he never said. Jack never asked, and did not intend to, for in spite of words spoken at the trial that the entire incident was an unhappy accident, Jack knew that Nolly blamed himself equally, if not more so, than he blamed McCready. To bring it up at all would push Nolly through a wall of gloom. And Jack needed him thinking straight, so they could close their business in Lyme and determine wither they would go.

But if needs must, then Jack would pick up the burden of memory and share Kayema with Nolly to distract him from his personal woes. And Jack would tell how he had joined in friendship with a black native with whom Jack had shared the bond of servitude and an armful of words: *go, come, stay, stop, wash, carry, hurry, idiot, filthy,* and so on, with an increasing frequency toward the cruel end of the spectrum. For in that life, so long ago it seemed, Nolly might be surprised, shocked even, to discover that Jack had been the obedient one, who forever fretted that, one day, Kayema would disobey one order too many or take it upon herself to forage amongst the skinny, almost bare trees that abutted the farmstead, and come back in her own sweet, self-determined time.

Jack rolled over in the bed, trying to pull back from the memories of that time, from this particular memory, before it became too real, too clearly outlined with the lurid red color lacing the farmer's machete. Farmer Wilson had required fresh meat for his dogs, and well, what further use had he for a black child who could not keep her place?

Were he to tell Nolly of this or of all that had come after, he was not sure what Nolly would say. Whether there would be judgment, as might be expected of someone with Nolly's loftier background. Or whether Nolly would be sympathetic and with a troubled furrow to his brow, say, *Oh, Jack*, in the tenderest of tones and offer whatever comfort Jack might accept. Pull Jack to him and enfold him in warm, steady arms. Or maybe what he'd say would be a reflection of the time when Nolly had brought his concerns about Martin to Jack. Dismissively, Jack had asked whether Martin was being buggered, because boys were buggered every day, what of it? Maybe Nolly would be like that, he'd give Jack a look, derisive and hard, and snap out something about how heathen black girls were only fit for dog food anyway.

Jack could not tell a soul that this kind of remark from his beloved Nolly would well and truly fell him. But Nolly had wondered what language was *black* and whether you could learn it, so Jack let himself be reassured that Nolly's response to Kayema would be somewhat more kind than that.

Kayema, who would take a mouthful of water at the pump with Jack and let the water settle in her mouth, rather than swallowing it straight down as Jack did. Then she would look at the hard blue sky with the sunlight breaking over the tops of the spare trees, scattering light like hard bits of glass. Then she would have looked at Jack and nodded as she swallowed, and if the nod could translate, it might have said, *this moment is beautiful.*

Though Jack would never know for certain, the word to describe something she found pleasing had never passed her lips. Just that nod, straightforward and dignified, her mouth wet, her eyes sparkling.

Jack wanted to tell Nolly more about her, awfully so, but that might require him to speak of what had come after. *What happened after she died, Jack?* Nolly would ask, for he did love stories, as Jack did, even the sad ones. But the remaining pages in that book were sordid and ugly, and too besmirched for one with Nolly's tender sensibilities.

16

CHORES IN THE AFTERNOON

T he fact that Jack could have counted on the fingers of one hand the number of days he'd lain a-bed on account of being ill, the slightness of this number was offset by the very fine view offered by a backside clothed in country trousers. Even more so was the fairness of that face, brows furrowed together as Nolly concentrated on the task at hand, that of waiting on him, Jack Dawkins, hand and foot.

"Can you manage this?" asked Nolly. He had helped Jack to sit, fluffing and propping pillows with great dignity and care. And now he held the bowl, steaming with dark beef tea, a delicate bowl that would have fetched no more than sixpence for the chipped paint and worn edge. Though in Nolly's hands, his long fingers curving around the bowl, it was a beautiful object.

Jack knew he was on the mend; the dark fog of the day before had faded, along with the fever. His headache was with him still but not enough to keep him from any activity except those that displeased him. And that, at the moment, was to have Nolly depart from his side. Which he would do if Jack didn't need anything.

"No, I cannot," said Jack, "for I fear I could not hold it an' what a dreadful mess that would make."

He kept very still and did not wink, nor even smile. Only watched as Nolly looked confused, his lower lip pushing out. It only took a moment, however, before Nolly straightened up. There was a flicker of amusement in his eyes, but it was apparent that he'd determined to go along with Jack's ploy for reasons of his own, which Jack could only hope was based on his affection for Jack that he sometimes neglected to display.

In spite of this, Nolly's expression became gentle as he dipped the spoon into the broth and brought it to Jack's mouth. He was as attentive as he was serious as he spooned Jack mouthfuls of broth, and then he had to set the bowl down on the napkin in Jack's lap as he shook his head and sighed, smiling.

"You are incorrigible," said Nolly. His eyes took on that ocean-blue hue that bespoke a contented attitude rather than a cross one.

"There's nowt wrong with wantin' you near," said Jack, stoutly. "It aids my digestion an' improved state of health, an' has many other benefits, besides."

Nolly was struggling with the desire, even the obligation, to scold, but the way his gaze flicked over Jack, like a deep generous caress, Jack knew that the urge was fleeting.

Nolly picked up the bowl once more and proceeded to dose Jack with the beef tea.

"I am indeed glad that you are on the mend," said Nolly, keeping his focus on what his hands were doing rather than meeting Jack's eyes.

This was often the way with Nolly, the more intense his feeling, the more he seemed to back away from them. As he was doing now, in the quiet solitude of the sickroom, even with the lack of any witness, Nolly's sense of propriety marched ever to the fore, leaving a shield of not only distance but decorum, behind which Nolly would disappear. It might take a sassy word or two, a wink, or some of Jack's ever-sparkling wit to draw Nolly out. It had happened before, a release brought on by a sudden abundance of

gin and pure exhaustion, at which point Nolly had been felled by
his own base desires and impulses, for which combination Jack
would be eternally grateful, for it had wrung from Nolly a quite
unexpected kiss, and all that had followed after.

Here, though, in this place, with its inauspicious beginning and
the awkward interlude of Jack's illness, Jack had to start anew.
Well, perhaps not completely from the very beginning. Not with
the current evidence of care and affection as Nolly lowered the
bowl and gently used a snowy-white napkin to tap along Jack's
lower lip. That Nolly might show the same care to anybody in
need, this was true. But it was the way his eyes followed his own
hand and the contemplative pause as his eyes flicked up and now
he looked at Jack properly.

"Oh, Nolly, just say it, for pity's sake. Always holdin' back on
me, ain't you."

Nolly licked his lips, and after a moment, looked down at his
hands. "I've never taken care of anyone before, not like this."

Now Jack felt badly for teasing; Nolly was sensitive in that way,
with all those deep thoughts of his, living in his own head, cut off
until he let Jack in.

"I knows it," said Jack. "An' both me an the doctor, even the
missus, would say you've done a fine job." Jack gestured to his
chest. "Ain't I well? Ain't I thrivin'?"

"Yes," said Nolly, after a moment, looking up to give Jack a
small smile with his eyes. "You are." Then he looked away, fiddling
with the napkin in his lap, as if abashed to be heard admitting it.

But Jack could stand for none of it. He took Nolly's hand, and
wouldn't let Nolly pull away, even when that little wrinkle formed
between his brow.

"Ain't nobody in the world could do what you did," said Jack,
sternly, shaking his finger at Nolly. "You understand me? *Nobody*.
Carryin' me down that hill in the rain, me half dead, you
exhausted. An' here I am, bright an' pink an' alive. Now give us a
kiss, you slacker, an' get back to work."

Surprisingly, Nolly obliged him, getting up off the bed, but not all the way, kneeling on one knee, so that he could hold Jack's face in his hand and land a chaste peck on his forehead.

"Get some rest, Jack," said Nolly, his throat sounding a bit clogged. "I'll check back, but you're to call if you need anything. Anything at all."

With a grand wave of his hand Jack dismissed him, smiling. Then he slunk down beneath the covers and remarked to himself that being abed wasn't all that bad.

～

The afternoon chore assigned to Oliver was something of a miracle, though Mrs. Heyland could not be aware of it. Not that it would have stopped her from giving it to Oliver, had she known. Still, as he stepped into the library on the second floor, where the arched wooden beams rose above him and the shelves spread before him, a sense of gratitude and delight filled him.

Shelves lined every wall, and there was a rolling ladder that went all the way around the room, even over the shelves along the window. In the middle of the room was a heavy, round table upon which several large atlases were laid out; the fat, sleek leather chairs on either side of the table were worn in a way that spoke of many a night spent reading in front of the blue and white china-fronted fireplace. The patterned rugs kept the room from being too scholarly, and the pile of books hastily stacked on one of the side tables told Oliver that the room had been in active use right up to the point when the family had gone to Brighton.

His job was to dust the shelves and the spines of the books and to check the floor for scuff marks. One of the maidservants would sweep and polish the floor and beat the carpet and clean the grate. Mrs. Heyland also wanted someone to make sure that, after being wiped down, the books were put back in the correct order. The implication was that the maidservants were either uneducated or silly, or perchance it was that they had no love of books. And so here Oliver was, surrounded by them.

"I'll start at the shelves by the fireplace," Oliver said out loud, as if there was someone he was conferring with. "And work my way around.

This job would be a pleasure.

He moved the ladder to the fireplace, taking care not to grind the rollers too hard into the shiny wood flooring. Then, with a slightly damp cloth over one shoulder, he climbed to the top shelf and began his task, taking out each book and wiping the cover with the cloth before putting it back. Some of the books were old, their edges crackling, the pages brown with time. Others were new, with green and red covers of bright leather or shiny cloth, with gold-gilt letters proclaiming the title and the writer.

He could not help himself; he opened each book and scanned the contents, looking for pictures and maps, sounding out the French when he came across it, grimacing when he encountered the German. For a good half hour, he was caught up in a child's fairy tale book, with the predictable, comforting stories and the brightly drawn pictures. Each book was a treasure that might, one day, be welcome in the shop he would own. What would sell? What would customers want to read? How many books could he afford to acquire as stock? And would owning a bookshop ever be as pleasurable as sitting in a corner and reading?

Perhaps not, but the current task was a great deal less complicated than much that Oliver had recently encountered, so it went like silk, the books glowing under the cloth, and almost putting themselves away. His whole body relaxed to a point where he realized how tense he'd been; perhaps later Jack might give him a sip of the horrid willow bark tea.

He stopped mid-afternoon to check on Jack, even though Mrs. Heyland said that she would take care of it. It wasn't that he didn't trust her, she seemed a kind woman right enough, but the scare of watching Jack's blood flow into a crescent-shaped bowl was too recent and sharp to let the care of Jack go so easily to another.

He crept down the back stairs and slipped past Edith in the kitchen, who was at the table scraping away at candlestick holders.

Then, when he opened the door to the sickroom, he saw Jack struggling to sit up, and went to his side to help him.

"Gettin' dreadful borin', sleepin'," said Jack, scrubbing at one eye. "I tell you I'm well."

"And I tell you," said Oliver, "the doctor said another two days in bed and that's that."

"You just like fussin' over me, tell the truth, now."

That was the truth, so he was not caught out falsely. But as he sat on the bed and patted the counterpane over Jack's leg, he could not express the relief in his heart that Jack had pulled through. Jack would only mock Oliver for being so soft-hearted and then go on about how he, Jack, was as tough as a sailor. But Jack must have seen something in Oliver's face, for he stroked Oliver's arm with the back of his fingers.

"They got you workin', I see. Not too hard, I hope."

"No," said Oliver. "I'm in the library, of all places, dusting book spines and making sure the books are in order before we cover everything with sheets. To keep out the dust." He explained this last, for he was quite certain that Jack would have no experience with how the finer folk protected their furniture when moving to one of their other houses.

"Must be a lot of dust they're expectin'," said Jack. "Hey," he added suddenly, his fingers tightening on Oliver's wrist. "Bring us a book, an' read it out, like you did back home."

"What?"

"Just a borrow," said Jack. "To be put back after. Say you will."

It was within Jack's ability to get Oliver to do just about anything for him, and Jack had to know that. To ask for something that Oliver wanted himself, with the opportunity of a good read so close to hand, well, it was almost a forgone conclusion.

"Just to borrow, mind," Oliver said, agreeing.

He looked away from Jack for a moment, thinking of the books he'd so recently dusted. The heavy, serious tomes would not have any entertainment value or fairy tales that might suit Jack. When he went back, he would look for the novels and the sonnets, some-

thing lively to distract, and then, something soothing to ease Jack
into sleep. It wouldn't cause any harm, as no one was reading any
of the books anyway. And surely someone who loved books as
much as Sir John seemed to, to have such a huge collection, would
not mind a fellow book lover taking down a volume or two.

"I'll look for something," said Oliver. "And now I must get back
to it. Do you need anything, Jack? Anything?"

He could see it in Jack's eyes that he would ask for a kiss just
then, so Oliver beat him to it, standing up, and then bending close,
closing his eyes at the last moment, seeing that flash of green
behind his lids as he pressed his mouth quickly to Jack's.

Then he opened his eyes and found himself smiling. It was odd
that such a simple thing as kissing Jack made something shimmer
inside of him, but it did. And in Jack's eyes as, unbidden, he slid
back down beneath the covers and put his head on the pillow, dark
hair spreading out, his smile hid by the counterpane's edge.

"Get somethin' good," said Jack, almost whispering as Oliver
opened the door.

"I will," said Oliver. "Something good, just for you."

There were other tasks around the house that day, but Oliver
insisted that the library was taking longer than it was, though, if he
was honest with himself, he'd done more reading than dusting. But
the books he examined to determine if they might be entertaining
for Jack kept drawing him in.

There was a book by Byron that he'd never read before, as well
as a book about a monster that was brought to life by lightning,
written by, of all things, a woman. These he carried down the
ladder to put on the nearest table, along with a slender volume of
love sonnets by Shakespeare; a book of fairy tales; *The Deerslayer;*
and also, an adventure tale about a young man wrongfully impris-
oned, called *The Count of Monte Cristo.*

He doubted they would get through all of the books, and Jack, perhaps, might not have a taste for poetry, but there was no harm in trying. Besides, Oliver could continue to read by candlelight, if Jack fell asleep.

Feeling only a little bad about borrowing without asking, he made several trips to the sickroom, each time with a book stuffed into his trousers, hurrying down the passageway to the sickroom to deposit the books beneath the mattress, without waking Jack. He succeeded each time, thinking that perhaps it might perk Jack up to learn that Oliver had taken something without asking.

Later, while Oliver was at the top of the ladder, Gussie came in, and while he did not greet her by name, he nodded at her and went on working. She, for her part, went to the fireplace at the end of the room, and started banging her bucket and her shovel, drawing out the ashes, and using a blacking brush to clean the grate. It meant a companionable hour or so, though she was noisy; the feeling of working together towards something was comforting. It would have been even better had Jack been in the room, and while it might be possible that Mrs. Heyland would allow Jack to recuperate where Oliver was working, he did not feel at ease to ask her. Maybe when they'd been there a while.

Soon Gussie went away, leaving Oliver in the large, empty library.

He spent the latter part of the day taking a soft cloth and a bottle of oil and wiping the baseboards in the library, relaxed and warm as beams of sun broke through the clouds and streamed into the room. There was a grand fireplace of marble, and high ceilings. There were long tapestries hanging from one wall, and an overly busy arrangement of various sizes of paintings on the other. In the middle of the room was the round table with the atlases, and Oliver dutifully oiled the table and dried it before carefully dusting, and examining each atlas, to lay them in an attractive arrangement.

Oliver took his cleaning supplies and the last book, the slim copy of Shakespeare's sonnets, which just fit into his pocket, and hurried down to the kitchen, where he gave Gussie the bottle and cloths. He then got her to heat up some beef tea, which he carried on a tray to the sickroom, to be in keeping with the formal practices of the staff. As he crept into the room, thinking Jack was asleep, he placed the bowl on the table, and leaned the tray up against the wall. When he turned, Jack was awake, his eyes bright, but not with fever.

"Are you laughing at me, Jack?"

"No," said Jack, though he was. "I still can't get over it—did you really think I was goin' to die? Would you have cried if I did?"

For a moment, Oliver couldn't answer. It was too cruel of Jack to mock him like this; his illness had been quite serious, although he didn't seem to know that.

"You might have died," Oliver said, sternly. "Had we not found shelter, somewhere warm and dry."

"You would have come to my funeral, wouldn't you have," Jack continued, rolling up the sleeves of the fancy shirt they'd given him. "You'd have dressed in somber black, with a black cravat, and a shiny black top hat, which would have set your beautiful eyes off a treat, and caused all the ladies to swoon."

Then he sat up, by himself, pulling the counterpane up to his waist and smiling at Oliver, as if his almost having died was the fairest joke in the world.

But Oliver didn't feel like laughing, even for Jack. He blinked away the dampness in his eyes, and turned his head, as though looking for something in the room. But not only was Jack canny, there was nowhere for Oliver to go; Jack reached out and circled his fingers around Oliver's wrist.

"There now," said Jack, tugging. "I'm only messin' with you." When Oliver allowed himself to be tugged close to sit on the bed beside Jack, Jack added, "Although, you do look rather lovely in funeral garb."

"How would you know?" asked Oliver, half-prepared to give Jack a piece of his mind.

"Saw you," said Jack. He gave Oliver's thigh a long pet with his hand and then sat back, the pillows plumping around his shoulders.

"Pardon me?"

"At the funeral for your uncle, back just when I came home. Saw you."

"Saw me where?"

"At the cemetery, dear Nolly. The one by the river. It had snowed, an' you were all in black. Well, everyone was in black, but you were standin' a little ways by yourself, without anybody around you, an' I recognized you directly."

This made Oliver sit up. He'd not known— "You were there? On the day of Uncle Brownlow's funeral?"

"I came lookin' for you, like I said. You and that other fellow, the nasty one with the cane, you had words, you and he. I was close enough to hear the tone, and to see the folks pretendin' that they couldn't hear. And you never cried, did you Nolly. Not there out in the open."

Oliver'd not known. All this time and he'd not known. The day of the funeral had been cold and miserable and sad, but what had kept him from crying was not stoic restraint. No, it had been Mr. Grimwig and his pointed remarks that Oliver had broken Uncle Brownlow's heart and that was why he died. Anger had taken over sorrow, and it had taken everything Oliver had not to lash out; Uncle wouldn't have liked it and their guests would have been shocked.

"Let's not talk about it," he said.

Jack looked at him, and blinked slowly, like a cat, and pulled Oliver to him, quick enough to put Oliver off balance so he landed half on Jack. Jack's arm came around him and held him close; Oliver could hear Jack's heartbeat, steady and sure, and so Oliver slipped his arms around Jack's waist, and he let himself stay like that, in the warm curve of Jack's arms. Until, that is, Jack reached around and pulled the book out of Oliver's pocket.

"I thought somethin' was pokin' me," Jack said.

Oliver sat up.

"It's a book of sonnets by Shakespeare," Oliver said.

"It's got a funny-looking fellow on the front, so I'm sure it can't be much good." Jack flipped the book at Oliver. "What did you bring this for? Why didn't you bring me a story?"

"I did bring you stories," said Oliver, taking the book. He turned the pages for a moment, and then looked up. Jack was watching him. "They're under the mattress," he said now. "I tucked them there. A good collection, if I do say so myself, and I thought you might enjoy the sonnets, as well."

"Poetry," said Jack. "You want to read me poetry, ain't that true?"

Heat crept along the back of Oliver's neck. He did not know how this was done, or even what he was doing. And now to have Jack catch him in his fumbling attempts to court was the worst misery. He ducked his head and placed the book in his lap. "I'll put it back," he said.

"No, you bloody well won't." With a smack to Oliver's shoulder, Jack gave a little laugh. "You're goin' to read them to me. Every single bloody one."

"Oh, just the best ones, I think," said Oliver. "The books will be better."

"You should read me one of each. First a poem."

"They're sonnets."

"First a sonnet, then a story, then a sonnet an' so on."

"Do you imagine you'll be in bed that long?" For all Jack had been complaining, he looked fairly comfortable.

"Naturally."

Hearing Mrs. Heyland call from the kitchen, Oliver stood up. But it felt better now. Jack was getting well, and Oliver's overtures, or whatever they were, and however clumsy they were, had been accepted.

"I'll light a candle and you can look at the drawings," said Oliver. He put the book of fairy tales in Jack's hands, and lit the candle, and kissed the top of Jack's head. It felt domestic and sweet, that moment between them. He liked it like that; there should be more of that.

"I'll be back after supper with more tea," he said, as he went to the door.

"I could stand something more than broth, you know," said Jack. "Like a beefsteak, or a roasted joint."

"I'll see what I can do."

Oliver smiled as he went down the passageway. They were safe, and Jack was getting well, and surely the weather would one day turn to spring.

After supper, Oliver offered to help Mrs. Heyland with any kitchen chores she might have, but the housekeeper looked taken aback.

"You're a young man, and you've done your share today, even with you taking care of your manservant. The girls can manage. You go along, take the tray to him and bring it back when you're done."

Oliver got up from the table, almost overwhelmed with the treasure of the evening he could share with Jack. Edith gave him a tray with the beef broth and willow bark tea, as usual, but since he'd asked for something else, they'd given him toast and butter and jam. To which Jack would probably remark that he would have preferred a slice of roast beef, but this would have to do.

He carried the tray down the passageway, setting it on the floor to open the door. Then he picked up the tray to see that Jack was partly out from beneath the bedclothes, in only his shirt with his legs crossed before him. He'd pulled all the books out from beneath the mattress and spread them around him, where they bobbed up and down on the counterpane as though riding on waves. Looking sweet, if half-naked in his shirt, his hair rumpled, Jack was thumbing through one of them, slowly, scanning the page.

"Are you *reading* that?" Oliver asked without thinking.

"Sure enough," said Jack, looking up. "Why? Ain't I supposed to be able to read?"

"Oh," said Oliver. He felt his face heat up. "Well, it's not that I thought you couldn't read, it's just that I didn't know that you—*could.*"

"'Course I can," said Jack, stoutly. "Not as well as you, o' course, but Fagin taught me, taught all the lads, to read our letters. So we could be lookin' at what the bills bein' posted was about, read the headlines."

"I see," said Oliver, and it did make a strange sort of sense. Fagin had always seemed to keen to get the boys out into the streets each day, rather than having them sit about, though Oliver had never seen Fagin and any boy bent over a book together, the master's hand pointing out the letters so the boy could read them aloud.

"Then with nothin' to do on the boat to Haustralia, the preacher taught lessons, an' it was better than goin' mad with boredom. Then, after that, the farmer wanted us to read aloud a passage on Sundays, so there you go. I know how to read the Bible an' all. But you read better than I, so, c'mon an' read to us."

Secretly pleased at Jack's eagerness, Oliver carried the tray to the small stand on the far side of the bed.

"Will you eat first? I'll read to you while you do. And look, toast and butter and jam for after you drink your broth. That's all I could get, I'm afraid."

"Well, you did try," said Jack, in a tone that suggested he was trying to be cruel and failing. "I am rather tired of beef broth, truth be told."

"Just drink it. Here."

Oliver handed Jack the bowl and the spoon, though he wouldn't have minded feeding Jack by hand. But it was good to see him able to sit up and eat, even if he did disdain the spoon and tipped the bowl to his mouth like a heathen. Then, before Oliver could even look at the books to pick one, Jack inhaled the tea, and then stuffed both slices of toast into his mouth, almost at the same time.

"Which one, then?" Jack asked with his mouth full, so it came out muffled, crumbs flying.

Oliver gazed at the books, trailing his fingers across the titles. He should not have borrowed so many, to make the choice so hard. Indeed, he should not have borrowed them at all.

"What are they about?"

Jack's voice came from far away, and Oliver had to tear himself away from the titles.

"Let's see," he said, rushing to cover his distracted state. "There's one about a monster, an Indian in America, and this one about an escaped prisoner—"

"That one sounds good."

Whether or not Jack was merely humoring him, Oliver agreed. The cover was of green leather, with gold scrollwork for the title and along the spine. When he opened it, the paper was fine and thin, the ink coal-black and crisp.

He took the other books and stuck them back beneath the mattress, including the much-maligned book of sonnets. Then he took Jack's bowl and tray and carried them quickly back to the kitchen. By the time he returned, Jack had the book in his hands and had already left a smudge with his thumb on the frontispiece, leaving a soup stain that any who saw it would remark upon and wonder from whence it had come.

But he'd not the heart to scold Jack, who didn't love books as Oliver did. Yes, he loved the stories, but whether from a book or a broadsheet, apparently, it was all the same to him.

"Come on an' sit, or will you stand and read?"

"No," said Oliver. "Will you move your legs, then?"

Jack agreed, and shifted his legs so that after Oliver unlaced his boots, he could stretch out on the counterpane. Jack stretched out as well, moving close, feeling warm through Oliver's shirt. Then, pausing to plant a gentle kiss on the side of Jack's head, Oliver took *The Count of Monte Cristo* from Jack's hands, settled the edges of the book on his hips, and began to read.

It began with a young man named Edmond, and his proud arrival into the French coastal town of Marseilles. But by the time Oliver had reached the point where Edmond was going to visit his father, Jack's eyes were closing.

"No, you go on," Jack said, when Oliver began to shut the book.

"You're tired," said Oliver. "You should go to sleep."

"As long as you come with me."

Oliver placed the book across his thighs, and reached across to lay his hand on Jack's dark head, where it stayed for a long moment, until he was sure that Jack was fully asleep.

"I will always come with you," he said. "Always.

17

AT WORK BY THE SEASIDE

A t breakfast, after the porridge had been polished off and the bacon shared around, and they all lingered at the table with their mostly finished cups of tea, Mrs. Heyland surprised him.

"I daresay, Oliver, I must spare you today."

"I beg your pardon, Mrs. Heyland?" This was the second time she'd caught him off guard, making him feel more like a foolish boy than even Mrs. Sowerberry ever had. Her statements and questions came out of nowhere, zinging by like bats at dusk.

"You must go to village today, for I found you work."

"*Today*, Mrs. Heyland?"

"Indeed, it must be today, for I have had a note from Mr. Thurly, who states that he will take you this morning to help the men with the first spring rush of mackerel."

Half of this went over his head, as he knew nothing about spring rushes, or mackerel, or who Mr. Thurly was. What must be left unremarked, of course, for it wouldn't do to question an honorable woman such as the housekeeper of a manor house why she'd gone and made all these arrangements, and was now ordering the very moments of his days about, as if—not to mention the fact that he'd be leaving Jack on his own.

"One doesn't give up a position with Mr. Thurly, when it's been so kindly offered, you know," said Mrs. Heyland. "Unless you're ill?"

"Indeed, I am quite well," said Oliver. He swallowed the last bit of his cold and almost bitter tea, and allowed himself to put the cup in the saucer with a very crisp clink. "Shall I go now, this very moment? Or might I take time to see to Jack's comfort?" The asperity in his voice seemed very clear to him, but Mrs. Heyland merely nodded.

"Yes, you should, for none of the girls can be spared; we're quite behind as it is."

Oliver got up, thinking that while spring cleaning was all very well and good, there was nothing more important than looking after a guest who was ill. Surely tasks or schedules could be moved about, especially as the master and the mistress and most of the servants were away, and not expected back for quite some time. But he only nodded at the maidservants and at Gerald and Tim, and marched down the passageway to the sickroom.

There he opened the door, quietly, which was unnecessary as Jack was sitting up on his own, with his knees bent under the counterpane, the pillows splayed behind his head. In his hands he held the bowl of broth, which was steaming in soft, round rings into the air. So someone had brought him his broth while Oliver wasn't looking; he wished he knew which maidservant to thank for that.

"You didn't wake me," said Jack, taking a sip of the broth. His fingers were curled around the pale yellow bowl, which just fit into his hands. "What're you up and dressed so early for?"

Oliver wanted to tell him that he'd be earning their keep by going into a strange village to meet someone by the name of Thurly who would set him to doing heaven knows what for wages. Wages that were needed to pay the medical bills. But perhaps Jack didn't need to know that Oliver would be working while he was resting; it might make him want to get up and offer aid, long before he was able. Or perhaps not. Jack had never, to Oliver's awareness, willingly taken up a full day's work in his life, so why would he start now? Still, with a caution he did not quite understand, Oliver shook this off.

"Oh, just running errands to assist Mrs. Heyland; to pay her back for her charity to us, as she was so kind to take us in."

"It ain't charity if you have to pay it back, Nolly," said Jack, taking another sip of his broth.

There was an expression on Jack's face for a moment; it seemed to speak of more opinions that Jack had on the matter, or perhaps a request for another kiss, something Oliver did not dare do. Not with the door open, and all the household moving about and within earshot. Or maybe it was something else, that Jack would not reveal even if Oliver questioned him. Besides, Oliver was just about to step out the door, so that would be an end to it.

"Have a care, Nolly, they don't work you too hard, you've barely had rest since we got here. On account o' me, might I add."

"But you would do the same for me, I think," said Oliver, feeling on more firm footing. "Though were it me in the bed, and you out in the house, you'd be a good deal more clever about it than I have been."

"What did they have you doin', then?"

"Carrying sheets. Catching the pony. Nothing I can't manage, so far."

"A pony?" Jack asked with uncommon interest. "They got a pony?"

"A lady's pony; one of the lord's daughters, and the pony is in the charge of young Tim, who, in a lax moment, let the pony's lead go, and off it ran."

"An' you caught it, then. Good for you. Now you'll win the heart of this daughter of the house, an' off you'll go."

"Jack, for pity's sake—"

Then he realized that Jack was teasing him, and stopped. "I must be going," he said.

Jack dropped his teasing tones, and his street voice, into the one he used when it was only him and Oliver. "Don't catch cold, you hear? This broth isn't as good as it looks."

"Of that I'm aware," said Oliver. But he stopped himself from sharing the atrocities of Mrs. Heyland's cooking, or from comparing it to Mrs. Pierson's, for to do so would not only detain him from his job, it might reveal too much altogether. He missed London and his life at the haberdashery, missed it so painfully that his heart might break if he let it. But now that they were here, and Jack was on the mend, the differences between this world, this place, and the one they had left, were quite stark.

Jack jerked his chin at Oliver, but whether in understanding or because Oliver was about to leave, Oliver didn't know. Also, he needn't take his nervousness out on Jack.

"Are you settled, do you need anything?" He couldn't ask much more than this, his throat felt so tight. He needed to be on his way, down to the village along as yet unseen roads to brace himself for rough work amongst unknown strangers.

"No, nothin' needed here. Though, if you could see your way to getting me some real grub to eat, I'd be mightily obliged. An' my clothes; they took 'em away to wash and I ain't seen 'em since. So with no clothes an' nothin' to eat, I might have to walk out there in nothin' but my shirt, an' what a scandal that would be."

Of course Jack meant it, he was afraid of nothing, followed the rules of no man. At the same time, the spark in his eyes made Oliver smile. Soothed the trouble within his breast. Allowed him to relax his shoulders.

"I'll see what I can do. Meanwhile, try to stay quiet. We wouldn't want any bad reports to get back to the doctor, however much Mrs. Heyland might enjoy delivering them."

"No indeed," said Jack with a raised eyebrow, which in turned raised Oliver's spirits even more, but he ducked his head to hide his smile as he left the room and closed the door behind him.

~

With his breakfast sitting like a rock in his belly, Oliver made his way, as instructed, in the soft rain, under the greening branches of the trees, downhill and into the village along Gage Lane. Gage Lane was narrow, but the hedges were trimmed all the way down to the gatehouse, as was befitting a manor house in the country. Beyond the hedges were tidy fields, with tips of new green tasting the air above the winter muck and mud. Beyond that, along the curve of the hill, he saw the haze of brightness at the edge of the clouds, but whether this was the sea or flicks of the sun, he could not tell.

So he kept walking, his head down in the misting rain, with drops falling off the brim of his hat, a strange, round, high affair that must be worn by men only in this part of the country, for he'd not seen the likes of it before. The hat, and the borrowed trousers that chafed his knees, were thick, for which he was grateful, as his city clothes would not have kept the rain off, which was a good thing, for it was constant and never ceasing. As was the smell of the sea, a tangy, distant salt that he'd sometimes vaguely sensed in London, on late summer days, when the new fresh breeze of autumn would come in from the west, bringing the sea air with it. This was like that, only cleaner, and more vibrant on the tongue.

At the bend in the road, where it headed out along the hills, he'd been instructed to take the footpath that went along the edge of something called Sleech Wood, which was only a narrow band of trees with much underbrush and no way through; some ancient tithe probably controlled the wood and much of it had been recently felled. He kept walking, with the spring trees dripping rain, and the whole sky a mournful mouth of grey and swirling light.

At Middle Mill Farm, he took the road that headed downhill, through the growth of trees on either side. The lane sank below the level of the ground so that it felt as though he were going through a straight, shallow trough. The effect, with the wind cut off by the soft edge of land on either side, was to block off the wind and a bit of the rain, giving him some respite from the weather. Still, by the time he got to the bottom of Middle Mill Lane, his clothes were beaded with rain.

Though Mrs. Heyland had given him instructions, and he was sure he was lost, the spires of St. Michael's church, the tallest thing in the village, continued to poke up above the tree line, so he must be going in the right direction. But at least, under the trees, with their leafless branches, the rain spattered above his head instead of upon it.

By the time he came to the dip in the road, a deep one, Mrs. Heyland had said, from all the years of people and carts passing along it, he knew he must be close. Sure enough, the next turning around the hedgerows showed him the first cobbled lane, still leading downhill. He followed it, his heart beating a little bit fast at the thought of him, a gentleman's son, gutting fish and packing salt, or whatever it was that he would be required to do. But mostly, more than that, it was the idea of being so far from Jack, on his own in this strange place, with so many people he didn't know, so far from anywhere he knew.

He was surprised to see a sliver of the sea along the top of the fence line, a grey-blue line at the far edges, as flat as though someone with a skilled and steady hand had drawn it, and a churning blue-white curve closer to shore. The smell of the sea was stronger, too, tart with salt, and the tang of something stronger, a secretive smell that was dark and made the inside of his nose burn. The wind kept a brisk pace, with dashes of rain, though the clouds seemed to be letting in small tumbles of yellow-grey light.

As he passed it, the churchyard of St. Michael's was old, as churchyards tended to be; places of moss and grey stone, and trees that cast shadows thick enough to need a lit candle to better see the markings on the gravestones by. The church itself, a grand building of spires and thick grey stone, seemed to weigh heavy on the earth, creating mounds of earth all around, as if the church had sunk into a pillow.

The main street was a wide one, and started on the other side of St. Michaels' and showed him the sea against the stone seawall, a waist-high ledge capped with large, flat stones. The sea was tossing in the morning rain, spraying up foam and bits of seaweed on the rocks not far below the road. The road continued along, wending its way around shops made of stone, their doors being opened, their stone steps swept, and everywhere the haze of salt air, with salt on his lips, on his skin. Oliver took a deep breath. He'd never been to the sea before, and Jack's comments about it had been few and unprepossessing.

He kept walking as the road curved around the bay. In the bay's shelter were several fishing smacks; he'd seen pictures of those, in books, or in broadsheets bought for a penny, and in newspapers, the kind Uncle Brownlow used to read when they'd sit by the fire together. The water was in close to the shore, and the smacks were close enough to see the brass fittings on the sails, the turns of rope around pins along the edges of each vessel. There were also little rowing boats, and a larger, three-masted barque that was just having her sails taken down in the rigging.

Up ahead, through the mist of rain, he could see the edge of the stone harbor where it connected with the road. This, as Mrs. Heyland had explained to him, was the Cobb, which curved into the sea like a human arm. It was at the end of the Cobb that he was to find Mr. Thurly's tent shed, and the tarpaulin pinned to poles over tables along the shore where the men worked, gutting and salting fish.

It had sounded interesting when she'd explained it, but now, coming close, the tarp was black with grease, and the men, huddled under it, looked rough with their baggy trousers and broad belts. They didn't even have jackets or hats, not even in the rain, with their sleeves rolled up on their thick shirts, with kerchiefs around their necks, and long leather aprons tied about their middles. One man looked up at Oliver spat into the sea, and elbowed the man nearby. Oliver looked away from him and kept walking. Made himself keep walking. Licked the salt from his lips and kept walking.

By the time he got to the shed, the tarpaulin was flapping in a sudden gust of wind that sent the foam curling over the rocks at the end of the Cobb, but at least it distracted a few of the men, allowing Oliver to walk up to them with somewhat less notice.

"What you want?" barked one of the men. His beard was black around his chin, and he looked quite unwashed.

"I'm looking for Mr. Thurly," said Oliver. He took off his hat and clutched it to his chest; his voice sounded small in his ears, so he coughed and tried again. "Mrs. Heyland sent me to be an extra hand."

"An extra hand," said the man with the beard, and he snorted a laugh. "With that face and you come down to work for old Thurly?"

Oliver felt his face flush at this remark, and the sniggers that followed it.

A gust of wind followed through with a spray of seawater that pelted his whole left side, and he couldn't even begin to think why anyone would want to spend a day at the seaside, as he'd so often heard, for relaxation. It was wet and cold and quite grey; the crude gesture of one of the men, his hand pumping at his crotch, made Oliver want to turn away, to go back to Rhode Hill House and tell Mrs. Heyland that he would work off what he owed her by scrubbing the chamberpots and privies. That would be far better than putting up with the insolence of such men.

"Now, then, what's this?"

From behind him came a question in a thick low voice, and Oliver turned. A man in a hat, much like the one Oliver was now gripping, and a thick woolen jacket, came up to him, his boots clanging on the cobblestones. A large, grey cat wove in and out between his legs, but he appeared not to notice it.

"Are you from Mrs. Heyland, then, boy?" the man asked. He, too, spat into the ocean, just past Oliver's shoulder.

"Yes, sir, I'm Oliver Twist, and she sent me to—"

"Yes, yes," said the man, waving the rest of Oliver's words away. "I'll set you to scrubbing barrels, there's plenty of water to be had today. And you lot!" The man, Mr. Thurly, it seemed, went on. "Standing about like a bunch of imbeciles who've never seen a stranger before. You three, start hauling the barrels down from the Cobb, and you two, set out the tables and knives and salt-buckets —do I have to tell you everything? And Leander, get them smacks to start unloading fish; we get our pick this morning; anything not of size we can give back to them to deal with. Now get moving!"

At this string of orders, the men unfurled from their huddle under the tarpaulin, and spread out to various tasks. Then Mr. Thurly, barely watching this, as if it was of no matter to him what anyone did, turned to Oliver.

"Oliver," he said, cocking his head at the length of the Cobb. "Them barrels'll be lined up along the shore here. Get a bucket and brush from Leander, he's the tall one, and get some seawater and scrub the insides. Tip 'em upside-down so they can drain and dry, at least as much as they can in this weather. Then, later, we'll have you packing salt; have you ever gutted a mackerel?" Mr. Thurly looked at Oliver, shaking his head and then went on without waiting for an answer. "I can see by your hands that you've not done much hard work, but that'll soon change. Leander! Get this boy a bucket and brush, and set up the first row of barrels."

The first row of barrels appeared in short order, with the racket of wooden wheels against stone, in wheelbarrows wielded by the men. The barrels were lined up against the Cobb, on the beach, ten along and two deep. The barrels were tall, almost up to Oliver's breastbone. And they were old, caked with rust along the rings around the staves, and weathered by salt to an almost black color.

Oliver was distracted for a moment as a man, freshly shaven and grinning, came up to him.

"You the new boy?" said the man. "I'm Leander Warren, and

I'm in charge after Thurly. And 'ere's you a bucket and a brush," he said, slamming both against Oliver's chest.

Oliver took them, hiding his grunt of pain behind his clenched jaw. It was completely foreign to him why someone would be so rude upon first acquaintance, but then, Noah Claypole had been like this, rough and rude, and grinning at the fun to be had from tormenting someone smaller and weaker than him.

"You need supplies, come to me," said Leander. "You need a break, just piss in the sea."

Leander laughed, and walked off, leaving Oliver to look at the barrels lined up like empty bodies. He looked at the brush and bucket in his hands and wondered how it always came to this, him scrubbing and cleaning like this when he could read quite well and write with an elegant hand—but what did that matter now? This was how it was, for Jack's continued health, and the doctor's bills, depended on Oliver to carry on as though none of this bothered him. Not the rough men, nor the smell of fish being unloaded from the first smack, nor the spray of the ocean curling over the edge of the Cobb and dampening everything it could reach.

Oliver licked his lips, tasting the salt and the wildness of the sea, wishing Jack were here with him, to help him navigate the strangeness of a new place, a new occupation. Then he picked up the bucket, and, taking a deep breath, wondered from where he should draw water.

He looked up. Leander was laying boards across trestles beneath the tarpaulin, and saw Oliver standing there.

"Go around, idiot, go around!" With a jerk of his head, Leander pointed along the Cobb to the shore. "There's a bit of a pool at the bottom of the stairs there, use that."

Oliver hefted the bucket and came close to the men under the tarpaulin. There was now a pile of narrow white fish attempting to flip out of the high confines of the wooden frame they'd been poured in. Without hesitation, one of the men grabbed a mackerel, laid it on the table to slit it open, still breathing and flipping, and then reached in to tear out its guts and the white line of its spine.

This mess he flung right in front of Oliver, directly into the sea, leaving a fine spray of blood across Oliver's shirt bosom.

As Oliver looked down at the blood, the men howled; when Oliver wiped the back of his hand across his mouth, they doubled over until they were out of breath. He wanted to shout at them all, but his glare only caught Leander's eye. Leander touched his forelock in a mockery of respect.

"Welcome to the Cobb, Oliver Twist. You can consider yourself baptized."

Oliver held on to his temper as best he could, marching on as if the stink of fish guts wasn't making his stomach turn, and the thought of days of this wasn't making him want to run to the hills till he could not be found. But he was well past the days where he might calculate that running away was his best option. Besides, it was only a little blood, and the men were rough; this was their idea of fun. It couldn't get too out of hand; a little fish guts wouldn't hurt him.

After taking off his jacket and hat and rolling up his shirt sleeves, Oliver spent the best part of the morning hauling icy-cold salt water up from the calmer waters of the little bay, and then on his knees inside of barrels, scrubbing them. He had to find a way to brace the barrels between two rough stones so that they wouldn't roll with him inside them; he managed that, but only barely. Mostly it was him on his knees; he had to brace his legs to steady the barrel from within, and by the time he'd done two barrels, his knees were raw and his thighs shook.

That wasn't the worst part; it was the smell and the dampness, closed in, and the strain on his shoulders as he scrubbed over his head. Round and round with the rough-bristled brush in his right hand until the cramp came in, and he had to switch to his left. Water dripped down on him from the staves of the barrel, half of it rain, half of it sea spray, and the other half from the brush. That was three halves, but it didn't matter, because that's how wet he became, soaked through in short order, the borrowed trousers quite ruined by barrel number five, and there were fifteen more to go. Except each time Oliver managed to tip two barrels upside down to dry, there were three *additional* barrels waiting for him when he came back with another bucket of water.

He'd just finished barrel number six and was heading down the stairs for more water when he felt a splat of a warm mass in the middle of his back. He twisted to see the red globules and the white shard of a spine rolling down the back of his legs, leaving a dark trail of blood and dark matter along the buff-colored cloth of his trousers. But when he looked up, all the men were involved in their tasks, and Mr. Thurly was looking the other way.

There was nothing he could do about this but scowl and continue on his way, head held high, as though there was nothing amiss but a slight odor, and that he could easily contend with. He went down the three, green-slicked steps and got his bucket of water, then went back to his barrels, noting, with some grim satisfaction, that the remaining count was no more than twenty, so at least he'd not fallen behind. And if he could continue keeping up, then Mr. Thurly wouldn't have any reason to make any complaints to Mrs. Heyland about him.

So he gritted his teeth and scrubbed barrels, carving blisters on the webbing of both hands, between his thumbs and his forefingers, and prayed that they didn't break open. Which they did, eventually, slowing him down. He sucked at the raw flesh, wincing as the salt air got to them.

He was through fifteen of the barrels and climbing the stairs with another full bucket of water, and crossing over the top of the Cobb so as to avoid the men scrambling to control the net of fish coming overhead. But then when something knocked against him, he went flying through the damp air. He expected to land with a thud on the cobblestones, but instead fell with a splat, his head going under the cold foamy waves, his hand losing the bucket as he drew in a mouthful of salt water.

Choking and gasping he kicked, his boots dragging him down, but his head broke above the foam. His arms splayed wide, as if they wanted, unconsciously, to grab hold of something, but the side of the Cobb was flat and slimy with seaweed, the height of it too far beyond his arms' reach.

Above him, standing on the edge of the Cobb, were Leander and two of the men, slapping their knees, and pointing. Oliver could swim, had learned to swim in the calm, bending River Bourne in Chertsey, but this was different. Swells of salty foam went over his head, and the pull and push of the sea battered him, as if it couldn't decide whether to smash him against the side of the Cobb or pull him out to disappear against a grey, rain-flecked horizon.

Oliver thought he should make to shore, and began to kick and to use his arms, aching as they were, to carve him a path to safety. But the sea pulled at him, and he went under. Holding his mouth closed, he thrashed with his hands, his arms, kicking all the while, and broke the surface to find himself even further out. His heart was racing, and then he heard shouts and saw the figures on the Cobb moving in different directions. This was dire; he was going to be swept out to sea on his first day—he was going to drown, and Jack would be waiting for his Nolly, who would never come home to him.

Kicking and moving his arms, Oliver kept himself afloat, tasting salt water in the back of his throat, his chest heaving with the effort not to go under. There was more shouting, and behind him he heard the creak of wood and the flap of something damp, and all of a sudden, rough hands grabbed his hair, and pulled at him. Then more hands were under his arms, hauling him up over the side of a fishing smack, where he landed with a tangled flop amidst the bits of sail and a puddle of seawater, and found himself looking at two pairs of oiled boots.

"Look what we caught," said one voice.

"What d'you imagine Thurly might pay for this lot?" asked a

second voice. "He's surely of a size we can keep, rather than throwing back overboard."

Oliver tried to sit up, his mind racing to come up with a clever reply to put the two men in their place, but his teeth were chattering so hard he could barely take a breath, let alone think of anything to say. But the comments were all that was teasing; everything else that they did to him was practical and kind. Two pairs of hands pulled him up to sit on a bench, out of the puddle, then someone started rubbing him all over with what felt like hemp sacking, and when he looked up, water dripping into his eyes, one of the men was bending toward him with a grey-wool blanket and a flask.

"'Ere you go, lad, get that into you."

The man lifted the flask to Oliver's lips and wrapped the blanket around him. Oliver kept shivering, and every movement made his clothes squelch against him.

"You'll be all right in a moment," the man said.

"You fell off the Cobb, I reckon; well, there's nothing wrong with a sea dip," said the first man, "as long as you can get dry after." He seemed to find this funny, laughing at Oliver, his mouth wide, yellow teeth shining through his beard.

Oliver nodded, attempting to flex his frozen fingers around the woolen blanket, rough against his neck, seawater stinging in his eyes, trying to still the shudders that coursed through him. Of course he had fallen, and he would never say otherwise. It wouldn't do any good anyhow, even if he did suspect Leander and his mates had planned the entire thing. Roughing up the new boy was probably an amusing pastime to them, and Thurly wouldn't think the better of Oliver for having carried any tales.

"S-slipped," he managed. "Wet stones."

This made the men laugh all the more, as one of them sat on the bench beside Oliver and began rowing towards the shore. With strong strokes, they were soon there, with the other man jumping out on the stone-lined shore to pull the dory in with jerks and stops. The boat continued to rock as Oliver stood up. He could see

Thurly marching over, his face like thunder, his hat pushed back on his head.

Oliver unfolded the blanket and handed it to one of the men, getting out of the boat just as Thurly came up.

"And I suppose you lost the bucket with that little stunt, you miserable whelp."

Without waiting for an answer, Mr. Thurly grabbed Oliver by the collar of his shirt and dragged him over the stones, away from the boat, and didn't stop his angry marching till they were at the tent. A few of the men, Leander among them, were pretending to work, but their movements were slow, and Oliver knew they were watching and laughing.

"You think we have time to waste and that supplies grow on trees?" Thurly let go of him to poke him in the chest with a gnarled finger. "That you jumping into the water is amusing? That men have time to waste to haul your sorry arse out of the ocean?"

Oliver wanted to back away, but didn't.

"I slipped, Mr. Thurly; it was an accident." Only the words came out through stiff lips, making him sound as though he was lisping, and the men on the Cobb laughed out loud. "I'll pay for the bucket," he said, not adding that the bucket had been old anyway. His hair dripped water on his face, salt water in his eyes, and the wind whistled through his wet clothes; all the shivering his body could muster wasn't helping.

Mr. Thurly looked him over as he shivered; there was no sympathy in his expression, but he narrowed his eyes a fraction and looked over at the men, still sniggering, but busy with the pile of fish on the boards in front of them. The wind flapped at the tarpaulin over their heads, and the smell of blood was sharp in the air. Then Mr. Thurly turned back to look at Oliver.

"You slipped, you say. You weren't pushed."

Oliver shook his head, tasting salt, clenching his fists against his thighs. "No, I slipped. The stones were wet, you see—"

"Here's the bucket, Mr. Thurly," shouted one of the men, and indeed he was holding the bucket high in the air, dangling from a long hook whereby he'd caught it out of the ocean.

Mr. Thurly closed his mouth hard, and his eyes, as well, sighing, as if gathering all of his strength not to lose his patience with the new boy. Then he opened his eyes, and patted Oliver on the chest.

"You be more careful in future; I don't have time to waste with this nonsense, I've a load of fish to get salted in those barrels, and there's money to be made. Never mind." Mr. Thurly shook his head. "It's dinnertime anyhow; you'll just have to stay in those wet clothes till they dry on you, but I reckon that'll teach you to be more careful next time."

Oliver followed Mr. Thurly back up the slant of the Cobb till they were high over the sea again. Oliver saw his bucket and brush sitting neatly together by the last barrel he'd been working on. At least the cost of the bucket wouldn't be added to the money he owed.

Besides, Mr. Thurly had opened the shed a little wider, and Oliver saw there was a small, square stove in there, with fat blocks of red coal burning inside of it. He wanted to stand close to it to get warm, but Mr. Thurly pushed past him, pulling Oliver out of the tent.

One of the men was pulling out benches beneath the tarpaulin, and a woman from the shore was carrying a stewpot to the table, where she began ladling out bowls of stew and handing them around the table. By the time Oliver got his bowl all the places on the bench were taken, and Oliver had to eat his stew standing up, with the men looking up at him. It wasn't bad stew, mutton and barley mixed in a dark broth, and after he'd finished the stew, he got a pint of beer drink with it; at least no one begrudged him that.

Someone smacked him on the back good-naturedly, it seemed, and offered him another lug of beer from the pitcher, and Oliver held out his tin pot, and nodded. It had been a rite of passage, that was easy to see, for one of the men got up from the bench and nodded at him, and Oliver was allowed, wet clothes and all, to sit down and drink his second pint of beer with a more relaxed air. That is, if a stiff wind racing through his bones, sealing the salt to his skin, could be called relaxed.

The willingness of the sun to come out from behind the clouds sweeping overhead was only outdone by Oliver's willingness to move on to something other than scrubbing the inside of rusty, salt-caked barrels. His knees were raw from kneeling on the hard wooden slats inside of the barrels, and his hands were splintered through. As he stood at the edge of the Cobb, the far end from Leander Warren, he waited while Mr. Thurly appraised his work.

"Ever gutted an' packed a fish before, one as slender as a mackerel?" Mr. Thurly eyed Oliver as Oliver watched what the fish gutters were doing.

It seemed straightforward enough, even though there was a great deal of blood spray and the strong, warm smell of fish guts as they were tossed into buckets that were later dumped into the sea. Rangy cats wove in and out of the table legs; the men seemed rather patient with them, often dropping bits of guts straight down, so the cats could have them. The fish heads went into long troughs to be carted down to where the women were, with their thick skirts and woven shawls tucked into mannish belts around their waists.

"No, sir," said Oliver. "But I reckon I could do it, if someone would teach me."

"Ain't squeamish, are you? Bein' a gentleman an' all from the big city?"

"No, sir," said Oliver again. He was far from being a gentleman these days, at least not a respectable one.

"Right you go, then. Leander, get over here, bring a spare apron and one of them knives. A sharp one. Teach Oliver here what's it about, an' mind you, no tricks, for I'll be watching you both. We've got fish to get ready."

Leander, with his bulky shoulders and leather apron, which was worn through where it had been tied and tightened so often about his waist, came up. He held two knives, one his own, smeared with guts, and another one, sharp and shiny in the glittering, sea-tossed air. He made a feint with it, as if expecting Oliver to be startled. Oliver jerked his head back, but remained where he was, to show Leander that he would not be put off.

"Here, you," said Leander. "Come by here, and mind you don't fall in again." He laughed, but only a few men joined him. It might be that while there was a tradition of initiation, as with the flying fish guts, shoving someone into the icy-cold waters outside of the Cobb, where he might get bashed against the rocks, was not within that tradition.

But rather than explain to Leander that he understood this, Oliver stood beside Leander, and took the knife's handle when it was offered to him. He put the knife on the blood-streaked deal table, tied the stiff leather apron about his waist, squared his feet, and nodded to show that he was ready.

"Roll up them sleeves up further, boy, else you'll be getting that knife tangled."

Oliver did as he was told, folding the muslin cloth up, and Leander gave each sleeve an extra fold, so the cloth was tight around Oliver's biceps. The sleeve crackled with salt.

"Easier to get bloodstains off your skin than out of your shirt. Just ask my wife."

This civil remark was only because Mr. Thurly was indeed watching them closely, so Oliver nodded. He would hold no grudges if Leander would teach him what he knew, so that he could make the three shillings and sixpence that he owed for each of the doctors' visits, so that was ten shillings and sixpence altogether, over half a pound, all told. He could make four shillings by Saturday, but that would only discharge less than half the debt. But if Leander taught him properly, Oliver could keep up with the rest of the men and be able to pay his debt by the end of the next week.

"Hold the fish like this, belly up." Leander grabbed a mackerel, quite dead, slender and silver in his hand, and turned it over with a twitch of his wrist, so that it landed in his palm, right where he wanted it. "Slit the belly open, throat to arse, and dig at the top knob there with your thumb to pull out the spine and the guts. If you cuts the head off first, you won't get a clean pull, an' it'll leave guts behind. Got it?"

"Yes, but do you cut the head off after, then?"

"You've been payin' attention, you have, even washin' them barrels. Yes, put the mackerel down, at an angle, like this, and cut, back of the head, to the front, top of the belly."

"What about the tail?"

"Stays attached, for ease o' washin' and also, the packin'. We hand this over to the lad who is rinsin' in salt water, and then, they get packed in barrels, newly washed by you, with salt between for each layer."

"And the head?"

"Well, if this were a haddock or a fish to sell directly, we'd keep the head on. We can sell it for soup today, per'aps tomorrow, otherwise, it's good for nowt but bait and cat food. Here, puss, here you go."

Leander bent down with the chopped-off head of the mackerel and gave the whole thing to a rather sleek beast that wound its way among his boots, reaching up with a silent mew, to race off with the prize in its mouth.

"Bloody cats," said Leander, but he was smiling as he watched a large tabby go up to Mr. Thurly, who bent to pet the animal's head, and give it a scrap of fish. "They keep the mice and rats at bay, so they earn their supper."

He handed Oliver a mackerel from the pile; it had been caught early in the morning, and by now was stiff and cold to the touch, though it didn't smell of anything but the sea. Oliver hefted it in his palm, watching the silver-blue scales litter his fingers. Oliver tried holding the mackerel in the air to cut it, his hand shaking a little at the sharpness of the knife, but Leander pressed on Oliver's wrist to get him to put the balance of the weight on the table, so that the cut would be even and straight.

"No, that ain't it," said Leander. "You want to cut your fingers off?"

He demonstrated how to cut the belly open, and how to break the knob at the top of the spine with his thumb, and how to pull the spine out. It looked much easier when the back of Leander's hand rested against the table.

"Mind you," said Leander. "You tip your hand a bit sideways, so if the knife slips, it might get a finger or two, but you won't be cutting open the whole of your palm. Messy business, that. So try again."

Oliver rested his hand on the table, with the fish in it, and dug in with the tip of the knife, making a fairly straight cut all the way to the belly. The smell of the fish's innards misted up at him, along with a freshet of blood that reeked of salt. He considered that since Leander was nodding, he was doing it right, so he went on to the next step, taking his thumb to feel up inside of the fish's head, to the slippery point of the top of the spine. The bone broke easily with a bit of pressure, and he crooked his thumb and pulled out the entire spine. It seemed to zip out cleanly.

"Now, cut off the head, put it in the bucket there, and put the rest in the tub over here. Someone'll rinse it, and then we salt. And you and I keep doing it over and over again, till the day's catch is done. Right?" Leander bent to feed a bit of fish to a passing cat.

"Yes," said Oliver, nodding.

Someone came up and put a pile of fish in front of him, insurmountably high, except Leander's pile was higher; they were using him lightly for the moment, until he showed he'd got the hang of it. The wind whisked over the pile of fish, bringing the coppery, salty smell of fresh blood, the ruddy, almost palpable smell of guts starting to rot, while cats tore at scraps, and the men cut and tossed and flung the fish about to get through the pile of fish by day's end.

Oliver worked slowly at first, taking care with the initial cut, learning where was too high and he cut into the head, and too low, where he half-sliced up the tail. His pile began to shrink, but then someone in a leather apron came along and dumped more fish in front of him. Leander looked at him as though he expected that the city boy would complain, or whine until he was let off.

But gutting fish was a damn sight better than scrubbing barrels. And, if anyone had asked him, more satisfying than counting buttons or winding silk ribbons in the warehouse at the haberdashery. Which surprised him a great deal as he'd not thought that manual labor such as gutting fish would have given him so much pleasure.

The crisp air off the churning sea felt good in his lungs, and any sense of being stifled or too warm was swept from his skin with each skiff of air. Sometimes the rain spattered down, or a truly cold bit of wind gusted across the Cobb from far out to sea. But though it was windy, with the smell of seaweed rotting along the shore at low tide, the air felt good. Welcoming, almost.

"Summer is a-comin' in," said Leander, pausing to tilt his head back to smell the wind.

"Pardon, what did you say?" Putting his knife down on the table, for what seemed like the first time that morning, Oliver looked at Leander.

"'Tis an old poem, you see," said Leander. "About summer. That's all I know of it, though. That first line. But you can smell it, can't you?"

"Yes," said Oliver. "I think so."

Leander's friendliness was driven by the fact that Mr. Thurly was watching them, and so Leander could not be fully trusted. But, with the slight warmth that drove the swells across the stones at the end of the Cobb, it was still pleasurable indeed to be in such a place.

"Ah, pick it up again, lad, before Mr. Thurly gets cross."

Oliver picked up the next fish, and as he wasn't watching where his knife was going, he cut a scrawl across the fish's belly, causing a streak of body-warm fish blood to spray across half of his face.

Leander laughed, and the men watched as Leander used the back of his hand to deftly smear the blood even further into Oliver's skin.

"You're one of us now," he said. "Now that you've been blood-ied. Go on, taste it. That's life, that is."

For a moment, Oliver considered spitting the blood from his lips, but perhaps this was part of the initiation. So he licked his lips from end to end with his tongue, and used his teeth, as well, to get the warm blood into his mouth. It tasted like salt, and like the sea, with a spark of something else he couldn't name.

"That's life, that is," said Leander again. All the men along the row saluted Oliver with the tips of their knives, and in that moment Oliver felt the kind of belonging he'd never had at the haberdashery. Where all the men were doing what he was doing, and while he might be newer and slower than them, he was able, and was expected, to catch up. Which he would.

Sometimes the women came up the table, as if they needed something. But their slow stroll with empty baskets on hips did no more than to pass the time, as there was always someone to run the buckets of fish heads down to them. But come they did, cats flitting between their booted feet, to get the buckets of water for themselves and to look at Oliver from beneath the brims of their thick, calico-lined straw bonnets, whose ribbons were blacked with grease, but which were tied beneath their chins with some flair.

"Get along with you, you saucy thing," said Leander to one girl bold enough to stare openly, and then to Oliver. "Never mind them; they ain't never seen a gentleman before, you'd think. But they come every summer, to use the bathing machines, and dance at the hall, and throw their gold about. But you ain't got no coin, 'ave you."

Oliver shook his head. He was used to being looked at, and to be ogled by a fisher-girl with no mother about to keep her from being too forward was no hardship at all. None of the men were looking at him in that way; they looked at his hands, and at the pile of fish, as if watching to see that he did the full day's work expected of him. Which was only fair; everyone was paid a percentage of the total day's profit, and Mr. Thurly seemed well aware of how much fish each man was processing.

Oliver smiled to himself, and returned to his work, content even in the rough company he now shared, for he was earning honest money, and would soon be able to pay the doctors for healing Jack.

18

BETWEEN WORK AND IDLENESS

While Jack enjoyed the laziness of sleeping in, by mid-morning the absence of Nolly, who had gone off to do errands for the missus, created so much empti-ness that Jack could stand it no longer. And who was he to be ordered about by a doctor he did not know and a housekeeper who ruled as though she were a tyrant? So though Nolly might be disap-pointed that Jack was disobeying orders by getting out of bed a day too early, surely he would be pleased to see Jack up and about. Besides, his headache was only a dim murmur in the back of his head.

He slithered out of the bed, pushing the bedclothes to the side, scratching his belly through his shirt. On the floor next to the chair were his clothes; while he'd slept, someone had returned them to him. As he pulled on his stockings and shoved his legs into the trousers, he noted that while the garments had been washed and dried, they'd not been mended, nor were they like the thicker, more weather-brave clothes that Nolly had received, probably without asking for them.

But such was the way of things. Compared to Nolly, in anyone's eyes, Jack was the mongrel, not worthy of a fine collar, let alone a new set of clothes. But what did that matter, and besides, Nolly did look handsome as he'd left that morning, having enjoyed a country breakfast before going off to gain that rosy flush to his cheeks that the sea air would bring.

Tucking in his shirttail and doing up the buttons on the front of his trousers, Jack walked down the passage toward the warm smells and sounds of crockery that must be the kitchen. As he stepped from the passage into the larger room, he spied his coat on a hook near the door.

He imagined that he might not be noticed by anybody, but the moment he was halfway across the room, the young woman standing at the stove turned and saw him. She shrieked and dropped the bowl she was holding. There was a loud smack as the bowl struck the stone floor, and shards of crockery and strings of some unknown food spread to all areas of the kitchen floor. She put her apron to her mouth and was all but sobbing into it.

Before Jack could even open his mouth to make a sly remark to ease her distress, the tyrant, Mrs. Heyland, stormed into the kitchen, clucking and fussing over the maid. Then she saw the mess, and then she saw Jack, and her irritation turned to fury.

"What are you doing in my kitchen upsetting my girls?" She advanced, pointing an angry finger at him. "You're to be a-bed till the doctor gives you leave to rise."

"I fuckin' felt better an' wanted to get up, so I did," said Jack, calmly in this face of this, for who was she to him?

Her gasp could have cut through wire.

"Besides I'm sick of drinkin' shite-tastin' tea," he said, even more calmly. "I was hoping to get a bite to eat, though Nolly says the food ain't so good."

Though Nolly might have a greater respect for manners, he was also bound by them. Jack, however, was not, but he knew how to use them for his own gain. And he knew that for the housekeeper to do aught but feed him now would be a terrible breach of those manners. Especially since the other two maids had obviously heard the racket and had descended the stairs to see what it was about.

He gave them both a wink and boldly strode to the table and sat down.

There were lumps of cloth and spools of thread from the morning's sewing, and what might be an uncut loaf of bread arrayed with a clean cloth, as well as a quarter of cheese.

"You're so kind, missus," he said, reaching for the food, though he had no plate, "to offer me food an' drink. My master told me of your generous nature, and 'tis true, I see."

"I'll cut it for you," said Mrs. Heyland. She snatched the bread from his hands, her mouth pursed in anger.

As she sliced the bread, one of the serving maids came over with a bowl of butter, which she quickly placed on the table and backed away. The slices of bread were slammed on a plate, but Jack ignored this, and went on buttering his bread. At one point, he bit into the block of cheese for the pleasure of it, and ignored their startled stares. But in the end, the portions of food had been small, as if Mrs. Heyland meant to snub him, or wanted him to ask for more, for the pleasure of refusing him.

Jack removed himself from the table just the same when he finished, wiping his mouth with the back of his hand just to see her wince. Besides, he was full enough for now; after so many meals of beef tea, his stomach had the capacity of a walnut.

The out-of-doors beckoned. Jack grabbed his coat and flung it on with as much style as he could muster; the maids must be entertained even if Mrs. Heyland was impervious to his charm.

The weather in the large courtyard was brisk and breezy and, for all its air of tidiness, there were scraps of leaves and bits of twig swirling around, as if astride the current of a small, damp ocean. The sky spangled down rain in snatches, starting and stopping, as if it wasn't quite sure what weather it wanted.

He wondered at Nolly's errands for Mrs. Heyland. Surely it would have been more efficient to send one of the house servants who knew the lay of the land. That Nolly had gone made little sense. Yet, if Nolly felt that this was the best way to earn their keep, then who was Jack to deny him?

Wandering about, Jack touched the cart that had been left askew, and the wheel that needed mending, and eyed the path that led off to a large fenced orchard, scraggly with springtime growth. The yard was open with high walls of brick abutting a barn and a stable and the main house, but the gates were flung wide open, to admit the freshening breezes.

Jack noted the smell of the sea air, salty and clean, with the thick, brackish scent of burning pitch and old seaweed. During his fever, the smell had eased into his dreams, making him feel that he was many places at once, with his skin overly sensitive to any scent, any sound. Unsettled, he stepped into the barn, which, with the doors also wide open, felt as though he were stepping into a tidy cave that smelled of old hay and fresh manure.

The number of open doors and gates all around bespoke of a country tendency to trust, which might have been their downfall, had anyone been in less-than-appropriate awe of the local gentry. It was obvious from the lack of bustle that the family, along with most of the staff, had removed from the house. Though to whither, Jack did not know. Nor did he care because, frankly, while this might be a good stopping-off place, their stay was surely temporary.

His eyes adjusted to the darkness of the barn, the shapes and lines of various shades of black rendering themselves into box stalls, wooden beams, and a tidy assemblage of tools hung on wooden frames on the far wall. And a man who was busily sorting metal objects on a table.

"Might I help you, stranger?" asked the man. He paused in his employment, and though he wiped his hands on his apron, he did not offer to shake Jack's hand. While he seemed alert, he was not alarmed, nor very concerned at all at Jack's presence.

If Jack had not already known it, that behavior would have told him he was in the country.

"I'm up at the house," said Jack, jerking his thumb over his shoulder. "The missus was kind enough to take us in."

"Then you're the manservant," said the man, as he took in the state of Jack's clothes.

"I'm Jack, the one who was ill with the fever, so I'm to be restin'. My master's off doin' errands, to repay the kindness of the missus."

"Well, I'm Gerald, the second groomsman," said Gerald. "But your master's not doing errands, he's down at the Cobb, gutting and packing fish."

Jack felt his eyebrows rise. "Gutting fish? As a favor?" He scratched the back of his head, as though clearing his thoughts, but felt something raw in his gut that Nolly had lied to him.

"No," said Gerald. "'Tis for the doctor's bills. I don't know what they are in the city, but here, they're three and six each time, so it's over ten shillings he owes, Mrs. Heyland said. He's earning money for that."

Gerald went back to his sorting, leaving Jack befuddled in a way that he could not put down to his recent fever. Nolly had not only lied about where he'd been headed, he'd told another lie about why he needed to go there. This was not the first time, of course, that Nolly had played it close to the chest, particularly when he obviously felt that the revelation might bring ill will or a less than kindly reflection. But while Nolly was not that good a liar, that morning he'd managed to look Jack straight in the eyes and tell not one but two lies. Jack had not known about the debt; he'd imagined if rich folk offered shelter to the needy, there would be no attempt to tally the cost.

The unease in Jack's breast cast corrosion on the perfect patina that encircled Nolly's place in his heart. Nolly, being Nolly, would be quite concerned about the entire nature of the debt, the hospitality, which cost nobody nothing, and the bloody doctor's bill, which if it were anyone's duty, it would be Jack's.

"Will you be needing anything, young Jack?" asked Gerald. He was leaning to pick up some folded horse blankets, banging them against his knees to knock out the dust.

"Only to get out of the way of the missus," said Jack, in a tone that was meant to invite Gerald to join him in chiding her less-than-welcoming nature.

As it did; Gerald smiled.

"Well, if you're out and about and looking for something to do, you could grab a broom. Tim and I cleaned out the stalls, but the cobwebs and stray straw need a good whacking."

In the moment of silence that fell, Jack examined his options. At one end, he could feign a return of sickness and go back into the house, which would be incredibly boring. At the other end, he could accept the task and not work very hard at it, which could be put down to his recent illness. Dancing behind this was the easily imagined picture of Nolly's reaction to Gerald's request. A quick *yes, sir, be pleased to, sir*, and then Nolly'd be all elbows and arseholes, grateful for the chance to get filthy from head to toe for someone else's benefit.

But who was he, Jack Dawkins, to engage in manual labor for no pay? Yes, when he'd been in Port Jackson, he'd been forced to work, but since his return to England, all had been as it once was. He'd been the street thief, picking pockets, helping polish silver in preparation for melting or selling. While that had been work, Jack's portion of the payout had been fair and hadn't felt like work. More, it had been a taste of the old days, with the flavor of melted silver in the air, and the hard-born heat from the blazing coal required to melt it, making the cellar as warm as summer. But this? It was work fit for a servant, and that Jack most definitely was not.

Had Nolly been present, he most certainly would have given Jack a look to tell him that the polite thing to do was to take up the offer of work. And, in doing so, to repay the kindness of Mrs. Heyland. But while Jack knew what Nolly would do, Jack could not agree.

Mrs. Heyland had given them shelter, but she had plenty of it to give. Besides, her generosity was uneven; Nolly got the lion's share of charity and goodwill, while Jack had gotten hard looks and a turned shoulder. Not that he begrudged Nolly the wealth of the world, for Nolly deserved it. But he could be sometimes blind to the inequalities of the world when not directly confronted by them. And he did his best, did Nolly, to view the world as he thought it should be, with country fields, green grass, and the abundance of plenty for everyone.

Meanwhile, Gerald awaited an answer, it seemed. But then he shrugged.

"I beg your pardon. You've been ill; I shouldn't have asked it of you."

For a brief moment, Jack thought to correct Gerald and take up the work. Then he thought better of it.

"I am gettin' better," said Jack. "Besides, my head is thick from bein' indoors, so I'm in need of fresh air. Might be able to manage somethin' small."

"I got these nails," said Gerald, gesturing at the pile of metal on the table. "We tore down a shed and there were old pegs and different sizes and types of nails. Perhaps you might sort them."

To sit inside a warm, still barn on a damp, chilly day was a damn better prospect than lying abed. Besides, he'd learned one truth from Gerald, so there was no telling what else he might glean.

"You could sit on that stool while you do it," said Gerald as he pulled out a low, three-legged stool. "To conserve your strength."

"I don't mind if I do," said Jack. He doffed his jacket and laid it over the wooden edge of an empty stall. He could sort nails; it would tax him not at all, and besides, if he found tidbits of anything valuable, he could pocket those as easily as anything. So, pulling a handful of nails and the boxes toward him, Jack got to work.

While Jack sorted nails, the rain came and went, sometimes falling in sheets that skittered past the open door. Thus the air remained fresh in the barn, with the faint taste of old hay, corn for absent horses, and the sweet, dry barn dust on Jack's tongue. He took the time to stretch out on the hay in one of the empty, clean stalls and awoke with a horse blanket draped over him. He wasn't hungry for dinner and wasn't sorry he missed it, and, anyway, eating beneath the wasp-sting of the missus's gaze took the appetite right out of him. So absent direction from Gerald, Jack puttered around the barn and the yard, out in the fresh air, trying to think of what he'd say to Nolly when he came back from the village.

Late in the afternoon, a young boy came with a pony, and tied her up to one of the iron rings in the wall. He began to pull out a brush and a hoof pick, when Gerald called him over.

"This is Tim, our new stablehand; Tim, say hello to our visitor, Jack."

"Hello," said Tim.

"And this is Daisy, who Tim has brought to groom in our company, rather than all alone in the empty stables. Right, Tim?"

"Yes," said Tim.

"Daisy belongs to Sir John's youngest daughter, who's away with the rest of the family in Brighton, and Tim's been left in charge of her, and doing quite a good job, I'd say."

Jack nodded. He couldn't see the sense of brushing an animal that no one had ridden, any more than he could see the sense in washing one's hands every day. But young Tim seemed earnest in his task, using various brushes to make her coat sleek, with oil for her hooves, and all under the watchful eye of Gerald.

"She seems a bit fractious, Tim," said Gerald. "Why don't you take her for a walk around the orchard when you're finished there."

"Yes, sir," Tim said, nodding. Solemnly, as though pleased at the prospect of this simple task.

Jack was done with the nails, so when Tim took Daisy out into the courtyard on a lead, Jack got up and motioned to the boxes of nails.

"That's done, then," he said. "Going to stretch my legs." He wasn't asking permission, for only a servant did that, but it was companionable, he decided, to state his inclinations.

He put on his coat and wandered into the cobblestoned yard,

feeling fairly contented, in spite of the fact that he'd found nothing of value amidst the nails. The rain had let up, leaving damp and silvery-black puddles among the slick cobbles. The air outside the barn was fresh on his face.

"Have a care, Master Jack," said young Tim, "as them cobbles are wet."

He was leading Daisy around the large yard, his small hand firmly on the pony's lead as they walked.

"Ain't you supposed to be takin' her around the orchard?" Not that Jack cared, he was only making conversation.

"I will," said Tim, though he looked rather shy beneath the brim of his wool cap. "But I'm getting a bit of the spring out of her step, as she can go wild when she's on ground rather than cobblestones."

"You should give her a good long ride, that'll settle her." Not that Jack had overly much experience with riding, but he'd seen the marines ride, which wore out the horses and made them calm. And he'd groomed many a horse after a marine had ridden it, so he should know.

"Oh, I can't do that, Master Jack," said Tim. "As much as I'd like to." He took a moment to halt the pony as he petted her shiny neck with long, soft strokes. The animal leaned into the touch, and seemed contented to have him nearby.

"An' why-ever not?" Jack came up slowly, so as not to spook the pony, and reached past Tim to stroke her on the neck, near her ears, where the muscle was most solid.

Tim looked up at him, rosy-cheeked and bright-eyed, so sweet and young in that way that reminded Jack of Nolly in his more relaxed moments. But Timothy had the expression that seemed to indicate that Jack was quite daft for asking this.

"Why, this is the mistress's pony, and she's not to be ridden by a servant."

"Bollocks," said Jack. "I'll give you a leg up and I can lead you around the orchard. Nobody needs to know."

Jack could see that the boy was tempted, and surely the pony needed more exercise rather than less.

"C'mon then, here's a leg up for you." Lacing his rust-dusted fingers together, Jack nodded. "You'll be fine, I'll lead you."

Tim must have been starved for it, as he quickly gestured Jack closer so that he could use Jack's cupped hands as a stirrup to lift himself up and settle on the pony's bare back. The pony, rather than being fretful, tucked her head, as if she'd been wearing a proper bridle and was eagerly awaiting her rider's command.

"You've got the legs for this, I see," said Jack.

He gave Tim's laced boot a pat, then took up the pony's head and led her through the half-open gate and into the orchard. The pony reacted to the soft ground thick with winter-dead grass-growth and squelches of mud just as Tim had said she would. Her head flew up and her polished hooves lifted a bit higher than they had in the yard. But at Tim's low murmur, she quieted down, and Jack found her to be responsive and obedient.

He led her along the line of the hand-stacked stone wall, tugging on the leather lead every so often, but Daisy seemed to want to follow him naturally. Besides, a human boy that she knew was astride her; every so often she would turn to nuzzle at Tim's leg, and Jack marveled at the peacefulness of it. The damp air, the straight rows of apple trees almost tempted to bud as spring came. The soft breaths of the pony. The excited light in Tim's eyes.

They circled around the long slope of the orchard, never once catching a glimpse of Gerald. The third time they'd gone around, at the bottom of the orchard, Jack paused, to lift his hat and push the hair back from his forehead with his arm. He was a bit tired from the walking and the fresh air, but his mind felt clearer for the first time since they'd left London.

Tim looked at him, as if about to ask a question, but Jack waved him off.

"I reckon her nose is soft enough for a hack bridle," said Jack. "Seein' as how she doesn't get rode much."

"Do you reckon so?" asked Tim.

Jack unhooked the lead and looped it around the pony's neck into makeshift reins. Jack tugged on it to test it, and watched as the pony's neck bent down with the pressure. Then he handed the circle of the rein to Tim.

"You hold it like regular. See? Just guide her as you would a horse with a bit. I'll get you started."

Jack held the makeshift bridle, then slipped one hand down the lead, and patted the pony's shoulder. Tim shifted forward, tucking his knees up to the pony's withers, as if in preparation for a quick race up through the orchard.

But just as Jack was about to lead the pony on, his foot slipped in the mud, and a pair of winter-lean rabbits sprang out of a clump of dry grass. The pony shied, pushing Jack to the stone wall and tearing the reins from Jack's hand. With Tim just barely astride and starting to slip, Daisy bolted up the orchard, shattering the half-open gate, the planks splintering. Tim flew off to land, luckily, in the relatively soft mud, while Daisy slipped on the cobblestones. The lead, which had come undone, tangled about her near foreleg, and she went down on her elegant knees before scrambling up to stand trembling, her sides heaving, her mud-spattered mane hanging in her eyes. Head lowered, a soft whicker was her only complaint.

Aghast, Jack scrambled to his feet and ran to Tim, who was still trying to get up from the mud.

"Oh, Master Jack," said Tim, between his bloody nose and snuffles. "Is Daisy all right, did she get hurt, is she hurt?"

With a swift pull, Jack got Tim to his feet, giving him a once-over to be certain that the bloody nose was perhaps the worse of the bruises and bangs he had received.

"I'm not your master," said Jack, gruffly. "But here he comes, I reckon."

Gerald, shirt half undone, apron strings fluttering behind him, disturbed perhaps from an afternoon's snooze in the barn, went straight to Daisy. He went up to her, securing the lead in his hand before petting her neck, making soft *shhh shhh* noises to her as he rubbed her neck. Then, as slowly as he might, he bent forward to run his large hand carefully over each of her forelegs, then her back, her belly, her flanks, and then back up to her poll, talking to her the while until she stopped quivering.

"Tim," said Gerald, without looking over his shoulder, and Tim shuddered beneath Jack's hand and went white about the mouth.

Of course, it could have been worse, as Tim could have broken his neck, or the pony her leg. But it was bad enough, and Jack accompanied Tim as he walked the remainder of the way to the gate, his feet slopping in the mud, the squelching sound accompanied by rather piteous sniffing on Tim's part.

As they reached the point in the courtyard where Gerald and the pony were, Jack opened his mouth to explain. Not that he normally would; what happened was obvious, and even young stablehands might be expected to bear up to the consequences of a bolted pony. But this was on Jack, and surely the absent owners of said pony wouldn't begrudge a wee lad a ride.

"Hey, Mister Gerald, you mustn't be cross with Tim, for the idea to ride was mine," said Jack.

Jack made to pat Tim on the shoulder, but Gerald reached out to yank young Tim by the collar, glaring at Jack.

"You might have brought your city ways from London," said Gerald, "but we don't take kindly to it. Besides," he gave Tim a rough shake, "Tim knows better—*ought* to know better—than to dare ride his mistress's pony."

"He does, I'm sure he does," said Jack, and he reached for Tim just as Gerald pulled him out of range. "But I convinced him, I talked him into it."

"Are you not listening?" asked Gerald, rage glittering in his eyes. "Tim should know better, but the fact that you're trying to influence him, to make him accustomed to activities not suited to his station? All the defenses you might give me could not equal the pain you have given him; you've given him a taste of something that is not his to have. Do you understand what I'm saying? You've done him a worse disservice than if you'd not allowed him to ride the pony in the first place!"

Jack took a step back, his ears practically ringing, feeling a cool rush of fury along the sides of his face, an anger in his belly at what would forever be denied young Tim, that a simple ride on a fine pony should never be his.

But there was nothing to be said, as Gerald handed the pony's lead to Jack, as he tightened his grip on Tim's collar.

"Take her into the stables; her stall is at the far end, with rosettes and daises carved into the lintel. Slowly, mind. I'll check her over again, when I'm done with this."

This was Tim, who Gerald marched into the barn, casting aside his apron, and drawing off his belt. Jack went into the empty stable, as quickly as he could, to put the pony safely in her stall before he hurried out. But he hadn't gotten more than two steps when he heard the whipping in the barn begin, the hard slap of leather, and Tim's muffled whimpers.

The sound of it carried, circling around him; the injustice of it stung down to his very core. And then to make it worse, Nolly came striding into the yard. He looked less like a young man who'd been doing errands and more as though he'd been keelhauled. As Jack came face to face with the truth of Nolly's lie, Jack's simmering anger focused, and as Nolly's eyebrows came down, Jack's shoulders came up.

19

THE FIRST QUARREL

T he road to the manor was empty as Oliver walked along it, exhausted. The air was cold, but it was fresh, laced with evening cook-fires as the village sat at their suppers and drank their tea. His clothes were crusted with salt, and had dried in hard folds. He reeked of seaweed and blood.

In the fading light, he looked down at his hands. They were raw, the pads of his hands all blistered and laced with streaks of blood and grime. They were a working man's hands, and he'd done a full day's work. Not spent organizing shelves or carrying a basket of a woman's dainty luxuries, but from rough scrubbing, hauling, and bracing himself on his knees in a time-blackened barrel. What was he going to tell Jack about where he'd been?

His hands were sticky in spite of the quick wash he'd had in the basin of fresh water that one of the fisher-girls had brought him, and the message from Mr. Thurly and his desire for blackberry tarts from Mrs. Heyland rang in his ears. He passed the gatehouse, and took the narrow dirt lane that led around the back of the main house, where the stables and the yard were. As he came into the yard, he was distracted by harsh sounds coming from the barn, and by the sight of Jack, dressed in his own clothes, which were tattered but clean. He was staring at the barn, where the doors hung open.

As Oliver got closer, he could see that Jack was still pale, and wondered why Mrs. Heyland had seen fit to let Jack out of bed. Surely it was too soon?

But that question was soon squelched as from out of the stables came Gerald, with a folded leather belt in one hand, and a reluctant Tim in the other. Tim was crying, silently, wiping his face in the crook of his sleeve, tripping as he attempted to keep up with Gerald's long strides. Gerald took Tim in through the back door, and into the kitchen.

"What has happened?" asked Oliver.

Jack turned to him, a little wide-eyed, and bareheaded even though it was starting to drizzle.

"Nolly."

"And what was that?" Oliver gestured to the barn and then to the house. "And why are you out?"

"You're cross today," said Jack, taking a step back.

Keeping a rein on his temper, Oliver nodded. "I only want to know why you are out of doors? You shouldn't be."

"Well," said Jack. He looked as though he wanted to touch Oliver's arm.

"Do tell me, Jack, so that we can go in—"

"You look a fright, Nolly," said Jack, tipping his head to one side. "Were you in a fight? It looks like you was."

"*Jack.*"

"I might have upset the maids a bit, an' been a bit rude to Mrs. Heyland. An' then I encouraged Tim to ride the pony instead of just leadin' her, an' then—"

"I should not have left you alone." Oliver's jaw tightened. "Of course you can't be trusted to behave one single moment while out of my sight."

"What are you on about? I was perfectly well behaved, it was just that things didn't turn out like I expected."

"It's not enough, Jack, it's not enough. What if she kicks us out, and you still ill? Where will we go then? I owe her money, and as you so blithely pointed out, we can't live under a hedge, not in this weather!" Oliver's breath came hard. He kept his fists clenched at his sides, which made them throb as hard as his heart was beating. He'd had the worst day he could ever imagine, and he would have to go through it again tomorrow. And all the while, Jack insisted on stirring up trouble.

"We could just leave, you know," said Jack. "I'm well enough, an' they won't be able to follow us. We can dodge the debt easy."

"No." Oliver attempted to take a deep breath but it just made him feel shaky. "We must stay here until the letter comes."

"What letter?"

"The letter I *told* you about. The parson is writing to the church in Barnet, to inquire after your family. I told you about this."

"And I told *you* I wanted no part of that."

If Jack meant to walk off, then Oliver would stop him. He grabbed hold of Jack's arm, and held it tight. "Of course you want to find your family, to know where you come from. Don't you?"

"You're the one who wants to find my family, not me. An' besides, who said you were in charge of me? Takin' the master and servant lie a bit too far, I'd say, makin' plans when I've said no."

"Jack—"

"Never you mind tryin' to sweet-talk me into it, neither. If that letter comes, I'll rip it up, d'you hear?"

There was no denying that Jack meant what he said. He barely seemed to notice that he was shivering in the cool, damp air as it began to rain again, but if he caught another chill, it was not for certain that beef broth and willow bark tea would cure him. There was no way Jack could stand being ill again, and no way that Oliver could bear watching him suffer.

The moment arced between them, almost like a visible thing, sharp, stabbing straight through Oliver's heart. But before he could say anything to convince Jack or apologize to him, he didn't know which, Mrs. Heyland came to the door.

"You've come late to supper, and I've a mind to tell you to give your manservant a good thrashing. Do you know the trouble he's caused today?"

For a moment Oliver could only gawp at her, was amazed that she would shout at him as though she were a fishwife.

"Mrs. Heyland—" he began, but she raised a finger at him and shook it.

"He scared the maid, Gussie, into shattering crockery, and who is going to pay for that, I ask you? And he was rude to me, with all his filthy words. Then he earned Tim a sound beating; the poor lad's got a heart of gold and wouldn't have gone wrong except for *him*." Now she pointed at Jack, and her scowl darkened. "Where you found this bit of rough trade I'll never know; it breaks my heart to see you putting up with it."

Jack moved slowly closer to him, and Oliver had the sense that he meant to make a dash for it if Mrs. Heyland came any closer.

"I've half a mind to throw you both out, and would, too, if it weren't for the parson reminding me of my Christian duty."

"I'm sorry," said Oliver, and he couldn't imagine what else he might say to her. Besides, there was no way he was going to continue his quarrel with Jack in front of Mrs. Heyland, and, frankly, the idea of arguing with Jack at *all* was making his stomach twist. "Truly, I'm sorry, I'm just finding our current situation to be a bit daunting."

This seemed to stop her from being angry, as she looked at him, then at Jack, and then back at him again.

"Never mind it now," she said. "Come in now; the rain's starting up again, and I don't want it on the floor and soaking the mats."

Oliver nodded at Jack, and followed her into the house, hanging up their jackets and Oliver's hat on the hooks by the door.

"You're as wet as hunting dogs," she said, as she began to fuss at the stove. "Go and wash so you don't hold supper up any further."

Housekeepers, it turned out, were cut from the same basic cloth. Mrs. Heyland didn't *tutt* nor *tsk*, but she gave an astonished scoff, which served just about the same purpose, and pointed at the basin of water, where Gussie was pouring warm water from a pitcher. And while it wasn't scented, it was hot; steam wafted up from it in tempting grey curls.

With a deep sigh, one he'd been holding back all day, Oliver went to the basin waiting on a stand with white soap and a pale brown towel. He rolled up his sleeves, and set his hands in the bottom of the basin, the water up to his wrists as it stung in his open blisters. He felt his palms throbbing. His shoulders throbbed too, and his legs and hips, muscles jittering as if they'd only just realized they could stop. He closed his eyes for a moment, and then sighed. It was good to be warm and dry.

He washed his hands, even though they stung, and the back of his neck, and his face till he'd got the salt off. When he was drying his hands, he looked up, finally focusing, to see Jack staring at him.

"Was it terribly dirty guttin' fish?" asked Jack, with some ire in his voice, eyes glittering. "I'll wager you were as fussy as a miss about it, all that blood and the guts spillin' out all over."

"It was better than sitting around all day, scaring the maidservants," Oliver snapped, though he kept his voice low so that no one else could hear. He wasn't actually surprised that Jack had found out, and was rather relieved that his current occupation was in the open. "Now, wash your hands, and don't make any more trouble."

Jack barely washed the tips of his fingers, preferring to wipe his hands on his trousers. Which nobody saw, because everyone was purposefully not looking at Jack.

Mrs. Heyland came up with some folded clothes, and put them on the stand next to the basin.

"Those are for tomorrow, Master Oliver, so give me those salty ones tonight and I'll wash them." She said this with clipped tones, but she didn't seem angry, just in a hurry, with much to do, and then she went back to the stove.

By the time Jack was finished splashing about, everyone was seated at the table, the three maidservants on one side, Mrs. Heyland at the end, and Gerald and Tim on the other side. There were two seats next to Tim, so Oliver led Jack to sit down there, bowing their heads through prayers, with Oliver saying a prayer of his own that Jack's table manners would have improved since they'd last eaten together.

As they sat down to supper, Jack made sure to sit in the chair next to Nolly, so that he would not have to look at the simmering fury in Nolly's eyes. Nor would he have to school his own features as carefully, since none of the country dolts around the table would be able to discern Jack's thoughts in the slightest. But Nolly might, if he could see Jack's expression, hence his choice of seat.

It was all new, Nolly and him, out in the world. The tenseness between them in the yard, Nolly's anger at Jack's behavior, Jack's sense of betrayal at Nolly's lies, and the letter sent without his permission—Jack had no idea what to think. It was all too domestic complicated.

Though now that he thought of it, Bill and Nancy had quarreled several times a week. So had Fagin and Bill. Frankly, Bill had quarrels with almost everyone. Only among Fagin's boys had there been a sense of order and peace, the unspoken laws of the pack: who slept where, who determined which street they would work, how much they would hold back when handing over the goods to Fagin. All of this lay beneath each boy's skin like a tribal mark, an agreement to which demonstrated by their complicit obedience.

But with Nolly, it was coming to light that the balance between them would be more of a struggle than Jack had heretofore encountered. It was not right for Nolly to have purposefully kept so small a thing as gutting fish from Jack. They needed to have truth between them. And if that was not the route to go, and Jack knew of no other, then indeed it might be that he and Nolly would quarrel like Bill and Nancy had, and maybe they would come to blows. Jack hoped not, but how else to clear the air?

Jack copied everyone around him and bent his head to listen to

Mrs. Heyland's quick mumble of grace. The supper was certainly not what Jack would have expected of such a great house, with everything looking like it had been boiled without enough salt. That being said, Jack took whatever food was passed to him, and put it on his plate; cold ham, braised celery, boiled potatoes. Then he began eating, only faintly conscious of the looks he was getting from around the table, until Nolly gave him a rude elbow to his ribs.

Except instead of making him care, this made him care less. He could so very easily march into the center of the village, pick some pockets, and quickly have the money to buy himself a supper much more desirable than this, and the devil take the hindmost. Nolly might be Jack's mate, but he was not his master, no matter what had been said to Mrs. Heyland upon their arrival. So Jack gave his table manners a push in the direction that he knew they ought *not* to go.

While everyone else held their knife and fork properly, Jack plunked his elbows on the table and, holding the fork in his fist, speared a potato and shoved the whole thing in his mouth. Mrs. Heyland's eyebrows went up, but she managed to restrain herself and instead of scolding, began to pass around brown bread, sliced on a platter.

"You do have an appetite, Master Oliver," said Mrs. Heyland. "But that's to be expected, all that fresh sea air."

If this was meant to be a veiled hint that Jack was practically invisible, it was not going to work. Jack let out a brassy belch, and didn't even cover his mouth for it.

"Jack," said Nolly. He gave Jack another dig in the ribs with his elbow. "We're in company now, and not on the road, so perhaps better table manners might be more appropriate."

Mid-chew, Jack looked at Nolly and the gawping faces of the maidservants. With his mouth full of food, he said, "You mean we ain't still livin' in a barn, then? I quite forgot." Then, as if the idea had been all his own, with great dignity, he took his elbows off the table, and picked up his knife in his other hand to cut the next potato into smaller pieces. Albeit still huge pieces, but smaller than the first one.

Mrs. Heyland coughed out loud to alert the maidservants that they'd best tend to their own meals, but this relaxed no one, and the meal continued in a pained silence. She couldn't throw out Jack without throwing out his *master*, so they would be allowed to stay, in spite of her wanting them elsewhere.

In the silence of the warm kitchen, Jack watched as the housekeeper gave young Tim an extra spoonful of rice pudding. The issue of the pony might not be brought up at supper, but Jack supposed that Nolly would call him to task for it. That would be playing the master a bit too freely, thinking that he ought to be in charge of Jack, to make sure that Jack fit in. And if Jack fit in, then was he still Jack? Or was he someone else?

But the question couldn't be answered in the kitchen, so Jack stood up, scraping his chair across the stone floor, and shoved his plate away. He dusted his hands over his plate in a mockery of wiping them on his napkin, and sighed, as if well contented, as he'd often done at the Three Cripples. He knew his manners were those of a sailor, but he couldn't sit here and be shamed by their silence, as if he should squirm under their recrimination.

Jack looked at the oh-so-politely attentive table. Nolly was laying his cutlery across his plate and taking a last daub with his hands with the napkin before folding it on the table.

"You should take him out to the barn and give him a good thrashing," said Mrs. Heyland, hissed to Nolly in a way that took Jack quite aback. "And then have him tend to your person and your clothes, as a good manservant should."

"I believe we will go and have a chat, Jack and I," said Nolly, with a little bow at the table.

"There's no light out there, like there is in the city," said Gerald unexpectedly. "Will you take the candle-lantern by the door?"

"I might, if I may," said Nolly, seemingly unsurprised by the offer. He stood as calmly, as if he'd been in church, and seemed not at all concerned that Mrs. Heyland had suggested that he actually *beat* Jack. "Thank you for the good meal, Mrs. Heyland, and for tending to my clothes. I'll appreciate them in the morning, I'm sure."

Everyone said a vague goodnight. Jack could sense their disappointment that Nolly would not administer the beating in their midst, but evidently, Nolly had other plans, though Jack could not imagine that Nolly thought he actually *deserved* whipping.

"Goodnight," Nolly said.

"'Till the mornin','" said Jack, making himself follow Nolly to the door without saying anything else that would set Mrs. Heyland off. Not that she didn't deserve it, oh no.

And when Nolly walked to the door, stopping to take down the candle-lantern and light it, Jack was close behind.

Jack donned his coat and, taking the candle-lantern from Nolly, stepped out into the yard. The air was brisk, moving about, and damp upon the stones as a matter of course, though it was not raining. As he crossed the yard, the light from the candle-lantern cast long, oval circles on the dark ground. Jack felt Nolly come up to walk beside him, their shoulders almost touching as they approached the barn door.

Jack made to shift the candle-lantern to his other hand, when Nolly stepped up to undo the latch.

"I'll get it," said Nolly.

He did not look at Jack as he moved beyond the circle of light into the darkness of the quiet barn, with its dry smell of hay, dusty with a bit of something green beneath. The table next to the stacks of hay bales and straw bales had been cleared of the boxes of nails so Jack put the candle-lantern there, and watched while the candlelight jumped and then settled. He was as solicitous of the danger of fire in such a place as anybody might be. But he was even more conscious of Nolly standing just outside the pale circle of light, could sense the tenseness that ran through him. Which made Jack feel somewhat more at ease, since it appeared that Nolly did not know what to do either.

"So," said Jack. He kept himself quite still so as to see which way Nolly might jump.

Naturally, Nolly jumped right into it.

"What were you thinking, Jack?" asked Nolly. It was a demand more than a question. "Letting a stable boy ride a lady's pony?"

"What of it?" asked Jack. "A cat may look at a king, after all." It was something Fagin had said to the boys, when encouraging them to go after the plushest swells.

"Whatever are you on about?" Now Nolly strode into the light, which cast his hair into burnished gold. He moved as if he were stepping onto a stage where his word, and only that, would hold sway. "That has nothing to do with this, nothing at all."

"He was sloggin' about, the wee thing, to give the pony some exercise, so he might as well have been astride her."

"But he's a servant."

"He tends to that animal every day, why shouldn't he ride her?" asked Jack. He understood the issue at hand, though for all of Nolly's championing Martin, Nolly seemed unaware that this was the same. Not that Jack generally spent any time in the struggle of the oppressed against the oppressor, seeing as how it was easier to slide through that particular fence than to break it down.

"Because he's a *servant!*"

There was a strident tone in Nolly's voice that Jack took to mean that Nolly intended not only to make him understand, but to make him agree as well. Well, Jack did understand but he could not agree, no, he could not. Nolly's view on how these things worked was based, it seemed, upon how he felt he fit inside of it. Jack, on the other hand, fit nowhere at the best of times and so did not need to fit at all. And this he needed to make Nolly understand.

"That's up to you," said Jack. "But it's not how I see it, nor will I ever."

"But he got a whipping because of it." Nolly scowled hard, looking desperately unhappy about it. The boy, Timothy, had received a thrashing of ten strokes at most and had shown no fear of Gerard at the supper table; the matter seemed resolved between them. But for Nolly, the shame of it lingered.

"An' the whippin' is done with," countered Jack. He settled himself along the edge of the table, crossing his arms over his chest.

The candlelight flickered, and Jack caught a glimpse of the distress on Nolly's face, the furl of his brow, the sad downward tilt to his eyes. It became apparent to Jack, in some wordless way, that if Jack was unwilling to take responsibility for the ill-used stable boy, then Nolly would. Because that was how he was. If he was quick to point the finger of blame at Jack, then he would be even quicker to lay blame upon himself. Someone must do it, after all, at least in Nolly's world.

Well, not in Jack's, and Jack found himself unwilling to let Nolly pound himself into the ground for something like this.

"I did not imagine it would occasion as it had," said Jack, relaxing his arms, though still holding them across his chest. "I was plannin' on assistin' him to the ground before much longer. Only the pony bolted, y'see."

Jack waited a moment, sensing Nolly's indrawn breath and expecting another scolding, and was surprised to see Nolly nod his head. Jack's explanation had served as an apology, which Nolly had accepted. However, Jack was not about to let the other matter slide.

"Though I might consider giving a stable boy a ride on a lady's pony somewhat less offensive than you lyin' to me."

"Lying?" asked Nolly, but he was a terrible liar; his face went tight and he took a step backwards, because he knew exactly what lie Jack was talking about. And while Jack almost felt, almost, bad enough to let up, he was equally surprised that Nolly had not clenched his fists and come out swinging. Jack had seen that flash-paper temper and what being on the wrong end of it could bring.

"You lied where you were today. If we're sweethearts, we shouldn't lie to each other. But you did when you didn't have to." Jack's heart sped up a little as he said this.

All the pride and strength that Nolly always carried in his shoulders left him.

"Was it on account of the doctor's bill, bein' at three and six three times over?" Jack got up from the table and dropped his arms to his side. "Or was it because guttin' fish is beneath you an' you didn't want me to know?"

Nolly didn't even ask how Jack knew; it must have been obvious that the servants had talked, though Jack had a sudden glimpse of the events in a way he'd not examined them before. Nolly had been confronted by his fear that Jack might die, and then had been presented with a bill for an amount that he simply did not have. And all the while Jack had lain unconscious in bed, likely to expire at any moment.

"I was so worried," said Nolly, softly, looking at the ground between them, as if almost afraid to admit it again, as if that would occasion the fear to arise once more. He scrubbed at his temple with his thumb. "I was worried enough for both of us, and could not task you with the bill, not when you were so ill."

"You could have mentioned it when the doctor declared I was on the mend, night before last. Or yesterday. Or this morning. You mentioned that letter easy enough, eh?"

As Jack took a step forward into the midst of the candlelight, Nolly stumbled back, tripping his heel on something in the near dark. He flayed at the air before tumbling back on a single bale of hay that stuck out from the others. A cloud of sharp dust plumed into the light as he landed, a slight fall of green-tinted rain.

Oh, but now Nolly was distracted, brought low by a hillock on the floor of the barn. And, seated, he looked up as Jack came closer. Jack could not begrudge any of this, if only Nolly would stop looking so ashamed of himself. For there was no shame in taking care of a friend, only in the lie.

"You should not have lied to me," Jack said, standing squarely in front of Nolly. His body blocked the light somewhat, but the flare of temper in Nolly's eyes was clear enough.

"But thieves lie all the time!" Nolly's voice rose, becoming strident again.

"Not to each other," said Jack. "Leastways if they do, it's for a rightful purpose. But I don't want it—" Jack reached out to touch Nolly—somewhere, *anywhere*—but pulled back at the last moment, almost shivering at the thickness in his throat. But if this was how it was done, then this was how he would do it. "Not between me an' thee, Nolly."

Nolly tipped his head down, his face obscured, disconcertingly unaware that Jack, too, had lied. When they'd been in London, about where Jack had been, what he'd thieved or traded, because it would have alarmed Nolly to the point of abandoning Jack to the Three Cripples, leaving Jack Nolly-less to the end of his days. But that had been before; Jack knew it was different between them now, it felt different. He could not have put words to it to explain exactly how, but he felt it. So he reached out to curve his fingers along the strands of Nolly's hair, behind his ear, wanting Nolly to look up.

"I only meant to spare you," said Nolly, low.

"I reckon I knows that," said Jack, in return.

Nolly pressed his head briefly into Jack's hand, and Jack realized that they were too far away in sensibility on account of something foolish that didn't matter anyway. So he moved quickly and straddled Nolly's thighs with his own, catching his arms around Nolly's shoulders so he wouldn't tumble back in surprise. But he was surprised, tilting his head back to look up at Jack, eyes wide, mouth a little open, as Jack's jacket settled around them both, like a rough cape, capturing their warmth, their bodies, together in a hidden hollow, a deeper shadow, in the barn.

"Jack?" he asked.

Jack laughed a little and smoothed Nolly's hair, feeling a touch of coarseness that must have come from so many hours in the salt air.

"This is what comes after a quarrel between sweethearts, you see," said Jack. "A spat is always mended by a kiss."

Jack curled forward to kiss Nolly on the mouth, tasting the salt from the sea that supper and a cloth napkin hadn't quite erased, enjoying the softness of those ashen-rose lips, feeling a little daring as he did so. And pleased, a rush of warmth going through him, when Nolly didn't pull away, but indeed pushed forward, touching Jack in return, his hands smoothing up Jack's thighs to settle on his hips. The near-darkness of the barn, like a large private sleeping chamber, seemed to ease Nolly as a tot of gin might have, and Jack stored fact this away, as he might have need of it later.

Yet Jack wanted to be sure, so he shifted back, settling his backside more solidly on Nolly's thighs, to check. To glean the expression in Nolly's face, that he was as relaxed and calmed from his earlier temper, as he seemed to be. And while Jack looked, he ran his hands down Nolly's shoulders to his arms. The cloth was rough now, though it had been soft only that morning. Speckled with points almost and stiff at the folds.

"What ails your shirt, Nolly?" Jack asked. He tested a fold of it between his finger and thumb, as if he might consider its purchase. "Why did the missus give you a new set of clothes, then? And why the talk of me doin' what a manservant should?"

"Oh," said Nolly, and there was a flicker of a lie in his voice that, to Jack's gratitude, died unborn. "Someone shoved me into the sea. A prank of sorts, I imagine, on my first day. They fished me out in a little dory, and afterwards the fellows were more accommodating."

Either Nolly was unaware, or was choosing to be unaware, that a rescue at sea that required a boat, even a small one, was more than a mere initiation. Jack smoothed his hand along the side of Nolly's face, enjoying the warmth growing between them, the long line where their bodies met. The small sigh from Nolly that he seemed completely unaware of.

"I shall sign up for work with you tomorrow," Jack said. "And I will spot this hooligan who dared to lay hands upon you, my very own."

He lighted a kiss, an innocent one, upon Nolly's forehead, and was pleased, as he pulled back again, to see the corner of Nolly's mouth curl up in a smile. So indeed, it seemed for all that Nolly enjoyed the role of hero, he was not above a little rescuing himself. What stories abounded in Nolly's head; if Jack had known this, back on that Barnet high street of long ago, then he could have made a better story of it to tempt wee Nolly whose recruitment might not have ended so disastrously. Still, that was neither here nor there, what mattered now was teaching Nolly the right of it. That he was no longer on his own. As Jack would no longer be, once Nolly knew it in his heart.

As Nolly shifted beneath him, Jack had a new thought.

"Ain't them clothes chafin' you, all dried with salt?"

"A little," said Nolly. "It wasn't so bad until they really dried."

But Jack knew it had to be more than a little. He'd been at sea and knew the abrasive nature of saltwater, how cloth chafed when dried with it. It was especially horrid at the bends of the knees, the waist, the neckline, where it left red patches that almost would not heal, unless one was prepared to go buck naked and could bathe in cool, fresh water.

Well Jack could make that happen, at least in part. He slid back to swing up from Nolly's lap, to stand and pull him to his feet.

"Come along, you gutter-and-packer-of-fish, for as your obedient manservant, I've a mind to give you a dousin' with fresh water. It'll mean doin' as I say, so none of your objections. You've been workin' and toilin', all elbows an' arseholes, so it's my turn now."

Without allowing Nolly to object, Jack picked up the lantern and tugged Nolly out of the barn. Pausing while Nolly latched the barn door, Jack led the way across the yard to the house. The night had grown blustery, the rain spattering down in waves, and Jack imagined the clouds closing over the stars, the rounded grey folds locking out the light, replacing star-glimmer with slivers of rain.

Once inside, they blew out the candle-lantern and replaced it on the hook, and doffed their jackets. Jack looked at the three maids, who sat around the table engaged in various employments, sewing and knitting, as women did, at the cleared and scrubbed table with the kettle on the stove steaming gently away.

"Where's the missus?" he asked, grabbing the clothes she'd laid out for Nolly. They were thick and well made, able to take the weather, as the first set had been.

"In the housekeeper's room," said the dark-haired one, the bold beauty that she was, daring to speak to such as him. He gave her a smile as a reward, and went over to the door to the housekeeper's room and knocked, conscious of Nolly, the entire time, watching him as though he were a story unfolding right there in front of him.

In an instant, she opened the door, ready to be affronted at his boldness, the edges of her cap fluttering.

"Mrs. Heyland, I'm goin' to borrow some fresh water from the laundry, like you told me." He said this as sweetly as he could. "'Tis for Master Oliver, on account of he's taken a dunk in the ocean and his clothes is all salt. I'll take care of them so you don't have to."

Her face made amusing contortions, but Jack did not let himself laugh, even though he knew she could not refuse him. Not with so many witnesses.

"You may," she said, dignified as a queen. "But make the laundry tidy after, for I'll not be having you give my girls extra work."

To keep everything moving, as it should, toward Nolly's comfort and ease, Jack only nodded.

"Yes, missus," he said, and before she could close the door, Jack was through the kitchen, past the maids, dragging Nolly with him, down the passage and to the laundry at the end.

At the door to the laundry, beyond which waited the promised water, Nolly stopped, half-turning toward Jack but not looking at him, his hand on the china knob. Jack could feel it before he realized it the way Nolly tried to pull back. The way his shoulders and the line of his back was so stiff, his discomfort vibrating like an over-plucked string.

"I don't need any assistance washing, Jack, truly I don't. I'm quite capable."

It took Jack a moment, a flicker, as Nolly looked back up the passageway, where the soft after-supper activity could still be heard, and the way Nolly was specifically not looking at him. The way his shoulders curved forward, with a lack of grace and something high-strung, uncomfortable. Jack couldn't understand what the problem was, only that Nolly didn't like it, wasn't warming up to the idea.

When Jack opened the door, he found a low-ceilinged room with a copper boiler over a squat stove, a deal table along the far wall, with slatted buckets beneath, and a wooden shelf with stacks of wash basins that looked ready to topple over, as well as several low-sided pans. The room had matches stacked in a box on the shelf and several blue and white china candlesticks with stubs of beeswax candles in them; Jack lit them all, and placed them on the deal table, and hang the expense.

Candlelight reflected on the pale-blue whitewashed walls, and the lack of windows made it seem like a sea grotto, cozy in spite of the slight damp, the still, cool air. There were two buckets of water by the boiler, from which a little bit of steam rose. Behind him Nolly was following close at Jack's heels and silent at Jack's extravagant use of candles.

"It'll be mostly cold," Jack said, as he grabbed an empty bucket and started pumping water into it. The pump squeaked the first few pumps, but soon was pulling up water and splashing it into the bucket. "But it'll be better than sleeping in salt."

"Jack, you shouldn't bother," said Nolly.

Jack paused to pour the full bucket of cool water into one of the ones with warm water one to look at Nolly.

"While I imagine you looked rakishly handsome whilst guttin' fish," Jack began, "you can't go to bed like a salted mackerel." At Nolly's furrowed brow, he went on. "You're crusted w'salt, an' I aim to make it better."

To emphasize that he meant business, Jack unbuttoned his own waistcoat, and draped it over the end of the table. Then he rolled up his shirt sleeves.

"You'll get washed, an' I'll dress you in the clean shirt that the missus gave you. We'll sneak you down the passage, it's not far, no one will see." Belatedly, Jack reached out with his foot and kicked the door shut. "An' I'll rinse out your salty clothes to help the missus."

As Nolly began unbuttoning his shirt buttons, he said, "You're not my manservant, Jack." This in low tones, as if in apology.

"Long as you know it," said Jack, mentally counting the buckets, eyeing the ones that were filled with warmer water. "Besides, it ain't any different than what I did when I was hextricated."

"How do you mean?" Nolly slid off his shirt, and Jack took it to the table, and took a basin and filled it with water from the bucket of cold water. He began soaking the shirt, pushing the thick cloth to the bottom of the basin with his fingers, then swirled the it around for a moment, before letting it settle.

"I used to fetch an' carry for the marines at the barracks in Port Jackson," Jack said, though the memory of those days gave him some troubles, enough so that he instantly regretted having brought it up. For Nolly was sure to inquire about it.

"Like a real manservant, you mean," Nolly said as he crouched down to unlace his boots. His tone sounded a bit teasing, so Jack answered in turn.

"Like a houseboy."

This earned him a laugh, and though Nolly might ask more about it later, Jack sensed the subject was dropped for now. Thus he could concentrate on giving Nolly's shirt another swirl in the basin, and the stockings that were added to the same basin. As Jack wiped his hands on his trousers, Nolly merely stood there, shirtless, stockingless.

"How am I to bathe, then?" Nolly asked, his fingers worrying the tabs at his trouser waist, his loose suspenders hanging to his thighs. "With no tub?"

Now Jack could clearly see the chafe marks at Nolly's neck and wrists, the speckled red lines along all the delicate places, the curve of his elbow, the tops of his shoulders. So many places; it made Jack want to haul up the bloody lunatic who'd done this and give him a taste of his own foolishness.

"You stand in this, you see." Jack pulled out one of the low-sided pans, and set it on the stone floor in front of Nolly's cold-curled toes. "An' I scrub you down. You'll sleep easier for it, I promise."

"You just want to see me in the altogether," said Nolly, balking, as if fighting the deep pink flush that was spreading up his neck to his face.

"Of course." Jack let himself smile. "Chance found to get my hands on you, my bright jewel? Couldn't bear passin' it up."

"There's no hot water; I'll be cold."

This insistence was accompanied by a quick frown that reminded Jack, as if he needed reminding, that however Nolly might be willing to kill a man with a cleaver, or work for hours up to his elbows in fish blood with a pack of rough, strange men, his sensibilities were too finely spun to easily admit the touch of cold water to wash his skin.

"I've mixed the warm with the cold so it won't be so bad. An' I'll be quick," Jack said. "'Tis a promise, now, come on. You're exhausted, an' my headache's comin' on."

This was true, and it seemed to be the key to Nolly's continued obedience. So when Nolly wiggled out of his trousers and under-drawers, Jack took the garments and tried not to stare as he dumped them in the washing basin. However, even if Jack's eyes had been nailed shut and his neck clamped in a vise causing him to look the other way, he still would not have failed to see what was before him.

There was a slight, jerky rhythm to Nolly's ribs, as he seemed to struggle to prepare himself for some horrible fate. Then Jack realized that the staring wasn't the only issue with Nolly. The issue was that Nolly'd stepped into the metal circle of a bathing pan, and

Jack, not also naked, had a bucket of barely warm water in his hands.

So Jack put the bucket down and stepped close, his booted toes banging the side of the pan. He put his hands on Nolly's neck and leaned in close to give him a quick kiss on the nose.

"You feel my hands? All cool and sweet from the water? That is how you will feel all over when I'm done. I've been to sea, Nolly. I know what it feels like."

With a quick swipe of his thumb along Nolly's jaw, Jack stepped back and gave a little laugh.

"You're brave as a lion when faced with a man who could kill you, but a little cold water?"

Jack bent to gather a soft cloth and soaked it in the bucket of water, shaking his head as if in dismay. He straightened up, the dripping cloth in his hand and let his eyes linger.

Over the curls on Nolly's head, growing out from the crop Jack had given him, the blushing sweet rose of his jaw, the slope of Nolly's neck. And then Jack let his eyes catch the bullet scar, half a palm in length, but narrow, of pulled flesh, just above the elbow. The slope of Nolly's waist, into his hips and the plush of dark-gold private hair between his legs, the nest upon which his cock lay, the now-soft skin pale in the candlelight.

For a long moment, Nolly had turned his head away, looking at the wall, looking at nothing, letting Jack look. But as he sensed Jack's eyes moving lower down his body, he jerked his hand in front of himself, to hide his cock, his private hair, and perhaps the rush of dark blood that was causing it to stiffen.

"Nolly," said Jack, and as he reached out to touch, Nolly's whole body bowed away like a hand-shy hound.

Jack finally understood. It was the idea of Jack touching Nolly here in this house. A sweet kiss here or there was one thing, but they were alone in a room together, and one of them was naked, while the servants, only a few feet away, were aware of this. That was what was bothering Nolly, that awareness. And while the servants would, in Jack's opinion, think only the obvious, in Nolly's mind, that intimacy, innocent in many forms, would be turned inside out. Jack was well and Nolly was naked, and it had all come down to this moment: Nolly thought that Jack would press him for more than a kiss. Or at least it seemed that way.

Of course Jack would have enjoyed this in a different way, had Nolly been willing. But he so obviously was not, and nothing on earth could induce Jack to force Nolly, not into anything, not when he was neither ready nor willing. Jack knew directly what it was like to be on the other end of that, when passion and power came together to overcome any resistance, with no heed to whether or not there was reflected desire, or fear, or—no, Jack would never do that to Nolly. Never.

The question now was how to make Nolly certain of this so that the fine tremors in his hand would stop.

"Nolly," said Jack, and Nolly reacted as if Jack had actually touched him. He shifted his whole body, his back to the wall, facing Jack head on, as if Jack had suddenly walked in on him disrobing, rather than having been there the whole time. Nolly's world had taught him many things, but this shame was not useful, not with Jack. It was ugly when Nolly was so beautiful, and Jack wanted only to look, and would touch only with permission. And he needed to make Nolly aware of this.

"Nolly," said Jack again, staying right where he was. "I'm only goin' to help you, an' I ain't goin' to do nothin' you don't want me to. You know that, don't you?"

Nolly's eyes flicked to the door, a rush of color coming to his face, and his shame made itself plain.

"I know it, Jack, I do, but with them just down the passage, I can *hear* them—"

Scrubbing at his forehead, the dampness of the room making Nolly's hair stick up in awkward places, making Nolly resemble a young duckling, but Jack couldn't laugh at him; mocking Nolly when he was so serious would be a cruel thing to do. Later, yes, this could be grounds for teasing, but not now.

"No," said Jack. "There's no need for shame, not between you an' me." He moved close and took Nolly's free hand in his and did not remove Nolly's hand from where he hid himself.

"It feels strange," said Nolly. "Having you look at me like that. With all these candles. Wouldn't it make you feel strange? Or do street thieves commonly go about in a state of nature?"

This last was said in clipped tones; Nolly was agitated and trying to hide it. But Jack ducked his head, not wanting to remember those times, the first time on board ship when he'd had to take off his clothes for the ship's doctor, and then casually, on the decks when the rain came, when they used it to rinse the salt off their skins. It had been strange, but by the time they'd reached Australia, it hadn't been strange anymore. Then at the farm, and then at the barracks—well, that was different. Jack made himself stop thinking about it, and wetting the flannel cloth, he began washing Nolly's hand and arm, moving calmly, using sure strokes.

"I might, an' I might not, dependin'," Jack allowed. "An' if it does you, it does, so you keep your hand there, if it suits you, an' I won't mock you for it."

At this Nolly gave a slight shiver, and tried to move his hand away, but he couldn't manage it. So Jack worked around it, sluicing and washing parts of Nolly that perhaps weren't so sensitive to being bare, and all the while Jack felt a pang of sympathy in his heart. It was enough that Nolly trusted him this far; Jack made his expression businesslike as he washed Nolly all over, from the damp curls at the back of his head, low on his skull, to the sculpted length of his ankles, taking the salt away and leaving smooth skin that he wanted to kiss all over but didn't.

Then, taking the very wet flannel cloth, he dipped it in the warmer water and wrung it out to wash the breadth of Nolly's shoulders, the trim curve of his waist, his round backside, and those long legs. Finally, he eased Nolly's hand away and washed him, down his front and between his thighs, being gentle always, and giving Nolly a quick smile when he caught Nolly peeking from behind his half-closed lashes.

When he was done, Jack gave one final rinse, tipping an entire bucket of warm water over Nolly's head, watching the blush of Nolly's skin climb and fade, and the muscles in Nolly's neck ease as Jack put the bucket down and buffed Nolly all over with a towel. And at last, Jack picked up the new shirt and dressed Nolly in it. And was gratified to see Nolly's eyes close as he wrapped his newly clothed arms around himself and bent his head to bury his nose in a fold of the shirt.

Then he opened his eyes and looked at Jack, eyes almost blazing, like a blue-hot coal fire.

"Thank you," Nolly said. His voice was low and solemn and deep, and it made Jack blink.

"You're most welcome," said Jack, and it took everything he could not to roll himself in Nolly's arms and beg him to speak in that way again. Instead he concentrated on rinsing out Nolly's clothing, wringing each item with his hands before he laid it out on a wooden rack near the wall. They dripped a bit, but better here than in the sickroom.

"Grab those boots of yours," Jack said, picking up the rest of the new clothes from Mrs. Heyland, and grabbing one of the candlesticks. "And don't worry, I'll guard the way."

For if Nolly hated cold water, it would be even worse to be seen walking down the passage dressed only in a shirt. But as Jack opened the door, swinging back against it, holding it open with his hip, he saw that the passage was dark, with no light coming from the kitchen. Which meant that the maids had gone to bed, and Nolly had nothing to fear. Still, Jack raced ahead and flung open the door to the sickroom.

"Quick, in you go," said Jack. "There's nobody to see."

Nolly scurried into the room, as if there were peering eyes about. But as Nolly lifted up the bedclothes, Jack himself was there to see, the curve of that backside, the dimples at the rise before his waist, a bit of dark-gold hair between his legs, and Jack could let himself smile only because Nolly was so preoccupied at getting himself covered up.

"I'll be a moment," said Jack, as polite as any manservant ever could be, hiding his smile as he laid the clothes on the chair, the candlestick on the table. Then he went back to the laundry to dump the water in the drain and arrange the basins and buckets as they had been. Then he blew out the remainder of the candles but one, making sure to pinch the wicks tight between his finger and his thumb before grabbing a still-lit candle, he closed the door to the laundry to go back to the sickroom.

Which wasn't quite a sickroom anymore, with Nolly in the bed, looking sleek and clean. He sat up in the bed, with a book in his hands, the one, Jack was pleased to see, about the old man and the young sailor, and Jack was glad he'd brought the extra candle, which he put next to the other one on the table between the bed and the wall. And caught the glint in Nolly's eyes, as he bent to untie his own boots and pull off his stockings, which next to the clean smell of Nolly's now saltless skin, he could now tell smelled like the funk of a laborer's shirt. When he straightened up to undo his trousers, Nolly was looking straight at him, smirking.

"It's terribly bright in here, Jack," said Nolly. "And yet I fail to see any tattoos whatsoever."

This was a little joke between them now, for surely Nolly knew that there never had been any tattoos. But as he pulled down his trousers, naked except for his shirt and the thin, ragged bit of cloth that served as undergarments, he slid his hand down his hip, his fingers sweeping beneath his cock, his balls, to soothe them into restfulness.

"Perhaps they're hidden somewhere you've not seen yet," said Jack, for he was almost completely naked, and chilly, despite the warmth of Nolly's eyes, and the lovely blush that had crept up behind his ears.

But he couldn't tease Nolly too much, or force him into a corner where Nolly would push back, because they'd be right back at that day, when Jack had Nolly buried in the snow, and when Nolly had fought back as if it had been he and not Jack who had the upper hand. Jack had fallen for his lion's heart then and there, for you couldn't tame that, and Jack never wanted to. But he could coax it, coax Nolly to him, gentle and quiet, so that when he came, it would be willingly. Though, true to his heart, Jack was ever taken in by Nolly's sweet blushes.

"Will you read, then?" asked Jack.

"Yes, if you will get under the covers before you freeze to death."

Jack obediently did as he was told, lifting the bedclothes only high enough so that he could slide into the bed next to Nolly. Scooting close, bringing their legs together, resting his head on Nolly's shoulder, and pointing at the book as he pulled the bedclothes up over his shoulder.

"Come on now, Nolly," said Jack. He took a deep inhale of Nolly's scent, now clean, and sweet, saw that the red marks on his neck were fading, and wanted to reach up and stroke the skin there, to make sure. But he didn't, for Nolly had opened the book and was scanning the page.

"The Abbe had shown up in Dantes's cell, when we left off, I believe." Nolly licked his thumb to test the page, in case he needed to turn it, and also, slowly, licked his bottom lip, sliding off into the world he was about to read about, where his voice would become low and firm and sure, and even if a whole passel of country idiots had found their way into the room, they would not have disturbed Nolly.

"Yes," said Jack, letting his weight relax against Nolly. "He's teachin' him all them other languages."

"Oh, we've already gone through that bit," said Nolly, turning the page. Licking his bottom lip, driving Jack quite mad. "He's teaching him maths now."

"Just read, Nolly," said Jack. "And I shall fall asleep."

"Yes, Jack," said Nolly, with soft words and a pet to Jack's hair.

Nolly began to read, in the still, warm room, with the smell of beeswax and the faraway patter of rain. The words that Nolly read, slowly and carefully, hummed in Jack's brain like a faraway lullaby, spoken true, and even and quiet, until he fell asleep.

20

JACK BE NIMBLE

At the breakfast table, Nolly ate an entire bowl of porridge before saying anything. He even sat back and drank his tea, and Jack thought he was never going to say it, and Jack would be stuck all day at the house again, without Nolly.

"Mrs. Heyland," Nolly said finally, wiping his mouth with his napkin. "I'll be taking Jack with me to the Cobb today. Mr. Thurly said he could use an extra hand, and, oh, by the way, one of your tarts wouldn't go amiss."

This said in a singular way, as if it were nothing out of the ordinary when in fact, Mrs. Heyland looked at him as if he'd proposed an activity that was beneath not just him, but her, and the entire household as well.

"He should be suited for the rough work, though I don't imagine Mr. Thurly would abide his low manners," she said.

The implication that Jack heard was that she felt Mr. Thurly would be quick to take him in hand, should he step out of line. But Jack held his breath and didn't say what he wanted to say; it would be better to be there instead of here, even if there was work.

"I'll look after him," said Nolly, in tones that told Jack, at least, that Nolly considered that no one could do it better than he, though it did ring a bit as though Nolly actually *were* Jack's master.

They pulled back from the table, leaving their plates, their cutlery, and put on their jackets. Nolly put on the hat he was wearing from the day before, a sad, salt-speckled thing that Jack wanted to point and mock, but the staff was watching, and Jack could see, also, that Nolly was trying to get them out of the house before an argument erupted.

They took their leave, and once out of sight of the manor house, Jack felt his shoulders come down. He took a breath of the damp air with the sea tang and the faraway flavor of spring. Even better than being out and about and feeling well was watching Nolly lead the way, with a jaunty lift in his step and the wind tossing through his flaxen curls beneath the brim of his country hat, and a smile lurking about. As if he was not trudging towards some horrible employment, where he might yet again be cast into the sea, or be smacked about or stand up to his elbows in fish guts. No, none of this was visible. Instead he seemed pleased at the duties that awaited him.

"You know, Nolly," said Jack, ducking beneath a branch to walk at Nolly's side. "If it's money you're after, there are easier ways to get it than this."

He meant it half as a joke, but less in jest than might otherwise be expected. But Nolly, true to his nature, shook his head and marched somewhat faster, the sound of his boot heels echoing against the stone walls along the edge of the lane.

"That wouldn't be right, you know it wouldn't. Dr. McMurtry deserves honest pay for bringing you to health."

Jack knew that would be the answer, but wasn't bothered; that's just how Nolly was.

They kept walking and, as they ascended a small hillock, they could see the village, from church to Cobb, spread out before them, surrounded by the grey and rolling cape of the sea.

"Besides, in a village such as this, they'd quickly be able to find you," said Nolly.

Giving Nolly a quick, light jab of his elbow to announce that he was just teasing, Jack also took care to hide his smile. While Nolly might not be the most savvy of criminals, and was perhaps still green around the ears, he was not without a keenness of observation. In a small village, it would be easier to nab a pickpocket; however, Nolly would be shocked to have it pointed out to him that he had figured this out. He would be horrified and ashamed and all the easiness between them from the night before would fade away.

So Jack didn't point it out, and only walked when Nolly walked, downhill the whole while, and looked at the slate roofs of the tidy cottages, the sparkling rain dripping from the eaves as the church bell rang the hour, bonging out brass clangs as if attempting to out-shout the clash of waves upon the stony shore.

He could see why Nolly was drawn to a place like this, but it was not a place for Jack. There wasn't enough movement, and it looked all too placid for his taste, though he did like the churn of the sea and the wide expanse of the horizon beyond, grey and white-curled and the fresh, frozen-edged air that rushed toward the land in a never-ending sweep. But to Nolly's mind the scope of the village, compared to London, was a bare armful, easy on the eye and as sweet as a summer morning. Jack figured he could endure it for a while, as watching the roses bloom in Nolly's cheeks with all the fresh air was a treat in itself.

They rounded the curve in the road at the bottom of the hill, and walked along a cream-colored stone wall that shielded the town from the dashing sea and walked along the edge of town, along the flint-strewn path by the shore, until they came to the Cobb.

Jack scanned the bay, protected by the curved arms of the Cobb and an adjacent stone wall. The masts of the smacks and barques, their sails being folded neatly by the different crews, bobbed back and forth as the sea rolled beneath them. But Nolly seemed obvious to them, marching right up to a small canvas tent, eager, it seemed, to set things in order and assist Jack in getting his spot for the day. Jack didn't have the heart to mention that he didn't need a plan, not when he had Nolly by his side. But Nolly was talking with a man in a canvas coat and hat, his beard yellowed with time and tobacco, a long-haired cat hefted carefully in the crook of his arm.

Jack waited until Nolly raised his hand to gesture him over, the ever-elegant master calling to his manservant. Jack reckoned he could manage for a day or two, putting up with Nolly doing that, and taking orders from a fellow he did not know, performing tasks for which he might earn barely a shilling. But needs must, especially when Nolly looked so pleading, so bright-eyed to make such introductions.

"Mr. Thurly, this is my good friend, Jack Dawkins."

Jack prepared himself to shake the man's hand, but Mr. Thurly only nodded and scruffed his fingers through the cat's long fur, while the cat appraised Jack with narrow, green eyes.

"You're the manservant what's been ill, I hear," said Mr. Thurly in a gruff voice. "Will you be up for much? Or will you collapse after hefting the first bucket?"

"I'll manage, right enough, Mr. Thurly," said Jack, confident, pushing his chest out. "I've been nursed completely back to health, under Mrs. Heyland's tender care."

This was the right tack; Mr. Thurly lit up, plainly in awe of the housekeeper of the big house, and perhaps willing to show some kindness to a young man under her care. Even better, Nolly relaxed a bit, for Jack would have a job to do that would keep him out of trouble, and everything was well on its way to being taken care of. Though when Jack determined everyone else in the world was pleased with him, he was not so pleased with himself, playing their game like he was. It was an ill feeling, being thought suitable for something so menial. Still it was only for the nonce, and so inconsequential that he knew he could bear it.

"Pay's a shilling a day, same as t'others. You can help the women unload the salt from that cart into the bins."

There was a cart ladened with salt, pulled right up to where the marled sand began. The women were sifting the salt in long, flat tubs, and one of them was tugging a barrel into an upright position. They didn't look as to need that much help, but Jack was willing just the same.

"And when you're done with that, you can cart fish from the cutting table to where the women will pack. You see? And no feeding the cats."

This last was surely a false order, for the cats were everywhere, spilling from under the table to follow whomever carried buckets of cut, bleeding fish. Women leaned to pet them; men fed them scraps.

But Jack ducked his head, nodding his agreement, and, without doffing his jacket, went to help unload salt for the women, while Nolly went off to help set up tables where he would be cutting fish. Watching Nolly do such rough work would be a sight worth seeing, but meanwhile, Jack was attentive and helpful to the women, who were far from helpless, and could have unloaded the salt on their own. He wanted to keep his place, so he did as he was told, and didn't complain, lest he lose it, if only for Nolly's sake.

When the salt was unloaded, Mr. Thurly directed Jack to start carrying the fish from the men's table to the women's bins. The piles of gutted fish had built up in front of each man, and so Jack, with an empty bucket in his hand, was pleased to step directly in front of where Nolly was working.

Nolly's collar was unbuttoned, showing his throat, his sleeves rolled up just to his elbow, scar discretely hidden, and his front was covered with a leather apron that hung from his neck and was already glistening with a bit of blood. Nolly was looking at his hands, concentrating on making the slices, up the fish's belly, then slicing off the head with a twist of his wrist.

He wore a serious expression on his face, a pleased contentedness that Jack felt was new. Even the work at the haberdashery had not wrought this expression, this ease of movement, as Nolly worked shoulder to shoulder with rough men, seeming at home, as if he'd been reading in his own parlor. And then, when perhaps sensing someone was waiting upon his newly cut fish, Nolly looked up and saw Jack.

Perhaps forgetting that there were others near, Nolly smiled at Jack. With his mouth, with his eyes. There was a sweet glow about him that could not be dampened, not even the smell of newly cut fish belly, spewing up some dark fluid over Nolly's fingers.

This made Nolly happy, this industry, this simple, messy task. Jack could not fathom it, nor suss the reason why, but he welcomed the result. Perhaps it was the rhythm of it, or the sense of purpose, things that Jack understood but had never experienced the need for. But Nolly did, and the awareness of it gave Jack a small pang, low in his belly. He'd tossed his hat in the same ring as a workhouse boy with a flash-quick temper and a strong sense of manners. But did that mean he had ascribe to doing the same?

It was a question that Jack couldn't answer, though he could admit he didn't *want* to answer. In the meantime, through the morning, as the rain came and went like sheets of grey lace being pulled through the sky, Jack soldiered on. He took Nolly's fish, piling the pieces in the long, narrow bucket, took the next man's as well, and the next, skidding across the cobbles, and sinking up to his ankles in the marled sand, delivering the fish quickly to the women so that the bubbling warm blood could be washed away, and the pink flesh could be salted in barrels before it went bad.

Back and forth Jack went, his city boots taking the bite of it, the edges of his jacket and the cuffs getting stained and torn from the rough work. This was not for him, most definitely not for him, and he would have left it. Cast aside the bucket, turned on his heel, and marched straight out of town.

But for that smile.

It was a sunburst among the clouds, that smile, frequent and easy enough to draw attention to itself; Nolly would need protection from unwanted attention. But it was more than that—those smiles were for Jack, aimed at Jack alone. And no matter who else borrowed pleasure from seeing them, they belonged to Jack. Not that smiles truly belonged to anyone, Jack knew that. Still. *Still.*

At one point, Mr. Thurly rang the bell for dinner, though Jack had lost track of the sun behind the film of clouds overhead. Obediently he went to the table with Nolly and the other men, debating for a moment before taking a spot at the table on the bench across from Nolly. Perhaps Nolly remembered their conversation, where Jack explained how he needed to have all in his sights, including Nolly, before he could relax enough to eat. Not that there was much danger to be had here, but Jack needed to be attentive to it just the same.

Mr. Thurly stood at the head of the plank table, and muttered a prayer and nodded at the two women, one who carried a pitcher and a platter of bread, and the other who hefted a steaming iron kettle with a long dipper with which to serve stew into the bowls, the spices and grease rising up clear and sharp in the salt air.

Jack watched as Nolly eagerly lifted his chin, holding up his bowl, waiting for his turn, his share. That is, until he lowered the bowl to the table in front of him. Just as Jack was served, the smell of eel, the oil from the skin having been boiled through, steamed up at him. It was as good a meal as any, and Jack would be content enough to eat it. But Nolly was not. The memory of the meal of eel stew, once served at the Three Cripples, that Nolly simply would not eat, had stayed with Jack, as he'd never seen Nolly refuse any other meal.

As Jack dug into the stew, he watched Nolly's brow furrow and watched the pleasure fade from his face. He didn't even look to Jack for help, but merely traced the surface of the stew with his spoon and stared at the contents of the metal bowl, as if it contained the entire of the world's troubles and he unable to solve them.

Perhaps there were some things people didn't warrant being saved from, and Nolly was what he was. On the other hand, Jack couldn't bear to watch Nolly suffer when there was anything Jack could do about it. Besides, sometimes, the easiest way to hide something, was to show it.

"Ah, 'tis a pity about that, Nolly," said Jack, reaching for a chunk of bread from the platter that was now in the middle of the table. He gestured to Nolly with it.

"What's that then, Jack?" asked Nolly, in that voice that would have not been the least bit amazing in a parlor, yet stood out here, as a sheet of fine lace might among straps of leather.

"That you can't abide eel." Jack dunked the bread into his stew and sucked happily on it, ignoring the startled looks, not least of which came from Nolly at having his shameful secret so exposed.

"Is that so," said Mr. Thurly, sopping his bread in the same manner as Jack.

"He ain't fussy about much," said Jack, slurping more stew loudly, "but it was a bad bit of eel that put him off it forever. Or maybe it was him spewin' eel for three whole days. Three *whole* days." Now Jack had everyone's complete attention. "Mind you," said Jack, waving his spoon like it was a bandleader's baton, "he tried to aim for the bucket as any gentleman would, but vomit goes where it will, and there was quite the mess to clean up, I can tell you."

"I've got a bit of leftover meat pie 'e could have," said one of the woman, wiping her hands on her apron. "That'd do you better, I should think."

Within a moment, and without asking anybody's leave, the woman had taken up the bowl of uneaten stew and plonked down a plate with a slice of meat pie. It was dry at the edges and perhaps not as new as it might be, but Nolly looked grateful for it just the same. Just as the men looked grateful they would not be subject to days of vomiting by a fellow who couldn't quite hit the bucket. For this reason, perhaps, Jack didn't get any sense that the men resented the special treatment for Nolly. Plus, Jack got one of those smiles, as Nolly caught his gaze, and it was fond and private, and Jack knew that this smile belonged only to him, for he had earned it fair and square.

～

After dinner was over, the men went back to their places, and as Jack continued to haul salt and bring fresh water from a pump that was a hefty hike from the shore, he kept his eyes open to what was around him. From Nolly's description of his workmates the day before, Jack could sense that while Nolly wasn't completely welcomed with open arms at the Cobb, there was a general acceptance of him. It was partly Nolly's own fault; any distance was created by him using table manners that befitted a young lord, rather than stuffing it in like everyone else did, Jack included. Plus the gentle treatment of the meat pie might have made some jealous, which Jack might regret later, only he couldn't bear to watch Nolly suffer through eel stew.

But there really only one pair of disapproving eyes cast Nolly's way, and it occurred to Jack that they belonged to the fellow who'd pushed Nolly into the drink. By the height of the Cobb and the way the top of it leaned ever so slightly toward the bayside rather than the ocean side, the man really must have wanted Nolly to fall, so the accident had to have happened on purpose.

So, while hauling gutted fish to the women along the shore, Jack kept watch. Particularly when Mr. Thurly sent Nolly on an errand to the harbormaster, who watched the mouth of the harbor and made sure the vessels in the fleet paid their tax and gave proper estimates of their catches. Jack could hear Mr. Thurly complain that the weight of fish did not equal what was paid for, and so they were being shorted.

"You ask them, boy," Jack could hear quite clearly as the wind shifted. "You ask them when on earth a standard English barrel began to hold only five stone of fish? Are they packing the bottom with wool? Here, take this slate."

Nolly was sent because he was new boy, and also because he presented a tidy picture as he hurried along the Cobb. Jack enjoyed the view, Nolly's legs moving so gracefully, that backside ever a treat. And his serious expression, though how Jack loved to see him smile.

When Nolly came back to shore, crossing over the rocks to

Mr. Thurly to pass along a message, Jack was watching. The dark-eyed fellow caught Nolly with a rude elbow that almost sent him tumbling to the rocks. Jack saw Nolly turn to the other man, ire narrowing his eyes as he took it up, as any lad would. Only this wasn't a lad Nolly was up against but a full grown man. But while Jack determined that the other fellow deserved his comeuppance, perhaps he wasn't quite aware of who he'd just shoved, and how angry Nolly could get. Whether or not this was the same man who'd almost drowned Nolly, Nolly needed to be pulled out of it.

Jack hurried over and laid his empty basket on the table and waded in, elbows and shoulders creating a space between the man's glare and Nolly's flashing eyes.

"Job be damned, eh, fellows?" asked Jack, equably giving both of them a hard shove in the chest. "It's nowt to do with me, but I gots to put in my time, debts to pay an' that."

Now Mr. Thurly's attention was drawn, and Jack grabbed each one by the collar of his shirt, Nolly and the man both. The man was solid and broad and half a head taller than Mr. Thurly, but he seemed more startled by Jack's actions, but not enough to restrain from lashing out.

"Let go, you *bloody*—"

Then he reached out to smack Nolly, but struck Jack with the back of his hand instead. Jack was rocked back on his heels and let go of the man's shirt, his ears ringing, almost falling to the stones, headache starting right up, as if every stone in the Cobb had been launched at him.

There was a spare moment when nobody moved and even the ocean seemed hushed, then Jack's ears started to ring, and there was a clamor of voices such that Jack was unable to discern the difference between; he only knew that he needed to draw Nolly away before something bad happened. He turned, slamming his hands on Nolly's shoulders, making him back up. Mr. Thurly nodded at Jack and grabbed the other fellow by the neck of his leather apron.

"What are you doing, Leander, mucking about on the job? Unsettling these cats? Eh?"

"He near ran me over!" shouted Leander, mouth open, his face red.

"What? This lad here?" Mr. Thurly pointed to Jack, whose face was now stinging, as if hit were on fire. Jack desperately wanted a cool hand laid to it, kisses pressed there, Nolly's kisses, but it was more important to be part of the argument to clear Nolly of any wrongdoing. But Nolly, with a low animal sound, pushed at Jack as if he were a gate that needed smashing through; Jack held him fast.

"No, that one, the prat who thinks he's better'n us!" said Leander.

"Yet this is the lad you struck?"

Mr. Thurly pointed at Jack, and of a sudden all the men were looking and quite still. Blood pounded across Jack's face, though the ringing in his ears was already fading.

"You make a wreck of my operations, Leander Warren," said Mr. Thurly, giving Leander a shake, "and you'll be needing to find yourself a new situation."

Leander grunted as he tipped his head, touching the brim of his cap.

"No, sir, that wasn't my intention, sir, but he—"

"Ain't done nothin' to you," said Jack into the bit of silence provided him. "Even when you shoved him into the water, he ain't done nothin'."

Because nobody spoke to naysay him, this brought an uncomfortable moment where everyone was silent, and Jack knew, *knew*, that Leander was the one who'd done it. And never mind that you weren't supposed to peach to the master, even though every man's face clearly stated that they'd known how it had happened. And now the master knew because Jack had peached. Well, Jack didn't give a damn, not even when the men stepped away and Mr. Thurly barked orders and nobody spoke to him.

Except when Jack turned as the men went back to work, Nolly

remained where he was. Neck damp from his having run from the harbormaster's, and in his eyes, a funny, quirky gratitude.

"You just peached, Jack," said Nolly, an unaccustomed smirk curling the edge of his mouth. "That's against Fagin's rules, I'd say."

Jack felt a quick rush of shame, and was about to open his mouth for a hasty explanation as to why, when he saw a glint in those ocean-blue eyes.

"Havin' me on, are you?" asked Jack, moving close to pat Nolly's shoulder, a pat that turned into a quick caress that Jack reckoned nobody would notice.

"Yes," said Nolly, quickly, dipping his chin, and in a quiet voice meant only for Jack, said, "I'd thrash him right here and now for touching you, if you wanted me to. If *you* wanted it."

It was not quite what Jack had been expecting to hear, but it didn't truly surprise him. The last person to lay hard hands upon Jack had been hacked to death with a meat cleaver, and while Jack was still awed deep inside, the current matter did not warrant such a hasty act.

Jack shook his head. "I know it, but no." He dodged Nolly's hand as it rose to comfort his cheek, in spite of him wanting it, in case looks were being aimed their way. "Back at it or old Thurly will discharge us for slackin', an' then I *will* have to hit the streets for cash."

He gave Nolly a push back to the table and hurried to grab his bucket. The work would settle Nolly just as Leander's attack had unsettled him. As for Jack, he was used to unpredictable outbursts and tavern brawls that erupted over a slight of no consequence and either ended with black eyes and busted teeth, or disbursed into drinking contests and off-key singing. What Jack wasn't used to was hustling under the watchful eye of a man who could break up a fight with a mere word, and who with a snap of his fingers and a look, could make Jack hustle and scurry over slippery stones with a bucket of slopping fish parts, growing blisters, and a coat of sweat that no man of dignity should ever be subject to, no sir.

But he soldiered on with each bump of the bucket against his thigh, and the long cluster of blisters in the crook of his fingers on both hands, and the indelicate limp that he was developing from a sore heel from where he'd come down too hard on a stone. He envied the men's sturdy boots, even Nolly wore a pair, but he kept his mouth shut about it. He was already known to be a small boy crying to his governess, but he would not also be a complainer. Not and be associated with Nolly, who never complained. Well, almost never, except when a wee workhouse boy died on his watch, and he'd thought he'd killed a man for it. Only then. So Jack could do no less.

"Here, boy," shouted one of the men, not Leander.

Jack scurried as obediently as ever he had, half laughing at himself, half ashamed, and so very glad that neither Fagin nor Charlie nor any of the boys from the gang could see him now. For he would look a proper dancing monkey to them, and they would fall about until they just about pissed themselves. Nor would they care to hear that Jack toiled for only one reason. And that was the lad who caught Jack's eye and gave him a smile, some sympathy in those eyes. Jack got the feeling that while Nolly was pleased with working on the Cobb, he did not, at the same time, expect that their current situation would continue. At least Jack hoped that was true. If he knew any prayers, he'd be on his knees in a heart-beat, raising his head to the heavens to whatever god might be listening that Nolly did not intend their current servitude to continue forever.

21

SAUCE FOR THE GOOSE

As the day lengthened into afternoon, the wind wicking through his hair, Oliver rested his knife on the table, and watched Jack. Jack was taking a bucket of fish down to the ladies by the shoreline. Above Jack's boot, one of his stockings was worn quite through to the skin, and his trousers were starting to wear to the point that a rent along his leg was turning into a full-blown gap. The jacket he wore was stained so as to darken it.

Oliver didn't know why he'd not noticed before. Perhaps Jack's illness had distracted him, but then, Mrs. Heyland had provided Oliver with thick trousers, the kind the other fish-gutters wore, and a thick muslin shirt, and a seaman's coat and hat and boots. He fit in here, at the Cobb, with the other men. Jack, on the other hand, looked out of place, not just because he wasn't doing the work of the other men and merely carried around the buckets, but also because he looked half done, as if there was no one at home to look after him.

Well, the only person to do that was Oliver himself. He'd been so worried about earning money to repay their debt and making sure Jack was well, he'd neglected to make sure that Jack was comfortable. Jack was not a helpless orphan, to be sure, but he'd lived on the streets so long that holes in his stockings and rents in his trousers were the ordinary way of things.

Oliver remembered well those days, and how that felt. If your feet were cold because there were holes in your boots, then you kept your mouth shut because it would only earn you a beating. Though Fagin had been the type, when he learned of a boy going hungry or cold because his clothes were too thin, well, he would shout and bang about, and curse the day he was born to be burdened with such a lot. But then he would find some odd coin, or make a trade, and that boy had thicker stockings, or a bit of woolen felt to put in the bottom of his boots to keep out the rain. Something. Fagin always found a way, when he could.

And now that was Oliver's job. Jack, whether or not he might complain, would not actually expect anyone to do anything about it. Cold feet or catching a chill from torn clothing was just how it was. But that wasn't how it should be. So Oliver would change that.

He put down his knife and nodded at Leander, who frowned at him and wiped some blood from his forehead.

"What're you doin'?" asked Leander.

"Stepping away for a moment," said Oliver. He waited until Jack was all the way to the shore before he went up to the hut that juddered in the wind. Inside, Mr. Thurly was sitting beside a little portable stove, from which emanated the most delicious heat. He was drinking coffee and although he nodded that Oliver might come in, he didn't offer him anything to drink.

"Why aren't you working?" asked Mr. Thurly. He waved his coffee mug at the cove and the stone dock and the men working hard in the brisk breeze.

"I was wondering, Mr. Thurly, if I could get an advance on my pay packet for the week."

"Eh? You want a loan? I hardly know you."

"Well, I reckon that Jack and I will have earned about seven shillings all told, by Saturday," said Oliver, refusing to let Mr. Thurly's gruff manner dissuade him.

"What do you want it for? Don't Mrs. Heyland give you room and board?"

"I just need the money." Oliver said this as patiently as he could. "We *have* earned it."

Taking a sip of his coffee, Mr. Thurly grunted. "That's all well and good," he said. "But if I do it for you, all them other fellows will want the same. Do you think I've got bank enough for that?"

Biting his lip, Oliver turned and saw Jack coming up with two empty buckets, his wet boots slipping on the stones. Having been so long abed, Jack shouldn't be working so hard, though Oliver knew that to remind Jack of this might have Jack stubbornly working all the harder. He vowed to keep an eye out, just the same.

"Very well. Jack needs new clothes. Mrs. Heyland gave me these," he pointed at his trousers and jacket, "but had nothing for Jack. He's been ill, as you know, and I want to buy him some stockings, at the very least."

"Stockings won't be enough," said Mr. Thurly, quite unexpectedly. His eyes flicked to where Jack was going up to the deal table. In a moment, it was apparent, Jack would be looking for Oliver and where he'd gotten to. "That lad needs a whole new kit. Mrs. Heyland didn't have it for him, then."

Hardly knowing what Mr. Thurly was getting at, Oliver shook his head and prepared to tell Mr. Thurly that it didn't matter, that it wasn't important. But Mr. Thurly stopped him, tapping his warm mug against Oliver's arm.

"My sister has a boy, he went off to be a sailor. He left some clothes behind. How much do you owe them doctors?"

"Ten shillings and sixpence," said Oliver. He did not let himself think of Jack's suggestion of getting the amount another way.

"I can give you the clothes for three shillings; boots, shirt, trousers, and jacket."

"Three shillings is too much," said Oliver. "Besides, I need stockings as well." A true gentleman would not stoop to haggle with the likes of Mr. Thurly, no, he'd be above it, and toss his coins about like petals in the wind. But for Jack, Oliver was willing. "Please, Mr. Thurly. It's not for anything but Jack's health."

There were footsteps coming up behind him, and he knew without looking that they belonged to Jack. There was a touch on his shoulder, and however much he wanted to lean into it, he couldn't let himself. So he reached up to clasp Jack's hand, to tell him that all was well.

"You slackin' off, Nolly?" asked Jack.

Oliver turned to smile at him, as brightly as he could. "No, indeed, but Mr. Thurly wanted to know whether we wanted our pay combined or separated. Saturday is payday."

"Oh, yes," said Jack. He squeezed Oliver's hand back, a silent signal, and then let go. "The bloody money for the bloody doctors, when Nolly here did the nursin', as fine a nurse as ever there was."

Mr. Thurly seemed to look at them with some sharpness, his eyes narrowing. But then he took a sip of coffee and looked out at the sea. "Come by the house, after work," he said. "I'm off Gage Street, one over from the church, halfway down. It's got a blue door."

"Thank you," said Oliver. He wasn't sure whether or not they'd agreed about the stockings, but perhaps something could be done to get a pair. The next issue was how to make Jack accept the gift, without getting peevish and outright refusing to put any of the garments on.

"What was that about, then?"

As they walked back to the bit of shore where the Cobb rose out of the sea to meet the land, and the seagulls wove over their heads to land on bits of fish guts, Oliver shook his head.

"It's about the pay," he said, pretending to be more cross than he truly was. "He's somewhat fussy, it seems, about his accounts."

"Seems a rather long conversation to have about a simple seven shillings." Jack looked at him askance, his head tilted back. "Is this another one of those letter things, where you say one thing, yet do another?"

"No, no," said Oliver. "Look, I've got to get back to gutting fish; Leander will torment me if he sees I'm not keeping up."

There was nothing Jack could do but let him go back to work, leaving a taste in Oliver's mouth that was entirely unpleasant. Not just that he had again lied to Jack, but that Jack had caught him at it. The only rescue from this was if Jack liked the clothes and if stockings could be had somewhere in the village for ninepence.

When the day's work was done, and they were walking home, Oliver tried to be casual, but he was terribly bad at it. As he led them up Gage Street and then one over from St. Michael's church, Jack was looking at him in a way that made Oliver quite, quite sure that Jack knew that something was amiss. Oliver was a creature of habit, for him to take a different route than the way they'd come, well, Jack was shaking his head but he followed Oliver anyway.

As Oliver stopped to knock on the blue door of a house halfway down the slanted street, Jack looked up and down the street, as if he were wondering which direction he might head and shed himself of this unwelcome errand.

The door opened, and a woman stood there. She was as old as Mr. Thurly, with a deeply creased face, and a tidy cap that kept back her grey hair. Her whole dress, sensible and dark, was covered with a spotless white apron. Here was a woman, Oliver knew at a glance, who could make the best blackberry tarts anybody had ever tasted.

"Good evening, Mrs. Thurly?"

"Yes, that be me. You come about the clothes?"

Oliver nodded, and she turned into the dark, narrow hallway, pulled out a bundle, and shoved them into his arms. Without even a nod, she shut the door. Good manners would not be on offer, nor any tarts, blackberry or otherwise. Swallowing, Oliver tucked the bundle under his arm. He could see the tips of boots tucked in the middle, and the tail end of what might be a pair of hand-knitted stockings.

"What did you just do?"

But Jack knew exactly what had happened. His mouth turned down into a scowl, and he turned up his collar, showing his displeasure. Which would have found a more vocal display, except that they were passing two lads with hand carts who were pulling piles of shells down the street toward the center of town.

"Your stockings were worn through," said Oliver, trudging on, keeping his head down, his eyes focused on the road.

"That bundle's a lot more than stockin's, Nolly." Jack bumped into him with his shoulder. "How much?"

"Never mind that now, you needed them."

"I said how much?"

There was no avoiding the question; if Oliver was to sweet-talk Jack into accepting the gift, then he needed to do it quickly.

"Only three shillings; it's a very good trade, and you won't be shivering down at the Cobb. I won't have to watch you shiver."

"Now we're *three* shillin's behind," said Jack, almost spitting it. "Now you'll be expectin' that we'll be stayin' at the Cobb forever to earn the money to pay those doctors their bloody money. "

And so they'd come to it.

"There's no need to hurry, until we decide what we're doing," said Oliver, unsettled by Jack's ire.

"And that bloody letter comes."

Oliver walked a little faster, his back stiff, the bundle tucked very securely under his arm.

"Nolly. Nolly, wait."

Jack rushed up beside him, half slipping on the wet streets. "You know I could have stolen what I wanted, what I needed. You don't like that workin' man's coat? I'll get you another'n, as easy as anythin'."

"You don't need to steal, Jack, not when we're earning money."

"But we ain't earnin' *nothin'*." Jack almost shouted, jerking on Oliver's arm and pulling him to a stop. They stepped to the edge of the road as a woman with a basket hurried past them, as if eager to avoid two drunks on the street.

"But we earned—"

"We barely earned enough to pay what we owe, Nolly. An' next week, it'll be more of the same. A regular fellow's got no luck to get ahead, none atall. We can, but not if we do it your way."

They were back to the old question, the one where they came to a crossroads, but Oliver felt it in his breast that they should not steal to live. Not in such a nice village as this.

"Mrs. Heyland—" he began, but Jack interrupted him.

"Mrs. Heyland won't be shelterin' us forever. I'm workin' on the Cobb—do you know why I'm workin' at the Cobb? It ain't for money. Not by half."

Oliver knew why. He didn't have to ask. The way Jack was looking at him twisted in his heart; the issue of how they came by money to live was not settled between them, and it couldn't be. Not in this world, this lifetime. Yet to be without Jack was impossible. He looked down and petted the bundle in his arms, his fingers moving across the mist of rain that had fallen on the jacket.

"I just wanted you to be warm," Oliver said, as steadily as he could.

"I'm used to being cold; I'm *used* to it," said Jack.

"You don't have to be; I don't *want* you to be."

"An' I don't need you to take care of me. You think you have everythin' figured out? Well, you don't. So stop tryin' to act as if you're the one in charge. Makin' decisions, writin' letters I don't want written."

"I told you why I had him write it," said Oliver, thinking that if he could explain it clearly, just once, Jack would see the sense of it. Certain things just needed to be, like Jack's comfort, his well being, and having a family was part of that. "I needed to know—"

"Well, I *don't* need to know." Jack actually gave the bundle in Oliver's arm a shove, almost hard enough to knock it into the muddy gutter along the side of the street.

"Will you take the clothes? *Please* take the clothes, Jack."

Now Jack's chin jutted out, just as large plops of rain came down on the top of his head, a crisp wind skittering along the back of his neck, tossing his untidy hair.

"You 'shamed of me, Nolly?" Jack asked this, his mouth tight against his teeth.

"No, of course not."

"Well, I don't give a bloody fuck if you are." Jack's voice sounded thick and there was a small, downward pull to his mouth. "You think I'd be better if I wore *that*?" He gave the clothes a poke with his finger. "And had *them*? That family you think I should have?"

"What?" Now it made sense, but he wasn't ashamed of Jack. "No. No. The clothes are to keep you warm. And I had the parson write to find your family, in case you died, which you haven't. All I want, you know this, Jack, you *know* it, is for you to be well. The clothes will stop you from becoming ill again." He saw the expression on Jack's face, the frown, the drawn-together brows.

"Do you remember," said Oliver, beginning it like a story to make Jack listen. "When I came to you at the Three Cripples, and the first thing you did was get me new clothes. And then you cut my hair, and rubbed soot from the fireplace on my skin. Do you remember?"

"'Course I do, you're such a bleedin' covey that I had to—" Suddenly Jack stopped and he looked at Oliver without even blinking.

"Yes, you had to change me so that I wouldn't stick out. I couldn't even bathe for days, you wouldn't let me because it would make me different from everyone else. You didn't want me to get caught, so you made me like you. At least on the outside."

"So you want me to do the same, to be like you. On the outside."

"At least for a little while." Now that he'd explained it, Oliver could breathe a little easier.

"With all the fussy manners, like at the table an' suchlike."

"And the words."

"Got my own words," said Jack, stoutly, sticking out his chin. "An' they're good enough for anybody, I reckon. Thought they was good enough for you, even. Besides, ain't nobody givin' us half a notice, if you ask me." Wiping his upper lip on his coat sleeve, Jack turned and started walking up the road.

Oliver followed. The problem was that they didn't know if anyone was watching them, or wondering what they were doing there. Half the village probably knew by now who Oliver was, who his family was. Even if that were true, his bastard status hadn't seemed to affect anyone, least of all the men at the Cobb, or Mr. Thurly, or even the parson. But he didn't like the way that they looked at Jack, looked askance as if asking what a gentleman's son was doing with such a coarse person. Their lie about the manservant and master had only taken them so far.

"And I don't want them to." Oliver hurried to catch up. Jack was indeed better if he could walk so swiftly, and uphill with the rain in his face. "Jack, wait."

Jack slowed down a little bit, casting a look at Oliver out of the corner of his eyes. They were completely alone on the road now, as it wound its way out of the village and under the branches reaching out over the road, newly budded with leaves in the spring. It wasn't enough to shelter them from the rain, but it did cut off the wind a bit.

"I wanted you to have better stockings." Oliver tugged at Jack's jacket sleeve with his fingers. "That's how it started. Your leg was bare above your boot, and I only noticed it today. I should have noticed it before."

"You did notice," said Jack, giving Oliver a poke with his elbow. "When you was rubbin' my feet, like one of them fancy ladies, after she takes a gent up from the parlor."

"Are you calling me a fancy lady?" Oliver pretended ire, but he knew he was forgiven, that Jack had forgiven him for spending all of their money on clothes for Jack. He knew Jack would have done the same if he'd needed it, though Jack would have stolen the clothes and pocketed the shillings.

Jack made a face, and Oliver tossed the bundle at him, which luckily Jack caught, in the curve of his elbow. With his other hand, he petted the wool of the coat, much as Oliver had. "That's nice cloth, that is. Too fine for the likes of me, I'm thinkin'."

"No," said Oliver. He licked his lips, wanting to find a way to say that no coat was too fine for Jack; Jack was liable to mock him forever more for saying something so pathetically kind. "It'll keep you warm," he said instead. "And it'll look good on you, besides."

"I'll match you, in that getup."

They walked, the rain starting to fall harder now, just at the point where they turned into the lane that would take them into the stable yard of Rhode Hill House. Crossing the yard, they went up to the house, and, pausing a little at the door, Oliver took off his hat and shook it. Jack moved in beside him, beneath the small overhang, where they could be alone for a moment.

"Would you mind if you did?" asked Oliver.

Shaking his head, Jack smacked Oliver on the arm, almost losing the bundle, which Oliver caught and held in his hands, pressing it against Jack's chest.

"Not on your life," said Jack. "Lookin' as fine as you? Why, that's been my dream since I were a wee lad. Although." He paused to tousle Oliver's hair, which tickled Oliver's ears, though he didn't pull away. Not when Jack was touching him like that, gently, as he might do to someone dear to him.

"I don't know how I might get my hair to be like yours," said Jack, as he tugged on his own dark hair, and opened the door. "Black as soot it is, nothin' like your flaxen locks."

The way he said it was different to anyone else in the world. Other people, when they stared and pointed, or remarked outright about Oliver's looks, made him feel as thought he were an ornament on display, or an object rather than a living boy.

But when Jack said it, something stirred to life inside of him. Oliver liked it, liked the way Jack's fingers curled around his skull, liked the way Jack's eyes lingered on his mouth, or even when Jack looked when he pretended he wasn't looking. Which happened a lot, as it was happening now, as they went inside, and shook out their jackets and Oliver's hat to hang them. Jack hurried off to deposit his new clothes in the sickroom before coming back to wash with Oliver.

"Good evening, Oliver," said Mrs. Heyland, as she and the maidservants set the table and brought over the food.

For Jack she only had a bare nod, and from Gerald there was nothing but a grunt. As for young Tim, he kept his eyes on the floor or his hands, and must have received quite a lecture to have dimmed his sweet smile. The three maidservants ignored Jack entirely. This could not continue much longer; Mrs. Heyland might not throw them out, but Oliver didn't know how much of this he could stand of Jack getting treated as if he weren't even there.

Oliver sat down, and Jack sat in the chair beside him. Jack's eyes seemed overly bright, as if his head ailed him and his fever had returned.

"Will you need some willow bark tea?" Oliver asked him, dipping his chin down to keep the conversation between them. "I could get Mrs. Heyland to make some. Or I could make you some."

"No," said Jack. "Don't need no tea, an' I reckon I could eat a horse, as well." He wiped his damp hands on his trousers, as usual, making Oliver want to scold him about it. But, with so ready an audience, that was the last thing he wanted to do. Besides, Jack had been making an effort to tame his table manners, at least when it mattered.

The entire time they ate, Jack was looking but not looking, as if Oliver was a secret that only Jack knew the telling of. That was the secret between them, a live thing that must be kept in a cage when others were about. He hoped they were doing fairly well, as Mr. Thurly's grimace could have been only that he was contentious of someone being so generous with their wages.

It was impossible to tell, and they could ask no one whether it showed, what was between him and Jack. Although Oliver was sometimes quite certain, as he was now, as Jack passed him the bowl of steaming boiled potatoes, that Jack stared too long, and that his eyes brightened when he caught Oliver's eye. That anyone would suspect them was a disaster in the making, especially in such close quarters around the table in the kitchen, one housekeeper, one groom, one stableboy, and three maidservants. All looking at Oliver and expecting him to get on with passing the potatoes.

"Will you care for some peas, Master Oliver?" asked Mrs. Heyland.

The peas looked as though they'd been dried last year, and boiled up in butter that left a greasy film on their grey, wrinkled skins. But to be polite, he took some peas, and passed them along.

And while they were eating, he felt his knee brush Jack's under the table. There wasn't a tablecloth to hide what they were doing, but nobody was looking. So instead of pulling his leg away, he shifted in his chair, and purposefully pushed his thigh outward, where it met Jack's. Jack's eyebrows rose, and the food in his mouth almost fell out on his plate. That would be the worst of bad manners, so it might be best to take his leg away, but he saw Jack close his mouth to keep carefully chewing, and felt the pressure of Jack, pushing back, just slightly.

Oliver didn't know why he'd done it. Surely someone would notice what they were doing and chide them; even if no one knew what they were *really* doing, such a thing at a table while people were eating was the worst sort of manners, and Oliver had no doubt that Jack would be blamed.

As well, he longed to see Jack in his new clothes, feeling a swell of pride that was its own kind of sin, that he had done this for Jack. He should have done it days ago, should have insisted that Mrs. Heyland provide for Jack the way she'd provided for Oliver. But Mrs. Heyland saw in Jack what everyone in Oliver's world did. Mr. McCready had known what kind of person Jack was the moment he'd seen him. It was clear; Jack was not suitable. Even Mrs. Bedwin would have been alarmed—

But what did that matter; Jack was the only one who was here, with his thigh cozy and close to Oliver's thigh. There was the hot meal, the warmth of the stove, and the glowing light of the two candles on the table. Amidst that was Jack, who had come with Oliver, and who had not left, even when he was cross. And later, there would be the darkness of the sickroom, and the single candle where he could watch Jack try on the clothes, and then bade him to take them off again—

Oliver stopped and concentrated on his food. He was grown quite warm among these thoughts, and he felt a rush in his belly, and the tightness of the flesh between his legs. This had not happened before; always it had been when Jack was touching him, reaching for him, with Jack's arms around, and in the darkness where no one could see them.

He felt Jack looking at him, more boldly now. He took a breath and nodded at Jack, to let him know that all was well. The meal was almost over; he could make it that long before he felt he might jump to his feet and drag Jack bodily away from the table. Boldly and loudly and without a care that anybody was watching.

To distract himself, Oliver said, "Mrs. Heyland, did you know that Mr. Thurly's son went off to be a sailor?"

"Indeed I did," said Mrs. Heyland, sounding indignant that Oliver imagined there was anything about anybody in the village that she did not know. "A year ago March, it was. Terrible storm we had, with water battering the Cobb, but off he went, bright as a sprite. He's a bosun's mate, I believe."

"Yes," said Oliver, nodding as if this story were very interesting to him. "Well, I've bought his clothes from Mrs. Thurly, for Jack, to give him something more suitable to wear." He looked at her, not saying it, but thinking that when she had given Oliver clothes, she might have considered giving some to Jack, as well.

"I see," said Mrs. Heyland. She busied herself with her plate without looking at Jack, who was the very subject of the conversation.

Oliver looked over to where Jack was finishing off his stew. He had lifted the bowl with one hand and was actually swiping his thumb around the inside and then stuck his thumb in his mouth to suck on it, to get at the last of the stew.

It would have been better if he'd used a spoon or a bit of bread, it would have been better if he'd left it, as only the coarsest sort of person had to dig for the smallest bits of food left behind. But Oliver would not rebuke Jack, not in front of Mrs. Heyland or the maidservants. If Jack didn't know any better, it was because of the way he was raised, and if Jack didn't know any better, it was because Oliver had not properly taught him. So this was Oliver's fault. Not that he would take the time to explain it to someone such as Mrs. Heyland.

"I'd like Jack to have a bath, seeing as he's been so ill, before he puts on his new clothes."

This stopped her mid-chew, and she looked a bit fierce with her lace cap casting shadows over her beetled brows. But she couldn't say no, at least Oliver didn't think that she could.

"I suppose that could be done," she said, and Oliver told himself that he didn't care she was displeased with him.

"There is hot water, ma'am," said Gussie. "From the sheets we washed today, why, the boiler is still half full, and they could use that."

"Yes, certainly," said Mrs. Heyland. "Now, is everyone done with their supper? I've sewing to do and lists to make up for tomorrow, and we don't have time to sit here chatting."

Oliver didn't let her see him smile. It would be rude, and besides, he had to concentrate his energy on getting Jack *into* the bath that he'd so craftily arranged for him.

22

THE BATH AND WHAT HAPPENED
AFTER

They were alone in the laundry, with the door closed, as Nolly poured the last of the hot water into a tin tub that Jack was quite sure had not been there the day before. But it was there now, all steaming, creating a warm damp in the air, like a swamp but much nicer-smelling. But the closed door meant that there would be no interruptions, nor any audience, and Nolly could do and think as he liked. Could do what he liked with Jack, if only he didn't make as though he was in charge of Jack, as it had sounded when he'd announced his intention for Jack to have a bath.

There was a queer sensation in Jack's middle, such as when he'd see the ladies from some church or other, or the gentlemen with their starched collars and their expressions of distaste as they marched along narrow streets and muddy, damp lanes, looking for someone to save. It was always easy to spot them, those Christians with their black Bibles and haughty, nose-up expressions. Where Jack had seen home and territory and folk that he knew, the would-be rescuers saw only how *helping the needy* would elevate them. But they only delivered false hope, and the price to pay for hot food and free lodgings was an enforced set of rules that took all the joy out of everything.

Nolly had those same rules, carried them in his heart, like a well-loved psalter. But if he thought that Jack would follow them, then he had another thing coming.

"I ain't a charity case, Nolly," said Jack.

Since the door was closed, Jack wasn't surprised to see Nolly look straight at him, unguarded, the flicker in his eyes unveiled. And then Jack knew, could see that Nolly understood this.

"No, you're not," said Nolly, in a steady way, as if he were considering his words very carefully. But then something seemed to whisk itself away in his expression, and for another idea to rose in its stead. Nolly put down the towel he was holding and in three bold steps, had his arms around Jack. So close, their faces were so close, Jack could see the pulse of heat in Nolly's face.

"But you're mine to care for," Nolly said, serious and low, and pulled Jack to him even tighter, an embrace that felt almost too much to bear, until it sank into Jack's skin like an anchor.

If Jack had heretofore considered himself a one-man island, a stable place to Nolly's flared sails, he began to think of it differently, just then. His hands came up to circle around Nolly's waist in a way that brought their hips together; their thighs, all sealed up and down, were warm, like something constant and true.

Nolly drew back a little bit, his mouth on Jack's ear, whispering as if he were shy.

"I wouldn't care what anybody thinks, Jack, but I can't bear to imagine you chilled from a rent in your trousers, or see you shiver because your jacket is too thin. Besides," added Nolly, and his voice went low as a blush spread across his cheeks. "You helped me yesterday with the bath, and it was so—"

Nolly stopped altogether, and Jack watched him swallow and swallow again. He wanted to make Nolly say what he was thinking, but a gentle hand was ever the way to go about things with Nolly, so Jack didn't say anything, and just waited.

"—so tender, I wanted to do the same for you."

Oh.

This was a fierce love indeed, for all Nolly so seldom expressed it. There might be some price eventually, but Jack always knew that there would be. And not just with Nolly, but with the world. You always had to pay in the end. An early ticket home had been paid for by a winter London bereft of almost everybody he knew. A bright-sky friendship with a bush-born black girl ended with death. The protection offered by a courtly marine meant dire retribution. Jack never wondered *whether*, it was more a question of when and what.

Not that Nolly needed to know this; he'd be aghast to find that Jack believed it. Not now, anyway, when Nolly's hands were gentle and quick as he stood back and began divesting Jack of his clothes.

"Come along, then, you," he said. "You can't bathe wearing all of this."

He undid each button on Jack's shirt as carefully as if they might break and, taking off the shirt, laid it on the table. Then, in a businesslike fashion, Nolly helped him with his boots, kneeling at Jack's feet, the perfect manservant, though he'd surely never had a day's training, all serious, his dark brows drawn together in concentration. Then he took off Jack's boots and stockings, and unbuttoned and slid off his trousers, and finally, the bit of cloth that served as Jack's undergarment.

Jack had never been as shy as Nolly, he'd lived too much in the streets for that, but he did flinch now, standing in a state of nature, as Nolly's eyes swept him up and down, and he wondered whether Nolly would find fault. Nolly was so particular, after all.

"In you get," was all Nolly said, as severe as any governess Jack had ever heard. Though he sensed that the severity was a cover for Nolly's tender nature, as standing in a closed room with a naked man not his relation was not something he'd ever been subjected to enough to be comfortable with. Well, it was sweet, so Jack couldn't bear to tease him about it. Maybe later.

So, instead, Jack tapped his forehead, a mock salute, and tendered himself into the tub. His skin seemed to draw against his bones at the hot water for a moment, as the steam rose around him with curling fingers. That the water was almost too hot was not a shock. What was different was the softness of the water, the smooth surface of the tub beneath his legs and backside.

Nolly knelt on the stone floor, his sleeves rolled up, looking quite pleased with himself. His lashes swept down over his blushed cheeks, a little smile curving his eyes, as if this moment was his greatest pleasure, the moment where he shared his joy in hot water and soap. Jack considered Nolly could do as he pleased, forever 'n ever, long as he continued smiling like that.

"I'm sure I'll die from all this hot water," Jack said, looking up at Nolly.

"You will not die," said Nolly. "I promise."

Baths were not unknown to Jack, but they weren't commonplace, at least not the all-over kind. Fagin had liked to have a little warm water around to daub his hands, and encouraged his boys to do the same, as dirty fingers were the sure ruin of a many a pickpocket. Then on the ship, there'd been one bath before he'd debarked at Port Jackson, to make him presentable, and though the water had been fresh, it had been cold. At the farm and the barracks, there'd been bathing on Saturdays, though the same cold water prevailed, and the sourest of soaps that stung the skin and seemed to abrade the dirt away in the most painful manner. So that was his attitude, and for good reason, and although he knew that Nolly had a thing for washing, Jack had never understood why.

But now, as Nolly wet the flannel cloth, swirling it around in the steaming tub next to Jack's legs, Jack thought this bath might be different. Nolly soaped the cloth and, ever so carefully, lifted it to Jack's neck, where he rubbed the skin there, soft and slow, and then all up and down Jack's back, and across his chest. The soap slid in long, drifting bubbles, shiny in the candlelight, with a perfume Jack couldn't identify. The slippery feel of it made him shudder with pleasure. He gripped the edges of the tub, sitting very still so that Nolly would do that, do that again, keep doing *that*.

And Nolly did, with more soap, and streams of hot water along Jack's shoulders and arms, and the steam rose up, coming down in sweat dripping from Jack's nose, Nolly's expression was serious in the soapy-sweet air, his attention on what his hands were doing.

"What's this?" asked Nolly.

Jack looked to where Nolly was tracing a finger along the back of his arm, where the skin was reddened and sore, and along his ribs on that side.

"It's from before," said Jack. "When they was puttin' us on the boat to come home. On the dock, you got stripped bare, an' sprinkled with powder. I didn't get in the barrel fast enough, an' it just kept burnin'."

"Does it hurt?"

"Itches sometimes," said Jack, completely undone by the dark light in Nolly's eyes that meant he was concerned and wanted to do something about it. "Never mind," Jack said, because there was nothing Nolly could do about it except get some expensive balm to treat it, and they hadn't enough to pay the doctors as it was. "You can keep goin', afore the water gets cold."

"Very well," said Nolly, dunking the flannel cloth in the water once more. "I'll wash your hair in a moment."

Jack could not respond, not even to protest, for Nolly had taken the cloth and was running it along Jack's leg. The tub wasn't as long as a man, so Jack's knees were two, heat-pink islands in the water that was quickly turning grey. The cloth in Nolly's hands went along Jack's thighs and over his knees and down to Jack's feet, which he normally didn't like to have touched, but Nolly's hand was firm and slow, so it didn't tickle, and as Nolly scrubbed both of Jack's ankles beneath the water, Jack did not once think of kicking him away.

Then Nolly soaped the cloth again, his face turning a fine shade of rose as he washed Jack between his legs, his brow furrowed with this most personal undertaking. Jack never moved, though his mind raced with a million ways to tease. But if he did, Nolly would stop. And certainly feeling clean like this, with the hot water and soap that Nolly loved so well, was an entirely new sensation.

Nolly put the washcloth between Jack's legs one last time, and Jack leered a bit, because it wouldn't do to let Nolly get too complacent Never think that Jack was completely tame. Satisfyingly, Nolly scowled, and placed the cloth over the edge of the tub.

Without warning, he took the tin pitcher and plopped it in the water, scooping it up full and dumping it over Jack's head. Jack pretended to be shocked, sputtering and speaking garbled words that nobody would understand. In a moment, Nolly's hands were on his head, sweeping his wet hair back, lathering up the soap and gently, oh, so gently, washed Jack's hair. Some of the soap ran into his eyes and stung, but he just blinked this away, tasting the soap on his lips, and looked at Nolly, and imagined what his kiss would taste like, with soap, his lips damp with water.

That would come, to be certain, for if Nolly was with him, there would be baths. Baths such as this one, though this wasn't like the quick wash he'd given Nolly. And then a new thought occurred. What if it were he outside the tub, and Nolly were the one within it? How would it be then? Just as good? Or better? Jack couldn't decide; either would be delightful. He groaned, his cock tightening in spite of the heated water.

"You best be finishin' up," Jack said, his voice clogging in his throat, "so I can have at you, now that I'm all worked up like this."

Nolly paused, his hands on Jack's head.

The privacy of the laundry held fast, as if this moment were enchanted, for normally that sort of comment would have Nolly scolding and pulling back and making things difficult in the name of chastity, and all for a world that would never know the difference whether Nolly had come in another man's hand or not. But Nolly did none of those things and instead a soft smile curled his mouth.

Eager to be at it, Jack let go of the tub and splashed some water around.

"Come on, come on, will you?"

Rinsing his hands in the bathwater, Nolly stood up and got some more hot water in the bucket.

"Now you must stand up," Nolly said, "so I can rinse you off properly."

Jack's cock was hard as a pole against his belly, and there was no denying it, so he stood up, taking Nolly's proffered arm to steady himself, and refused to be shy about it. Nolly was shy enough for five lads, and that was the truth of it. Maybe if he saw how easy it was, how natural, he would become less shy, in time. At least with Jack.

But even as Nolly poured several buckets of warm water over Jack's head to rinse him, he avoided looking where Jack wanted him to look.

"Ain't you never seen another man like this, Nolly?" asked Jack.

Nolly shook his head, the action full of shame, it seemed, and pathetic that was, in Jack's mind.

"Never looked at yourself then? Not even once?"

"Maybe once or twice," said Nolly. "But it's not how they teach you in church—"

"Well, blast the church, for making you blind like that. It's no different than a leg or an arm, 'ceptin' it gives so much pleasure."

For a moment it looked as though Nolly was going to pull back, drop the bucket, and march out of the room in a fit of piety. It made Jack cross to think of it, and he didn't like it. So he stepped out of the tub, and took the bucket from Nolly to put it on the ground. Then he pressed up close, all wet and dripping, his body against Nolly's, sharing himself, but not making his cock something Nolly had to look at if he weren't ready.

"I won't tease you," said Jack, because he'd never felt sorrier for anyone in his life. "It's just me, after all, an' pleased to see you."

"Yes, I gathered," said Nolly, with a little rueful laugh as he let Jack hold him, and circled his arms around Jack in return. "I don't know how it's done, you know. Not sober anyway. Is this how it's done? What you an' me are doin'?"

Oh, that tender little slip in Nolly's words, that quick taste of street language, made Jack's heart feel good, full through. It was like a tiny taste of Nolly unguarded, how it might be if he wasn't so stiff all the time with a rod up his arse, making like a respectable gentleman was all there was to be, or know, or do. Surely there were advantages to it, but it shouldn't keep anyone from pleasure, especially not his Nolly. And Jack could show him this, by-and-bye, in this warm room, with its simple pleasures of hot water and soap and the promise of something afterwards. But slowly, so as not to startle him off.

But Nolly pulled back and dried Jack, and made him put on his new clothes. Of course, *made* wasn't the exact word, as Jack never took orders from anybody. Except that Nolly had a way of getting his way. Besides, Nolly looked so sweet when pleased with himself, and his hands were gentle as he helped Jack put on his new clothes, even though it was bedtime.

"What're you fussin' with anyhow?" sputtered Jack, as Nolly dressed him in the sturdy stockings, the thick trousers and waist-coat, the collarless shirt of striped cotton. But this was just for the effect of it, as if he were truly bewildered instead of undone by the attention, feeling the heat of the bath pulling at his bones, exhausted. "I'm to take them off in a moment—an' just how many buttons are there?"

"Many," said Nolly, with unaccustomed dryness. "Seven." He tucked the thick shirt in Jack's trousers, and did the last button. Then he stood up, patting Jack's belly.

"You look a fine treat in that," said Nolly, stepping back. "It's not what you ever wore in the City, to be sure, but it's a good effect."

"You ain't tryin' to make me like you, are you, Nolly?"

Nolly's eyes widened and he shook his head.

"No indeed. I rather like you as you are, in your brightly

colored waistcoat and shiny top hat. But, well, while we're here, you should be warm instead of cold."

"An' I like you as you are," said Jack, smiling. "Especially since them trousers you got on make your arse look ever so sweet." Jack liked the way those words tasted, having wanted to say them since he'd first clapped eyes on Nolly so long ago in that graveyard in the snow.

But Nolly backed away, brow furrowed, his hands coming down, spread at his sides as if to hide himself from the world. That was a misstep, then; of course, Nolly didn't like talk like that, as might come out of the mouth of any coarse sailor, or from the people who stared at him as if he were something they might own. And while normally Jack might feel stung at having such a compliment, his first *real* compliment, practically refused, he knew there was a way around this.

"Say, say, say," said Jack, coming close, cupping Nolly's shoulders then moving with soft hands up to his face. "Nobody's noticed but me, an' that's a promise. They just look so fine on you, is all. But only for my eyes. Mine alone."

He'd thought that he'd gone too far, making a claim like that, but Nolly's eyes went dark and he nodded, seeming to understand at least a little what Jack meant. So Jack kissed him on the mouth light and quick and then gave Nolly's cheek a gentle pat.

"I'm half wrung out from that bath an' these new clothes, never mind all that work today. But will you take up that book an' read to me? The one about the sailor, not them fuckin' sonnets."

If there were ways into Nolly's heart, one of them was surely books. Jack would have said, had anybody asked him six months ago, whether he would have demanded a book be read to him, he would have denied it quite strongly. But now being read to was no a hardship, now that he understood why Nolly loved it

"Come on, then," said Nolly, as pleased as if this had been his own idea.

Jack slung his arm around Nolly's neck, pausing while Nolly picked up the candle. They left Jack's old clothes for Mrs. Heyland to deal with, and together went to their room. Jack thought of it that way now, though it was still the sickroom, a disused corner of an enormous empty house. He made himself ignore the question of what price they might be made to pay for the use of it. Besides, it was better to watch Nolly fuss with the candle and the buttons on his trousers, the laces on his boots. It was a more enticing prospect to watch Nolly disrobe at any hour of the day or night, and Jack would never question that.

Watching Nolly, standing there in only his shirt, pulling the book out from under the mattress with a contented sigh, was just the crowning glory on the treat. Jack quickly took off his new clothes, except for the shirt, so soft against his skin and threw them in a pile in the corner. Ignoring Nolly's scowl, which Jack returned with a broad, toothy smile, he climbed into bed, and patted the space beside him.

"In you get, start readin'. I'll be asleep afore the old man tells that sailor his secret, else."

"The Abbe and Dantes," said Nolly, pretending to be stern. He took his place in the bed, his back cushioned by the pillows. Then Jack took Nolly's shoulder for a pillow, which was enough for him, and pulled the bedclothes up, taking care not to muss the lower edge of the book.

"Do it," said Jack, pushing his thumb at the book. "Do what you always do. Lick your finger, turn the page. Read."

So Nolly did. He read about the priest and the young sailor becoming friends and master and pupil, the old man teaching the sailor everything he knew. After the harrowing beginning of the story, the schoolroom of the prison must was like a balm, and indeed, to Jack, it seemed like the pleasantest of interludes, and as desirable as a stolen kiss on a warm afternoon.

Listening to Nolly read aloud, voice sweet and low, watching him, eyes half-lidded, so damn relaxed, was as beatific a thing as Jack had ever seen. And he'd seen a lot. Nolly was so relaxed that Jack was able to snug down, resting his cheek on Nolly's belly, his arm looped across Nolly's hips. But this made it difficult for Nolly to turn the pages, with Jack's chin almost brushing the edge of the book.

"Jack, what *are* you doing? I cannot get on with your head in the way."

"You smell like a posy," said Jack, not perturbed in the slightest. He squeezed Nolly's hips. "How do you manage after a day with the guts of fish all around you?"

"I'd smell better if I'd had the bath," said Nolly, licking his finger and attempting to tug the page gently around Jack's chin. "But you're the one who did, so I'd say you're the one smelling like flowers."

"Don't," said Jack. He reached up to still Nolly's hand with his own. "Don't *ever* say that. I'm a street thief who don't smell like no posy."

"Oh, but you do," said Nolly, and as Jack tilted his head up, Nolly was looking down at him, fond, one eyebrow arched, as if he meant to be fierce. "You very much do."

As Oliver turned the page, he almost tore it, barely able to feel the texture of the edge of it. His arm curved as he reached around Jack's head, but he could barely manage that, his heart was pounding so. The weight of Jack's head was against his belly, arm curved round him, Jack's hair drying like black ink spread out over his shirt and the white counterpane, as if it had been spilled. Oliver's mouth went dry as Jack pressed closer, as if apologizing for an argument that made no sense whatsoever. Because Jack didn't really smell like a posy, didn't smell like the street, or smoke from a tavern—there was the scent of soap, and beneath that, something else.

Oliver tried to swallow, but his nose was filled with Jack's clean scent, like a low murmur that filled the ears and drew the listener in. But he couldn't blame Jack for being a distraction; the bath had been his idea after all, a small story with hot water and soap and a kindness that he could repay to Jack. He'd not counted on Jack standing straight up in the bath, skin streaming, water dappled on his lashes, slicking his mouth, and dripping from the base of Jack's cock.

He'd had to focus on Jack's face, in spite of the overwhelming sense of it, how he wanted to kiss Jack and never stop. But one didn't *stare*, one simply didn't. And Jack had taken pity on him in the laundry and had not teased. Rather, he had folded himself against Oliver so his tumescent state could be felt rather than seen.

But now Oliver was excited as well, though he shifted, taking his hand a moment to tug down his shirt, to pull up the sheet. He knew Jack was looking at him; Jack wasn't blind, and Oliver took a deep breath, hoping to find a way to douse his excitement, for they couldn't, they could *not* engage in carnal pleasures with the rest of the household sleeping above them. But how to stop it? What could he do, but keep reading? So he turned the page.

"You skipped a bit there, Nolly," said Jack, and Oliver almost jumped out of his skin.

"No, I didn't, it's—" But then he looked and realized Jack was right, and hopelessly shrugged his shoulders, wanting to toss the book aside and pull Jack to him, only he didn't dare. Jack was well again, but the last time they'd done anything like this, it had been in the cover of darkness, in a room over a noisy tavern, and Oliver had been stone blind with drink. It was much easier to let go when no one, not even yourself, could see what you were doing.

Oliver jumped again when Jack cupped his arm and began to stroke it slowly.

"Hey, easy, *easy*. You're all torqued up," said Jack, softly. He kissed Oliver, planting a kiss in the middle of his belly, as if he were kissing the shirt. "I could take care of that for you. Would you like me to?"

The question, as bare as it was, was typical of Jack. Of course he would suggest it, straight out like that. Of course the answer should be no.

"We can't, Jack," Oliver said, concentrating on the book, though the words were jumping about, as though someone had let them out of a box. "It'll mess the sheets, and everybody will know."

"Bother that," said Jack. "Anyhow, I know a way so it won't."

Oliver opened his mouth to ask how that could even be possible, but was distracted by Jack taking the book to dog-ear the page, and then, as he leaned to put the book on the floor, the sheets got pulled, baring Oliver's legs to the candlelight. Oliver jerked the sheets back in place, and Jack along with them.

"It won't, I promise," said Jack.

"How can you promise that, Jack, how?" Oliver knew his voice came out sharply, but he didn't know how to stop it.

"Tell you what," said Jack, with a little smile, half winking at Oliver. "A wager. If I mess up these sheets, I'll go to church with you on Sunday."

"Will it hurt?" Oliver found himself asking. He was giving in without much of a fight, but how could he do otherwise with Jack looking up at him like that, his hands already tugging at the bedclothes. That dimple when he smiled, a dimple that Oliver had never seen before.

"Would never hurt you, Nolly," said Jack. "It'll be good, I promise."

Barely able to think in a straight line, let alone answer out loud, Oliver nodded. His lips were numb and his heart raced as though it wanted to explode out of his chest, but he couldn't take his eyes off of what Jack was doing.

"Come down like this," Jack said, tugging at him, making Oliver slip down from a sitting position, pulling the pillow so his head could rest upon it. The sheets and blankets were now a-tumble, but Jack pulled those straight as well, away from Oliver's middle, and Oliver couldn't help the gasp that escaped him.

Jack knelt up, on all fours, his shirt gaping away from his body, giving Oliver a glimpse of his naked chest and legs through the hole of the neck. Then Jack dipped down, kissing Oliver's thigh, a mere brush of his mouth.

"You know I won't hurt you, Nolly," said Jack. "I only want to give you some ease, but you may tell me to stop if you like. Tell me to stop, an' I will. This moment."

There wasn't a bit of a tease in Jack's eyes, green and flickering in the candlelight. He was perfectly serious and holding himself quite still, and there was a sense of something else that Oliver couldn't interpret. A tenderness that only Jack could express, in stillness, in waiting, that Oliver knew that were he to wave him off, to say *no*, Jack would pick up the book from the floor, curl up at Oliver's side, and bid him to go on reading.

But Oliver's heart was pounding, each breath drawing in Jack's scent, the promise in his eyes, the closeness of him. And that closeness vibrated within him, in his chest, down the back of his legs, in his belly, his groin. Everywhere. He didn't know how to make it go away, but Jack did.

"Yes—I mean—no." Oliver took a breath. "Don't stop."

Jack nodded, not mocking, not even laughing, just serious and quiet, and Oliver let out the breath he was holding. Then, moving slowly, Jack slid down, taking the counterpane, the sheet and blanket, with him, tucked himself against Oliver's legs, and curled his fingers around the bottom of Oliver's shirt. He did all of this in an ordinary way, as if people did this every day, and Oliver supposed that they did, though he'd never even gotten a hint that they did what Jack was doing. For Jack was stroking Oliver's thighs, first one thigh, then the other, using one hand only, resting on his elbow, his weight against Oliver. But this weight felt steadying, keeping him anchored to the bed, reminding him that this was Jack, and that there was no need for fear.

Even when Jack pulled Oliver's shirt up, exposing the part of himself that he'd never much subjected to observation; even in the bath, it wasn't done, it simply wasn't done. But Jack was looking as he stroked and petted at the thin dark line that led from Oliver's belly button to the tangle of Oliver's private hair, and the line of his hardness, standing up pink and straight, the tip of it a darker red, and Oliver had to blink several times at what Jack was doing. Reaching for Oliver's cock, cupping it in his hand to stroke it up and down. If he did that for much longer, Oliver knew he was going to ejaculate all over the sheets, and how would Jack keep his promise then?

He was about to say something, to muster up everything he had to get the words out of his mouth, when Jack moved back onto his knees, his shirt coming off one shoulder, his neck bent so that Oliver could see the top of his dark head. Then, all at once, from amidst the bedclothes, Oliver felt something wet and warm upon him. As Jack shifted back, supporting himself on one arm, Oliver could see that while Jack had one hand around him, he had his mouth upon him also, and before Oliver could say anything, anything, Jack swiped his tongue around the dark red top, and sank down, swallowing him up.

Any words, any words at all, that Oliver had known left him, all at once, and went racing out of his mind, leaving him breathless, open mouthed, his head arching back as Jack did this thing to him, this sweet, sinful thing. Jack's mouth was tight on Oliver's cock, slick and tight, a wet sucking that slid up and down, Jack's hand was at the base of him, anchoring him as his mouth pulled, the pad of his tongue sweeping along. It felt as if every single nerve in Oliver's body was collecting at whatever spot Jack was attending to.

And then Jack's hand turned, a flick of his wrist, and he tucked his fingers around the flesh that had tightened between Oliver's legs—and Jack shouldn't be *doing* that—but he was, tickling and petting, and with a quick, hard suck of his mouth, pulled Oliver to where his whole body seemed to tighten, and his back arched, his head tipping back, releasing his seed into Jack's mouth, not even able to breathe, or see anything but the ceiling, which flickered as the bed bumped the table with the candle upon it. He felt Jack's throat move and swallow, and Jack's hand, petting the inside of his thigh as Oliver's body shivered on the bed. Jack's mouth came off him gently, and Jack settled Oliver's spent cock against his private hair.

Oliver sensed rather than saw Jack lick his lips, could almost feel him smile.

"Reckon there's no church for me then, eh, Nolly?"

He felt Jack flick his thumb across the inside of his thigh, and blinked at the ceiling, watching the candlelight as it become steady and still. For a moment, he thought of the shame of it, of what they'd just done, him and Jack, even as it had saved the sheets. Then he caught Jack's eyes with his own, saw the way that Jack was still over him, as if protecting him from his own doubts, or from the world's castigation, and the struggle, and the shame, which was his own and not Jack's, left him. Oh, it would be back, but for now, with Jack there above him, it vanished, a vapor, burned away.

"You want to taste what you taste like, then?" Jack licked his lips, as if savoring them, and the wetness of them drew Oliver's attention, and he nodded, not really thinking about what he was doing.

Jack leaned in with care and, scooting up, planted an arm on either side of Oliver's shoulders, and kissed Oliver on the mouth. Jack's lips tasted of salt, so intense and unfamiliar that Oliver could hardly bear the thought of what it was that Jack had swallowed.

As Jack's arms scooped around him, his mouth wet and soft and careful, Oliver closed his eyes, and pulled Jack on top of him, holding him close, tasting himself and Jack, and felt shivers running through Jack, who, though so recently ill, had done this for him. Had brought him such pleasure, much the sweeter for having been experienced without the drink. This lovely thing his Jack had brought him, had *wrung* from him, tender and careful.

Jack's weight felt good upon him, and as Jack took his mouth away, Oliver opened his eyes.

"No church for me, ever," said Jack.

"No," agreed Oliver, smiling because he felt like it. He didn't need to hide it, not when it was just him and Jack.

He pushed away the dark hair that had spilled across Jack's

forehead, and thought now he might be able to understand how Jack saw the world, the way it might be, the good things, that nothing, not even church, could approach. His throat tightened up as he struggled for a way to express this, but the words remained coy and refused to come near.

Jack hefted his weight so he was on his elbow, half-resting on Oliver's chest. He pulled the bedclothes up, smiling, cocky, proud of himself. Oliver reached out and held his hand.

"Should I—should I do the same for you? Do you want me to, Jack?" The prospect of it terrified him, but up till now, it had mostly been Jack pleasuring him, Jack's hands on him, and now Jack's mouth—with Oliver almost never doing anything for Jack in return. It was selfish. "Shall I? I could do it, if you'd teach me."

His reward was a smile, and a short, almost silent laugh; Jack's mouth open, the crinkle beside his eyes.

"You are sweet to ask, my dear Nolly, so sweet." Jack bent to kiss Oliver again, his tongue sweeping across his own mouth before doing it. "But I'm as worn as a bottle rag after a day like today. But I'll hold you to it, teach you everythin' I know. Everythin'."

It occurred to Oliver as Jack slid down in the bed, pulling up the bedclothes to wrap around them both, to ask where it was that Jack had learned what he knew and promised to teach. All the touching, the ways of it, how fingers and hands moved, what mouths could do.

Of course, Jack had lived in the streets most of his life, had traveled on a long voyage at sea, had lived among strangers. But as Oliver looked down where Jack was snug against him, his eyes already closing, lashes fanning against his cheeks, he could not bring himself to ask. For Jack was worn out, it was easy to see, and asking more of him would be a cruel, and more of a sin than what Jack had done to him.

"Promise you will, Jack, for it can't just be you doing—doing things for me."

"Oh," said Jack, a yawn breaking off his words. "I promise. All kinds of things, especially since you were so brave in trustin' me."

"How can I not," said Oliver, almost missing Jack's small smile of pleasure as he burrowed against him.

Oliver reached up to pinch out the light, as he'd seen Jack do, the sizzle of wax between his fingers scenting the air with honey. He slid down beneath the bedclothes, adjusting the pillows beneath his head, drawing a full breath. The weight of Jack's head on his shoulder felt right, felt comforting. His whole body, in fact, felt more relaxed than he could recall being in such a long time.

"Thank you, Jack," he said in the darkness, his mind slipping into a spin that would soon lead to sleep. "I had no idea, not even the slightest."

"Nobody does till they know," said Jack, with a sleepy slowness.

Oliver bent down to kiss the top of Jack's head, tasting the moisture of the water, the scent of soap, and, drowsily, Jack said something that Oliver couldn't quite hear. It didn't matter, for Jack would say it to him again in the morning, Oliver was sure of it.

❧ 23 ❧

A WORKADAY WORLD HOLDS
SOME SURPRISES

I n the morning, Oliver awoke, feeling as though he'd been tied
to the bed, only when he opened his eyes, it was Jack curled
around him, his arm across Oliver's belly. Holding him, while
he'd slept better than he'd thought possible. There was a calmness
to his limbs, a low rumble of pleasure, the memory of Jack's mouth
on him the night before. And a smile he did not even trouble
himself to suppress.

Suddenly, there was a knock at the door, and Oliver sat up
quickly to dislodge Jack before anyone saw. Though perhaps the
closeness of their bodies might be taken at face value, that Jack
and Oliver were only huddled together for warmth. In a village
such as this, the most obvious thing would be what was accepted.
The only thing that would give them away would be the expression
on his face as the door opened. He struggled to tame from the
florid heat in his cheeks.

"Did you not hear the missus calling?" asked Melinda, as she
poked her head through the doorway, no doubt getting an eyeful of
them both. "All the bacon'll be gone if you don't hurry."

She shut the door behind her, leaving Oliver to struggle into
his clothes, and to rouse Jack. Who, as seemed usual, awoke slowly,

with all the casualness of a well-born gentleman who knows that his breakfast will be held for him, no matter how delayed the hour.

"Hurry, Jack, you must hurry." Oliver tucked his shirttails into his trousers, and made sure he had the buttons snug in their proper places.

"There will be bacon aplenty, Nolly," said Jack. "Even if she'll charge you a penny a slice, that one."

"She must stick to her budget, surely." He didn't want to get into an argument with Jack so early in the morning.

"Oh, all right. Ha'penny, then. On account of your pretty face." Jack managed to get into his trousers, sat down to lace his boots, and stood up to stamp them on the floor, to get his heels to slide all the way in. "Come on, then, before your stomach deafens us with its growlin'."

As Oliver finished dressing, he admired Jack in his new attire, trying to stem the feeling of pride but failing. Jack saw him failing, and reached out to pat his cheek in a slow lingering way that started Oliver's heartbeat racing.

"Never mind that now, you tease," said Jack, who gave him a swift peck on the brow as he helped Oliver with his suspenders.

Still smiling, Oliver followed Jack into the kitchen, where the smell of bacon frying, and slabs of ham with a drizzle of brown sugar on top were being carried to the table. There was also porridge and sugar and cream.

"It's raining today, already," Mrs. Heyland said in answer to his unasked question. "Thought you lads might like a bit of warmth in your stomachs before you go down to the Cobb."

Looking out the window at the sheet of grey, the rain was more like a fine mist, but if it encouraged Mrs. Heyland to fry the ham instead of serving it to them cold, then he was all for it. He ate everything that was put in front of him, and encouraged Jack to eat his share, tapping the edge of his plate when Jack's attention wandered, and pulling the stout pitcher of cream towards Jack when he faltered on finishing his porridge.

"Would you like sugar as well?" Oliver beckoned for the bowl with the flakes of sugar in it, and then realized that the maidservants and Mrs. Heyland were staring at him. "He really does need to keep his strength up," he said to them. "That's what Dr. McMurtry said."

With a slight shake of her head, Mrs. Heyland returned to her breakfast, drinking her tea with the utmost concentration. There was nothing she could say, nothing that would contradict a well-educated doctor at any rate. Which left Oliver in peace to prod Jack to eat more, to take another swallow of hot tea, to finish his bacon.

"You can have it," said Jack. "Truly, I've had enough."

Oliver let himself have the last slice of bacon on Jack's plate, conscious of the startled stare of Tim from across the table. Fine-bred people didn't share food like this; he knew that, but had chosen to forget.

"Thank you for breakfast, Mrs. Heyland," said Oliver as he stood up. "We'll do a good day's work now, and will have your shillings for you by Saturday, I should think."

"Indeed," said Mrs. Heyland. "I'll see you at supper, then. Give Mr. Thurly my regards."

"We will," said Jack.

After he put his coat and hat on, Oliver waited while Jack raced back to the room to grab his coat, but upon his return, Oliver opened the door, letting the slanting rain came in, splashing on the threshold. It would be a dreary day on the Cobb, nothing like the sprightly day they'd had the day before. He shivered as he pulled his collar up, wishing he had some sort of cloak to keep the rain off. As they stepped outside, Jack pulled up his collar, and Oliver looked at him.

"You can stay here, where it's dry. Help Mrs. Heyland out, instead of coming with me."

"I should say not," said Jack. He shook his head and tugged on Oliver's arm to get him to start walking along the lane toward town. "Not if it means stayin' here with that lot an' worryin' about you fallin' in again. I don't care if he was your work mate, that was a vicious thing to do."

"It was only a prank, after all," said Oliver.

"A prank," said Jack. "One that tossed you into the drink to get smashed against the Cobb. The Cobb is wide, Nolly." Jack stopped at the point where the road began to dip down, and pointed. "Do you see from here how wide it is? There's no way he could mistake which side he was pushing you off of."

Oliver looked at the arm of the Cobb stretching out into the boiling, rain-grey sea. It was a wide, thick beam of rocks, from side to side, as solid as could be, enough to keep the inside of the Cobb fairly still, where the fishing smacks and a small three-masted barque were hove to. What Jack said was true; the Cobb was too wide for forgetting which side you were on. But perhaps it had just been an error in judgment, that the sea would have been so rough that the waves would roil over his head and pull him under so quickly.

"Never mind," said Oliver. "It's done now, so come on, or we'll be late."

The storm rolled away at dinnertime, with breezy skies that played hide and seek with the sun between patches of misty grey and clear blue sky. With the bits of sunlight, Oliver was able to warm up for the first time that day, and the blood on his hands from the fish didn't feel quite so cold.

"You," said Mr. Thurly to Jack. "Bring that last bucket; c'mon lads, time for a break."

Once they were seated at the table, Oliver watched to make sure that Jack ate his fair share today, which was fish and potatoes fried in lard with onion. In the swiftly moving open air, it was delicious and Oliver was tempted to ask for seconds, except that every scrap was accounted for. The sleek dockside cats wove in and around their feet, and were given special scraps by Mr. Thurly.

Taking a swallow of small beer from the tin tumbler beside his plate, Oliver truly felt like smiling. Just outright, on account of nothing.

He caught Jack watching him out of the corner of his eyes, and did smile. When Jack smiled back, a patch of sunlight sprayed across the Cobb, and for a moment, it was like summer, with a breeze cooling the salt-spiced air, and Jack, there beside him, looking as though he was feeling better.

Jack ducked his head to whisper a confidence near Oliver's ear.

"You quit starin' at me like that," he said. "Or they'll start to talk."

"What?" Oliver sat upright and took a hurried assessment of their present company. To a man, they were scraping the last of the fried fish from tin plates, and no one was paying them any mind. He wanted to glower at Jack and started to, but Jack just smiled and Oliver couldn't quite manage it.

"Jack," he said.

"What, then?"

There was something inside of him that he wanted to say, only he didn't know how. Not with an audience of rough fish-gutters, but that was the least of it. It was the sight of Jack beside him, on a windy day, with no evidence of anyone chasing them, and the future full of his bookshop and Jack. He only had to make it through the next few years, and he could easily manage this, as long as he had Jack with him. Of this he was sure.

"Nothing," he said, smiling back. "Nothing at all."

At the end of the day, with Jack at his side, Oliver took off his apron and laid it on the deal table with the rest of the aprons, and rolled down his sleeves. Jack handed him his jacket and his hat, and gave Oliver's shoulder a pat to show that all was well. Of course, Jack shouldn't have tried to do any work, even something as simple as rinsing gutted fish so that they could be properly packed in barrels with salt. Even with the speckles of sunlight coming from behind the clouds, he looked a little pale, with circles under his eyes. But when he saw Oliver looking at him, he managed a smile and a nod.

"That's us, then. D'you reckon the missus will wait supper for us? I know you don't want to miss her good cookin'."

This was meant to amuse, and it did, making Oliver smile even as he attempted to find a way to deny that Mrs. Heyland's cooking was less than delicious. "It's hot and it's filling," he said, finally. "And that's better than as might be, though Mrs. Pierson could make far better use of that kitchen than Mrs. Heyland. If you'd ever tasted Mrs. Pierson's roasted chicken or even her bread, with fresh butter on it, you'd agree."

Jack gave him a smile, and then they made their way across the slippery stairs that led from the Cobb to the shorefront, which was wide for the traffic, but muddy and potted with stones.

"You think the old man was playin' us for fools?" asked Jack. "Or do folks actually bathe in these waters?"

Oliver surveyed the surf. The entire day it had boiled and moved, running out to sea and baring the muddy flats beneath, but always moving and sending up sprays of cold, icy water. A late smack was limping in, its sails half down, and on the swirling breeze, he could smell the cargo of half-rotted and worthless fish.

"That's in the summertime," said Oliver. "And they use little bathing huts on wheels, or something."

"Madness," said Jack. "That's what that is. There's fish in there that will eat you alive."

"I expect you're right," said Oliver, too tired to contemplate it further than that. "Here, we go up this way."

They turned to go up the lane, passing the church and the parsonage, and the tidy, green cemetery, with its moss-speckled headstones and gathering of marble tombs. The wind came from behind them, keeping the smell of the sea close around them, making Oliver shiver as his body, used to constant movement, now slowed to the simple task of walking.

"We've never worked together before," he said to Jack, thinking of that sense of companionship and satisfaction that he'd really never had at the haberdashery. "It isn't so bad, is it?"

Jack answered Oliver's smile with one of his own, but there was a wickedness in it. "Yes, we did. You an' me, at that house, Mrs. Whats-her-name, when we took her silver plate an' that."

"That was different," said Oliver, but the spell was broken. Jack was right, of course, to remind him of his singular attempt at house breaking. Even the fact that they were miles away, and that Mrs. Acton had almost deserved it, nothing would change the fact that it had been illegal. Just another token in his pile of sins. But if he said this out loud, then Jack was liable to tell him that no one was counting but him.

"What did you say we owed?" Jack asked, not because he cared, Oliver could see, but to distract him.

"Ten shillings and sixpence, all told," said Oliver. "We'll have four shillings to give Mrs. Heyland on Saturday, with none left over."

"That won't buy nothin'," said Jack, as they started uphill to go along the tree-lined Gage Lane.

Jack took a breath, probably to explain, that, of course, there were easier ways to make money, other than working themselves to death for it, but along behind them came the sound of footsteps. At first Oliver thought it was some errand boy late for a delivery, but when he turned, he saw that it was Leander Warren, whose attention Oliver had been at pains to avoid.

Leander came right up to them, and grabbed Oliver's arm.

"Whoa there, Oliver, I've a word to say to you."

Jack opened his mouth, as if he were about to launch at Leander. Oliver shook his head at Jack; if there was to be a fight, they were already bested, Leander was just that big. Besides, he let go of Oliver as soon as he and Jack had stopped. Then he wiped his forehead with the back of his shirtsleeve, leaving a streak of grime that would surely displease his wife. On top of that, Leander looked quite bestirred.

"I came to say," began Leander. He crumpled his hat in his hands. "I came to say that I were only havin' a bit of fun, t'other day, you see. You being the new boy, and all. You were meant to go into the water on the inside of the Cobb, not the outside. You see?"

For a moment Oliver could only look at him, for, as Jack had pointed out, pushing somebody off the Cobb on the outside could not have been done by accident.

"My wife nearly had my hide, when she heard about it. I tried all day to tell you, couldn't manage it in front of me mates. Right?"

"Oh." Oliver thought about this. "On the inside."

"Yes, where the muck goes and the seaweed and such. But you can swim right out, or climb up the ladder, nice and easy. You'll just stink a bit the rest of the day, an' it's worth a laugh."

It was quite something that this big, burly fellow was actually taking the time to apologize, or at least explain, what had happened. And it made sense, as compared to the rest of the ocean, the water on the inside of the Cobb was as calm as a pond.

"Thank you for explaining," he said, using his best manners, trying to avoid looking at Jack's expressive eyebrows, mocking him for doing such a thing. "I can swim well enough, but not in that sort of water."

"Dressed, an' with boots on," said Leander, nodding. "You should have sunk like a stone. I'm glad you didn't."

"Why-ever for?" Jack asked with some astonishment. "Why should you be glad? Why should you care atall?"

"Well," said Leander. He put his hat back on and straightened his jacket. "I don't know, really. I reckon it's because you look like someone I know."

"But I've never met you before."

This was true and Leander nodded, scratching the back of his head. "Mr. Thurly said that Mrs. Heyland told him that the parson told her that you'd come lookin' for your people. Only you didn't find 'em."

"Yes," said Oliver, ignoring the fact that it was rather queer to be having this conversation with an almost perfect stranger who had tried to drown him. "I came looking for my mother's people, the Flemings. My mother, Agnes, well, you see—"

"Bloody Christ."

At the words from Leander, stopped Oliver short.

"You're the baby. You're *that* baby." Leander was bleached white, his eyes wide and dark.

All in one motion, Jack grabbed Oliver's arm. "Let's go, Nolly, let's go now. He doesn't know, he can't know."

But it appeared that he did.

"That's it," Leander said reverently, looking at Oliver, as if he'd suddenly seen the sun rise on a pitch-black and endless night. "That's you, then. I knew it, I knew there was something. I should have seen it when I saw you laughing today. You've got her eyes, and that elegant look, like a painting she was. And guts. Oh, how that girl could dance." For a moment, Leander's attention veered off to some inner place, where the memories of a dancing girl wove in and out.

"Nolly," said Jack. He sounded desperate.

"You knew my *mother?*" asked Oliver. He couldn't understand why he'd not thought of this before, that there were people in this village who were the same age as his mother would have been, had she lived. And here was one of them, who he'd been standing shoulder to shoulder with for days.

"She were the girl of my heart," said Leander, focusing on Oliver once more. "And of all the lads in the village, I was hers, at least for a time. Such a bright thing, she was, until the man in the long blue coat came a-knocking at her door. Then she only saw him, it were like the rest of us just vanished."

Oliver felt Jack tug on his sleeve, but it came from a distance, as if Jack were standing very far away, rather than right at his side like he was. Oliver looked at Leander to see if there was any recrimination on his face. After all, Agnes had gone off with someone not of the town, and had a bastard child.

"Me mam knew," said Leander, as if answering an unanswered

question. "She said it was a shame he'd cast such a spell over her, and then left, without waitin' for her, when he found out. About the baby."

"Did—did everyone know?" Oliver couldn't imagine what it must have been like, being with child in such a small village as this.

"Me mam," said Leander. "Maybe some others. And Captain Fleming, but that was after she left, and me mam went to him to offer comfort. He cried such great big tears, like a baby, me mam said. Only—" Here Leander paused to make sure that Oliver was paying attention. "Only not because of the disgrace of it, but because she'd gone off, and he'd likely never see you. Him an' Rose left quite soon after, a-lookin' for her. Her and the baby."

Leander pressed his thumb in the center of Oliver's chest. "She'd be quite proud to know you had such guts, to come all this way, lookin' for her. And not squallin' 'cause you got tossed into the drink." With a nod, Leander tipped the brim of his hat at them. "I must be off before my wife has my hide. See you on the morrow, Oliver. You too, Jack."

Leander turned and went back the way he'd come, down the damp lane and into the village, just as the rain began to fall.

Walking the rest of the way home, with Jack silently watching him, Oliver felt as though he were walking in a cocoon of air, where even the rain could not touch him. He'd not thought that anyone in Lyme would know his mother, or remember the time before she left. Aunt Rose and Uncle Brownlow had both refused to talk about that time, or about his mother. When they did talk about Agnes, it was couched in terms of the tragedy of a young girl, her womanhood cut off too soon. And never about how she'd been elegant and brave, or that she liked to dance, or that all the lads in the village fancied themselves in love with her.

Oliver had stared at the portrait of her, long lost now, for great stretches of time, but had never been able to glean what kind of girl she had been, nor why she'd fallen for a stranger in a long blue coat. Had she stayed in town and borne the reproach of the village, then he would have grown up here, perhaps in a small house in town, or on one of the farms that clung to the hillsides. It was impossible to know.

It wasn't until they arrived at the servants' entrance of Rhode Hill House that he realized he'd not spoken a single word to Jack as they'd walked. Jack who was looking at him with careful eyes, as if Oliver might sprout wings and fly back to Leander to hear more about Agnes, and the time that she'd lived.

Oliver wanted to say something reassuring, but as they went inside and shook off their jackets and hung them and Oliver's hat on the peg just inside the door, he couldn't imagine what he might say. *Did you hear? He said she was elegant, like a painting. And that everyone loved her. Did you hear?*

Jack, who had no mother, nor any interest in discovering who she might be, would likely be disinclined to hear Oliver go on about his long-dead one. Besides, Oliver wanted to collect his own feelings first, before saying anything out loud. And he wanted to hear more, whatever it was that Leander had to say.

"Would you go with me?" asked Oliver, as they hurried into the kitchen to wash for supper.

"Go?" asked Jack, pretending to splash in the basin while Oliver dried his hands. "Go where?"

"To talk to him again, to ask him about my mother."

"Of course I'll go," said Jack in a whisper as they sat down together. But he didn't sound as if he meant it. Rather, he sounded as if he'd expected this, and anticipated it to be a dreary affair.

"You lads, did you wash?" Mrs. Heyland stood over them with a tureen of soup. "Move that butter dish, there. Tim, pull your chair up to the table, you're liable to spill it all down your front."

Jack opened his mouth, as if to continue with a slight about Mrs. Heyland's cooking, Oliver was sure of it, so he pulled up his napkin and flicked it to settled it in his lap, making a great show of it to distract Jack. Obligingly, Jack was distracted, and also put his napkin in his lap, clasping his hands and bowing his head for grace.

When that was done, Mrs. Heyland served the soup. Oliver eyed the bits of cabbage and boiled potato floating in the brown broth. At least it wasn't eel; he could eat anything but eel. The table went silent, as everyone ate; the soup was welcome on such a cold day, and Oliver kept his eye on Jack to make sure he was eating his share. Then Mrs. Heyland dished up steak and kidney pie, with the robust juices sliding onto each plate.

And all the while, Oliver's heart thudded in his chest; he felt warm from the inside out at the thought that he had been walking the very streets and paths where his mother had walked. Along the Cobb, along the shoreline, in front of St. Michael's. Perhaps she'd even come to Rhode Hill House, for a country party, done by the gentry for the local village. Anything was possible.

"You want puddin'?" Jack jabbed him with an elbow, and Oliver looked up to see everyone staring at him.

"Are you coming down with something, young master?" asked Mrs. Heyland. "It's not like you to refuse something sweet."

"I'm sorry, Mrs. Heyland." Oliver wiped his palms on his trousers. "I'm a bit tired, but yes, I would like some pudding."

She dished out the pudding, and Oliver resolved to be more alert to the company he was in until he and Jack were alone together, and then, perhaps, he could talk about his mother.

But when supper ended, and they took themselves to the sick-room and shut the door behind them, he could see that Jack was too tired to be pleased for him. Or maybe it was that he was simply not interested, on account of not knowing about his own mother.

"You'll feel differently," said Oliver. The room was chilly and his shirt collar was damp. Would that the small room had a fireplace, even a little one. He lit the candle, and the flickering light brought to life all the shadows on the wall.

"About what?" asked Jack. He sat on the bed, shoulders slumped, and Oliver knew that Jack had done too much that day and the day before.

"Let me help you," said Oliver, as he came around the bed and knelt at Jack's feet to untie the laces on his boots.

"I'm not a cripple," said Jack, trying to pull his foot out of Oliver's grasp.

"I know that." Oliver undid the laces and pulled off both of Jack's boots. Jack's stockings were quite black along the bottoms. "We should get you an extra pair of stockings."

"Or we could just wander into a shop as if lookin' for somethin' else and then—"

"Jack."

"Stockings don't cost no three shillin's anyhow." Jack tore off his stockings and threw them at the bedrail at the bottom of the bed, much like he used to do at the Three Cripples, throwing clothes any old where, and completely disinterested in their state.

Oliver ignored this. He warmed Jack's cold feet by cupping each one between two palms and breathing over them.

"What did you mean, I'll feel differently?" asked Jack, watching him.

Standing up, Oliver sat on the bed next to Jack, and bent over to undo his own laces. His back was tired from bending over the table gutting fish all day, and he knew that Jack was tired; Oliver did not want them to argue about it, so he replied, gently, "When the letter comes, and you have the opportunity to find your mother."

All at once, Jack shoved Oliver away, and stood, his bare feet curling on the stone floor, his chin jutted out. "I'm not interested in knowin' her. I told you that, I *know* I did."

"Not even a little?"

"Oh, Nolly," said Jack, but it was completely without affection. "I know you would give just about anythin' if your mam were here an' you could walk arm in arm an' point out the sights to each other. But me? I don't want to know."

There was something in his voice that made Oliver stand up and brave the certainty in Jack's eyes. Jack was usually so easygoing that it was hard to see beyond the fierceness there.

"But why, Jack? Why?" He almost reached out to touch Jack's arm, but stopped at the last moment.

Seeing the gesture, Jack turned his gaze elsewhere, at his feet, at the bed, the flickering candle. It was to the latter that he spoke; and the light made slender lines of shadow from his eyelashes upon his cheeks. "You're all agog about this. But you see, Nolly. I know some of the story, I know what Fagin told me. What the gypsies told him. That some woman left her boy-child sitting on the edge of a stone fountain. And then went off dancin'."

Now he looked at Oliver, his eyes flat, his jawline firm, as if there were no room for argument.

"I was there for hours, an' there was no goin' home for me. Now I ask you, Nolly. What would I want with a mother who would cast her child aside like that? That's not what mothers do. You should know that more than anyone, with all those stories you read."

There was not even the slightest quaver in Jack's voice as he said this. His gaze was steady and he was most certain about it. While Fagin might have dressed up the story for Jack's benefit, the detail about the length of time that Jack had sat on the fountain was too specific to ignore. Oliver considered, for the first time, that while Jack might have gone all the way up to Barnet, it had not been to find his mother, but rather to rebuke her.

Oliver wished he'd had known this when he'd talked to the parson, but who knew whether or not it would have made a difference. Even more, he wished that he could take that expression from Jack's face, and the feeling from his breast, that his own mother had been indifferent enough to deposit him at a fountain, as if he were nothing more than a package. At least Oliver had the fantasy that his mother had loved him, and no fact on earth could be found to refute that. But Jack? His only certainty was that his mother had not.

"But you've already sent the letter, ain't you, Nolly." Jack grimaced, his face showing his exhaustion from the day. "I'll rip it up when it arrives. If it arrives."

"Yes," said Oliver. "It's done now." He took off his trousers and stockings, folding them carefully and putting them on the floor, out of the way. He had hoped that Jack would change his mind, but, from the looks of it, he would not waver from his stance.

"I could leave before it gets here, you know." Jack gestured to the door. "I could leave this instant. My name's not the one on the bill."

Oliver found his muscles starting to quiver from the strain of holding himself so still, and not launching full body at Jack to beg him not to go. But it was true; Jack had no ties, not to Lyme, nor to any debt, and indeed, no real reason to stay away from London. He, after all, was not a murderer. So Jack could go, this instant, take up his new coat and stride out into the rainy night. Back the way he'd come, picking pockets to pay for his journey home. Oliver felt the feelings in his chest explode into a harried, scurrying worry, that Jack would go, and he would be all alone.

"It's unkind of you, Jack." Oliver tried to breathe beyond the panic in his chest. "To threaten me with that, with your leaving. Don't ever—" But he couldn't speak. He could only look at Jack, at the pale lines of Jack's face, and the green eyes glittering at him, as he attempted to quell his fear that Jack might leave. "Please."

"I ain't doin' that, an' don't know why I said it. Can't leave in the middle of the night, anyhow," said Jack. "Don't know why we're squabblin'. Just tired, I reckon."

He collapsed on the bed. "Now dig out that book, the one about the fellow in the prison, an' read to me. This instant." Jack shifted his head to the pillow, pulling off his salt-stained trousers and shoving them off the nicely folded counterpane with his bare foot. "I always know that while you're readin' you don't have that look on your face."

"What look?"

"The one that tells me your little house of carefully planned cards is tumblin' down an' things ain't the way you like 'em. I can't bear to see that look."

Jack looked so tired, so relieved to be lying still, in a soft bed, that Oliver tucked away the fierce words about what he did not like to see on Jack's face, and reached under the bed for the largest book, *The Count of Monte Cristo*. Then he arranged himself on the bed next to Jack, taking up the pillow to tuck behind his head. Taking a deep breath, he fanned through the pages, until he came to the tiny dog-ear Jack had left the night before. With the edge of his thumbnail, he unfolded the crease, spread the book across his bent knees, and began to read

～

Jack felt better, lying still. He couldn't understand why they had quarreled, but it was over now and Nolly was reading. Listening to Nolly reading was better than a pint of beer. As for Nolly, Jack thought his relaxed state was due to putting in a hard day's work, an honest day's work, which would tire any man out and for no good purpose other than to earn some brass that would need to be handed over to yet someone else. Still, Nolly didn't like hearing about the alternatives, so Jack determined not to mention that.

Instead, he let Nolly's voice float over him for a bit, following the story somewhat, but mostly watching Nolly's mouth as it moved, looking at his skin, all white and gold in the candlelight, or how Nolly's eyes flickered when he caught Jack watching him, as if he didn't quite know what to do with that. After a while of this, Jack reached up and put his hand on the page in front of Nolly, to keep him from reading.

"I ain't goin' nowhere, not without you," he said, looking at his hand and not at Nolly. "Ain't leavin', 'cause I ain't like that. The only way I'll go is if you sent me. Got it?"

Nodding, looking a little shaken still by their quarrel, Nolly inched Jack's hand away, carefully with the tips of his fingers, and continued to read until his voice smoothed out. Now and then he gave Jack a look, such as to make Jack feel warm inside, and frankly, a little bit worked up, as though he was a virgin miss. He was about to sink his head full into the pillow of Nolly's side, when Nolly stopped reading again.

"Jack."

"Yes, Nolly."

Clearing his throat, resting the book on his bent knees, Nolly took Jack's hand and pulled it to him, clasping it to his belly.

"My world," Nolly said, looking down at Jack's hand, "is different now that you're in it. But I'm uncertain who or what I'm supposed to be, when I'm with you."

Nolly gave a bit of a laugh, and Jack felt his eyebrows go up, somewhat astonished to hear Nolly make such a revelation, so slowly and carefully, as if he'd been thinking all day about how to say it.

"Just be happy," said Jack. It was so straightforward, so terribly easy to understand. Unless you were Nolly, in which case, everything was complicated and difficult.

"That's easy, when it's just you and I, as it is now. Then the world intrudes and it's confusing."

"Nowt to be confused about," said Jack, completely assured of the fact. "'Tis only you an' I now, anyhow."

"That's true," said Nolly, and for a moment, his mouth pressed together, that crease appearing between his eyes, as it sometimes did when he was burdened with heavy thoughts, the heaviness of his own making, but, of course, a burden nonetheless. "We are alone."

"That we are," said Jack, though he didn't understand why Nolly was making saying something so obvious.

Nolly was putting the book down, was leaning over to put it on the floor in fact, which left him with no book to read from. Which was a shame, because the story was just getting good, with the sailor's escape from a horrible jail, and him finding the island full of jewels.

When Nolly leaned back up again, Jack was certain he could hear Nolly's heart pounding, and could see the flush on his cheek. And even before Nolly touched his face, Jack knew that his best beloved was preparing himself to cross over into uncharted territory.

"I want to pay you back," Nolly said. "To do something for you as you've done for me. D'you understand?"

There it was, that little slip of street coarseness, where Nolly spoke more like Jack than he did the young gentleman he considered himself to be, making Jack's heart feel more tender than he'd thought possible. But there was something that needed clearing up, if they were to go on, which Jack dearly wished them to do.

"What you need to understand," said Jack, sitting up, pressing Nolly's hand so that his palm cupped Jack's face. "An' mind me when I tell you, this is not payment, 'tis *never* a payment. I don't know how to say it more plain than that. If it is, there's somethin' wrong, an' besides, that's not how it's to be between us. 'Tis only ever a gift."

Now Jack's heart was pounding. But he never wanted Nolly going down that road, where the pleasures of the body became a coin in a system of barter that would leave him drained and wanting. Not when Jack was nearby, and could give him anything he wanted, anything.

"Promise me." Jack pulled Nolly's hand up to his mouth and kissed the center of the palm.

"I promise, Jack. Upon my honor, I promise."

It was such a solemn moment, and Jack ever preferred to see a smile on that sweet face, so he kissed Nolly on the mouth, and gave him a wink as he stole the pillow and leaned back on it, propping his hands behind his head.

"So what did you 'ave in mind then, this gift. For it is a gift, remember. Not a trade."

Nolly seemed bestilled by the task of thinking this through, but, after a moment, he leaned forward and tugged on the sheet and blanket, looking at his hands, casting about, as if for an explanation as to what he was about to do.

"I thought I'd—start the way you started. That first night, when we were together. Would you mind, d'you think?"

"Bloody hell, Nolly," said Jack, squeezing his eyes shut, and pressing his head back into his hands. "You could pour a bucket of snow over my head an' bugger me senseless, an' I wouldn't mind. Long as it was you. Don't you see?" He opened his eyes, to see Nolly had drawn back, and Jack gentled his tone.

"Anythin' you want to do, I'm game, all right?" He brought his hands down as well, to reach out and touch Nolly's thigh, just exposed beneath his shirt. "Just tell me what it is an' I'll say yes."

"I'm fairly certain that this is a sin," said Nolly, with continued solemness.

"An' I'm fairly certain you're right," said Jack, unable to keep himself from smiling. This made Nolly smile back, which was all to the better. "An' I'll hold still an' all, won't thrash about, or push at you, or anythin'—" Jack stopped explaining what it was he wouldn't do, and made himself stay still to see what Nolly *would* do.

A braver lad there never was, for Nolly moved close lay down next to Jack, so close that Jack could feel that Nolly's cock was hard against his thigh, feel the warmth of blood in it, feel how Nolly's chest shuddered a bit. Just lying together, just from this, and Nolly was worked up. Now Jack's body was in the shadow of Nolly's, with Nolly slipping his hand beneath Jack's waist to draw him even closer, tucking his head in the curve of Jack's neck. And, given where his other hand was, Jack had a fair idea of what Nolly was going to try.

"You'll tell me if I do it wrong," said Nolly as he bent down, his breath puffing along the curve of Jack's collarbone. "Won't you, Jack?"

"You're already doin' it right, from what I can tell."

With great care, Nolly pulled down the sheet, and pulled up Jack's shirt, and gave Jack's belly a tender pet, and Jack felt his own skin prickle and jump beneath the caress. When Nolly's fingers curved down, Jack pressed his cheek to the top of Nolly's head.

"Give your palm a lick first, that'll do best, you see. Like primin' a pump."

With a nod, Nolly did as Jack suggested, and Jack wished he had a thousand pair of eyes to see this from all angles, his sweet Nolly, slavering up his own palm to give Jack a good, fast ride with his hand. No one else, alive or dead, would ever see this, Nolly taking Jack's cock in his hand, and for a moment, when palm touched hot skin, Jack closed his eyes, to savor it. Then he opened them, he tucked his head down, to kiss the top of Nolly's head, and moved his hips up, just a fraction, to show Nolly how it was done, how his cock would slide up and down in Nolly's grip.

"You're very warm," said Nolly, in a low voice, not quite a whisper.

"'Tis my blood," said Jack. "Gets all excited and rushes down to that one spot."

Nolly was moving his palm up and down Jack's cock, tightening it, curling his fingers closed and open as he went, as if experimenting. Jack hoped Nolly wouldn't get shy about the fluid building at the slit, because that was what was supposed to happen, only he didn't have the voice, suddenly, to explain this.

Nolly took his hand off and licked it again, and then, drew the breadth of it over the top of Jack's cock, and, smearing the fluid, slid his hand down the length of it, all the way to Jack's private hair in one long, careful, and precise slide. Jack could only moan, quite undone, his head tilting back to bang against the headboard, which knocked against the wall. Which was, luckily, stone and absorbed the sound.

"Is that right, Jack, am I doing it right?" Nolly paused a moment, pressing close, his other arm around Jack's waist tightening.

"Oh, my Lord," said Jack. He had no idea Nolly had a grip like that, had wrists that could do that. If only Fagin had known, he'd have had Nolly knocking out patterns on sheets of silver, using a stamp to forge money; Nolly would have made them a fortune with hands that strong. "Only go on, only do, please, please, *please*—"

And Nolly did, with his clever hand moving up and down, the grip tightening and loosening, as if he knew, somehow knew the exact spot where it would drive Jack mad.

Jack's eyes were rolling up in his head at the sheer touch of

Nolly's palm; Nolly had a series of calluses and they were tumbling along the underside of Jack's cock, over and over, until it was too much and Jack's spine crumbled inward and he was too late to warn Nolly, he was coming in cream-white streams over Nolly's hand, his moving fist, and the blasted sheets.

"Oh fuck," said Jack, his hips twitching, pulling Nolly's hand off from too-sensitive flesh. "Do stop, then, that's right, give us your hand." Jack pulled Nolly's hand to his belly, where the tightness still quivered, and stroked his own belly with Nolly's hand.

"The sheets," said Nolly, but he rested his head on Jack's shoulder, breathing apace with Jack, but not moving away. As if, Jack was pleased to note, shame had no refuge between them.

"Never mind them," said Jack. "They'll wash." He took the tail end of his shirt, and wiped his leg, his belly. "You can have a taste, you know, it's on your thumb."

Nolly could hardly be aware of the picture he presented, as he looked up at Jack, his hair sticking to his forehead with a thin line of sweat, his eyes a bright china-blue. But he was not by nature a flirt, and so very likely had no idea how the sight of him gripped at Jack's heart. Then he looked at his palm, and up at Jack, and slowly, very slowly, as if he did know what this was doing to Jack, brought up his hand and licked across the tops of three of his fingers. With a rapid blink he pulled his hand back, then, pausing, licked his fingers again, his tongue moving the whole length of his forefinger.

"It tastes different," he said, almost as if to himself. Once more he looked at Jack. "Shall I kiss you now, with the taste of it on my tongue?"

"C'mere to me," said Jack, and he pulled Nolly up, settling him between his legs where he could get his hands on Nolly's cock, and pleasure him till he came, and kiss him all the while. He kissed Nolly, pushing his tongue in, tasting himself, and the salt of Nolly's mouth, and cradled his arm around Nolly's shoulders. When he reached down between Nolly's legs, impatient with the yards of cloth contained in Nolly's shirt, Nolly shifted himself, and pulled his own shirt up. Tucked himself into the curve of Jack's shoulders, all loose-limbed and supple, his head thrown back, blue sparks coming from his half-closed eyes. At surrender, and all Jack's. Just like this.

"'Tis a gift, now," Jack said, his voice shaking, as he curled his fingers in Nolly's private hair, felt Nolly's hips move between his spread thighs. "Not a tit for tat, you understand?"

Nolly tipped his head back, reaching up to pull Jack's head closer to his, and Jack felt Nolly's mouth on his ear, moist breath moving, his own heartbeat pounding.

"Yes," said Nolly. "A gift."

Kisses trailed down Jack's neck as Nolly settled himself to where Jack could kiss him directly, and stroke his cock and show him what words could not say. That love of this kind was not made of shame or guilt, but instead, of soft strokes, and hard ones, of a palm licked for an easy slide, of kisses shared, tasting like salt. Of them together, in spite of the world, which would never understand.

24

AMONG THE WILD BOYS IN TOWN

With the low wind coming across the water as they finished for the day, it was almost warm on the Cobb. Oliver found that he didn't have to roll down his shirt sleeves the moment he stopped working. Nor was he worried about Jack, who tended to go slavishly unbuttoned at any opportunity. Such as now, when he was taking off his apron and putting the buckets underneath the deal table. He must have felt Oliver looking at him, for as he stood up, he reached for his shirt, and pretended to unbutton it even more.

For all that Oliver tried to retain some sense of propriety, to come up with a lecture for Jack, Oliver could not make himself do it. Not with the memory from last night of Jack, white shirt rucked about his neck, holding Oliver between his legs, petting him, ruining the sheets even more. Not that the sheets mattered anyway; ejaculate looked like any other stain, and no one doing laundry would think anything of it. And why should he worry about that, when there was Jack to consider, with his soft hands, and firm touch, that sleepy glimmer in his eyes that told Oliver how well pleased he was. If he lived a hundred years, it would be impossible to forget that moment when, inexplicably, he had felt something shift within him, and he knew that it would never be the same between him and Jack.

Oliver shook his head and tried to pay attention to what Leander was saying to him.

"So, you're one of us, right? So you might consider coming to the tavern tonight. Just for a pint or two, bit of a laugh."

Oliver considered this; Leander thought Oliver was one of the village now, but that didn't mean he thought the same of Jack, otherwise, he would not have left off Jack from the invitation.

"I'll buy you a round or two of drinks," said Leander. "To make up for t'other day, your first day."

"Jack and I can come," said Oliver, glad that the issue of paying had been cleared up. "Perhaps after supper?"

"Reckon he can come along, at that," said Leander. He tilted his head to see around Oliver, to where Jack was standing. "See you both when you get back."

Just as Oliver was about to take off his own apron, Mr. Thurly came up to him.

"You already paid us this morning, Mr. Thurly, I mean, we're all square, aren't we?"

"Indeed," said Mr. Thurly. "But the parson came by with this letter for you. You were busy so I took it. Here you go."

Even before Oliver saw the return address on the back of the envelope, he knew it was the letter from Barnet. He felt a cold shock run through him. For the letter was thick rather than thin, and surely to give mere condolences would only have taken a single page. Looking to see that Jack was chatting with one of the fish-gutters, Oliver held the letter against his stomach. It snapped open easily, as if the wax had already been broken and resealed. It was addressed to the parson, who would have already broken the seal on it, but it was Oliver's to read just the same.

The paper was of good quality, thick between his fingers; the ink dark black in the sunlight as the wind wafted over the page. He made himself read what the letter had to say, instead of scanning. Then he had to read it again.

The first lines were the usual salutation and praises of God and queen, a general note about the weather and the conditions of the road that might delay the mail coach. Then it continued:

I am sad to inform you that in September, 1832, there was an incident such as you are inquiring after during the Barnet Fair. A young mother, Mrs. Juliette Dawkins, left her son, Jack, who was then four years old, at the side of Christ's Fountain. She then made merry with drink and with dance, and forgot the child for that time.

When she returned to the fountain with her husband, Mr. Seth Dawkins (a laborer), she found the child missing and became hysterical. However, eventually Mr. and Mrs. Dawkins went home. No amount of searching or posting of flyers or asking surrendered the location of the child. The boy, Jack, was never seen nor heard of again.

As the Barnet Fair is rather large and unrelentingly frequented by the lower orders, horse dealers, card sharps, and all the dregs of humanity, it is suspected that the child was taken by gypsies, as they are not uncommonly seen at the Barnet Fair.

After a time, Mr. and Mrs. Dawkins removed to Hale, near Liverpool, from whence the family had originally come. It is believed that they reside there still, and have since brought forth a young daughter who goes by the name of Delia (Cordelia). All future correspondence about this event and family, might be directed to St. Peter's Church in Hale, Cheshire County.

Oliver knew, from his lessons in geography, that Liverpool was up north. It was near the sea, and produced rough goods like salt and coal. It sounded as though Jack's family was actually from there, rather than Barnet, which he had assumed, particularly after Jack had admitted that he'd gone there to look for his family. Oliver had not thought much of it when Jack had first told him the story, but of course a four-year-old might remember the name of a place, even if he couldn't recall why he'd been there.

Hearing feet stomping up behind him, Oliver folded the letter and shoved it in his pocket. He could not bring himself to show it to Jack in front of all the men.

The thought of this entire family springing to life for Jack made Oliver feel unsteady. They'd existed before this moment, of course, but it was as though they appeared out of the mist, and stepped right through to where Oliver was standing. The hard part would be to let Jack be with that family, if he wanted to. It was a small comfort that he didn't seem to want; instead, he seemed to want, simply, to be with Oliver. But Oliver would be remiss in his duties as a friend if he did not inform Jack of these, his relations. The only question was how. And when. Perhaps the evening, anticipated to be full of talk and of drink, would provide its own direction. Oliver patted his pocket, and turned to Jack.

"Are you done, then?" asked Oliver, in what he hoped was an unremarkable way. "Shall we go back and have a wash, and let Mrs. Heyland know of our plans?"

"What plans?"

It was obvious that while Oliver had been occupied, Leander had not paid Jack the courtesy of inviting him personally. Well, Oliver would remedy that.

"Didn't you know?" he began, keeping his voice casual. "Leander and his mates go to the tavern of a Saturday evening, and they've invited us."

"Invited you, you mean," said Jack. But he smiled, tipping his head back as if to scoff at this and show that he didn't care that he'd not been invited.

"No, truly, he invited us both. I wouldn't go without you, besides."

"Nolly," said Jack, somewhat sternly. "You can't go turning down invitations simply on account of they don't want me along."

"I can," said Oliver stoutly. "I reckon I can go with whoever I like, same as you."

This made Jack laugh again, but more kindly, as he patted Oliver on the arm.

"Just messin' with you, Nolly." Jack's eyes did that thing that they did, though so seldom out in the open like this. He blinked, like a cat might who is dozing in the sun, content to be there. For a moment, as his lashes fanned across his cheeks, Oliver felt he might blush, for usually such an expression was only to be seen when he and Jack were alone with only one candle lighting the darkness.

"Come on, then," said Oliver. He thought he wanted to pet Jack, to touch his face with gentle fingers. But if they started walking, they would have to concentrate on that, instead of on each other. He tugged Jack's sleeve, needing a distraction. "We'll get a bite from Mrs. Heyland and wash. Do you suppose she'll leave the whole house unlocked for us?"

"Better she should give us the key," said Jack. "We could copy it and sell it."

Leaving to mystery how one might copy a key, Oliver started walking, Jack at his side.

The tavern was one block up from the shoreline, so the smash of sea against the Cobb echoed between the buildings, and the smell of salt air misted down onto the slippery street stones. Leander's directions took them directly to the tavern, which was an older building with a sagging roof, though the window frames looked new and the steps had been freshly scrubbed, at the very least, that afternoon. Oliver opened the door, and, with Jack close behind him, they entered the tavern. It was smoky, as taverns were, but the floor was swept with care and the counter along the far wall looked burnished in the candlelight.

Directly, they saw Leander waving them over between the loosely arranged chairs and round tables. He was spruced up for their convivial evening, with a Sunday jacket on and a clean cravat about his neck. He left the men he'd been with, and drew Oliver and Jack to a small table near the brightly lit coal fire. They sat down, and Oliver balanced his hat on his knee; he was grateful for the warmth, and the slight smile on Jack's face as he relaxed in what must be his favorite environment.

"Good of you to come, lads, so the first round'll be on me." He raised a hand to the pot boy. "Come, boy, bring us three pots of beer. And not that swill you keep in the back. The good stuff."

The pot boy went off, trotting between the other customers, who had just come in and were flocking to the bar to order drinks, raising the noise in the tavern to a more festive level. The boy was swiftly back. He placed the new tin pint pots down carefully, and he gave the edge of the table a swipe.

When he was gone, Leander lifted his pot and nodded once each at Oliver and Jack. "Here's to Agnes's boy, come back to us after so many years."

At last Oliver could pull the pot of beer to him and take a long, healthy swallow; the beer was cold and it had a bite he was not used to, but it went down his throat with ease, relaxing as the effects of it raced through him. He saw Jack relaxing as well, wiping off the foam from his upper lip with the back of his coat sleeve, which was a comforting sight, in its way. Jack would always be the same, no matter what the world would make of him, and for that Oliver was grateful. If everything around him changed, Jack would still be the same.

Oliver finished off his beer with three huge swallows, tipping his head back, and licking his upper lip with his tongue. He put the pot back on the table with a slight clink.

"Will you have another'n?" asked Leander, only looking at Oliver.

Leander began to raise his hand for the pot boy, and Oliver wanted to stop him, should, in fact, stop him, but didn't. Not when Jack was looking at him like that, and the room seemed a warm, convivial place, and he and Jack could be this way together.

"Here, take a shilling," Oliver said, instead. He took it out of his pocket and pushed it across the table at Leander. "As a sort of payment. And yes, we'll *both* have another."

He hadn't seen how much the beers had been, but Leander seemed pleased by the gesture and beckoned to the pot boy for another round of beers. Oliver looked at Jack, who smiled at him, as contented, it seemed, as Oliver was in the warm room, with the beer flowing. Around them, the collection of men, drinking beer or totting back glasses of gin, were of a better sort than had been found at the Three Cripples. Here were working men stopping at the tavern to have a drink with their mates, and Oliver reckoned that none of them would later be found skulking around the streets at night, hauling stolen goods, or making trouble, getting into trouble.

He felt Jack looking at him now, and cocked his ear to hear what Jack was about to say.

"You should own one of these," Jack said. "Instead of a bookshop."

"I would drink up my profits and stock inside of a week and you know it."

Jack tipped back his head and laughed, and Oliver smiled and reached for his beer with eager hands when the pot boy came over with his loaded tray. He drank his second beer more slowly, enjoying the slide of the beer over his tongue, licking his lips to taste the bitter edge of it. He watched Jack drink his beer slowly as well, and hid his smile behind his tin pot, for it would not do to be seen pulling together into a sudden and unexpected kiss.

Leander was talking to someone standing next to the table that Oliver didn't know, a grey-haired gentleman who was dressed as one might who worked indoors, perhaps with pen and ink, a clerk of some sorts. The pair of them were talking about the cliffs, and someone named Miss Anning, who dug up things as well as, if not better than, any man could.

Oliver wondered, with Leander distracted, if now was the time. He looked at Jack, handsome and content in the light of the fire and the robust and pleasant company, then reached into his pocket to feel the edges of the letter.

"Come and meet our own Oliver Twist and his man Jack," said Leander. "This here's Mr. Scrimm, he owns a basket shop down by the Cobb. Scrimmy, this is Agnes's boy child. The one she left for and gave birth to in a workhouse, and now he's come back to us.

Just look at him! Sweet-faced as an angel." Leander raised his pot of beer and the man did likewise, and both men took a healthy drink.

"How do you do," said Oliver, shaking the man's hand, noting that Jack was looking off, looking elsewhere, as if not caring that he'd not been part of the introductions.

"Knew your mam, I did," said Scrimmy, sitting down next to Leander. "She was a beauty, an' could have had any lad in the village. 'Spect Leander's told you, she kissed me once, an' I kissed her back, and didn't her pa have words with my pa."

Oliver could only raise his eyebrows at this. But the man was the same age as his mother would have been, had she been alive, except, having lived by the sea, he was a little more careworn and salt-speckled.

"Didn't mind the whipping after, neither. Agnes had lips as sweet as raspberry jam, didn't she, Leander?" Scrimmy pounded Leander on the back, and Leander, his mouth dripping with foam, nodded.

"Only one kiss, that's what you got back then," continued Scrimmy. "One kiss an' she'd move on."

"Now, don't bother the boy with them sort of details, Scrimmy." Leander shook his head, bits of foam flying to dot his coat. "That's not what the boy wants to hear. Tell him something else, about her singing."

"She could sing, she could," said Scrimmy, being obliging, smoothing his waistcoat as he leaned forward. "And with a mouth as that, every note was from heaven itself. And she had this bosom —" Scrimmy put his beer down to use his hands to carve out the shape of Agnes's endowments. "A bosom," said Scrimmy reverently, "as round and as white as a summer cloud."

Scrimmy threw back his head and laughed, inviting the attention of the men standing at the bar, who, when he told them what was so amusing, began to chuckle and nod their heads.

"Your mam was a bit of a looker, you see," said Leander to Oliver. "Maybe too much of one."

Scrimmy looked concerned at this, but then, when the next round of beer came to their table without him having to either order or pay, he continued to drink and seemed supremely happy.

One of the men came over to the table; he wore a cap, like most of the men, but his collar was white, and his shirt looked freshly pressed. He wore glasses and squinted a bit, and Leander shook his hand as soon as he came up.

"That last round of drinks from you, Walter? This is Oliver Twist, Agnes's whelp, an' this here's Walter Lorne, and he knew your old mam too!"

Oliver found his hand being shook with a great deal of force, and could hear Jack sniggering into his beer, even though Leander had not taken the time to acknowledge Jack's existence, let alone introduce him.

Walter thumped Oliver on the back and pointed to the beers.

"Yes, those are from me," said Walter. "And I don't want to say your mam could put it away, she was a lady an' that, but she could."

All three men, Leander, Scrimmy, and Walter, nodded at each other. Walter went so far as to take off his hat and place it over his heart. "Half the lads in the village had a taste of that mouth."

"An' a couple," said Scrimmy, "had a feel up her skirt, to hear them tell of it."

"There was a particular barn—d'you remember the springtime dance?" Walter gestured at the table, starting in on another story. "Well, there weren't much dancing on account of all the dancers had taken themselves away, to where Miss Agnes was taking callers." He clapped Scrimmy on the back, laughing, his mouth open, the beer spraying. "D'you remember waitin' your turn? Oh, but wasn't she quick, getting the lads off, one after t'other."

Oliver felt as though he'd been smacked on the head. He turned to stare at the far wall, next to the door. And pretended that the men were talking about something else altogether, as their jaws yapped and the beer spilled down their waistcoats.

This was not what he'd expected to hear about his mother. Though he'd been heartened to find people who knew her, the story that he'd been telling to himself about her had been a lie. He felt his jaw stiffen as he put his pot of beer on the table.

"Never mind, Nolly," said Jack.

Oliver could barely hear Jack above the din, though it seemed that he'd had been paying attention all along.

"What are you saying?"

"I said never mind them. Surely it's just their pipe dreams that she even looked at them, let alone kissed them. Although." Jack paused to finish off another pot of beer, again wiping the foam and beer from his mouth with the back of his hand. "Knowing she was your mam, I feel certain she was truly beautiful."

"It was a sad day when she left us," Walter said, jerking on Oliver's shoulder to pull him into the conversation again, oblivious to Oliver's discomfort. "She had a smile sweet as summer, and that hair, all—" Walter made a motion at his own hair, which was parted fiercely on the side to cover his bald pate. "Like golden strings from a fairy's harp, that hair. Well, anyway, there was a spring dance at the grange hall, an' I was to escort her. But along come this bloke in a long blue coat, an' that was it. Someone said they saw 'em fucking against the church wall, outside, of course."

"Ah, well," said Scrimmy. "'T'were a shame such a decent lass could be pulled down into the gutter so fast. She went to him like a collie to 'er master, an' he had her heart in his hand and he squeezed—an' then he left her, and she weren't never the same. She was soiled, an' hardly no one would talk to her. Except her own family, though Captain Fleming couldn't fight the whole village, now, could he? It was just after Easter that he told her she couldn't come back to church n'more."

"Who told her that?" Leander leaned forward, taking a swallow of his beer, and spilling it on his coat sleeve. "Her own father?"

"Why, the parson, o'course. She was ruined, that was for sure, an' with child. No man would touch 'er after that. She were a sinner, and no sinner can come to church."

This was like being slammed up against the Cobb with the water dragging him down. It was one thing to know that his mother was a bit of a flirt, and could sing and dance, and had a kissable mouth. But to know the village had turned against her? The cruelty of it seemed unrelenting, for the abasement of her reputation continued even now, and never mind that so many men had supposedly been a party to it, only Agnes was found to be the sinner.

Amidst the movement and smoke of the tavern, the candles glittering in their tin sconces on the wall, Oliver was bestilled. And quiet in that place, where resided his dearest memories of who he thought his mother was, someone who loved and who laughed, and who met a man in the long blue coat. And who then was cast out on account of she couldn't resist his charms, all of this was turned into one, long bawdy story. Though the part about her fornicating standing up against the church wall was probably a lie—

The three men seemed to be laughing at something else now, deeply embedded in talk about the shoreline, and how the Devil's Bellows wasn't safe anymore to take even a wheelbarrow across. And then about the sad fate of the *William & Anne*, a schooner that had wrecked at the Cobb ten years before. And on it went, with one of the men every now and then taking a swig of beer and having a glance at Oliver. And then, with a shake of his head, would toss out some comment to land at Oliver's feet as though it were a fine jewel instead of what it was, a faded, dusty, tarnished, worthless trinket.

"Your mam," said Scrimmy. "She was a beautiful woman, but loose morals will out, you know."

"Fucked like a rabbit, they do say," added Walter, punctuating this with a brassy belch.

"The mouth on her," said Leander, making beer-foamed kisses to the air.

Oliver did not know what to say to this. He could hardly lash out at all three men, as he once had lashed out at Noah, for saying such things about his mother. But it wasn't that there were three of them, it was the overwhelming evidence. Even if his mother had been beautiful, she'd let herself be mesmerized by a stranger. In spite of her background, her station in life.

And then she'd left. He could hardly blame her for that, leaving when she was heavy with a child. No, he could hardly blame her. But it did take some of the shine off, and the glimmer of the romantic story he'd carried for so long, had dulled into aged brass.

"Hey, Nolly," said Jack.

Oliver looked up and there was Jack, quite close at the table, looking at him with his head tipped down, and a sad turn to his mouth that echoed how Oliver's heart felt just then.

"She was your mam," Jack said. "An' she didn't want you growin' up in a village full of bloody idiots."

"It doesn't matter," said Oliver, though it did. He felt the huge chasm between now and only moments ago. Would that he could turn back time and not hear the story about his mother. He felt Jack squeeze his knee under the table. "It's done now."

"At least the beer's comin'. Hey, you," Jack tugged on Scrimmy's sleeve. "Since you're so easy castin' the first stone, an' all, you might see your way to earnin' back that ticket to heaven, an' get some more beer for me an' Agnes's sweet boy here. Who were raised in a workhouse, sufferin' away, an' all while—"

"Yes, yes," said Scrimmy. "We should all raise a glass and toast Agnes's workhouse boy!"

"For the love of God, Jack," said Oliver, teeth gritted, as almost all the men in the place lifted their tin pots and glasses and said "A toast, a toast!"

But when more beer came, Oliver drank it, just the same. There was no stopping the men from thinking what they wanted; his mother had died after giving birth to him, alone and in squalor.

"Shall I have 'em get you some gin, Nolly?" Jack had to fairly shout this above the noise.

"I've had enough!" Oliver shouted back, but he drank the next beer, and the one after that.

When the room was swimming about him, and the candles seemed to flash in and out of existence, he knew it was the moment. Such a gift as that, Jack's kind words when Oliver needed them most, deserved another kindness. So Oliver pulled out the letter and shoved it across the table to Jack. His aim was a little wobbly, but the letter got there, just the same. Jack picked it up and turned it over, the flakes from the wax seal littering his hand. Immediately his brows lowered, and he was scowling while not, Oliver noticed, actually opening the letter.

"What's this?"

"It's the letter," Oliver said, loudly so as to be heard. He pointed at Jack. "If I can't have a family, then you shall have one."

"I *told* you I didn't want this letter."

Jack put the letter on the table and pushed it back at Oliver. Who promptly pushed it back again at Jack.

"Well, you'll want this family. And they're respectable, too. They reside in Hale, a salt works town near Liverpool, which if you remember your geography—"

"I bloody don't care," said Jack. "Will you not listen? I've told you *afore*, an' there you go, with your grand airs thinkin' you have any say in what I want. Well, you don't."

What Jack was saying didn't make any sense.

"But there's a family waiting for you, Jack." Oliver ignored the stare that Leander was giving him, but he might have been imagining it. He couldn't be speaking that loudly.

"You have a family and a home—" Oliver's voice suddenly twisted on itself, and he had to swallow to get the words out. "And I'm sure they're waiting for you. We could write ahead, and then we could go—"

"No."

"But Jack—"

"Fuck off, Nolly," said Jack. "I don't want a family, other than the one I already got."

Jack's meaning was clear, but Oliver couldn't comprehend it; Jack had a family, now, and a home, and he didn't want it?

Oliver's heart pounded in his chest. The heat was rising up his cheeks, and felt as if the blood was boiling behind his eyes. This was his gift to Jack, and Jack was refusing it?

"Your mother probably left you at that fountain on *purpose*." The words tumbled past his numb lips before he could stop them.

Jack blinked, as if Oliver had struck him. Then he seemed to gather himself together. He stood up, ripped the letter in half, and threw it on the table. It slid across the wood surface and off the other side to land at Oliver's feet on the tavern floor.

"You don't know *fuck* all about any of it, on account of you never had no mam in the first place." His eyes were narrow slits, glaring at Oliver.

Before Oliver could even take a breath to retort to this, Leander stepped up and cuffed Jack hard across the top of his head.

"Don't you show no disrespect to your betters, Jack," he said, almost laughing, because of course, Agnes's boy's manservant must be kept in his place. "Don't you speak like that to him."

"And don't you speak like that to Jack."

Oliver was on his feet. He launched himself at Leander, his hands around Leander's neck, squeezing as tightly as he could, driving his knee into Leander's gut. The movements felt sloppy, but the result felt good and hard, and when Leander doubled over, Oliver smashed him in the face with an elbow, and threw a punch with his fist, feeling it slam into Leander's face with a brilliant, angry joy. No one touched *Jack*, no one.

Then hands were pulling him back.

"Nolly, Nolly, c'mon now, that's no way to behave in a tavern. Scrimmy, get him back."

The hands were insistent and the room flashed in and out of blackness and he wondered if someone had hit him or if the whole room was tipping sideways because he was flat out on the floor with Walter standing over him. Scrimmy dragged Leander away, and a circle of men formed around the spot on the floor that felt suddenly cold.

"I'll get him out of here, no, no, that's—"

Someone lifted him off the floor. It might have been Jack, but he was earnestly looking at Oliver, and tugging on Oliver's arm.

"Walk now, Nolly. Show them you can, that's a boy."

Jack said that he should walk, so that's what he must do. He felt the floor tip to the side and then swing back to center, and luckily there was a doorway and the cold fresh sea air coming up the street and whipping through the darkness. And at his side, slipping his arm around Oliver's waist, was Jack.

"Keep comin' on, that's it. That's my Nolly."

From somewhere behind, a door slammed and the warmth of a fire and the light of a candle was shut off as if they'd been doused in water. The air was full of mist and flecked with the smell of dark seaweed, and the deep, pressed earth along the shore.

"No, no, bend over like this, in the ditch now."

Jack's hand was curling around the back of Oliver's neck, bending him forward, so that he could throw up, hot, acid gushes of bitter country beer. When he stood up again, Jack wiped Oliver's mouth with the back of his sleeve and urged him to keep walking. The night was so dark, and each footstep on the cobbled road pounded all the way up to his skull. In between his feet and his head was a vast stretch of nothingness. He knew Jack was guiding him, up the road and along the lane that would take them to Rhode Hill House.

He opened his mouth to ask about Mrs. Heyland, some vague question that he couldn't quite form, maybe about the key to the back door, was there a key? Would she lend them a key?

"Bushes," said Jack, inexplicably. But there were warm hands guiding him, and he bent to throw up again.

After that, it was a lot more walking; the night and the road stretched on forever. The only reason to go on was because Jack was taking him there.

The punch that Nolly had thrown at Leander had hit home, a left hook so fast and sharp it had been a blur. It might have been that Jack had been too drunk to really see it for what it was, but he was sure that Nolly's skill, untrained though it might be, could have taken down any man. As it was, Leander had stumbled back, holding his nose as the blood streamed in ribbons across his teeth.

But had been drunk, so drunk, he must have barely felt it and seemed to be laughing as much as he was howling. His mates held him up, gripping under his arms, and Jack knew it was time to go, before Nolly could display anymore of his powerful but wild punches. If he'd had any schooling in boxing, even the least little bit, Jack would have been willing to place all of his currently nonexistent money on that left hook.

For now, he slung his arm around Nolly's shoulders. He was close enough to smell the beer on Nolly's breath, see the despair flash in his eyes. That Nolly would defend Jack so passionately and without reservation always came as a surprise, like an unexpected burst of light and warmth through the clouds on an otherwise rainy day. But Nolly was like that, all reserved and proper for the longest time, tame and tamped until something struck a spark and lit him on fire from within. A roar of passion that sent all the walls tumbling. Sent a fully grown man crashing to the floor, chopped to pieces, or pushed a sturdy fish packer back against his fellows, his face bleeding.

"He shouldn't speak to you so, Jack," said Nolly, insistent. Clasping the front of Jack's jacket with tender fingers for all that his teeth were gritted together with such fierceness, his language slipping into coarseness. "It's nowt to me how he speaks to his mates, but he cannot speak that way to mine."

The drunkenness brought on by too many beers made Nolly sprint forth with all the feelings of his heart, as was the way with drunks. Particularly in Jack's experience, Nolly was a drunk who liked to get close, to be close, with his hands all over the place, as he was now. He was not an angry drunk, except when something ill crossed his path. Leander's manner had set Nolly off. But it wasn't right that Nolly had taken up the battle over Leander's singular remark to Jack. Nolly should, rather, have fought for Agnes. That Oliver had accorded her less defense, his own mam, when they'd ripped her reputation to shreds, and talked of her so, as if she were a common girl, with her skirts up and her bosom on display for all to see. It wasn't right.

Jack looked up the hill as they walked, Nolly hanging off his neck, earnest, and oh-so-sincere.

"They're not allowed, Jack, d'you hear? Not allowed to touch you. Only me, only me *ever*. Right? Tell me that it's true. True. Only you 'n me. Me an' thee. *Tell* me, Jack."

It was a bit slippery as they waded through the dark as the road became bracketed by trees instead of buildings and cottages. Dark enough so that Nolly could bury his face in the curve of Jack's neck, between bouts of throwing up, his nose cold against the underside of Jack's jaw.

"'Tis all right, Nolly," said Jack, trying to keep them at a good pace. "It's always been me an' thee, just as you say."

He pulled Nolly close and patted his shoulder and imagined the hundred other soothing things he might say, even if Nolly would not remember them come morning. Except what Jack had just said was a lie. There had been others; you couldn't grow up on the streets of London and not encounter it. Or cross half the world in a rolling ship and not need it, and take it, willing or unwilling. Jack reached to stroke Nolly's face, a silent apology for words never spoken.

"When you do that, Jack," said Nolly, as they finally began crunching up the gravel drive that would lead them around the back of the house.

"What's that, sweetheart?" Jack asked, low. He stopped them at the back door, releasing Nolly to stand them both upright, settling Nolly so that when they did enter the house, Nolly wouldn't still be chattering on.

"When you do that," said Nolly, and the dark allowed only a dark grey impression of Nolly's face, as he kept talking, a stubborn, passionate drunk, stepping into the space of Jack's arms.

"I always meant to say it, but could never—when you do this." Nolly fumbled about and finally took Jack's hand and put it to his own face. Leaned into Jack's palm, a small, lost sound escaping his lips in a way that half-broke Jack's heart.

"Fell in love with you then," said Nolly. "I love you, Jack."

Jack had always expected that, if they ever came, these words would have been delivered in that distant polite way Nolly sometimes had. But not like this, when he was drunk. The words would have rung truer had he been sober.

"That's right, Nolly. Shall we go in and take care not to disturb the house?" Jack reached for the knob of the door, turning it, finding it unlocked, in a country way. Wanting to be already abed, the distance between the door and the bed was an unmapped battlefield.

Nolly, stepping close, pressed close, warm, fluid against Jack, and though Jack normally never considered it, he longed for temperance now. He had never had a problem with a raucous drunk until that very moment. What Nolly was doing was like a lie, a painful lie that shredded at Jack's heart.

"I never feel anythin' 'til you put your hands on me, Jack."

"Oh, that can't be," said Jack, keeping his voice low as they entered the silent dark house, past the housekeeper's room and across the empty space of the kitchen to the passage on the far side.

"No, no," said Nolly, adamant and loud, as if he were gearing up to sing his pronouncements to the very rooftop. Jack put his fingers over Nolly's mouth, his *warm* mouth, and almost yelped when Nolly opened his mouth, not to speak, but to kiss. To press Jack's hand to his mouth and kiss the palm, up to the tips of his fingers, the tip of his tongue pressing warm spots that blazed a trail up Jack's arm, setting sparked in his head. In his belly.

"Steady on, sweetheart," said Jack, wondering why it seemed to happen like this, Nolly catching him off guard with the sudden fire of kisses and affection.

Stumbling down the passage, with Nolly hanging about his

waist, nuzzling him, kissing his ear, Jack managed to get them to their little room, but barely able to get the door open before Nolly tripped on a bit of uneven flooring and Jack was forced to catch him before his head hit the floor. But as ever with drunks and children, the near miss meant nothing to Nolly; he stood up straight, as if completely sober, and gave a low bow, doffing his hat and tossing it across the room.

"Shall we light a candle, Jack?" said Nolly, now toe-to-toe with Jack, finding him unerringly. "Or shall we fuck in the dark?"

Jack felt himself start, Nolly's hands at his waist, and understood that the gates had truly been unlocked this night, with the country beer flowing like a river tide, and Nolly's head full of unhappy stories about his mam. But while Nolly could use a good fuck, and who didn't at the best of times, doing it while he was drunk was a line in the sand that Jack was unwilling to cross. It wasn't only that Nolly wouldn't remember, it was that he'd be unable to share it with Jack while it was happening, and Jack wanted him, to, oh, so very much. But not like this, not drunk and babbling and listing to one side, so that Jack had to grab him hard about the ribs and pull him close. Where Nolly's beer-laced breath whispered across his face. He might be beautiful, but he was drunk just the same.

"Let me light the candle, dear Nolly," said Jack. "And then we shall see, eh?"

He meant to do this, and then get Nolly to the bed, but it happened in backwards order, as when he stepped forward, Nolly stepped back, and the bed was suddenly there, with Nolly falling back upon it, arms spread wide, feet sprawled on the counterpane in a way that Jack knew there'd be black streaks upon it in the morning.

"In the light, then," said Nolly. "With a candle, an' you an' me, in a state o' nature, with your hands upon me. I love your hands, Jack, you know that, don't you? Jack?"

Hurrying to light the candle, Jack then stripped off his jacket and flung it upon the floor next to where Nolly's hat had landed.

Nolly's hair was spread upon the pillow, his face pale, a line of sweat sticking his hair to his forehead. His eyes were narrowed, focused on the ceiling, as if he were trying to find a spot to land on.

"D'you need the basin, Nolly?" Jack asked.

"Might do," said Nolly.

His throat moved over a large swallow, and Jack went to the laundry to grab the first basin he could get his hands on, hurrying back to hover at the bedside, hauling Nolly to a sitting position so he would vomit in the basin, rather than all over the floor. Jack's timing was good, and the beer-smelling sick splashed against the galvanized tin, covering the little flowers and the bright blue border that Jack found himself focusing on. That, rather than the fact that he was also drunk and the smell of vomit was making his stomach start to dance about.

Nolly sat up, the back of his hand wiping his mouth, wincing as if the back of his throat burned. He looked askance at Jack, as if Jack were to blame for his current state. Jack knew he was not, but felt badly about it just the same, the whole of it, everything from start to finish. Not that he'd come with Nolly out of London, no, he'd never regret that. But being ill, forcing Nolly into a position where he'd felt everything had depended on him. Getting them shelter. Calling for a doctor. Taking a job to pay the bills that had come in quick succession. Putting up with Mrs. Heyland's cooking.

This last bit made him smile, for he doubted that Nolly would be up to eating anything soon.

"I'll wash this out; can you do with a drink of water?"

Nolly would want one, even as he shook his head. Jack wanted one too, as his head was pounding, and that sharp, twisted sensation was crawling up his back again. There was nothing for it but that he took the basin and went to the laundry, feeling his way in the half-dark, to pull a bucket of water and tilt the basin over the drain in the floor to rinse it. Fumbling amongst the shelves, he grabbed what felt like a tin pitcher, and filled it from the pump. Taking the pitcher and the clean basin, he went back to the room.

Nolly was still sprawled on the bed, one leg hanging off, streaks on the counterpane, jacket off, his shirt undone, neck tilted back. Sweat sparked on his skin, and his eyes were closed.

"Jack?"

All of a sudden, Nolly sat up, and Jack was there with the basin, going through it all over again, except this time, his own reaction was even stronger. He'd have liked to have a good vomit in the basin himself, but Nolly was going about it as though he were the only one to have been affected by the beer. When Nolly was finished, Jack rinsed out the basin again, and brought it back, just in case.

"Is there water?" asked Nolly, sitting on the edge of the bed, slumped over, his hands clasped between his knees.

"Here," said Jack, his eyes burning, a sudden fatigue making him sit down next to Nolly. He handed over the pitcher.

"No tumbler?" Nolly took the pitcher with both hands, and Jack looked at him.

"No tumbler, an' no manservant to bring you one. Just drink it."

As he watched Nolly lift the pitcher, tilting his head back to account for the heft of it, the width of the brim, Jack knew he should not have been so harsh. Of course Nolly would expect a glass to drink out of, as anyone would.

Nolly handed him the pitcher, and Jack brought it to his mouth, taking several large swallows, and spilling a great deal more down his shirt bosom.

"They shouldn't have talked to you that way," said Nolly. His hands became fists against his knees. "You're not a manservant, you're no one's servant, an' even if you were—"

Jack groaned beneath his breath, resting the pitcher on the bed between them, more sorry than anything else in his life that he'd started that lie, a story to cover why they were together. Why on earth had Jack imagined that they needed a story? Why couldn't he have just left it as it was, that they were two friends traveling together? But no, he had to make a lie that although born quite small and innocent, had now turned into this. That Nolly would defend Jack because someone had dared to treat him like someone common born, which he was, and that rather than defend his own mam. It wasn't right. Moreover, it was coming into his awareness that Nolly was, perhaps, protesting a bit too much.

"You're not my manservant, you're *not*, d'you understand me, Jack?"

"Well, you can bloody well just shut up about it, then," said Jack, though he knew that Nolly probably wasn't even listening, which was ever the way with drunks. They tended to be very truthful, saying anything that came to them, even if it was, perhaps, a bit cruel. "You keep defendin' it as if there *were* somethin' to defend, so if there ain't, then shut up."

"You can make me if you kiss me, Jack," said Nolly.

He threw an arm around Jack's shoulders, which caused the pitcher tip forward, splashing the water all over the bedstead, and the floor. Leastways it wasn't on the bed itself, for which Jack was eternally grateful. He bent to pick up the pitcher, the blood pounding in his ears as he straightened up. The water on the floor would dry by morning.

"Ain't goin' to kiss you, Nolly. Not with you tastin' like beer-sick." Now Jack had to swallow, as his throat tightened up, threatening to follow Nolly's example. "Now, d'you mind takin' off your own clothes, as your manservant is off to get some more water, in case we need it in the night. An' there's the basin." Jack used his foot to push the basin across the floor closer to where Nolly was sitting. "'Case you needs it while I'm gone."

Nolly opened his mouth to say something, but if it was another admission of love, then Jack could hardly bear to look at him, with his head pounding, and his heart so crumpled. He concentrated on getting into the laundry without knocking anything over, and, finding the pump, drew up some water and stuck his head beneath the stream, smelling the leftover soap from the stone sink, the muck and mold from the drain. The last trace of sweet beer from his skin as he rinsed his head.

Shaking himself, he went back to the room and quietly shut the door. Nolly was studiously and carefully unlacing his boots. His hands were shaking but he was trying, so Jack knelt at his feet, and, pushing Nolly's hands away, unlaced his boots for him. Like a good manservant should. Then he stood up, taking Nolly with him, so he could undo Nolly's trousers and straighten his shirt to be more comfortable for sleeping in.

"Are you unhappy, Jack?" asked Nolly, his hands on Jack's face, a sweet blur to his eyes that told Jack that all was not lost, if he could get Nolly to face up what was before them. They were together in this world, both of them. All it needed was for Nolly to realize it while sober.

"You've got such a frown, shall I kiss it away, d'you want me to?"

"No," said Jack. He pulled Nolly's hands away from his face. "What I want is for you to get in bed, so I can go to bed. Can you do that, Nolly? Do that one thing?"

His words came out more harshly than he'd anticipated, causing the little smile playing around Nolly's rosy, vomit-stained mouth to tremble away. Jack licked his thumb, and wiped Nolly's lower lip with it, feeling a little unsteady on his own feet. Then he swept Nolly's hair back from his forehead.

"You want me in the bed, Jack?" asked Nolly, blinking, as if someone had lit more candles, and him unprepared for the brightness. But he seemed to be trying to focus on where he was, on what Jack was saying.

"Yes," said Jack. He stepped back to unbutton his own shirt, and wondered if he could manage to unlace his boots standing up. "If you go to bed, then I can go to bed, an' we can avoid the disaster of wakin' up the missus an' the rest of the household."

To his exhausted gratitude, Nolly seemed to see the sense in this, for he drew off his stockings and climbed into the bed, pulling the covers half up, and leaving them open for Jack, when he was ready. That this was unconsciously done made Jack feel a little better, but the morning would tell if Nolly, once sober, would be as considerate.

Jack sat on the edge of the bed, and bent to undo the laces on his boots, and the buttons on his trousers, before standing up to shuck everything off but his shirt. He could smell the tavern on him, the acid smoke from the coal fire, the salted air that had dried on his skin. He needed to get into bed and sleep off the beer, and determine, come morning what he, and they, needed to do. For he could not live in a town such as this, where the passion of a young girl could be pounded into the ground and turned into something so ugly, when it was *those* men—

In the morning, he would talk with Nolly about it. That was always best. For now, he needed to rest, and consider only the pillows and the blanket. And Nolly. And this he did, climbing into the bed, leaning over Nolly's chest, with Nolly's eyes half flickering open to watch what he was doing, to pinch the candle out, and fall back

Nolly curled sleepily into his arms, smelling like beer, the salt air, like Jack himself, their scents melding together in the dark. This at least, was peaceful and good; Nolly was almost asleep and Jack would be there soon. The morning, when it arrived, would bring at the very least a headache for them both. Nolly would bounce back, and Jack would as well, and thank goodness, he didn't have to go to church in the morning.

With a low laugh, he reached out to pet Nolly, who was sound asleep and snoring, his nose buried in Jack's armpit. Other than that, it was dark and still, and Jack felt sleep taking him. He let it.

25

IN THE BRIGHTNESS OF THE SEA'S LIGHT

There was a light in Oliver's face, and it burned like scouring acid. He rolled away, his head pounding, expecting to find Jack next to him in the bed. But the space was empty and, when he reached out, quite cold. Scrubbing his face, he tried to concentrate, squinting to focus on the ceiling in the blinding light that was pushing in through the window. The window must have been closed tightly, for the air smelled still and thick.

Sitting up, he pushed the bedclothes from him, and saw directly that Jack's clothes were gone. His heart went still, for where was Jack? He knew that there had been cruel words said about his mother, and then about Jack. A walk home in the dark that he could only remember through vague flashes. Him throwing up in the basin, and trying to get Jack to kiss him.

The sun was so high, the room so bright, the air so still and dry that he longed for a drink of cool water. He remembered Jack giving water to him last night, the thin edge of the pitcher against his lips.

But where was Jack?

Oliver jumped up, feeling the queasiness in his stomach and

stumbled around to find his clothes. There was a towel on the floor and a washcloth folded on top of it, as if someone had sat up during the night to perform nursing tasks.

Jack.

The trousers almost refused to go on, and his shirt was stained with beer; something had dried in a stiff line next to the buttons. He put his trousers on anyway, and his stockings, and then got all tangled when he laced up his boots. Tucking his shirt tails in and grabbing his jacket from the floor, he stumbled into the kitchen, to find Gussie, alone at the long, white-scrubbed table with a cup of tea and a large Bible spread out before her.

"Oh, it's you, Master Oliver."

Oliver licked his lips, but couldn't even find enough spit to do that. The kitchen was as bright as the sickroom; Gussie's white apron seemed to glow, and he had to look away.

"Where's Jack?" he asked, though his voice came out as though his throat had been clamped in a vise.

"I beg your pardon?"

Taking a breath, Oliver tried again.

"Do you know where Jack's gone? Did he leave or—?"

"Goodness," said Gussie. She pursed her lips together and made a face. "He didn't go to church, if that's what you're asking. No, he came through some time ago, and asked for directions to some place that overlooked the sea." She made a little sound under her breath. "As if that weren't the whole village."

Oliver felt his mouth fall open with a short, startled squeak.

"I told him to take the path through the woods to the Devil's Bellows. 'Tis a broad path, as folks walk it to catch the coach that goes from Charmouth right away to London, since there's no coach that goes through Lyme."

"Path?" asked Oliver. "To *London*?"

She made a motion with her hand. "It runs right past the house on the west side, and goes straight on out across the Black Ven to Charmouth. You can't miss it. Unless you're drunk, that is."

Without so much as a reply to her, and not caring what she

thought of him, Oliver threw on his coat and raced out the door, letting it bang shut behind him. He circled the entire house before he found the path, which was half-hidden by sturdy hedges that dripped with dew. He pushed his way through them and saw in the mid-morning glare, that there was indeed a path that led into the woods. He began to run, his coat flying open and his breath hitching in his side. He couldn't get any air, his heart jumping as he ran, stomach making awkward pushes upward, as if he was about to throw up.

And throw up he did, on the first bend out of the woods; he stood up after, saliva stringing from his hand as he wiped his mouth. He scrubbed his hand against his trousers and started trotting; there was nothing in his mouth to heal the acid in his throat, and his lip was split somehow, a crack that tasted red and stung up and down and back again. But he kept moving. If Jack was intending to take the coach to London, he'd be gone from Oliver, and he'd never let himself be found again.

Oliver couldn't stop to take even a breath, couldn't stop now. Had to keep going, even with the sea wind pushing against him, the sun in the blazing sky, making him hot, making his skin feel as though it was burning and there was nothing more he wanted than to crawl into a small, grassy hollow and let the sun bake him into nothingness.

It was where the path pitched upward and began to snake across a hillside, where half the earth had slipped toward the shore, that his legs almost gave out. If he'd not drunk so much the night before, it would have been easy. Only now it was hard, because his knees shook and the path was slippery with flinted stones and sliding gravel. He had to push up a steep part of the path, with the wind trying to suck him down. He had to go on hands and knees till he scrambled over a large mound and found himself on the path that led across a flat part of the hill.

On either side of the path were grasses, high and sweetly new-green, whispering and waving in the sea wind. The path stretched out a good long way, and if he squinted, he thought he could see a steeple rising above the far edge of the hill, and all along the horizon was the line of the ocean, deep and blue and endless.

And there, among the grasses, sitting in a hollow next to a boulder, was Jack. He hadn't seen Oliver yet, it seemed, for he was just sitting there with his arms wrapped around his bent knees. He was chewing on a stem of grass, the thin end of it dangling from his mouth, as if in replacement of his pipe, now long gone. Oliver realized he should have taken some of the shillings they'd been paid and bought a pipe and some tobacco for Jack. But he'd been careless, thinking of only things that were more practical than that.

Jack was staring at the sea; the wind pushed his hair into his eyes, and when he lifted his hand to wipe his dark forelock to one side, it was then that he saw Oliver.

Jack was as free as a wild thing and could go anywhere and be anything. And now, it looked as though he'd come halfway to Charmouth. Only he'd stopped and Oliver didn't know why.

"Jack." Oliver's voice came out thin, and was swallowed by the air above the cliff.

Jack turned his gaze back to the sea, the wind whipping his dark hair. Oliver walked closer, and looked at Jack, his eyes hot, hoping with everything he had that in the blackness that had swallowed the memory of the night before he'd not struck Jack. But along the curve of Jack's cheek, there was no bruise, so it had to have been something else. Though, with the lack of joy in Jack's expression at Oliver's presence, he had to have done something fearful and cruel.

"Jack." Now Oliver was close enough to see the circles under Jack's eyes, the exhaustion there. Jack looked careworn, and Oliver was to blame for it.

"Jack."

But Jack wasn't looking up. His shoulders hunched up even further and he stared at his knees, at the laces of the boots Oliver had got for him.

"Jack, I'm sorry, truly—"

"Anyone can say sorry," said Jack, suddenly picking up a stone and shying it down the hill toward the blue sea. "Even a child. Don't mean nothin'." He tugged the grass from his mouth and flicked it from him.

Oliver went to his knees in the grasses beside Jack. He reached for Jack, but then, at the last moment, just as his fingers brushed Jack's sleeve, he stilled his hand.

"Don't mean nothin'." Jack's mouth barely moved as he said this, the muscles so tight under his skin that the bones seemed to push through to the surface, and there were white circles around his knuckles.

Oliver moved forward on his knees. Jack reached out and with a single push, sent Oliver sprawling. Now he was face up to the sunny, almost cloudless sky, the wind whipping the grasses, green and bright, over his head, as if he were buried beneath them while they went on waving and waving, back and forth. He closed his eyes and wished himself far away. If Jack wouldn't let him apologize, then Jack would leave. And without Jack, there was no point, not in anything. The blood that had been pounding so close beneath his skin raced away, leaving a cold sear from which he felt he would never warm.

Oliver tightened his eyes until he was sunk in darkness, with only the fine whisper of the grasses above his head to let him know he was still in the world of the living.

"Whatever I said, Jack, I'm truly sorry for it."

For a moment there was silence, as if Jack hadn't heard him.

"No," said Jack's, finally. "You ain't."

The memory of the night before was a black weave, with flashes of Jack bending over him, bringing a cold pitcher of water to drink. A pillow that was too hot, and gentle hands lifting his head to turn the pillow over for him. Then blackness, and his own voice, scratchy in his throat as he talked to Jack. Because Jack would always listen, just like Jack was there for him when he'd had too much to drink.

Oliver made himself sit up, and opened his eyes, even though his stomach lurched and the sunlight was brighter than before. Scrubbing at his mouth, he tried to blink away his headache so he could concentrate.

"What did I say, Jack, what did I do? Tell me."

Jack sighed, and continued looking out at the sea, his eyes tracking the waves, and the white flash of winging seagulls overhead.

"You lied to me, to begin with," said Jack.

"Lied?" asked Oliver, squinting.

"About the money you owed, an' the work you were doin'."

"But you know about that," said Oliver, aghast that this small thing had upset Jack, and for no reason.

"I do now, but I didn't then," said Jack. His hands were clenched around his bent knees. "You kept it from me, an' I had to find out on my own—from a stranger."

This silenced Oliver. It was becoming painfully clear to him that to Jack a lie was a powerful thing, and nothing that should be told between people who were close.

"An' then there was the letter—"

"I didn't keep that a secret from you, Jack," said Oliver. The sun was so hot overhead, he felt like he was sweating all over.

"Told you I didn't want it, but you gave it to me anyhow."

"But you didn't even read it, so what does it matter?"

"It matters that you didn't listen when I said no." Jack's lower lip seemed to tremble as he said this, bringing all of Oliver's protestations to a halt.

Oliver bent his head and thought hard. Up from the dark, thumping cavern of his headache was a memory of them in bed together. There amidst the bedclothes, Jack was telling him that if he, Oliver, said no, that Jack would stop. What Jack had done for him was powerful and full of love; but in return, when Jack had said no, Oliver hadn't stopped.

"That was wrong of me," said Oliver. "Very wrong of me, and I'm sorry, but I don't see why you're so upset."

"It ain't even a thought for you, is it." Jack was finally looking at him, his eyes dull and tired, his eyebrows coming together in a sad scowl. "No, I don't reckon you remember anyway. You put enough beer away for three men."

Jack looked and sounded as if he were already trying to forgive Oliver already; that was like Jack. But there was something eating at Jack, and Oliver could not let that continue, not with Jack.

"Yes, I drank too much beer," agreed Oliver. "But Jack, please tell me what I said to hurt you so. It's got to be more than the lie I told, or the letter you didn't want."

Oliver's whole body was starting to shake; he wanted to move closer but didn't dare.

Jack's face crumpled just before he turned away. In a moment, Jack was scrubbing at his eyes, and Oliver swallowed hard, his stomach churning.

Jack never cried. Oliver had never seen him cry. Oliver scrambled to his side, holding Jack's face, wanting to comfort him. But Jack's hands gripped Oliver's wrists, digging into the cords of muscle with his fingertips, hard enough to hurt. Oliver moved back a little, letting go, but he stayed close, his knees against Jack's thigh, his chest to Jack's shoulder.

"Tell me what I've done, for the love of everything, tell me—"

Jack hid his face in the crook of his own elbow, and Oliver felt his whole body shudder. Then Jack took a breath and lifted his face. His eyelashes were speckled with tears, and his nose was running.

"You were so drunk," said Jack. "You were wide open, like you almost never are, except when you're drinkin'. Talkin' and wavin' your hands about."

"What did I say, Jack?" For that seemed to be the crux of it. What he'd said while drunk.

"You told me you loved me last night," said Jack. "You ain't never said it before then, but you were drunk, so it don't mean nothin'."

A cold horror filled Oliver. In the face of Jack's gentleness, his unwavering kindness—the way he made sure that Oliver always had something to eat so that he never, ever went hungry—Jack said *I love you* in so many ways, and Oliver had wounded him beyond all measure by not saying it in return. He'd only scorned Jack for his low manners, and kept things from him—and he'd made Jack feel like he didn't love him. Like a coward, he'd needed to be bolstered with beer before he could say it.

But instead of making excuses, Oliver tipped his head forward, the sunlight bright upon the back of his neck. What he was about to confess should be heard only by Jack, and not carried on the whispering wind. He took a breath, and had to swallow against the whistle in his throat.

"I love you, Jack. I should have said it before, but I was scared. Of the world. Of myself." He had to lick his lips, his mouth was so dry, but he had to finish, so that Jack would know he meant it. So that Jack would stay with him. "But I love you, I do. More than anything else, more than everything else."

Oliver found himself tumbled back on the grass, with two arms around him and Jack's head buried in his neck, and their legs tangled together as the wind whipped over their heads. Jack's face was wet against his neck, and he felt the flutter of Jack's eyelashes, every nerve brought to life by the brush of Jack's lips against his cheeks.

"Do you forgive me?" Oliver whispered into the spill of Jack's hair upon his face. "Please say you do."

Jack lifted himself up on his elbows, sprawling over Oliver's chest, becoming a pinwheeling spark of green eyes and flashing teeth against the radiance of the sun. So bright that Oliver had to squint until Jack moved his head so that Oliver could look up within Jack's shadow and see the last tear slip off of Jack's nose.

Now he could reach up to wipe away the tears from Jack's cheek, and Jack didn't mind. Jack's weight upon him was comforting and warm, steady and constant. He could feel Jack's heart thudding against his ribs, and the push and ebb of Jack's breathing.

"You goin' to say it again, ever?" asked Jack. "Or do I have to get you flattened with beer for you to own it?"

With his heart hammering, surely Jack could feel the terror in his breast, Oliver licked his lips again, praying for rain, or a nice cool glass of water. Not that there was any to be found. But there was Jack, who was, with his wide green eyes and a quirk of a grin that seemed now a little shy, waiting for an answer, who wanted it said without the influence of drink.

"I love you, Jack." Oliver's breath left him in a rush, so he nodded fiercely. "I do, I do indeed. And I'm sorry, for everything. For lying to you, and the letter. Everything."

Jack's smiled. It lit up his face, the brightness reaching into the dark parts of Oliver's soul, filling them with something sweet and good. And it was powerful, somehow, so powerful that he wrapped his arms around Jack and pulled him down so their hearts could be close, and tighter than that so that he could feel all of Jack up against him, the weight of Jack pushing him into the solid earth, so that it might hold them both until they died.

But they did not die. Instead Jack rolled off Oliver to rest his head in the curve of Oliver's shoulder, their heads close enough so that their hair twined together like wild sea grass. Oliver petted Jack with long strokes, never letting go. Letting himself think of all the things he might do for Jack, now with the world blazing open before them, now that Jack wasn't leaving him.

"D'you want me to say it again, Jack?" he asked, half-whispering, wishing there was a spring close by, where he could draw up a cool dipper of water for him and Jack to drink.

"Say it any time you like," murmured Jack into Oliver's skin. "Now, roll back around and make yourself my pillow, an' I'll use you, an' we can shut our eyes for a bit an' snooze in the sun, while it lasts."

Oliver did as was required of him, his back feeling the dampness of the grass seeping up through his jacket. But what did that matter, when Jack was resting his head on Oliver's shoulder, and looping his arm around Oliver's belly, sighing with a deep contentment, as if his dearest dream had been reached. That Oliver was anyone's dream, let alone on a windy hillside—

"You will stop thinkin' this instant," said Jack, his voice muffled against Oliver's jacket lapel. "For the love of *God* just stop thinkin'. Rest now. Shut your eyes, and rest now."

"Yes, sir," said Nolly, biting back his smile.

"*Nolly*," said Jack, his warning stern and sleepy all at once.

"Yes, Jack."

The warmth of the sun and the stillness of the hillside sank into them. The grasses waved over their heads, the wind a low hiss across them. Oliver let his eyes close, shifting his forearm high on his forehead, and allowed himself to fall asleep.

By the time they returned to the manor house, it had begun to rain, a clean, swift rain, that would make the fields green the way Nolly liked them, because in the spring, the world was a more gentle place, and in England, there was no place better, in spring. It'd been some time since Jack had been home in springtime, when everything came up new and soft; he was glad to be home for it this year.

Jack opened the door and they went down the passage to the kitchen, where they found the rest of the household sitting down to supper. It looked as though grace had already been said, the way they all had their cutlery in their hands, looking at them both, as if irritated at the delay in their meal.

"I'm terribly sorry that we're late, Mrs. Heyland," said Nolly. "We took a rather long walk this morning, Jack and I."

"And took the liberty of missing church, as well, I see. And dinner besides."

They made quick work of washing at the basin, and sat down.

"That was my fault, missus," said Jack, laying his napkin in his lap as he'd seen Nolly do. "I wasn't feelin' well, and Master Oliver determined that some fresh air would do me more good than church."

Nolly looked confused for a moment; Jack knew what he'd said on the hillside about never playing master and servant again, but they weren't really playing it, they were just finishing the story for Mrs. Heyland, who would be very confused if they suddenly stopped. But he'd have to explain that to Nolly later. He gave Nolly's ankle a kick.

"Why, yes, yes," said Nolly, hesitating a bit. "Since our Lord is omnipotent, I consider that He might be found as well on a hillside as in a church."

"The view was very beautiful," said Jack, nodding. "Very holy."

"Did you not make it to Charmouth, then?" asked Gussie, taking a platter of beef from Mrs. Heyland. "To look at you this morning, I thought you were running away, making your master come after you like he did."

"Oh no," said Nolly. He took the platter in his turn, forking a slice of boiled beef to his plate before passing the platter on to Jack, looking very serious as he did so. "I knew Jack had gone walking out—"

"No, you didn't," said Gussie. "You had no idea where he'd gone, absolutely no idea."

"I *knew* Jack had gone walking," said Nolly again, slower this time, his tone stern as if fully inheriting the role of Jack's master, but for good purpose this time. "I just didn't know where, and wanted to catch up with him."

The conversation was about to take an ugly turn, if Gussie continued to insist she saw and heard what she did. So as Jack took two slices of beef before passing on the platter to Gerald, he nodded quite vigorously, to grab everyone's attention.

"Did you happen to notice, Master Oliver, whilst we were on the hillside, how many smacks were in the harbor? Was it more or less than had been there yesterday?"

"There's sure to be less," said Gerald unexpectedly. He gave Jack a look that said that he knew what Jack was up to. "Some boats go down Weymouth way when the spring tides are high, like they were today. Makes for better fishing in the morning."

"There's a lot I need to learn about tides, I expect," said Nolly, and with that the discussion of that morning's activities, witnessed only by Gussie, died down.

But now Jack had a better idea how it had transpired that morning. How, after waking up alone, Nolly had determined that Jack had actually *left* him. Jack felt a pang of guilt. The next time he needed to get out in the fresh air, with no walls around him, he'd be leaving Nolly a message, some type of note, which would leave him with no doubt as to Jack's intention to return.

The meal continued with only an occasional comment about the service that day, or a request to pass the butter, or another slice of bread, please. The difficult part came after supper, as they stood up, and Nolly paused to speak to Mrs. Heyland.

"Mrs. Heyland, I meant to give this to you yesterday." He reached into his pocket to pull out three shillings, the remainder of their combined pay packets. The coins were bright in his hand as he held them out to her.

Mrs. Heyland's mouth worked as she looked at the money, but she didn't take it.

"The bill from the doctors, Dr. Rudge and Dr. McMurtry both, comes to *ten* shillings, sixpence. That is only three; whatever did you do with *four* shillings in this village? Since I know very well Mr. Thurly paid you seven between you."

The maidservants paused in their tasks, and Jack knew that even Gerald and young Tim, as they went out the door, were listening. And poor Nolly, with his hand outstretched to pay the blasted woman what he could, well, Jack couldn't bear witnessing it more than a moment.

"Well, 'tis true," said Jack. He scooped up the coins from Nolly's hand and grabbed the missus's hand, to press the coins to her palm, and roll her fingers over them. "But Master Oliver here determined his poor manservant needed a suit of clothes, since there were none to be had, and that's where his pay went. Such a lucky soul am I to have such a generous master. There's no one who can question that, I reckon."

Jack looked at her, daring her to naysay him. But she didn't. She pulled out a small, leather change purse from her apron pocket and put the coins in, closing the clasp with a snap.

"Very well," she said, lifting her chin at them. "But I shall expect the remainder by Thursday; you can tell Mr. Thurly that."

Nolly opened his mouth to apologize, and Jack could sense that he was about to say something about their continued residence at the house. And it might be good, with the entire staff within earshot, because the missus could do nothing but continue to be seen to be charitable toward them.

But Nolly didn't say anything, and Jack gave the waist of Nolly's trousers a small tug; it might be better to be out of eyeshot just now. Besides, they needed to talk; if the missus did throw them out, then where were they for next? They needed to agree on this, as it couldn't always be Nolly who determined their direction.

"Good night, Mrs. Heyland, thank you for the lovely supper."

Nolly almost bowed, but she scowled at him. Jack walked away, with no comment about the supper, nor any thanks, either. The supper hadn't been worth even the barest of thanks, but Nolly was like that, all manners, being the gentleman wherever they went.

"Come along, Master Oliver," said Jack, at last, to get Nolly walking with him and not lingering in the kitchen. "You know I need my rest."

"Yes, Jack," said Nolly, finally, *finally* walking where Jack wanted him to go. The kitchen was the territory of the missus, and Jack wanted out of it as soon as possible.

Jack had been right, Oliver did feel better now that he'd eaten. Not that the food had been very good, but it had been something to fill his belly, giving him energy to fight his exhaustion, and the headache, which was now a pale semblance of its former self. Both of them were in their shirts, tucked cozily beneath the blankets and Oliver knew he didn't want to be anywhere else at the moment.

As for Jack, he was curled up next to him in the bed, with his head on Oliver's arm, and his legs beneath Oliver's bent knees, upon which Oliver had balanced *The Count of Monte Cristo*. He was attempting to read about the exorbitant amount of money the Count was spending to seek revenge for the death of his father, and the fact that the woman he loved was married to another.

But as good as the story was, it was hard to focus on the words, with Jack pressed against him so that he was as warm as he might be on a summer day. Even the pages seemed warm beneath his fingertips, the words moving up and down, in a slow undulation, like a lazy wave. He blinked to focus his eyes, and wanted very much to stop reading. And would but for Jack, who was looking up at him, the expectation in his face that Oliver would continue.

"Jack," he said, laying both of his hands in the gutter of the book. "If she does kick us out, where will we go?"

"I was wonderin' the same thing durin' supper," said Jack, with a short laugh. "She weren't none too pleased gettin' only three shillin's."

"Well, if she'd given you clothes when she'd given them to me, we wouldn't have had to spend it." He wanted to shut the book with a snap, but Jack stopped him, laying his hand on Oliver's wrist.

"Could have done without, except for your soft heart, Nolly."

Oliver ducked his chin, feeling his face flush. "You could have stolen the money, or the clothes, I understand that, Jack. But I wanted to get them for you, because I didn't want you to be cold."

He was about to go on, because it had taken him till Thursday to realize that Jack had a rent in his trousers, that his stockings had holes. Again Jack stopped him, giving the book a tug, as if to ask that Oliver start to read again.

But then the words weren't as dear to him as Jack was, and Oliver took his hands out of the book and folded it closed.

Watching Jack watching him, Oliver leaned down to put the book beneath the mattress; his movements jarred the side table, and the candlelight flickered, sending sparks into the air, and the smell of burnt honey. Sliding down the pillow, so that his head was next to Jack's, he pulled the sheet up to his chin.

"What're you up to, then, Nolly?" But being Jack, he shifted down, too, rolling toward the center of the bed to face Oliver, even as Oliver rolled toward him.

"I'm not quite sure," Oliver said. "But if you would let me, I'd like to give you something."

He felt quite foolish even as he said it, but wanted to make it quite clear that this wasn't a payment, as Jack had requested he should never do. It didn't help that Jack's eyebrows flew up into his hairline, as if in a moment, he would begin to tease, and Oliver knew he would not be able to continue, not with his heart racing already, his face as hot as fire.

He was about to rescind his offer, or to lie about what he meant, when Jack laid his hand on Oliver's neck. Just that, but the contact alone was enough to tell him that Jack wouldn't tease. That Jack already knew what Oliver was offering. This personal, *intimate* thing.

"I'm about to get it all wrong, aren't I," said Oliver, almost panting. He was so hot he shoved the sheet and blanket away, and took a gulp of air.

"Oh, I doubt it," said Jack smiling with his eyes as well as his mouth. "For there's no way you could get it wrong."

Oliver looked down to where Jack's shirt collar moved against his neck, and realized that Jack's heart was beating quite fast, that a dapple of sweat curled along his hairline, making his dark hair stand up a bit. Jack might be pretending to be calm, but his body told a different story.

"Do you want that I should pinch out the candle, Nolly?" Jack asked in a low voice, one that didn't do anything to calm Oliver's nerves.

"No," he said, swallowing. Half sitting up, he raked his hand through his hair, then held it, palm out, to Jack. "Just stay—like that. Please. While I—figure it out."

"It ain't meant to be horrible, Nolly," said Jack, staying perfectly still. "You don't have to do it."

There was more that Oliver could say, but if the words came spilling out of him, it would create a barrier between this moment, and what he intended to do for Jack. Which he wanted to do before his nerve ran out. So, making another palm-out gesture, he slid lower in the bed, taking most of the bedclothes with him, though Jack, now uncovered almost to his knees, didn't seem to mind. Jack kept quite still, watching with patient eyes, though Oliver could see that his color was quite high, and his skin very warm to the touch. Oliver ran his hand up one of Jack's thighs, moving the tail end of Jack's shirt aside.

The sight of the skin along Jack's thigh goose-pimpling up froze him all over again, and he knew that if he didn't get going, that his intent, as well as Jack's pleasure, would be no more than tatters about him. So he took a breath, and swung his leg over so that he was straddling both of Jack's thighs. Jerking upward, Jack threw him off, head whipping to one side as he gasped. Oliver scurried off, and knelt on the bed with no idea of what had just happened, but knowing he'd done something terribly wrong.

"Jack, what did I do? Did I hurt you, did I—"

Curling to his side for a moment, his hair dark where it spread on the sheets, Jack seemed to make an effort to loosen his shoulders by shrugging them. "No," he said. "Just surprised me, that's all. My legs don't like bein' trapped, I think."

Oliver's heart was truly pounding, having made a mistake like that, not even thinking—

"I'm sorry, Jack," he said, wondering if he'd ruined everything.

"'Tis no matter," said Jack, rolling onto his back, though Oliver could see that it *did* matter. "I liked you like that, feelin' your skin on mine. But perhaps with only half of you."

Nodding, Oliver took a breath. Something had happened to Jack, if the weight of a body would startle him. Something had scared him. Perhaps Oliver would ask later, though Jack might not want to talk about it. For now, he bent down and kissed Jack's knee, pushing the shirt that Jack had pulled down up again. Straddling only one leg, feeling Jack's thigh between his, the silky, forbidden movement of their skin together.

He moved his hand between his own legs to ease the hardness there, his cock erect against his belly, and it seemed a forbidden thing, this touch, his own hand to himself. But Jack saw and gave him a wink.

"Standin' and posin'?" asked Jack. "Or doin'?"

"*Kneelin'* and posin' an' doin'," Oliver corrected, getting a very strong feeling that, even if they were to do this thing, that he were to do this *sinful* thing to Jack, everything else would, pretty much, remain the same between them.

He shifted back along Jack's leg oh-so-slowly to draw it out, feeling Jack shudder beneath him, and, silkily, moved his hands up between Jack's legs, pushing Jack's shirt up the rest of the way. He kissed the inside of Jack's thighs, closing his eyes for a moment, a brief flash of dark pink, and blood red framed in his memory, as he kissed alongside Jack's cock. It was warm against his lips, and he opened his mouth to let his tongue have a taste.

Remembering what Jack had done to him, he tipped his mouth up to encircle the top of it, the dark red part, the heat of it filling the roof of his mouth, almost making him pull back with surprise. He'd not expected such warmth, and the clear fluid that Jack seemed to think was helpful and useful, was there on his tongue. It was salty and a little sweet, and lovely for all that a part of him thought the entire of it somewhat strange, still.

Jack made a sound, and Oliver looked up. Jack's mouth was open, his cheeks flushed, his eyes half closed. As if aware that Oliver was looking at him, Jack shook his head, his eyes half-lidded and unfocused.

"'Tis just sound, Nolly, just sound. Go on w'what you're doin' an' never mind the noises I make."

Oliver took Jack's cock back in his mouth, the taste and feel of it more familiar now, and used his hand to circle it to the base, his wrist tickled by Jack's private hair, much darker than his own, more abundant. So many differences, but so much was the same, for as he did to Jack what Jack had done to him, Jack writhed beneath his touch, with long low groans, as if he liked very much what Oliver was doing to him.

Oliver made his mouth slick, sucking gently, and then with more force, pulsing his hand up and down, and then when he used his free hand to curve his fingers around the taut flesh between Jack's legs, and when Jack actually cried out and arched his back off the bed, Oliver felt as proud as he ever had from any other lesson he'd ever learned. For when he stroked Jack and sucked and slid his mouth about, Jack would sigh, and when he went gentle and used only his tongue, Jack would push into his mouth, as if powerless to stop himself. And when his jaw got tired, and he pulled off a bit, drawing back to use only his hand, Jack's whole body pushed into it.

When he began again, bending down, sucking Jack into his mouth, using his tongue to twirl around and around, as Jack had done to him, Jack actually began to weep, with soft, high cries that sent shivers up Oliver's spine. That was it, then, what Jack liked most of all, so Oliver did it again, drawing off for a moment, as if he meant to stop altogether, and then opening his mouth to suck Jack in, twirling his tongue and pulling Jack deep into his throat until Jack was practically sobbing, the back of his hand over his mouth to stifle the sound of it.

It became fluid, this touching, the connection between his mouth and hands, and Jack's body, fluid and welcoming, each touch received by Jack with movement and sound, and coming back to him, like a wave, moving through him, and going back into Jack. He twisted his wrist at the base of Jack's cock, and licked the whole of him in one long stroke. Then he put his mouth fully on Jack again, and almost jumped out of his skin when Jack's cock pulsed in his mouth, and the stream of ejaculate hit the back of his throat. But Jack had swallowed, to save the sheets, and so would he. The taste was stronger, a bit sour, but with Jack's soft cries in his ears, Jack's hand on the top of his head, almost pulling his hair, Oliver swallowed it all, gulping, pulling off when he thought Jack was finished.

But Jack was not, not quite. He circled his own fingers around his cock and stroked it hard two times, making a small amount of the milky fluid dribble down the side. Then Jack gasped and collapsed back on the bed, and Oliver gasped too, wiping his mouth with the back of his hand. His heart was pounding still, his lungs working, and he was sweaty everywhere, in a most ungentlemanly fashion, and he could not have cared less. Not when Jack's eyes opened as he pushed his dark hair off his damp forehead, smiling with his teeth as he crooked his finger for Oliver to come closer.

And this Oliver did willingly, kissing Jack open-mouthed, sharing Jack's taste with him. Licking his own lower lip before he did the same to Jack, teasing him about what Oliver had just done. Pushing his tongue in and licking the inside of Jack's mouth like the bold thing that he was. Smiling to himself to think he'd given this thing to Jack, and made him weep with pleasure.

Pulling back, he saw that the tender skin beneath Jack's eyes was still damp, so he licked there too, softly, drawing his tongue along Jack's eyelashes, tasting the salt there, feeling Jack's eyelids quiver.

"Oh," said Jack. "You're so *talented* now, so *talented* with that tongue of yours, are you?"

"It's been hidden," said Oliver, in kind. "Hidden these many years. Waiting," His voice went low, almost rumbling in his chest. "Waiting for you to find it."

Jack's eyes went soft and round, as if Oliver had said something quite remarkable, and then Jack carried on as if he had. Jack curled on his side and pulled Oliver to him, burying his face in Oliver's neck, whispering against his skin, as if in prayer, with worshipful kisses, with Jack's breath warm against his skin.

"What, Jack?" asked Oliver, clasping his hands over Jack's. "What are you saying?"

Tipping his head back, Jack cast him a glance, black lashes over bright green eyes, his expression stirring in Oliver's heart in an almost painful way. Jack wrapped both hands around Oliver's face and kissed him, then pulled back.

"My dear Nolly," he said. "You have no idea, do you. None atall. How precious you are to me."

It was astonishing to hear this, the way Jack said it, as if it were the most obvious thing in the world, the most important. The words wrapped themselves around Oliver's heart, and became part of it, and he hugged Jack as hard as he could, gritting his teeth with the pain of it, this affection Jack had for him, this love that Jack expressed, in simple words, a single touch.

"All right, Nolly, it's all right," said Jack, patting his back, soothing him, and Oliver realized he was shaking. Jack pushed him back, those green eyes taking in everything, missing nothing. "I can say it whenever you like, any time, *any* time. All right? Now how 'bout I take care of you, eh?" Jack shifted one hand to stroke between Oliver's legs, and Oliver's whole body twitched. But he felt shy, the blush burning his cheeks, and Jack shook his head.

"What did I tell you about that? There's no need for shame between you an' me, no need. 'Tis a gift, pure and simple. So, yes?"

Oliver nodded, and didn't even need to move, for Jack curled down to his waist and shifted Oliver's shirt around to his liking, and when Oliver felt Jack's mouth, warm and soft upon him, he tilted his head, closed his eyes, and let the pleasure begin within him.

AS THE STORM RISES

T he green-topped waves smashed into the Cobb, and brought the spray of the sea over the rims of the buckets, the edge of the deal table, the men's beards, their knives. Oliver was on the leeward side of the line of men, and he stood at the end of the table. Jack was at his side as they both cut fish and tossed the heads into the bucket or to one of the cats, which mewled and wove around the legs of the table and the men's boots.

Mr. Thurly, in his canvas hut with the little stove at his feet, kept an eye on the weather, as the storm that was rolling in might curtail the fishing smacks from coming in. The canvas was flapping, and the men had been making bets to each other as to whether or not the pegs would last the day. Jack wanted to bet the coming week's salary for both of them, but Oliver knew it was a bad risk. Men like Mr. Thurly knew how strong spring winds were; those pegs would outlast a force gale.

"'Tis comin' on dinnertime, lads," said Mr. Thurly. He stood up and walked over to the table, weaving in and out of the women who carried buckets of fish heads down to the shore and brought up buckets of salt. "I'll get the girl to set up the table on the low side, where the wind won't take away the dishes."

Jack reached over to pat Oliver's belly; Oliver gave him a shove away with his elbow, but he didn't shove very hard. After yesterday, he would have let Jack kiss him then and there, if it wouldn't have gotten them both arrested.

"Probably eel stew today," Jack said, winking broadly for effect, making the men laugh.

"You'll have mine, then," said Oliver, in return. Mock sternness was in his tone, as he meant it to be, but he didn't stop the smile that only Jack could see.

Jack's answering grin sent a raft of sparks shifting through him, warming him, making him feel tight through his middle and loose everywhere else. Even his feet felt fine, even after standing all morning on the rough stones of the Cobb.

They sat down to mutton stew. Around them the men grunted through their meal; Leander was telling someone about the fight in the tavern, and with good spirit. Which was better than it might have been, though Oliver wished there had been no story to tell in the first place.

"A quart of beer? No, it were more than that; he drank enough to sink that fishing smack over there." Leander pointed, waving his spoon around. "Could still hit worth a damn after that, though. Couldn't you, Oliver? Tried to take me down with a punch I never saw coming, he did."

The man sitting next to Oliver laughed and almost tumbled his bowl as he gave Oliver a hard nudge. But it was good natured, in that the man went back to his meal, and Leander went on talking about the dances to come when the weather was fine, and how the bathers would crowd the streets and rocky beaches in summer. At which point Oliver began to muse whether or not he and Jack would be in town, to see such a sight as the brightly painted bathing wagons and the high-born ladies and gentlemen who would use them to bathe in the sea. But he knew that he and Jack would determine their way together, so he nodded to himself, and continued eating.

"What's that, then?" asked Jack. "What's got you smilin'?"

Jack had bent his head down to catch Oliver's expression. His wide mouth was curved in a smile, and he looked ready to say yes to anything Oliver might recommend. And Oliver knew that this was how he should feel always.

"It's nothing," he said. But it was everything.

Down along the shore, along the gravel road, a plain, two-wheeled wagon was pulling up at the end of the Cobb, and two constables were getting out of it. In their dark blue suits, they were tidy against the buff-colored rocks on the shoreline. They seemed headed for the tent, and indeed walked along as though they had a destination in mind.

When they spotted Mr. Thurly, they came along the low side of the Cobb towards him. Mr. Thurly, seeing them, got up to meet them. Oliver didn't think anything of it, and went back to his dinner, pushing bits of stew around with a piece of buttered bread, and thinking about taking a swallow of beer.

"You want Jack?" asked Mr. Thurly. "What's he done, then?"

All at once Oliver felt Jack go still beside him on the bench, and felt a draft of cold air along his jaw.

"This one Jack Dawkins?" one of the constables asked, pointing at Jack, and at Mr. Thurly's nod, they came over and hauled Jack up by the collar of his jacket. His legs became tangled in the bench as they roughly drew him out, and then Oliver was on his feet, his bowl clattering on the table.

"What do you want with Jack?" He shouted, with his fists clenched at his sides, and all the men looking at him.

"That's none of your affair, boy," said the constable who had Jack.

"No." Oliver stepped out from the bench, marched over to the constable, and grabbed Jack's arm. "You can't take him, you have no right to take him!"

The constable attempted to pry Oliver's fingers away, with

enough force to bruise, but Oliver shifted to the other side, looking at Jack, catching his eyes. "This is wrong, Jack, this is a mistake."

"No mistake," said the constable, as if finding the last of his patience. He gave Jack a shake. "Mrs. Heyland says there was a pile of stolen books under the bed, which she found when collecting for her laundry."

"Valuable books were taken, she told us," said the other constable. "Valuable books stolen by this wretch, who she'd taken in and given shelter."

The men at the table had gone completely silent, and even Mr. Thurly seemed unable to give a gruff opinion. The wind whisked over the top of the Cobb, and as Oliver felt the first drafts of sea-tasting rain, he knew that he could not let them take Jack away from him.

"I took the books," Oliver said, because it was true.

"Nolly," said Jack. He could barely speak for the tight hold the constable had on his collar. But he tried, twitching in the constable's grip to look up at him. "He's lyin'; I'm the one who did it, not him."

For a moment, the constable's eyes narrowed as he looked at Oliver, seeing what everyone saw, a face too beautiful to commit a crime. The constable nodded to his companion and was about to walk away, taking Jack with him, when Oliver leaped at him, tearing at the fist that held Jack's collar, swinging a blow that smashed into the constable's chin. Astonished, he let go of Jack. Who, to Oliver's surprise, did not run.

"No, Nolly," Jack said, shaking his head. "This is not for you."

The second constable grabbed Jack again while the first one took out a snowy-white handkerchief to wipe his bloody mouth with.

"You want to do that again, boy?" he asked.

"Yes," said Oliver, his breast heaving, and he swung, as hard as he could, to land a blow in the middle of the constable's dark blue uniform. Then he gathered a mouthful of spit and sprayed the constable's face with it. "I took the books. In front of all these witnesses, I say it. Now, what are you doing to do about that?"

"We'll take you both," said the constable, wiping his face once more before putting his soiled handkerchief back in his pocket. "And let the magistrate at the quarter session decide."

With a shudder, Oliver felt the constable's hand clamping on his shirt collar, and saw the handcuffs come out, and the long, metal keys as they clinked on the ring at the constable's waist. Breathing through his nose, Oliver let the constable put the handcuffs on him, and let himself be led down the Cobb toward the cart. Jack was at his side, cuffed just the same, his jacket collar rumpled up to his ears, and Oliver longed to straighten it, longed to kiss Jack's cheek and whisper in his ear that everything would be all right.

But Jack looked surly, with high color streaking his face, muttering something under his breath. And when they were both shoved into the cart, and the cuffs were locked to the brackets in the wooden floor, Jack leaned close and kicked Oliver with his boot.

"You stupid bloody—stupid *fucking* fool."

The words were jerked out of Jack's mouth as the constables got into the cart and one of them picked up the reins and clucked to the horse to start. All of the men stopped gutting fish, and Mr. Thurly, and the women on the shore watched as the cart circled round, and began to go back along the road toward the church. The silence was broken by the roar of the ocean on the rocks, the green-whipped water clattering the stones, and the salt-spray rising into the air, curving over itself like the white-rounded back of a horse.

Jack's face was white, the faint freckles showing like dots, his eyes blinking as if something was in them.

"I wish to God you hadn't done that."

"I *had* to, Jack, I couldn't let you go alone. And be away from me."

"Be quiet, you," said the constable. He flicked the whip at the horse to get it going along the street as it began to follow the rise of the hill. But the horse had good sense to ignore the whip and pace itself, and so Oliver found himself rocking back and forth, his hands connected by iron cuffs, the chain pulled close to the floor between his legs. Jack was the same, and as soon as they reached the top of the hill, where the trees began to bend over the macadamed road, he realized he could not sit fully upright.

The horse broke into a low trot to get over the height of the hill, and it started to rain, a low, round-dappled rain, as the clouds closed over the sky, and the sun turned to grey-lit streaks through the trees. It was then that Oliver realized that they were well and truly leaving Lyme Regis.

"Where are you taking us?" he asked.

The constable he'd struck reached around and slapped Oliver across the face. It was so abrupt that Oliver swayed back, unable to raise his hands to ease the sting of his cheek. He felt Jack go very still beside him, and knew that he needed to walk very carefully through this dark place, or he'd make things worse for himself. Worse for Jack.

"Not that you've any say," the constable said, as if to himself. "There isn't any house of correction, so we're taking you to Axminster workhouse, until the magistrate can see you."

The world began to flicker in front of Oliver's eyes, as if someone were throwing a black hood over his head and then jerking it off again. He could not feel anything, not the seat beneath him, nor the pressure of the cuffs on his wrists, not anything. It was as if his entire body had vanished, and he was only a pair of burning, searching eyes, staring at the back of the constable's head, looking for some other truth.

But there wasn't any, and as the cart rattled on, he couldn't hear it, though he knew the wheels were clattering on the surface of the road, jouncing them when the road got rough, slipping in the puddles that were beginning to form. There was just a low humming that seemed to undulate, and finally smacked into him as he took a deep breath, his mouth wide open, the rain coming down.

"Nolly." Jack said his name, as though he'd been saying it over and over. "Nolly, Nolly."

But Oliver couldn't respond. He made himself breathe in and out, and tried to look at Jack, but couldn't turn his head. If he did, if he looked at Jack, then he would realize what he'd just done, and he'd scream at the constables to take Jack and leave him, because he could not go to a workhouse. Would not go. Would rather die on the roadside and let Jack—

He was shaking in the rain, the collar of his thick jacket open to the weather. And all at once he was cold, with the sharp stab of panic coming up from inside his ribs.

"Nolly, you all right?"

This was a whisper from Jack, sweet and low, and Oliver shook his head. He was not all right, but Jack did not deserve to go into this alone, with Oliver collapsing at the workhouse gates. So he swallowed and shifted his wrists to ease them in the cuffs. The metal was wet and dragged across his skin, and he had to close his eyes for a moment.

When he opened them, he looked at Jack. At the rain dripping from his forelock, and the roiling clouds behind his head as the cart took them beyond the woods and across a patch of open fields.

"Just don't leave me," Oliver said, low, so the constables couldn't hear them. "I couldn't bear it if you left me."

"Never," said Jack. "I'd never do that."

The cart trundled on.

～

The End

～

CHRISTINA'S CLUB

Click the link below to join Christina's Club.

Members are always the first to hear about my new books and publications.

You'll get free books, free behind the scenes information, and unique items to accompany the books.

It's completely free to sign up and you will never be spammed by me; you can opt out easily at any time.

To sign up, visit the following URL:

http://eepurl.com/coVgI1

PLEASE LEAVE A REVIEW

If you have enjoyed this book, it would be tremendous if you were able to leave a review.

Reviews help me get noticed and they can bring my books to the attention of other readers who might enjoy them.

Please leave a review at the online retailer of your choice.

Thank you!

ALSO BY CHRISTINA E. PILZ

The following are in the Oliver & Jack series:

Lightning Source UK Ltd.
Milton Keynes UK
UKHW021236250722
406337UK00010B/2553

9 780989 727334